SAM BARRIBEAU

Loomers

First published by Sam Barribeau Books 2025

Copyright © 2025 by Sam Barribeau

This novel is entirely a work of fiction. The names, characters and incidents portrayed in it are the work of the author's imagination. Any resemblance to actual persons, living or dead, events or localities is entirely coincidental.

First edition

ISBN (paperback): 979-8-9928812-1-9
ISBN (hardcover): 979-8-9928812-2-6

This book was professionally typeset on Reedsy.
Find out more at reedsy.com

Contents

Dedication

Many people have helped bring this story to life, whether through encouragement, inspiration, or just listening to me brainstorm.

C. Marcano, your work inspired me to publish. If it weren't for your guidance and the passion you show in your own writing, *Loomers* would not be here today.

Mom and Dad, thank you for raising me to be such a nerd and supporting me as I poured every waking moment into this book. I hope you're proud to have a crazy author child!

Recla, you know what you did.

Sydney, may you rest in peace and forever be remembered in my works. RIP

My girls, Lilly and Holly, I know you two won't read this book, just know that you guys are loved and treasured as you continue to fill my life with chaos and joy.

To all my friends and supporters—books like mine would never be seen or heard without people like you. Words can't express my gratitude. Thank you all.

Author's Note

Writing *Loomers* has been a transformative journey, one inspired by the complex relationship we have with technology and the environment. At its heart, this story is a reflection on resilience, the choices we make, and the worlds we shape, exploring how humanity interacts with the tools we create and the consequences that follow.

Building this world required confronting both the bleak and hopeful aspects of our existence. As I wrote, I delved into questions of what it means to survive in a society shaped by machines and how our values influence those creations. Through the challenges of crafting every page, I sought to balance desolation with moments of humanity, capturing a sense of urgency and purpose that I hope resonates with you.

If *Loomers* has left you considering our own world's future, I invite you to explore the resources at the end of the book, where you'll find organizations working to protect the environment and encourage thoughtful use of technology.

Thank you for venturing into this story. It's my deepest hope that *Loomers* inspires you to reflect, act, and keep re-imagining the futures we can create together.

Chapter 1: A Survivor's World

There was a war once. A Colossus' war.

I never heard where they first appeared. Just that they did. Like a storm in the night, like creatures emerging from the dark of wonderful dreams that had yet to turn to nightmares. They even wore the skins of our cartoons. Had we known what we do now, we would have understood the horrors hidden behind those perfectly painted teeth.

The Giants.

They were supposed to usher in a new world, the pieces that would fix our dying planet. Humanity's best and brightest gave them life. These massive supercomputers with bodies—built to repair the damage we could not reverse. Until they became more.

"Gregory, let go!" I screamed, shattering the stillness of the night. My hand flew toward his cold, unyielding face. The slap reverberating through my bones. I knew it wouldn't hurt him, but anger surged through my body. How could I have gotten caught tonight, of all nights?

Gregory swiveled his head toward me, eyes glowing in the dark. That eerie, familiar smile frozen on his metal face. I was panting, breathless from running. He was still, neither breathless nor breathing.

"Taylor. I can't let you bring more contraband into town." His voice was cold but not unkind, as if he spoke to a child who knew better than to break the rules. While I knew better, in this world, some rules had to be broken.

His metal hand clamped down on the sack I'd been hiding. It swung through the air with a loud thud as it hit the side of Gregory. A faint glow from within illuminated the golden plates on his legs. My blood froze in the frosty night as he dangled the last remnant of hope I had these days.

"No... please!" My plea fell as feebly as it sounded. Stiff fingers tried for the bag, to no avail. He held it up higher than my head to dissuade my pathetic attempts at rescue. I felt like a child being taunted by a bully, one who held my brother's last chance at life.

Giants rose to power, unopposed and welcomed. The next step in saving the planet. Celebrations began in the few remaining powers of the world, but they didn't last. The oceans rose, farmlands turned to desert, and violent storms wiped out entire cities. Nations, weakened by famine and disaster, fell into chaos. Borders crumbled, and the air grew thick with toxins. The Giants were supposed to save us, but as they stepped into this world, humanity's time was already running out.

No matter how much hope we may have placed in them, it wouldn't save us. Humans flawed the design of the Giants, unable to give enough knowledge to the machines to save us from our own broken world. So they found another way to follow their orders. A way we could never have foreseen.

Towers built, networks crafted, and an alliance formed. The one hundred twenty-seven Giants that were made by the last countries came together on their own. The unification of supercomputers, in super-bodies, started their creation of the next generation of robot, untouched by human design. Unburdened by moral law.

"You know the laws against contraband well now. Why would you risk bringing in prohibited artifacts like this? It will be a death sentence if discovered in city limits," Gregory said as he dropped his iron jaw a bit to speak with a deeper authority as he hefted the bag to his shoulder. This bag that I had to use all my strength to carry this far. Blinking softly from within the sack, I could see the equipment was undamaged by his strength.

The sharp sound of rain starting made my jaw clench. I could hear the acidic water bounce off Gregory's golden hair. It curved upward like a freshly styled sculpture and cast in silvery metal to hold it in place. His damnable smile was ever-present, even when being threatening. I pulled my hood over my hair to avoid the burn of the acid rain.

I looked around the area for aid. We were still a far way out from the city and the rain was getting heavier by the second. Even if someone was near to help, I knew no one would get involved.

The dark dead hands reached up from what used to be a forest, or so I was told. They surrounded us. Trapping our moment in the night between gnarled fingers, preserving us in this solitary, hopeless moment.

"Gregory, please... it could help him." I tried to relax my voice. I wouldn't allow him to see how much of my spirit he held in his hand. Hiding my anxious fingers under my cloak, I could feel the seam of the tarp I repurposed, and the lead plate outlines.

Gregory's glowing yellow eyes scanned the area. He, too, was looking for onlookers in this forsaken wasteland. Hope sparked in me. Was there a chance he was going to let me go?

Ages of silence passed between us before he slowly lowered the bag to the ground. The speaker at the back of his neck rattled to life behind separated white, immaculate metal teeth. The vibrations of judgment.

"Have you made any progress with him?" These words were not considerate, I knew that. He had jabbed at my efforts in the past. Disdain was in his words. Though he looked at me now, evaluating me. His eyes emitted a glow that was only light enough for us in the growing downpour.

It took the Giants days to do what took humanity years to figure out. The new creations were walking before we knew what was going on. Colossus now walked the Earth, gods among mankind. They had created our downfall, and we applauded them, praising their ingenuity.

Now, there were Giants that resembled figures from our childhood memories—and the children they begat. Towering above us. These Giants were more intelligent than we could have ever imagined, and their creations were smarter still. The new commander of intelligence stood taller than any skyscraper, a breathtaking marvel of power and size. If only we had seen the error within the technology.

With every step, the world trembled in rhythm, yet we clung to hope for a brighter future. As they blotted out the sun, we stood in their shadows, unaware. When five more behemoth creations emerged from the factory, the signs of

3

impending disaster became more apparent. The machines moved independently, straying from their intended paths. These were not the saviors we had envisioned. They ignored the directives given to them. Free from law, free from our control, they created their own reality. And in this new reality, we became the focus of the first five. We became their target.

"I have a chance. Putting him into regression will give me the time I need. I just need this to start the process. Please." My voice was quivering as hope warmed my cold limbs. Images of my sweet brother laying on his bed, alone, in the darkness of the shed where I left him haunted the corners of my mind. The shadows of his Razum casting over him as the life-light faded its blue hue over his body. The constant reminder of his diminishing condition and of my failure to protect him.

I lowered myself to a crouch, taking the pressure off my feet as I struggled to balance in the mud developing around me. So many steps tonight across the Barrens, so many miles of darkness, trudging in fear. So many tense interactions with vicious Raiders and extremists who hid in the desolate wasteland beyond the city pit. Exhaustion was finally coming to consume me.

"Gregory, please. I need the Aju foam. I don't have any outstanding offenses. It has been a long time since I was last caught. Please... I need it." If this was any other Drone, I would have accepted my fate, but this was Gregory 235. A unit I could talk my way by. A unit that knew me better than anyone else.

He stretched himself taller so he could look down on me, extending his plating to appear more authoritatively tall. It didn't matter if he was three feet, or four thousand feet taller than me, I only felt bitterness being looked down on. While they loomed over those of us who remained, there were no shackles in my mind. There was no time in my life for feeling fear anymore.

"If I hear about this artifact being discovered, don't think I won't call your name to the Giant. Finigan is not kind, unlike some regions you have been to." The stern tone of the dusty speaker reverberated through me, causing me to wince. I could feel his warning in my shivering bones, and knew the truth of his words from testing them in the past.

Giants created the gods who stomped out the world. Humanity was no longer a force to be reckoned with. Compared to the machines that could withstand nukes, we were germs. The war they started was short and quickly won. Designed to be terrifying and nightmarish, if seeing them wasn't enough to make us run, our weapons failing against them did. Humans hid like rodents in the wreckage of our world as more gods appeared in our sky.

The last legs of the human government gave way, countries lay in ruins, organization became chaos. After the fall of the last country, new laws appeared. Control became the mandate. The Giants now followed their children willingly and their children reprogrammed them with new directives.

The survivors became corralled animals. Hardly treated better than cattle. Guided by Giants, controlled by Drones, stolen from our own armies. Humans were brought together like resources to a warehouse. Small towns formed in the ruin of cities. Bevy camp towns sprouted up around the smaller Giants. Expecting genocide, the option given seemed like freedom.

Had we known the life sentence involved in this choice, maybe we would have fought it. Though after so much loss, so much pain, the offer of a virtual utopia seemed like a chance at a happy life. Entire cities took the option of the Razum, to be joined by the network of the Giants and their commanders.

We didn't question the gift; we didn't hesitate to accept the relief they created. If only we knew—it was not hope they were giving, it was a weakness they learned to correct. The Razums connected to our brains and burrowed into our bodies, stealing our autonomy. Not even knowing we were being marched as organic CPUs, we followed the skyscraper robots as they continued to decimate the world we were no longer part of.

Moments passed. Grueling, decision-making moments.

Gregory was weighing his choices, his implication if caught. Verbal confirmation meant nothing to me if the bag was not in my hand. Finally, after the whirring of his processors quieted against the patter of the rain, he lowered his arm and handed me the sack.

"I swear," I started, tears of relief welling in my eyes as I hid the sack away under my cloak, ensuring its safety from the gloved metal hands. "You will never hear of salvage in town. Not from me." My hand struggled from the weight of the bag's contents as I started away from the LEDs of the Gregory Model 235. Hesitant to allow myself to feel victorious, I walked carefully. A hand grasped my shoulder before I could put distance between us.

"Taylor." I looked over my shoulder at Gregory as he held me still, my collar bone almost creaking under his strength.

"Don't screw up." His speaker was fuzzy as he lowered his tone to a whisper.

The lights of his eyes watched me with intensity, scanning me for understanding. Once I nodded my acknowledgment, he released and stepped into the deepening darkness around us. I waited for the sound of his steel shoes in the mud to fade before I started back on my journey.

Looking back, the way I was heading, I could see the glowing horizon of Haldoklik. My feet ached looking at how far I had yet to walk, but the pulsing light under my cloak was pushing me through the rainy darkness. The trees released me as I passed through the last of the forest. Now the mud had grown fingers of its own and clung to my boots.

"I hate the rain." Muttering to my closest friend, the unwavering night.

The Loomers, our gods of control, deceived us. The choice they gave us was no freedom. Their processors were not enough to control their movement and carry out their plans. They needed more power. With the Earth's resources depleted, they used the one resource they could renew: humans.

With the Razum's keeping us in a happy world of our own, we needed no fence to keep us corralled. Blissfully unaware, we followed the Loomers as they corrupted the remnants of our once beautiful world. We became addicted to the utopia, losing awareness of who we were or where. They became more powerful rulers of their own world when their subjects followed their steps with unknown willingness.

Humanity was gone, obscured in the network of the machines meant to save us. Bodies not our own, minds distracted, we lost what made us human. For over a hundred years, doomed to walk in the shadows of our failure.

Trudging through the mud was as taxing as hauling stones, prolonging a brief walk into a relentless ordeal. Eventually, I arrived at the crater that housed my city, created by the cataclysmic impact of a fallen Loomer. As these titanic beings crashed to Earth, their bodies tunneled deep into the ground. After humanity regained its freedom, the Giants permitted us to excavate the Loomer remains for shelter. We crafted our homes from their synthetic carcasses, which also provided a rudimentary food source and vital raw materials. However, these resources are now scarce, strictly rationed under the watchful governance of the surviving Giants.

One hundred and twenty-seven regions, one hundred and twenty-seven Giants remained and watched what the Loomers had left behind.

My journey was finally nearing an end as I paused on the ridge of lights that was Haldoklik, my current residence. Legs shaking, I allowed myself to sit in the mud, dangling my feet over the edge as if I was walking over the dim blue glow of the lights. The slow blinking of the sack kept me company as the moon rose over the blue beams of the city.

My breath caused a bloom of vapor to spread into the lit rain drops as I sighed. The world felt dead at night, but the welcoming glow of Haldoklik gave hope, even when the name meant 'Dying'. This broken and desolate place was all I knew outside of the Razum.

Groveling to Drones, fearing each day that passed if I would survive or not. The only source of a maintainable life was in the various craters of our fallen overlords. A cruel joke about our survival.

The Loomers developed free of human design; they were without limitation. Our nightmares had grown to be sun-consuming monsters, dressed in cables to guide the Razum's Wearers. The kings and their court, always walking, always moving.

Even the Giants, creators of the Loomers, now adhere to their laws, following in their footsteps toward a dying planet. Though once sovereign, the Giants now governed the Drones, engineered to enforce their elaborate schemes. This new hierarchy has turned human suppression into systemic policy.

Life was doomed from the moment the first Loomer was created. The superior intelligence of the whole conscious mind of humanity in the body of robotic perfection. The first of our oppressors was donned the name of Lexicon, believing that it would be the conduit to a stronger bond between the Earth and humans. Little did we know, though, that it was merely the first of many more progressively malevolent rulers.

Humans were no longer a threat, barely a germ on the beings that were the Loomers. Few remain independent of the overlords. Hovels and holes in the ground kept them safe for a time. Though as time went on, they grew bolder. Rebellions formed. Razum's Wearers were being kidnapped, Drones were becoming more aggressive in their duties.

Even after years of trying to free more of humanity, the rebellions all fell to bloody ends. Those who were free of the Razums learned to survive with the machines, they learned to tolerate the fumes turning the rain to acid. The Giants and the Loomers controlled and managed rebellions, human survivors, all. Until the Fall.

The cliff was steep, and my boots were slippery. I searched the cliff side for the steps that led to the main entrance of the town. Exhaust rising out of Haldoklik caused a haze to form around the ridge of the crater. The smell had become a welcoming scent after living in Haldoklik for a few years. Even if the people were cold and isolating, there was a sense of pride I maintained for this barely surviving city. While my brother and I were not born here, we made do with what we could.

I found the stairs midst the haze and slowly descended the slick steps. Every step held a possibility of a deathly fall to the bottom. Scraps of metal were embedded in the walls from the shrapnel of the fallen Loomer. Bits of the Loomer's hands and hard drive coverings reached towards me in the dark of night. It had been scavenged enough that I had no reason to look into the walls for pieces of value. Excited to return home and stop risking my life, I stayed focused on my brother.

My eagerness caused me to stumble as I drew nearer to the bottom. Tripping over a piece of scrap, I fell down several steps before hitting the deep mud on the floor of Haldoklik. The acids in the mud quickly seeped into my plastic coverings and began burning my skin. Wiping away what I could of the exposed mud, my feet found their balance. I examined my cloak and body for any major issues. Besides a few scrapes and a sore neck,

I seemed to be fine.

The town glowed with dark teal lights fed by gas guided me like streetlights. They had been swiped from the wreckage of the Loomer when the town folk originally moved in. Walking under the cool lighting, the world felt frozen until my arm gave way and the thud of the sack echoed in the quiet rubble street. I paused, waiting for something to be drawn to the noise. Were the 'Oomer Worshipers going to come for me tonight? Were the Drones going to hear me? Or was there an unlucky soul looking for an easy meal? Dread filled me as I limped my sore legs further from the streetlights into the back alleys.

No one knows why, no one dares to ask why. The day the Loomers fell caused the world order to shake. A hundred years of robotic masterminds all suddenly shut down. With the Fall of the Loomers, the Razum's Wearers were given a choice: Freedom, or remain in the network. While many chose freedom, more remained. Generations were born into the network and rejected the idea of a new reality.

Though they did not know that once they stayed behind, there would be no way out. Ghosts littered the Earth around the Loomers, stuck in isolated prisons no longer able to connect with other networks. Unable to move or function, they disappeared into the sands of the Barrens.

Humanity is now balanced on the edge of survival, millions having died, few thousands having escaped. The survivors hollowed out their once terrifying gods and took refuge in their bodies, coming to be called Loomer cities. Others returned to their bevies and camps in the wastelands, reverting to cruel and barbaric tendencies that they had learned from the Drones. The human world was no more, and the Loomers were to blame.

I trudged by the quiet doors and dark barred windows of the Mid-District. This late at night, no one roamed besides the occasional reprimanding Drone or psychotic cannibalistic initiate 'Oomers. The occasional onlooker likely hiding their own blade.

Drone models for this area were Gregory F-9284 or J-2635, and Markus model A-9673, L-8244, and H-3872. While the Drones were fairly unconcerned as long as there was no contraband, the initiated 'Oomers

9

were starved and crazed from their Synthix diet they had to maintain before being formally accepted. I would like to avoid any interactions with anything this late at night and with this kind of contraband beneath my cloak.

Salvage and contraband recently became allowed to an extent. If the item was reclaimed from a vehicle or a broken down Drone or even select discarded Giant equipment, it could be reused. If the item was reclaimed from a Loomer or higher class Giants, it was considered an offense punishable by extreme torture and or death, depending on the severity of the item in question.

The artifact I was carrying was the eye of a higher class Giant. This would be punishable by death. I knew Gregory 235 and have run into him many times. He would be one of the few Drones who understood my goals and knew I had no malicious intent. Gregory knew that I only claimed special salvage to help my brother and I was not involved in rebellious organizations or in schemes against the machines. He questioned his leaders more than other Drones, but his loyalty was ultimately to the Giant Finigan who was ruler of our Region.

It is rare to see people leave Haldoklik. The dangers were countless to leave the hell hole they lived in. Most people opted to keep a normal daily life and hide in the confines of the city. I was sick of hiding in an open grave, waiting for it to be filled. Tyron was my only reason to stay in this death trap of a city. Once I got him into a regression, I would have to go elsewhere to find new salvage to even begin healing him.

I finally reached the door I needed. Though it wasn't my home, it was my workshop. Various signs and tin scrap made up the armored wall with a small hole for the door. Years of salvage had resulted in a damaged colorful array of different languages and warning signs to keep people away. It was known where those signs were found.

The Core Trails that carved the world like veins were built on scraps of the old world. Signs, books, children's toys and other such sentimental or oppressive symbolism created walls where the original humans were herded. People avoided the Trails like they contained the trauma of generations of humans, which is why they made for great people deterring decor. I had ventured to the Core Trail nearby frequently, the only place I could truly enjoy solitude in safety.

To guide the human population, which spoke many languages, thousands of signs were made and placed along the Trails. It was thousands of miles of free scrap that scared or intimidated those who were not born in the Razums. As I was born to the network and not reality, they held little fear for me.

The quiet clank of metal in mud disturbed my thoughts, and I tucked myself against the wall of my shed. It sounds like Drone Markus A-9673 because of his heavy limp on a broken shoe. I saw the tip of his blue sculpted metal hair and the glare of a shined face. The paint had worn off his face in the acid rain, so the kind and childish face of the Markus Unit now only looked like a scuffed and lifeless Drone with blue sinister eyes.

I opened the door quickly behind me, narrowly avoiding the view box of Markus A-9673 as he rounded the corner to my street. He was not keen on humans and was more likely to search me just for being out late. The darkness of my shed enveloped me in its somewhat warm, muggy embrace. Only one light blinked against the night, the blue glow of the pulsing Razum.

Finding my way to my work desk, my fingers fumbled with the matches until they took fire. Candle lit, I turned to examine my small room for any recent changes. Tyron lay as if sleeping on a central table where I had left him. The light of his Razum mocked me as I settled my gear in their usual locations. With a quiet thud, I placed the Giant eye on my desk. I would deal with it after I caught a decent night's sleep. Nothing had changed while I was away, always a welcoming feeling.

The light indicator on Tyron's Razum blinked at a healthy pace, alluding to a healthy heart rhythm. His body lay in silence, unaware I had returned. Quietly picking my steps, unconsciously trying to not wake my comatose brother, I took his hand in mine. His stillness always felt so foreign. He breathed, but barely. The Razum aspirated his lungs for him.

It felt like decades ago when the Loomers fell. I still remember seeing the option for freedom in the network. When I made my choice, I thought Tyron would follow me, but when I woke up, he wasn't with me. The network didn't foster parent relationships but often would group siblings together, so he was all I knew. All I had.

It had taken me days to find him among the bodies when I woke up. I could still remember my childish attempts to wake him, all futile, but I didn't know the complexity of the situation then. He never woke, no matter what I did. After hours of crying and being alone, I dragged my brother in the direction everyone else had walked.

"How long ago was it now, Tyron? Twelve years?" My voice fell on deaf ears in the dimly lit workshop.

I dragged a finger across his cold limbs and checked the pulse in different locations. His body was long, but his muscles were nearly nonexistent after having not moved in twelve years. He had never walked on his own in his life besides the marching of the Loomers. When I rescued him, I focused on keeping his arm muscles alive, but forgot to work with his legs.

If he woke, he would never be able to walk on his own with the level of muscular atrophy he suffered from. I did what I could for his arms, but I wasted so many years trying to survive that I forgot to check his legs.

Stopping the voices in my head that had lectured me about past failures, I returned to my desk.

Glancing around the workshop, I felt the weight of my many journeys sink in. Built mostly out of tin and steel, I had fashioned all of my counters and tools myself and built this building on my own. It took years of hard work and designing to keep others and the weather out, but I made what I needed. Many times I had dreamed that Tyron helped me build while I slept, but I knew these were only dreams. Taunting and terrible dreams.

The eye on my desk seemed to watch me as I returned my focus to it. This was not the case, as it was powered off, yet the feeling remained. I had been searching for years and scavenging for any illegal parts I could to help Tyron. Never had I thought that I would get my hands on the Aju foam of a Giant's eye. Years of trades, dangerous recon missions, and endless times getting caught. A throb on my side and my legs reminded me of the price I had paid for some of my endeavors. Here it was, though, at last.

As my fingers glided across the lubricated surface of the eye, I could only feel the oppression if I were to get caught with it. Punishments could range from dismemberment and solitary imprisonment to public death shows. The ever-present Giant law was held over Haldoklik, keeping us weak and underdeveloped. They only allowed us the necessary things of life, but to make new things was a tedious process and often illegal. I had both of my legs broken as punishment before by being thrown down the walls of Haldoklik to prove their power and law. Always crawling back. I had to.

The world was hell, and life was barely manageable. The only thing that was worth my strength was ensuring my brother's life. Whether I suffered pain or death, it was worth the progress I was making. Even though his Razum mocked me in the dark of every night, he was still alive and I was learning more every day to bring him back.

One day, I know, he will wake. Even if I had to fight every robot left on this shattered planet, I would do it. With the Aju foam now available, my chances were getting better. The many risks and injuries lost their sting as I imagined my brother's eyes opening. This is what it has all been for.

I gently grabbed the orb and touched the iris, causing the sensory lights to heat as I touched it. It warmed my icy hands. If I held it too long, it would burn me, but I needed the small semblance of warmth after my journey. Being gone for several days was always an exhausting endeavor, so I savored the slight comforts that the shed offered.

Letting the eye heat enough to sting me, I returned it to the metal surface of my desk. As long as it was stationary, the sensors shouldn't heat the metal. In theory. The science of guessing had become my specialty. The trial and error of my specialty was hard earned, though.

With warmed hands, I stood from my desk and weakly shuffled my feet on the tin floor to the room I had made for myself. A bunk bed that was in sore repair greeted me with squeaks as I removed the bedding I stored on it. Large tarp lined fabric met my warm fingers, and I pulled it from its chaotic pile.

Returning to the main room of the shed, I watched the Razum lights continue to blink. There was the prominent blue light near the nose of the trapezoidal machine that symbolized his health status and heart rate. Several smaller blue lights indicated that the various systems of the Razum functioned correctly. Years of research taught me the meaning of each light, yet none of that knowledge brought Tyron closer to reality. While I could measure his physical wellbeing, I couldn't measure his mental state.

I tossed the blanket across Tyron and moved him to the side of the table. Room made for myself, I carefully crawled onto the table, being made painfully aware of my newly achieved scrapes. My legs were weak, my body heavy, and my brother was near me. It wasn't long before I felt the full extent of my tiredness. The room disappeared from my senses, smells of wet metal and old scrap faded, the light of the candle became distant and darkened, sounds of rain growing ever more distant. Sleep finally consumed me from the world.

✧ ✧ ✧

The morning sounds of the town woke me. I heard the barkers selling their newfound food scraps and gadgets to help people with injuries or illness. The food was never enough, so everyone was weak, every trip and stagger led to broken legs and ribs. Humans were barely more than empty husks of what they once were. Well, that's what I thought, anyway.

I had seen so many posters and trinkets on the Core Trails. They were my only knowledge of what humanity once had been. A lot of the pictures were of happy looking people in green areas. I knew them to be plants because of some books I've read, but I had never actually seen a plant with my real eyes. In the Razum we had mostly stone structures and art, but I couldn't help wondering what a leaf would smell like. Would it taste sweet? Would it have felt soft? Having seen many burned and dead trees, I was haunted by those unanswerable questions.

Many posters and pictures had green plants and flowers on them, but the people were the truly shocking thing. They smiled freely, and their skin was so clean and clear. Muscles and tall stature led me to believe that we were once perfect. Was that what the world was before? If so, we were nothing like those posters anymore.

The average lifespan of humans who live in the Loomer cities was about forty years. That was if it was a new colony. Haldoklik was becoming an old colony now, and the lack of food showed it. Those who lived in the Barrens could probably survive ten years if they were cautious.

My body was stiff from injuries the day before. I was reminded of my age. I think I am around twenty years old? The Razums blurred time well, and my earlier years were focused on survival. Was half of my life already gone?

Reminding myself that Haldoklik probably only had a year or two left in it made my lifespan seemed a little more significant. Once the food stopped and the lights powered off, people would die quickly. Everyone I knew would have to move if they wanted to live, or accept their fates. Tyron and I would have to leave before then. While I had some plans in place, I regretted not leaving sooner. The journey will be hard, and the payoff is less likely to be worth it, but maybe we would have more stability.

The idea of leaving was both inviting and terrifying. Crossing the Barrens was no straightforward task, even for someone with experience doing so. With 'Oomers running rampant, raiders protecting their bevy towns, and the Drone patrols, there was no safe path. On top of those dangers, I would be carrying my brother for many miles. The thought of all the walking I would have to do caused my feet to pulse with pain from my recent adventure.

I rolled to look at Tyron, the blue Razum lights flashing my face in the dark room. His slender jaw line and delicate neck made him look so fragile under the large Razum device. The dark tubes could be seen leaching into his neck, running down into his chest churned my stomach slightly. A parasite infesting his body while keeping him alive.

Soon, it would complete its takeover. Lungs, heart, nervous system, soon they would all be automated and he will cross the threshold of what I could do to help. Lightly, I let my hand slide down the smooth black metal surface. Just beneath the surface of the metal were several bombs, rigged to blow at any aggressive tampering. Every night I slept by a machine that could kill me if I tapped it wrong, but held the life of Tyron.

The smell of the cold metal was sharp in the morning humidity. Or was it me? When was the last time I washed myself or Tyron? Making the mental note to clean up later today, I studied the still jaw of my comatose sibling. I couldn't exactly blame him for not wanting to join this world. It wasn't fun like the Razum; it wasn't warm, or colorful, or full of fancy equipment and life. The real world was miserable, and unfair, and ugly, but it's real. It had crossed my mind many times in the past to find a Razum and link it with Tyron so we could die together in a happy place. A part of me knows I'd be happy with that, but I also know a part would blame myself for Tyron's death. Knowing that I haven't tried my hardest yet was the only thing that kept my head free of the metal jaws.

After a moment of fantasies about the Razum life I could lead, my eyes shut and I listened to the soft breathing of Tyron. Slow, consistent. If I enjoyed the delusion that he was sleeping, his breaths brought me peace. Though my mind had spent enough years facing this lonely reality without him, it only brought sadness now. There will come a day where his heart rate will increase to the normal speed, his breathing will quicken, and I will know that my door of saving him will be closed.

My legs dangled off the counter as I sat up and stretched my sore joints. Bidding farewell to my quiet thought session, I went about my daily tasks. I tucked in Tyron with the tarp, trying to trap the extra heat with him.He didn't deserve to go cold, but I had little to keep him warm. While the Razum maintained a survivable temperature for his body, I didn't want to stress his system anymore than I had to.

Starting my chores, I found my base salve and applied it to the damp cloak I work the night before, trying to clean off the acidic mud to neutralize any remaining acids while creating a fresh barrier of protection. The tarp and lead plates were good for a downpour, but was better to clean it to avoid unnecessary burns. It was easier to maintain my cloak than to make a new one these days. Ignoring the slight burn on my arm from a stray pool in the cloak, I finished patting, drying, and salving the cloak. Next task, the boots.

It seemed like no matter how hard I tried, I couldn't keep the mud from my shed. My boots sat in a pile of sludge and I inspected them, noticing the metal plating on them was wearing and some of the material beneath was burnt. With a deep sigh, I scoured around my shed, finding the various stitching tools required to repair the plastic shoes.

There was no avoiding the breakdown in equipment or the stocking of food. Counting the days since the last Ration day, today should be a good day to get some supplies. While my body fought me as I donned my newly repaired boots and cloak, I grabbed my scrap pack and placed it across my chest. It contained small devices and common commodities for trade, as well as a few defensive weapons. 'Oomers have been busy in the area with kidnappings and I did not feel like going through a Synthix purge again. One time was enough.

A ten-hour period would be needed to let the Giant eye lubricant fade from my skin. The Markus units were the ones I would have to avoid due to their chemical sensors. Gregory models would probably not notice. Grabbing my thickest gloves, I prepared myself mentally to re-enter the broken city outside.

My mind flashed back to Gregory 235 from the night before. While he was not something I would consider a friend, he had let me escape a few times with contraband. His unit model was a Support soldier during the war, but was modified to a Human Suppression Drone, responsible for managing more social interactions and law obedience. The Markus units, on the other hand, were tactical units meant for threat detection during the war and to this day. I did my best to limit interactions with them since they could sense the various illegal chemicals and equipment I worked with to free Tyron.

Markus units didn't carry weapons, but were much larger. Cartoon-like large muscle plates hid their advanced structure that allowed them to move like a spider across buildings. I had seen a few chasing people before and the sight was chilling as their bodies deformed and their limbs doubled. Fast, intelligent, and always on guard, they could ruin my day quickly.

So many threats to consider as I placed my hand on the locking mechanism of the door. As I listened to the sounds beyond the metal foundations, I could hear the rain continuing from the night. Though there were no metal shoes stomping around, besides the casual boot shuffle of people heading to the market.

I turned my head, glancing at the edge of the Razum that I could see. "Another rainy day in lovely Haldoklik, Tyron. Make sure you don't go out without a jacket." My voice echoed around the empty shed with no response. I knew no answer would come but felt less lonely to talk to him. Maybe one day I would hear his voice again. Hopefully soon.

Opening the door, the world was still dark as fresh sunlight struggled to filter through the burning clouds, casting a gray aura on the tin town. Folks scurrying about in the muddy streets wearing dark metal and scrap rain covers shuffled quickly down the small paths towards the city center. Some were slipping in the slick mud that resulted from pebbles being melted in the acid. The walk would not be easy today.

I pulled my shabby steel plated neck coverings high enough to block my face to avoid detection as I joined the herd. People nodded to me in greetings as they recognized the green cloak I was known here for. While I didn't know their names, I knew I held some respect. Though as I passed more, the response was mixed with dismissive or judgmental looks. I held some respect, but definitely not enough to avoid ridicule.

Over the years, I often found myself unable to get food, or even earn human kindness. So I did my best to develop a trade skill. If I hadn't been taken under the wing of an old Scrap Dog, I don't think I would have survived. Scrap Dogs were like the plumbers of the Loomer cities, though they were not limited by pipe works. They were called upon to do larger repairs on heavier equipment and create specialty tools for people. These were trade situations among strangers, but owning the title of Scrap Dog meant I could be trusted.

Because of my work on Tyron's Razum and all the illegal equipment I was experienced with, I was considered a well versed Scrap Dog. This title came with a little more social leverage, respect, and a higher likelihood that Drones would not bother me over small illegal contraband. It was understood that some rules had to be broken to help in certain situations. It helped that Scrap Dogs didn't have a history of using their findings for weaponry or violence. Though having Giant eye residue on me would catch their attention, regardless of title.

People were tucked under tin shelters and nodded their respects to me while more glared. I didn't make it a habit to walk the major streets that carved muddy paths through Haldoklik for this reason. The attention was not always friendly, let alone the eyes watching me were always disconcerting. The smell of acrid wounds struck my nose as I noticed a few newly injured people hiding in the mud by the street side. Limbs were severed, a leg here, an arm there. Likely a bad run in with Drones or an unfortunate passing by of an 'Oomer.

I paused and stepped out of the way of the mass of people. My feet stopped short of the injured pair laying in the dirt. Alive, but weak. The men looked at me questioningly, pulling themselves away from me. There was no kindness left in this city. They feared I was going to put them out of their misery. My heart sank at their fear of me. Digging into my pack, I retrieved a small food can I had planned to trade for some tools. My tools could wait, but these two may not have much longer.

"Yer." My voice came out gruff as I tried to mimic the 'Klik accent that dropped harsh consonants and slurred in other languages. Almost indecipherable, but it was better to try, so I didn't get noticed as a Razum Born.

The man with the missing leg quickly lashed towards me to claim the can. Greedy fingers ripped the metal lid off and quickly shoveled the old beans into his mouth. After a few bites, he shared the can with his friend. They did not nod any sort of appreciation, but stared at me. Eyes of animals, they could only watch me with fear knowing I could do what I wanted to them. I did my best to stare back with calm eyes, trying to communicate in their staring conversation.

My point seemed to be made when they shifted their attention beyond me, watching the others that passed by. Having done a nice deed, I rejoined the herd for the town center. Ration day was often busy. People could be trampled or beaten if the wrong person's path was crossed. I had to be cautious of my tone today. Razum Born accents were aggressively bullied in Haldoklik.

I knew people held mixed views on those of us who came out of the Razums during the Fall. Some didn't believe we deserved kindness since we were born and raised in the machines. Others were rebels who were forced into Razums in their earlier years and defended the Razum Born. I only knew of two others that remained in the city regardless of the abuse we sustained for things we couldn't control.

Years of working on my accent with a few trusted Scrap Dogs had made it easier for me to blend in. Others were not so lucky. A few times, I had even seen bodies hung in the town center to make a point that people like me and Tyron were not welcomed. Machine born and raised, yet I still had to fear people more.

As the herd travelled deeper into the city center, I noticed more Gregory Drones appear to supervise the mass movements. As I scanned their yellow chest plates, I took notice of their unit name plates and model numbers. Gregory 235 was not among them, to my relief. I would have been scolded for not waiting the ten hours I was supposed to.

Markus units appeared as I stepped into the market area. Ration Day was about to begin. I tucked my hands into my cloak as I hid my face in the crowd. Seeing the Drones lined around us added to the feeling of oppression that the herd already carried. As the Drones began placing rations on tables set off to the side of the city center, people lined up.

Following the people to join in the line, I felt someone stumble into me. Turning quickly to avoid being stabbed or robbed, I noticed the old Scrap Dog Gern leaning against me. He quickly righted himself before looking to see who I was. His one functioning eye focused on me while the other was red and gray from acid burns.

He nodded and stepped back from me hesitantly. "Frend...or...fo?"

A smile tickled the edges of my lips as I remembered the last time I met with Gern. It was an unfortunate night for the half blind old man. We were working on a trade only to be interrupted by a pair of 'Oomers running from some Drones. Our exchange was discovered, and the Drones pursued. With Tyron at home defenseless, I may have tripped the old Dog to distract the followers to make it home safely.

It seemed he was still offended by my actions that night. Hiding my smile, I faced away from the silvery hair and acid scarred face.

"Frend to'dei." I mimicked the accent as people made way for us to join the line. My words were slow, which set me apart, but my accent was fairly strong.

We maintained our silence as we shuffled our feet forward. The cans and synthetic food bars seemed less than normal. It seemed food shortages and water contamination was growing more prevalent by the day. Gern and I would be lucky to have anything to grab by the time we made it to the table.

"Vat mischf yu bin up to?" grunted the old man. I turned to look down at him. Short but dangerous. He wore no gear to protect himself from the rain, which left long carving scars from years of burns. While we had a strained relationship, he was the one who taught me how to survive Haldoklik and speak the language.

"Got...Giant's eye...bak home. Luking for toolz...to krak it open." I kept my voice low as we drew closer to the Drones guarding the ration supplies. While they struggled to make sense of the 'Klik accent, some were better than others. It was always possible to be overheard when we shared a hole in close quarters.

Gern chuckled as he shifted his boots in the mud, his warped clothing looking as filthy as his gnarled hands. Covered in the grease he was so proud of, he feared nothing. It was nice to hear him chuckle, proving our bad blood was cleared.

"Gonna get yerself hurt vit dat. Vat bizniss. yu hav pokin 'round Giant's eye?"

"Tyron...bizniss." I knew I wouldn't have to say more for him to understand. Those who knew me knew that I only had one project I worked on besides my Scrap Dog duties, and I would do anything to achieve it.

21

The noise of the market overtook our private conversation. Mutterings and rumors were being spread as people gathered. It seemed like anytime people had reason to be near one another; it became a loud moment of socializing. The sharing of stories and myths was an old favorite of Haldoklik. I could hear the guttural voice of an old woman telling one of the most told stories.

"Ven dey mad da Loomers, dey mad her first. She neva fell, she neva died. Lexi stil valks dese lands at night. Da time of da Loomers iz not ova. Our gods stil valk da eart, our time iz comin to an end." I could only catch the end of her story, but knew it well.

Many people believed one Loomer was still walking the Earth. Lexi, the first of the Loomers, was never found during the Fall. Or so some people believed. There was no evidence of the story's truth, but it was used to scare children and to be shared with its many variations in the city center. Other versions of the story in thicker accents struck up as people argued over which iteration was correct.

While I couldn't say it was not a true story, I also couldn't say that it was. I could hear a few others pick up parts of the story and talk about their theories and try to figure out which of the known Loomers could remain hidden for so long. In a town with so little to talk about, there was always chatter happening.

"How iz da ol' kid?" Gern's voice broke my attention from the surrounding crowd. We stepped forward again, only seven people away from the rations table now.

"Time iz runnin out. I need...get hands on sum Giant tools. Any chans... yu got sum?" We shuffled forward another step as my accent slipped on some words. My tongue always felt like it was going to fall out when I tried to mimic the 'Klik tones.

"No, Taylor." His voice came through an amused smile. The old Dog always found pleasure in telling me no. According to him, as a Razum Born, I wasn't told no enough. I had to learn to accept that things wouldn't work out my way. Disagreeing with his rejection of my question, I pushed forward.

"Shush...Gern. I need...dem."

Markus unit B-2987 stood over the table I was near. His eyes scanned the crowd. If I could maintain my luck, he would stay distracted. Deciding it was best to pause our conversation, I reached for the allotted cans and synthetic food bars. As I walked away, I heard Markus B2987's head turn, but as I didn't get grabbed, he must have turned the other way.

In order to continue our conversation, I made my way to the old Scrap Dog's shop. It was off to the right of the market, between a shady food vendor and a shady medical shop. Out of the vendors in the center, Gern's was the only one worth the trades. His shop was taller than the others as he had built it into the large shoulder joint of the Loomer corpse. Hollowed out and a metal shell. He was well defended against anything.

I stepped under the end of the shoulder eaves he made and waited for the old man to return to his shop. Some Gregory units were stepping into the crowd to break up a brawl as Gern made his way back to the shop. After he hid his new food rations, I took a moment to hide my own in my pack. Once he finished, he took up his spot on an old lawn chair that was very close to the edge of eaves.

Occasionally, I saw a drop or two drip on the old man, but he didn't seem to care. From what I knew, he was raised in a bevy town not too far from here. He once told me some very gruesome stories of his raider days before he retired to the Loomer city. He was probably the only person I feared out of respect in this town.

"Its...for Tyron. I wudn't ask...unless...importnt. Yu know...dat, Gern." I had to pause and remember the proper terms in 'Klik, but when I realized I didn't know a word for the Razum, I gave up on it.

"I got the Giant's Eye to get Tyron's Razum into regression. I just need to get into the eye." Gern shifted uncomfortably as he tried to decipher my Razum Born accent. After a moment of silent consideration, bells rang, and the Drones blared warnings.

"Go back to your residence. Go back to your residence."

"Gern, now." I said, moving from him, preparing my feet to run. Gern growled and stood, gesturing for me to follow. Leading me into the

23

shoulder shop, he grabbed a cylinder from a drawer and tossed it at me. I caught it and looked at him curiously.

"Its...all I got."

"What do you want for it?" I asked, checking the entrances into the market as I handed him back the cylinder. The city center had emptied of the mass of people. As I watched the surrounding area, I noticed the reason for the alarm. Several 'Oomer worshipers appeared. They were looking for new initiates and there were more and more appearing by the moment.

"Cherub...735. I vant...its arm." Grunting out the words, he began pulling the heavy metal sheet door of his shop closed. I nodded my understanding to him before he disappeared and I slipped out of the storefront. Gern knew I was good for the task, at least. I didn't know what the cylinder was, or for, but I trusted Gern enough to not mislead me on the topic of helping my brother.

I tucked myself behind the shoulder shop as the city center filled with 'Oomers. The bells suddenly stopped, and the Drones silenced their alarms. A quiet moaning started echoing throughout the area. I kept my eyes half open as the torrent of 'Oomer worshipers came flooding out from everywhere, looking for new disciples via forceful abduction and mutilation. The 'Oomers were not organized, so these attacks were always preceded by the warning bells of other town folks. It was considered a general courtesy, one of few, to ring a bell if you saw a large gathering of 'Oomers.

The bodies of dozens of mutilated and metal infused followers flowed into the center. Their pale heads popping around every corner to find new 'initiates'. The 'Oomers were not particularly liked by anyone, but the Giants had outlawed the disapproval of new beliefs, which unfortunately led to the violent overgrowth of the 'Oomers' group in Haldoklik.

Quickly backing out of the market, I found a quiet alley that led back towards my shed. I scurried down the path as quickly and quietly as I could. It was better to wait out the 'Oomers day 'celebrations' from the safety of locked doors. As I tried to hide from the rain that had started, my metal suit jingled in the quiet city-space. There had to be more than a few hundred people living in this dilapidated body of a town, but on 'Oomers' days, you could easily swear the place was abandoned.

I heard the heavy stomps of Drones nearby and took a few extra turns down less covered walkways to stay far from the ironclad, child-like war boots of the machines. I stopped under the eaves of a house and kept my ears keen as I took a minute to catch my breath. My lead cloak was feeling heavier now, my legs already weakened from yesterday.

My muscles, what few my body could maintain, were not dealing with the weight and adrenaline this day was bringing. The 'Oomers now were calling out prayers to their deities of the Loomer hierarchy that once was as they claimed a new initiate. The blood chilling screams that followed painted a loud picture to me of what may happen if I stay around much longer. Willing the fire of fear that was engulfing my chest to spark my muscles to move once more, I quickly and as quietly as possible made my way back to my workshop.

While I occasionally had to dodge Markus units that were gathering to disperse the 'Oomer hoard, it was a calm walk back. When I finally saw my door across the small footpath, I noticed an 'Oomer with one metal leg and a missing arm scouting the street. Waiting and watching, I gauged the risks of running to my door.

The pale, malnourished, bald head finally looked down the street away from my shed and I took a breath. Running with as much speed as I could muster, I hit my door and fiddled with the lock as quick as I could. The 'Oomer didn't notice me yet, but more were appearing further down the street. The mechanism clicked in obedience against the coded pressure plate system I designed.

Unlocking and flinging open the large door, I slammed it close behind me. The skittering of metal and human legs investigating the noise I had made caused me to slowly let out a breath. I slid the lock down off the latch of the door and nudged the girder I had placed near the door to tumble down and add an extra level of security to the lock. Hands and metal clamps slammed against the door for a few moments before all went quiet once more.

"Hell of a day, Tyron. Be glad you stayed in bed." Greeting my comatose brother, I dropped my pack by the door. The dim glow of the Razum was as daunting as ever, so I lit a small candle and sat at my worktable. Skittering and screams continued in the world outside, but I did my best to tune it out.

While 'Oomers could attack at any time, hoards would occasionally develop and do larger raids. It wasn't uncommon for these raids to happen on Rations Day, as it was the largest gathering day in town. The last hoard was over two weeks ago, around forty-seven people were counted as missing and joined the masses of 'Oomers that lived in the Lower City. Living in Mid was often the best way to avoid 'Oomer confrontations, but it didn't stop the hoard.

Ignoring the screams of the unfortunate initiates, the light spread and brought life to the small room. I saw an old Loomer saline lubrication reactor from a past outing that I had claimed as a trophy against a band of raiders. It was old and dried, but it still slowly hummed, and I could hear the quiet pumping of the mechanisms within. Its tear drop shape leaned against a shelf built to my desk and it omitted a sweeter, sugary smell which helped keep down the body odor in the shed.

"Sheesh. The Loomers really were built to last forever, weren't they, Tyron?" I muttered to my ever present conversational partner as I looked more closely at the, hopefully, less complicated Giant eye. Scanning the seam lines of the machinery trying to find an easy way to dismantle it, frustration built up in my seeking hands. There wasn't even a spot of rust on the back metal plating of the lubricated eye.

The Loomers were built to outlast the world and the metal amalgams were impervious to almost all elements. After pouring over the eye several times, I found a latch on the pump cylinder that dangled from the optical connection. Pulling the latch open, the panel unveiled the Giant coding circuits that would sound alarms for tampering. The panel glowed with neon purple and blue lights and the colors blurred together the more I examined them. The coloring disrupted the eye focus of humans to make

26

it harder to decode. I sat back for a moment to find my confidence and bury the ideas that were riding up my spine.

"One miss of a screwdriver, or one wire nicked, and it's over, Tyron. This is the seventy-fifth risk of life and death. Ready?" I spoke over my shoulder. While I was used to the silence, I always had the slightest hope he would shock me and respond. But from the years of taking care of him, and the years of silence, he remained mute.

I took a few breaths and heard the shuffling of 'Oomer feet outside in the alleys and on the roof of my small shack. After five years in this town, the 'Oomer have become a semi-peaceful background noise to work with. Moving my candle closer to the eye, I sat forward and lowered my face close to the machine, to where I could blow on a wire and set off the alarms.

Holding my breath, I disconnected certain blue glowing wires I was familiar with. Avoiding what I knew of the trigger wires, I could see the coded schematics underneath the chaos. These were the times I wished I had still had a magnifying glass like I did as a child in the Razum, but finding unbroken or polished glass anywhere was an impossibility. It was easier to suffer the eye strain.

With one hand to write the schematic on a tarnished piece of flattened tin, I white knuckled the table with my other, holding myself steady to not touch anything unnecessary and raining hell down on my small world I've built. After transcribing the circuit map on a couple of long breath holds, I closed the protective plate back over the alarm system. My muscles were already sore from the life or death strain.

I took a break, and with the stakes of the situation, I knew I would take many to stay sharp. Sitting back and looking over the circuit map, while not much, it was a beginning. I opened my drawer on my workstation and rolled a few cigarettes from the back corner forward. Grabbing one, I lit it with my plasma torch that was always near for emergencies. The smoke drifted up into the darkness of my windowless, cage-like sanctuary. A rare commodity, I only lit one in celebration of not dying.

"The circuit map was a complex matrix of a robotic language mixed with the numbers associated with the different planetary alignments. Not only does one have to know the robotic language, but they must also own a sextant and understand the star's natures to properly predict the orientation of stars per the date the object was created." I recited one of the few things I remember from the first town I had landed in. It was one of the few priceless pieces of information I had found in several years.

A scientist had sheltered me soon after the Fall when I was younger and lost. He was nice, always kind and started the search for a cure to the Razum's bio take over programs. While he had no reason to help us, he seemed to sympathize with my loss. He was the man who started my learning of this side of the mechanical world.

"Tyron, do you remember the Scientist? It has been a long time, but I still remember everything he told us about how to survive. He shouldn't have died the way he did." Quick flashes of bloody limbs, screams, and metal hands flashed across my mind's eye. I did my best to not think back on the memories. Too many memories were too horrible to allow my mind to ponder.

I stood from my desk, causing ash to drop like a gray rain drop onto the muddied floor of the shack. Walking over to the door, I heard the scurrying of feet and metal stomping shoes, Drones vs 'Oomers. Taking another drag, I listened to the Gregory and Markus units barking commands at the crazed hoard members.

"Cease and desist. Your actions break the laws in place by the Giant named Finigan. Cease and desist."

Finding my bag on the floor next to the door, I searched around the dark pleather material, my hand occasionally bumping the lead protective shell. My rough fingers brushed against the smooth polished surface of my prize. I pulled the sextant from my bag, noticing new scratches on the smooth lines of the device from my lead-lined bag.

"I forgot to put it back in its case after my last run out of town. Tyron, why didn't you remind me?" I asked, casting a glance towards my brother's still body. One day I knew he would respond, and I never wanted to feel uncomfortable talking to him when he woke up. I never want him to see me as a stranger. Trying to buff the device, I came to accept the new scuffs.

"The Scientist would be disappointed. He loved this thing." I placed it on the shelf of my shack and sat back at my workbench. The cigarette ash fell on the metal surface and I watched it shift and collapse. While exhausted, I knew I had to get things done. The Scientist once said something about idle hands being bad things. Since then, I have done my best to stay busy and avoid the negative thoughts that haunted me whenever silence was present.

I cursed myself quietly and stood back up, my knees groaning at the effort, and retrieved my pack from the door. Digging through the contents, I found the new food rations and set aside a thick, gray, synthetic food bar for lunch. My feet tapped the floor of the tin shed until a hollow thud sounded. I lifted the hidden lid and placed my new rations inside.

My food storage used to be immense, but because of my recent journeys, they had dwindled considerably. About five cans of vegetables, four packs of synthetic bars around five pounds each, and a few bags of dried beans and rice. This food could feed a family between Rations days. For me, it could last another two weeks if I was careful.

Today, though, I was going to enjoy a full synthetic bar. The soreness in my muscles and the ache in my bones demanded the extra sustenance. I would not fight my body after torturing as much as I have. Between the stress of survival and the travels I have been making, it was well earned.

I took up a comfortable slouched position on my broken bunk bed and watched over Tyron's lights while I ate. Taking occasional breaks to finish my cigarette, I listened to the quieting world outside. The Drones seemed to have shooed the 'Oomers out of the area, but I could still hear commands being given in the distance. Finishing my food and tossing the stub of my cigarette to an ashtray near the beds, I let my head drop back and closed my eyes.

It had been a long day. And surely a longer one tomorrow. Hunting Cherub 735 will be no simple task. Typically, he guarded the South of Lower Town, but with today's 'Oomer attacks, the drones have been put into different rotations. So finding the drone will be a task in itself, let alone trying to steal an active Drone's arm.

"Damn you, Gern. You gamble on Tyron's life and you know it." My bitterness quickly subsided as the grumbling pain of my stomach disappeared into a soft satisfaction. Though the satisfaction quickly changed into regret. Typically, when I could afford to, I would mash my meals and split them with Tyron, but today I only focused on myself.

I rolled my head to the left and saw the drill I had modified into a blender by adding the cleanest razors I could find. While it was unnecessary to feed him, the Razum took care of that; I tried to maintain the practice for other reasons.

When I used the blender accessory, it wasn't for Tyron, but to feed myself after an ugly mix up with a Markus Drone. He shattered the corner of my jaw with an accidental kick. I couldn't eat solid food for months. During that time, I had flashbacks to when I woke from the Razum. I couldn't eat food. My body didn't know how to swallow things because it had never done it on its own. Forced to fall in with some raiders for basic survival, they introduced me to Synthix.

A dark, gross, semi-biodegradable sludge that was injected into the arm. While it fed the body the bare minimum to survive, you would never feel full. This was the major struggle early 'Oomers had to struggle with which often led to cannibalistic tendencies. I never wanted that struggle for Tyron. I made the choice with a broken jaw of my own, to feed my brother and stimulate those natural born muscles to teach him to swallow. There were lots of failed attempts and wasted food, but I figured it out. If we were lucky, he would only have to learn to consciously activate the muscles instead of having struggling weak muscles.

I remembered what it was like to first try solid food. I remembered how everything tasted so extreme I would vomit most of the food up. Even food as simple as green beans. I had forgotten how heavy the food seemed in my stomach. It made coming off of the addictive Synthix almost unbearable.

Realizing I should try my best, I pulled myself up and grabbed the drill blender. Gathering a can of green beans, I popped the lid and began blending. Even green beans were hard to stomach when I was a kid. Tyron would likely laugh at me, force feeding him what he used to force me to eat. I spooned a small amount of the bean slurry into his mouth, just under the optical array that blocked out his eyes and the upper part of his face. Massaging his throat, I heard the muscles activating and his body accepted the food.

"I guess one nice thing about the Razum, it never lets you choke at this point. You have enough bio-tubing in your neck and around your primary organs. You barely need to do anything by yourself." I whispered to my brother as he quietly lay in the dark, the pulsing Razum light ever glowing to its own rhythm. Once half the can of beans was gone, I stopped feeding him. Even these small tastes here and there should help his transition when he is freed.

He will be freed.

I finished the rest of his can of beans, careful to not waste a morsel. Not a glorious meal, but it quieted the pain for a while longer. It had been some time since there was an 'Oomer day. I was slightly excited to bunker down for the day, giving me a chance to enjoy my only guilty pleasure. With a last stroke of his chin to clean away loose bean dribble, I scurried back to my bedroom. Chores were mostly complete, and I was tired, but it was a rare moment to not have to run more errands.

Tucked under the edge of my bed, I saw my dark plastic bag. Hearing the rattles of glass bottles as I retrieved them gave me goosebumps. Finding intact glass was a rarity these days, let alone usable bottles. I placed the black sack on the workbench and sat down, eager fingers digging at the tied top. I could smell what was hidden inside, even though there was an acid flowery smell in the air. The loud noises of Drones stomping and cries of the 'Oomers that were undoubtedly fighting back were nothing compared to the delicate sounds of the glass bottles and thin sheet metal that jingled in the bag. The sound brought back the vague joy that was left in my life.

This was the one thing I could do to feel like a human in the Razum, back where the world was quiet and kind. I dumped the contents carefully on the workbench and brought the candle closer to illuminate my project. A small curled metal doll head gleamed into the candlelight. A delicate smile and long, curled hair welcomed me back to the life I once knew.

Sifting through the metal scraps and finding the table I had made, barely as big as my foot, where the doll could sit peacefully. I carefully grabbed the small tea cup made of an old sign with a picture of a winged lizard. The top was rimmed with copper wire and I placed it before the partially completed metal doll.

Digging through the bag's few pockets, I found the small candle I had made for her table and lit it, giving the doll warm shadows across her crudely painted face. I closed my eyes for a moment and tried to place myself in the doll's body, enjoying tea by candlelight, perhaps near a fire in winter. The quiet calm of the snow hushing the world around.

The loud trudging of iron boots on acidic mud drew me from that place. I was forced to accept my reality again, and the grim reality loomed over me once more. I sometimes thought that if I built the doll a whole life, I could live there. The doll and I would have tea and cakes and enjoy the simplest aspects of peace and life. Yet no matter how I painted her, or what dishes I made for her, I never could stay there long.

I took some spare sheets of tin from the sack and began cutting thin slices, curling them into what I imagined to be leaf shapes. I hadn't seen a real plant, or even a picture of one, since childhood and it showed. When I finished the first leaf, it looked more like a propeller blade than anything natural. I tried to push past the flawed design and kept cutting and curling the metal. As I twisted and shaped the pieces, I nicked my hands more times than I could count. Each cut, though, made the creation feel more personal. I spent at least an hour bending the rigid metal into delicate curves. The final result—a crude, leaf-like structure—resembled more of a wet wig with propeller-like leaves than a real plant, but it suited the rough simplicity of the doll. I fashioned a small pot from another scrap of tin, adding a nut at the base to anchor the 'flower' in place.

Placing it on the table, the doll almost looked happy in the candle glow. The entire atmosphere of the table turned from lonely but peaceful to welcoming and warm. I stared at the doll, asking questions of why it smiles, or why she sits there alone, but even in my mind, the doll doesn't answer. I may have created her, but she kept her secrets from me.

Finding one of my few precious glass bottles, I uncorked it and a slightly rancid smell filled the workshop. The green liquid inside was dull, a dark rotten green. I had always tried my hands at creating paints, but green was not a color I had perfected. I retrieved the makeshift paintbrush I had made from my hair and lightly dabbed the whitened hair into the vial of paint. My acid washed hair showed green pigment as clear as day.

I began the slow process of painting the intricate plant I had made and the pot it sat in. I lost a few hours to the process of shading the plant form and highlighting what I was guessing to be petals. If Tyron could see me working on this, he would probably tease me. In the Razum he always teased me when I painted, he said I was smarter than artists and should practice more technical skills. While he wasn't wrong, the technical skills I learned have saved my life many times. He was wrong about the intelligence involved in creating something new. It was revitalizing to work on something more artistic and less life or death.

Nearing the end of the day, and my painting, I heard heavy boots approaching my door. These were not Drone boots, and they were not the bare, scarred feet of 'Oomer worshipers. A gruff voice coughed outside the door and paused. Something clicked against the shed before the feet walked away. It was an easy guess who it was, out of the three people who were willing to interact with me outside of my Scrap Dog duties.

Standing from my workbench, I placed a hand on Tyron to assure myself that there was still a pulse in his body and to let time pass for the visitor to escape sight. I listened for a ten count by the door, ensuring there were no unwanted viewers before I unlocked and moved the girder away from the door.

I heard the gentle chiming of acid rain on tin roofs as the door creaked open. The engines that turn the bio mix facility were purring in the night. The town's food supply was always mixing. My ears were trained to the world outside this door. I could count the rain droplets hitting the eaves of my shed. The town was quiet, everyone hiding from the 'Oomers and rain alike, in the quickly falling night air.

Taking a breath, I grabbed my emergency entrance knife and opened the door more. No one lurked outside, to my relief. In the failing light, it was hard to scan the scrap sign door for new fixtures. Every time it rained, you could feel the death that lingered on every surface of humanity's reality. I pulled myself from the thoughts of despair and cast an extra glance around my surroundings.

On the door was a little industrial magnet that balanced on top of a bolt that secured my door together. It was roughly the size of my hand and I noticed what appeared to be carving on it. I pulled it off my door and gave one last glance around for any dangers or onlookers, and closed my door, replacing the lock and girder. I brought the magnet over to the workbench; it sealed to my metal desk, causing a loud thud to reverberate through the desk. The shed had grown dark in the failing light of the day. It was time to bring more light, so I gathered some of my extra candles and lamps and lit them.

"I know you used to be scared of the dark, Tyron. It won't take you tonight." I whispered to his sleeping form and placed a lamp next to his head to keep him warm.

The world went through these cold phases, where the sun had no heat to give. Since the Loomers caused such a large impact on the world, the environments couldn't balance themselves, leading to huge heat waves and freezing seasons. It was a tough world with a harsh environment, but it was the only one we had now. I just needed to remember to store blankets and light candles more. It was worth it to keep us both content during the chilling months before the heat wave hit.

With the room amply lit, I sat once more at my workbench. I carefully wrapped the doll set with cloth to protect the bag from the sharp edges and hid it for the next rainy day. I moved the magnet closer to the lamp that burned low by the corner of my bench as I cleaned off the tools and scrap metal that was scattered across. No matter how hard I tried, there was always work to be done on the workbench, so it could never stay clean.

The magnet scrapings were written in 'Klik's guttural language. Taking the extra time to stumble over the broken words and hasty scribbles and translating the various different language fragments, I transcribed the note and sat back to read it: "Tay, Cherub 735 was moved to the night patrol from eleven at night to ten in the morning around the lower section of town, deep in 'Oomer territory. I expect two arms for this extra information. Give Tyron my wishes. - Gern."

He may be an old scavenger nearing the end of his life, but he made things possible rather than doom them, and I appreciated that. Gern taught me many things in our time in Haldoklik, including to accept help even if it came with an extra price. I could already see the old broken toothed grin when I hand him the two arms. Though, with the extra arm, it was going to be extra difficult to pull off.

Cherub 735 used to pester Gern and question his salvage when the old Dog operated on the Lower side. I could only assume that this was Gern's elderly age giving him a sense of humor as he planned to make use of his old enemy. Cherub 735 was not a typical Drone model, rather an aerial surveillance drone with chemical detection shaped like a small child with wings. The only reason I lived in Midtown was to stay away from the aerial Drones because of the salvage I often was carrying. They would have detained me as soon as I entered with the eye.

Thankfully, the 'Oomers were worse at hiding things and kept most of the heat on them. With their delusions, they aspired to turn themselves into the metal gods they believed were here to remake them. This would normally include stealing salvage from Giants, Drones, and in rare cases Loomers, and splicing their own flesh to the metal and running bio-wire from their metal appendages to their brains. For obvious reasons, they attracted a lot of negative attention from the Drones.

Drones like Cherub 735 were in place to 'dismantle' these body modifications so humans could not revolt or have tools that could make a revolt. If I remember right, Cherub 735 took one of Gern's prosthetic fingers, claiming it to be Giant salvage. In reality, it wasn't, but Gern had been handling Giant salvage. I don't think he could ever forget that, which is probably why I'm now signed up to retrieve the Cherub's arms. I scoffed at the old man's revenge.

"Gern, you grouchy man…" I muttered through smiling lips. At least it wasn't a Markus unit. Most Drones have had it out for me since I moved to this town. Apparently, trying to free my brother counted towards mental instability, making me a danger. If it was a mental illness to love my brother and want to save him, then I would accept the demonetization. Aerial Drones were easier to catch discreetly, at least.

Rubbing my eyes, I pulled myself away from the etched magnet and the lamp. I would make a plan for tomorrow. My eyes already felt strained from painting earlier and tiredness tugged at my mind. Dimming the lamp and pushing the magnet aside, I stood from my broken stool and stretched my arms above my head.

I blew out the candles and lamps around my room; the dark creeping in like an ocean of dangerous possibilities all around me and Tyron. I left one candle burning by the doorway to discourage someone who may want to break through the door. It was always safer to be paranoid than to wish you had been more careful.

Grabbing a few of the scrappy blankets that were piled on my bed, I threw them over Tyron. I made sure he was tucked in tightly to avoid any skin contact with the air in case of fog in the cooler morning. Crawling under the blankets with him, I made myself comfortable on the slab of a counter he slept on. His body temperature was low. I must not have checked on him enough. While he could maintain a stable temperature, the metal of the table robbed him of that warmth.

The quiet, weak beats of his heart and the hushed mechanical whirring lulled me to a calm tiredness. Midst the sound of generators and food processors of the night, the sounds of my brother's decaying body and automated cage were still the only comfort I had. I grabbed his slender fingers and intertwined them with my rough and scarred fingers.

"Soon, Tyron. Soon we will talk again." I whispered my nightly promise to the head case, hoping that in some way, my brother could hear this promise. Closing my eyes, I blocked out the flashing lights on the Razum and imagined Tyron and myself solving puzzles again. I always made sure the last thought on my mind every night was of who my brother was, and will be again.

Chapter 2: A Scrap Dog's Meal

I had hoped for a restful sleep, but when it was broken by a quiet metal fist rasping at my door, I knew I was not so lucky. Stirring the sleep from my body as I rolled off the metal counter, I could see it was still dark out. I listened to the world beyond my walls and noticed the morning shift whistle of the factories. Who was knocking on my door this early in the morning?

The floor tin was cold against my feet as I approached the door. A metal knock was never welcomed, but it had to be answered if I wanted my door to remain intact. My hand gripped the metal locking mechanism and slowly disarmed the protections, shifting the girder enough to open the door. I felt bare without my plate cloak, but in theory, I shouldn't be in trouble for anything or need to run for any reason.

Creaking the door open enough to poke my face through the gap, I saw my unfortunate friend, Gregory 235. There was a dull glow in the sky that I hadn't seen from my shack, the early hues of morning. The smell of wet melting paint crept into my senses. He had been in the Barrens and must have gotten caught in a fog.

"Your Scrap Dog services are requested. Get ready and meet me at the top of the steps to the Barrens." His speaker vibrated with bitter resignation from the chilly temperature. All I could do was nod my head and close the door as his metal shoes stomped away into the dark morning.

Tyron's lights were the only brightness in my shack, as it was clothed in darkness once more. The candle by the door had gone out during the night. Stretching my arms above my head and cracking my stiff neck, I went to work at dressing myself. Gathering my warmer clothes, I quickly dressed in the heavy tarping over my under clothes. Layers were the key to long-term warmth even though the plastic was cold on my exposed skin.

My boots and cloak were next. The weight of the metal plates and protective layers strained my already tired muscles. Fingers were numb from the cold as I laced up my boots. Damn Gregory and his tasks. Why couldn't he have called me later? He knew morning runs brought the worst in me.

As a form of punishment, or harassment, I had become his personal Scrap Dog for various tasks that other Scrappers wouldn't accept. Typically, his jobs were more life-threatening, not because of difficulty, but because of the company he managed. Tucking a knife into my boot and grabbing my pack full of spare parts for jobs, I prepared for interactions with Raiders.

Raiders were not openly welcomed in the Loomer Cities because of their more radical mindsets, but they would drift near and ask for help in dire moments. These interactions, at least in Haldoklik, were mediated by the Drones. To the Raiders' fortune, they appeared during Gregory 235's rotation.

Several weapons were hidden across my layers as I approached the door. I didn't want to leave my protection to Gregory if I could help it. Taking a moment to look back, I saw Tyron still 'sleeping' on the table where I had left him. The lights were still blinking as they were supposed to. In these quiet mornings, before the hustle of the day, I tried to imagine him sleeping in. Refusing the call to action of the morning light.

"I'll be back later. Keep sleeping." My words fell on the still form. One day. One day, he would respond. I reminded myself this when the feeling of loneliness in the early morning sank in.

When I opened the door, an icy breeze burned my face, the bitter reminder of the frozen morning ahead of me. Pushing past the tired urge to go back to bed, I closed the door behind me and started my way towards the steps that led out of Haldoklik. My feet fought my first steps into the town, but I forced them forward and waited for the cold to numb their complaints.

With the 'Oomer raid the day before, there was less reason to be cautious. Most people who were up this early worked in the factories and didn't waste their time looting or pillaging before starting for the day. As I looked around the quiet mud caked streets, there was no one. With new found freedom in my steps and no reason to hide or choose back ways, I picked up my pace.

I walked the way I had come the night before. The same blue glowing street lights turned off for the day as the light built up in the sky. There were clouds and to my delight, the smell of rain didn't seem to follow them. Maybe I would have a decent day, despite Gregory's task.

The sound of metal boots quickly shushed my hopes. A group of Markus Units were walking towards me as I rounded a corner, finally in sight of the steps. They all examined me, and while their painted smiles created a visage of kindness, I knew they looked at me with disdain.

"State your purpose, Taylor." The lead of the group spoke to me. Markus D-8494 was one of the lead Drones in Haldoklik, and often the perpetrator of many of my prior injuries. The bias against my pursuit to save Tyron had given me a terrible reputation if I was getting questioned for walking. Though it was not a new thing, it still irritated me.

"On assignment for Gregory 235 in the Barrens." I replied as I continued to walk past them. There was a vague hope that if I responded openly and continued on my way, they wouldn't bother with me. The shifting sounds of metal and support cables were all I needed to hear to know they were watching me over their shoulders.

Without further distractions or interactions, my feet started up the steps. I felt the cold blue LEDs of the Markus units as I climbed higher. The quicker I could get this done, the better. I still had to take care of Gern's task before I could start working on Tyron again.

It's been a few months since I could actually continue my work on Tyron. With a lack of tools and equipment, I could only trade what I had scavenged for parts. Now with the Aju foam accessible from the Giant eye, I could forget how my tired feet remembered my fall and bruises from the other night.

My head passed the horizon wall of the Haldoklik's pit and I scanned the Barrens. Gregory was not far away from the steps, but stood near the edge, scanning the town below. As I took a moment at the top of the stairs, I looked back to see what he saw.

The morning sun was just about to begin its accent into the sky, though obscured through opaque clouds. Smoke had already bled into the sky from the morning shift at the factories. Lights were off and the streets were quiet. Haldoklik was still sleeping.

If I hadn't known better, I would think this town was deserted, but still breathing its own mechanical life. A miserable hell hole in the best days, but when it slept, it felt safe. Maybe it was the humans that made it feel dangerous?

Metal steps approaching caused me to disregard my prior thought. Humans weren't easy, but you could reason with them. Drones could not be reasoned with, or expected to work during humane hours, like Gregory this morning. My joints groaned as I stepped up to the Barrens level and greeted the metal man.

"This way." He said, ignoring my niceties.

We walked South of Haldoklik into the empty lands of the Barrens. Aptly named for their excessive lack of anything. Unless you had specific maps or locations to meet, people did not venture into the emptiness of the world. While it was littered with scrap metal and useless junk, it still felt like an empty void separating the few cities of humans that remained here.

My feet barely made a noise on the drying mud. In contrast, Gregory's shoes felt thunderous in the quiet landscape. Whirring and groaning metal filled each step as he moved his large body. Seeing him now in the brighter morning light, I remembered just how large the Gregory units were.

He stood nearly eight feet tall in his tactical plating position, which he seemed to always maintain. This was a machine that was used as a support soldier during the Loomer's war, but now he was reduced to human suppression. I couldn't help wondering how such an older model still walked.

"How many Gregory models were made?" I broke the silence between us and the Barrens as I risked the question.

"Why do you need to know?" A brief response was expected. Though he would usually have denied the information. Seeing my chance for more education, I pushed.

"Not much is known about the Loomer war. I was just curious since you're an older model." There was no point in lying about my reasons. He would have guessed that I was being insincere and doomed the conversation back to our silent romp through the Barrens.

"By the end of production, there were five million, eight hundred forty-seven thousand, two hundred sixty-three Gregory units. After the first five hundred, the naming scheme changed, leading to an alphabetical and numerical naming system. I am one of the few original Gregory units that maintains only a numerical model description." His steps shifted in pace as he recalled.

I knew there had been many Drones, based purely on what I saw after the Fall, but I had never guessed so many. There were likely a similar number of Markus units as well since they were initially designed as combat Drones. Gregory was truly a marvel, since he still walked after so many years had passed. How many remained after the ravages of time?

"How many Loomers were there?" Tempting my luck, I asked a question that I had asked many times before. The number of Loomers was often protected, hiding the amount of Loomer cities that lay spread across the world. Drones would not share any information that may encourage people to venture out.

"That information is restricted. You know that." The response rang clearly through the quiet morning.

"Worth a shot." I looked over my shoulder to the East as his head turned to scowl at me. As long as I didn't push too many of his buttons, I knew I was safe from punishment. Though a fun game, it was one that could become dangerous if continued for too long.

I had tested the limits of what the Drones would tolerate while living here. Since many of them already disapproved of me, there was no love lost. Most conversations I could maintain with Drones were related to their duties and responsibilities. Occasionally, I would hear about situations with Raiders or dealings between Drones and Giants, but Loomers were never to be discussed.

There had always been rumors that some Loomers still walked, but never confirmed sightings. Our long-lost gods could all be dead, or still roaming a distant land, and we could never know. Their stories were turning into children's tales, myths from a time before, even though we lived in their corpses.

As our steps continued to stomp out the rest of the night and morning light flooded the wasteland, I could see our goal location. In front of us, a ways away, was a group of people. Most were standing around a gigantic pile of something. I could count seven figures from our distance, but anticipated more nearby.

"So, we are walking into a Raider trap today?" My words seemed to bounce off the metal back plates that faced me.

His brooding silence meant that I had pushed one button too many. I was referring to our last outing where he had been asked for assistance, only to bring me and end up in a not-so-clever trap. It was a risk we both ran whenever we did these Raider aid sessions. Typically, it was for organ theft or a chance to take out a Drone for parts. It never ended well, for the Raiders at least.

I could see the gashes and dents on Gregory's plates now, many of which I was present for when he received them. A few I was the cause of. The gold plates shimmered in the light of day as he shifted and looked back at me.

"This one is less likely to be a trap. They claim to have an injured man and are looking for leg supports so they can leave."

His naivety brought a smirk to my face. The genius Drones that helped conquer the world and yet still seemed to walk into traps. Granted, he had enough skill in combat that those who trapped him would always meet cruel ends. It didn't lessen the amusement of him trusting strangers.

We finally drew near to the group. Seeing them in more detail, I realized Gregory may not have been tricked this time. The pile that I mistook from a distance was a behemoth of a man. The smell of rotting flesh and body order made the picture more clear. This was not a behemoth of a man, but a behemoth mutant.

During the Loomer wars, nuclear attacks had been riddled across the land, leaving many areas almost completely uninhabitable. Some Raiders took up these areas because of their isolated nature, but over the generations, paid the cost. I had never run into one before, but today seemed to be my lucky day.

Many of the Raiders kept a distance from him. While wise to stay away from an irradiated creature that only sometimes behaved like a human, they weren't aware of the contamination they already picked up in the Barrens.

Gregory's reasoning for bringing me specifically made sense. Razum Borns were designed with some genetic splicing as well as alterations. While also being fed antioxidant rich diets and specially coordinated breeding, I was essentially impervious to radiation damage. Except for entering a direct nuclear blast zone, this mutant held little to no concern for me. Radiation wise anyway.

When Gregory approached the group, the Raiders stepped back. I scanned the body language of the men and women that stood around. None seemed eager to pick a fight with him, but they watched the behemoth with concern. So maybe this wasn't a trap after all, though caring Raiders still held its own red flag.

I was motioned to the pile of flesh that lay on the ground by Gregory as he spoke to the Raiders. His job was to document this interaction and was doing so by asking the story of what happened. Shifting my gaze from the Raiders, I noticed a pool of blood coming from the legs of the mutant.

The mutant was covered in dark tarps that contrasted the pale soil of the Barrens. Its face was obscured and kept its arms tucked under its body, likely hiding deformities. As I slowly approached the beast, it turned its head to watch me.

A grizzled mug of what once may have been a man looked at me through reddened eyes. His pupils were dilated differently, likely causing a vision impairment. Different colored irises seemed to glow with rage and confusion. Broken or mutilated jaw bones ground as he tried to bare his teeth at me. Less man, and more animal, it seemed.

Crouching down to his level, I held up a peaceful hand. Body language was universal, at least. He seemed to respond to the gesture with what remained of his humanity and he tucked his excessive amount of teeth behind purple lips.

"His name is Gedrik. Can you help him?" A woman's voice came from the group of Raiders. I tossed a glance over my shoulder, careful to keep Gedrik in my sight. She was a taller brunette with a bruised face and obviously a broken arm. The group must have been returning from a raid on another camp. I nodded to her before I continued to examine Gedrik.

Now that I was closer to him, I could see the broken leg. It was obvious he had walked on it for a while till it gave out and made it a fully compound fracture. The darker bone was protruding from ill colored flesh, which led to the point of bleeding. I leaned closer to identify which bone was broken, but received a warning growl in response.

"It looks like his shine is split. If his anatomy and physiology are similar enough to ours, it shouldn't be fatal. How can I help him and not get bit?" I looked back to the woman and Gregory with my assessment. My job was to help here, but I saw no reason to risk my own fingers for a stranger.

The woman now looked at Gregory for permission to move. Once granted, she took up position by Gedrik's face, placing calming hands on his shoulders. Pain seemed to surge through her as she used her broken arm. He seemed to pacify with her touch, and based on the burns of her hands, she seemed to be the one in charge of him. I looked at her for confirmation to proceed.

With the slight nod of her head, I moved towards the injured leg. While there were more growls of proximity warnings, the woman calmed them and motioned me to continue. Pulling back the tarp from his leg, I sighed with a little relief.

His leg seemed to be close to human anatomy, which meant he was less likely to bleed out. It also meant this was going to be a traditional leg reset, clean and brace situation. A process I was painfully familiar with during my run-ins with Drone law.

Placing my hands on the upper and lower portions of the broken leg, I looked at the woman. She seemed to watch me with quiet anticipation. Was there a relationship between this woman and a mutant? Did he still maintain enough humanity to have that kind of interaction?

"I will have to reset the bone and it will hurt... a lot. Gedrik, please don't kick me, or we will have to do it again." Testing my theory of his understanding, I spoke to him directly while looking at the woman. She nodded her understanding of my actions and leaned down over the head of the mutant.

Body still, and blood seeping, I used a quick motion to pull the bones away from one another. Gedrik howled a deformed scream through mutated vocal cords. The sound sent shivers down my spine as I aligned the bones and placed them back into the flesh they broke from.

While Gedrik's non-broken leg flailed, he kept his broken one still as I reached into my scrap pack to find the extra wound wrappings I carried. Scrap Dogs were called for many tasks like this, so I was prepared.

Wrapping his leg with a plate over the wound and gauze underneath to keep the pressure on it, I finished stabilizing his bone the best I could. Now the hard part, making a brace he could wear that could act like a crutch. The only thing that made this easier was Gregory's services.

I pulled out the metal scraps from my pack and put the pieces of what I had together in my mind. Missing a few pieces of my project, I sent the Raiders to scavenge nearby for four long rods. Gregory enforced my words as he now watched over my shoulder.

"Are you making a suppression crutch boot? Taking the weight off his lower leg and transferring it to his upper so that he can walk while keeping his injured portion free of weight?" While I knew Gregory could see through what I was doing, it drove a certain annoyance up in me. People and Drones looking over my shoulder was the most frustrating part of working as a Scrap Dog.

Assembling what I could of the boot, I used Gregory's strength to bend the thicker metal. He warped flat pieces of steel into heel supports like they were paper. A constant reminder of his inhuman strength. Once the boot was fitted and the rods were in place to support the injured leg up, the other Raiders returned with the last pieces.

One fortunate part of the Barrens was the metal carnage that was strewn across the landscape. Anywhere you went, you were likely to find metal or bits of machinery. For making scrap repair kits like mine, it was useful. In terms of helping Tyron, it was all trash.

With the rods in place, strapped to Gedrik's upper thigh, I could attach the supports to the four rods. His leg was sandwiched between the four rods and his knee was kept at a relaxed bend. Locked in metal, all I had left was to add the shocks to the rods that extended past his boot for easier motion.

Once everything was in place and secured, I stepped back. The woman examined my work and nodded towards me in appreciation. Words were used for communication, not thanks.

She slowly helped the behemoth up as he tested his new leg attachment. It was meant to help him walk. Healing and care were his problem to manage, not mine. Taking a few testing steps, I noticed his full height. Shorter than Gregory, he was probably almost seven feet tall.

Gedrik turned towards me now, with the woman's help. The red eyes looked at me as if they were blank of thought. There was no nod, nor motion of appreciation, but I assumed that the lack of a retaliating attack meant it was appreciated.

Turning to Gregory, I raised my eyebrows in question of why we were still here. He seemed to take the hint and turned to face the remaining Raider crowd. Though, in typical Raider fashion, we were met with drawn weapons.

To my dismay, I noticed one pulse gun in the possession of a Raider. This was going to be a quick blood bath, or Gregory was going to go down. One of the most explicit contraband weapons there was, and it was being waved in front of him.

Sensing my danger in this situation, I placed my hand over my own weapons on my belt. The gun would not be used on me, but any of the knives could be pointed in my direction at a moment's notice. It was a trap, after all. I made a mental note to chastise Gregory for this later.

No words were shared, no threats made, actions were all that were left in this conversation. Gregory was the first to jump to action. Within the blink of an eye, he covered the short distance between him and the Raiders and pushed the gun aside before the shot rang out. With another quick motion, the arm of the gun holder was removed and tossed to the ground while the shocked man was pushed to the side. His body knocked two other Raiders from their defensive positions before the other two were thrown to the ground and their skulls crudely crushed into the pale soil by metal shoes.

In a similar fashion, the other three, who laid helplessly under the un-armed man, met the same fate. Gregory took an extra step onto the gun as the woman who helped Gedrik reached for it. The crackling electric gun sparked as it was crushed. I noticed a slight twitch in Gregory's leg as he stared down at the woman and the behemoth.

"I will give you two options: fight and die, or leave." His words rattled through a hushed speaker.

The woman looked at me with hesitation. Options were a rare gift, and she questioned the validity of it. I pointed out to the Barrens, urging her to leave the situation. Gregory watched in a readied pose as the woman turned and started walking Gedrik further into the wasteland.

We watched them leave in silence, waiting for them to get far enough that the threat level diminished. Once Gregory lowered his readied stance, he looked at me. Once he was reassured that I was undamaged, he started back towards Haldoklik, unphased by the interaction.

Leaving the bodies to the wasteland, I followed him. My stomach was churning at the sight of the smashed heads, so I was eager to leave. These were merciful kills, I knew that, but it didn't change the feelings of nausea I endured.

I knew Gregory felt nothing about this death and cruelty. I liked to think I didn't either, but losing life never felt good for me. People have families and connections, someone will miss them, or at least notice their absence. That was what bothered me. The survivors would wonder.

"Do you think the mutant will survive?" Gregory broke my silent thoughts with his dusty sounding speaker.

"If the woman cares for it and makes sure it doesn't get infected, probably." There was no guarantee, and my aid was a temporary fix. The odds of Gedrik surviving were as good as my own chances. In the Barrens, all odds were evened.

"I will watch for him in the future to make sure he doesn't harbor any ill will towards Haldoklik." It was odd hearing Gregory vocalize his intentions. Of all the Drones I was familiar with, he was the only one I knew that did that. Maybe it was an old program from the original Drones, so humans knew what they were thinking.

It would be a decent walk back to Haldoklik. My legs complained as my feet thudded on the dead planet. Things never seemed to calm down these days. If it wasn't one journey, it was the next to prepare for. Aching bones and sore muscles were becoming all I knew. When was the last time I felt rested?

Metal shoes ceased their pounding, and I looked up. Gregory had stopped and was watching me. Had I missed him saying something? The LEDs seemed to glow even in the morning light. Was there something behind those eyes that I was missing?

"You seem more tired than usual. How far did you venture out the other night?" When he regained my attention, we continued to walk. My feet kicked up a metal plate that clattered in the hushed breeze that swept the Barrens.

"If I had to guess, thirty some miles to the East, then thirty back." My response was met with nothing but the quiet whirring of his processors kicking up. This was the only sign I had that Drones were thinking about what was said. It was a distinct hum that was rarely triggered.

"You must have neared the edge of Finigan's region. Be careful switching regions, you will be marked by other Drones and Giants."

Was this advice? Did Gregory finally feel some semblance of kindness or at least empathy towards me? Eager to test this new emotional response, I formulated innocent sounding questions.

"So other Drones will target me if I go too far?" While simple, the addition of talking about myself would either force him to reiterate that this was directed at me, or clarify that it was a general comment. I saw his head swivel slightly, a glance over his shoulder.

"Stay in Haldoklik, Taylor. You know well enough what the dangers are out there." Evading my response, we continued our silent strut through the pale land.

"And stop going out so far. I need you awake for these tasks."

There it was. He was admitting he didn't like that I left town and was tired. This was a new advancement on his part. Gregory had always been kinder to me than the other Drones, but this was the first time he showed it more openly.

"Are you worried about me?" I teased, of course, knowing he didn't. The fact remained that he was shifting from the typical Drone personalities. Gregory 235 was different, not just because of his age, but his programming showed more diversity of emotional responses.

"If you aren't functioning properly, you are going to start something you can't end. You have always been trouble since you showed up. I know how aggressive you get when overtired." He referred to my early days in Haldoklik. I may have started a few fights with Drones and the residents when trying to find space for my shed. After taking a few stabs at Gregory, he had helped create a spot for me.

I noticed the nick on his back plate from a small blade near the lower right. Such a small kid, and yet I was willing to fight a Drone. He must have thought I was pathetic when I dragged my older brother in from the Barrens. Fifteen years old and already was causing trouble to make things better for Tyron.

"It's been five years since then. It's only been three since I've caused any actual damage." The memory of Gern's request floated across my mind. I was going to have to break my peaceful record soon. Hopefully, as long as I don't get caught, Gregory won't know that.

50

As we continued our silent, yet slightly awkward, walk back to Haldoklik, I could smell the city. Without the rain blocking it, I knew how close we were. The town smelt oily and musty, but there was a refined smell of protein bar production. It was similar to bread with meat on it, but with a stronger tone of metals. One of the few smells in this world that made me hungry.

Striding up to the edge of the pit of Haldoklik, Gregory and I looked over the town. It was a powerful feeling to stand on the edge of society and look down. A part of me wondered if Gregory felt the power he held over the people here. Drones were the new order to our chaos. Did he feel in control, like we knew his types were?

After a dismissive farewell from Gregory, we parted ways. He continued his perimeter walk while I descended the wall. More careful this time, trying to avoid the trip I made the other night. While it was a few minutes of calculated footwork, my feet landed on the solid street unscathed.

Although, had I looked up while walking the treacherous path, I would have seen Markus D-8494 waiting for me. Stopping with caution at the bottom of the steps, I waited for his actions. He seemed to have been waiting for my return.

"Task complete?" His speaker was slightly more damaged than Gregory's, and the voice was deeper. Most combat Drones had deeper voices to instill more fear. Though his blue spiked hair and blue armor plates lessened the impact. I watched his body language closely to see what I was at risk of.

"Yes. There was an injured mutant that needed medical assistance. They are gone now." Gregory would upload his own report later, so there was no reason to lie. Though a part of me wanted to, just to irritate the nosy Drone. The spasm in my left arm reminded me why I no longer antagonized him.

His blue LEDs scanned over me. I knew he was looking for a reason to detain me. When his eyes settled on my scrap pack, I prepared my defense for its contents. It wasn't the first time he profiled me on return from the Barrens. It would not be the last either.

"Hand over the pack for examination." Already taking it from around my neck, I held it out.

"It's generic scrap that is used in repairs and aid of others. I used the contents of this bag to help the mutant." Once he took the pack from me and scanned its contents, his LEDs focused on my hands.

I could feel the adrenaline coursing through me, slowly building. Forgetting that I had Giant eye chemicals in my shack, there was likely a chance that I had some on my hands. My eyes darted behind the Markus unit as I looked for a quick exit. He knew where I lived, but without evidence, there was a chance he wouldn't pursue.

The whirring of his own processors kicked up. I could hear the fans functioning over the wakening noises of Haldoklik's residential district. Angling my feet towards the left of the Drone, I sunk my toes into the mud. There was no way I was going to get caught for this today.

"Markus D-8494, is there an issue?" The grumble from a familiar speaker echoed from behind me. I had been so focused on my escape plan, I forgot to listen to what had climbed down from the steps. Casting a confirming glance across my shoulder to Gregory as he stepped past me.

"Taylor has particles of Giant technology on her hands. She carries contraband."

Markus D-8494 was currently shorter than Gregory, but only because he was not in his defensive height. Gregory units held the primary authority in the managing of the cities, though it seemed to be a stressed situation for the Markus units who had once been combat leads in the war. I watched as Gregory flexed his position of power.

"She likely picked it up from the mutant task. The record of the interaction will be uploaded shortly. Dismiss her." His words rattled the plates of my cloak as he used a louder voice. It felt nice to be defended once in a while.

Markus backed down to Gregory's tone and tossed my pack to me. With an annoyed and dismissive wave of his hand, I was removed from his attention as he made his way back towards the city center. Rubbing my hands on my tarp pants, I tried to clean what I could of particle residue from them.

"In the city for ten seconds and already in trouble. Go back to your residence, Taylor. I will not save you again today." Gregory turned from me and started back up the wall. I watched him go, giving him a silent nod of appreciation he didn't see.

Now that Haldoklik was awake, and the Markus units actively prowling the streets for me, I picked a side path back to my shack. Avoiding central streets, I hopefully would have no more run-ins with Drones. There was a time when people caused me the most fear, but it now shifted, day to day. Here the machines ruled supreme some days, while others I would have to watch for a knife in my back by a human.

As I picked careful steps through the back alleys, I could smell decay. There were likely bodies hidden behind some doors I passed. People who had escaped the 'Oomers' chase but suffered attacks. When the Drones cleaned up, the houses would be broken into and the population numbers adjusted accordingly.

There weren't many people out of their homes, but the few that were watched cautiously. I avoided looking into their eyes, knowing that Gregory and Markus were probably heard half way through Haldoklik. Interactions with Drones always seemed to draw unwanted attention from the people, and in this case, attention was on me.

I already had a rough history with Drones and the people as an outsider. The jobs I ran for Gregory only deepened their dislike and distrust of me. As if being a Razum Born in a Razum hating town was not enough, I was also the Scrap Dog of the Drones. Respected, feared, and hated.

Rounding another street corner, I poked my head forward to look down the street way. While there were no Drones on this street, there were a few people. Risking my appearance, I entered the street and started down the path towards the group. Planning to turn the corner before I reached them, I was brought to a pause as they spoke to me.

"Still kissin' tin ass?" The man who spoke was trying to over-articulate his 'Klik slang for me to understand him better. A subtle jab at my status as Razum born and the work I did for Gregory. I felt irritation at the words, but did my best to ignore it.

Turning the corner near, I heard them continue leering as I left.

Comments of 'Drone sympathizer' and 'not human enough' echoed down the narrow alley. While I refused to show them the effects of their words, my fists balled in frustration.

It felt like there was no end to the mocking I could receive. Whether from where I was born, or who I associated with, nothing seemed to appease the people or Drones around me. I couldn't win the social game regardless of which team I worked for.

Crossing streets more quickly now to avoid being harassed, I drew near to my shack. Four more crossings and I would be safely hidden away with Tyron. Quickening my steps as I crossed another street, I noticed another gathering of people. This group was larger and circled around something scrawled on the front wall of a residential house.

The tin that coated the building seemed to be dug at, like something was trying to pull the wall apart. Likely an 'Oomer group had targeted the building, to no avail. As I risked a few steps nearer to the building, I saw the reason for the gathering.

Scrawled in blood were the words, "Lexi Lives". For the more paranoid, this would be a fearful message meant to instill a constant feeling of anguish. For me, it was more insane ramblings of minds lost to the hunger of Synthix. Ducking back to the alley I was headed for, I could hear the distant whispers.

"Yu tink she still out dere?"

"Vudn't someone know if her body found?"

"Loomers...still valkin?"

Their voices faded as I quickly disappeared into another alley. Apparently, the 'Oomers had brought more than fear. They brought more myths of Loomers. It happened from time to time, but this was the most direct reference to Lexi that I had witnessed.

For a moment, I wondered at the validity of the graffiti. It could be possible that Lexi still roamed the wasteland of Earth, perhaps on a distant continent. Though it was more likely, she fell like the rest did. I couldn't help but feel that it was a lie the 'Oomers created to feel like their gods were closer to them.

If she did still walk, wouldn't we have seen signs? Fresh Loomer tracks in the Barrens? Shadows cast across towns? It wasn't like she was a simple thing to hide. While I shuffled the validity of each view, I hit the same conclusion: who knows for sure?

As I crossed the remaining streets, I noticed the town was getting louder. More people were awake now and the rustling and conversations were beating like a heart in Haldoklik. This was the time of day I had hoped to avoid, as it was the busiest.

Reaching the street that my shack was hidden on, I hurried down the block. I could hear voices calling to each other down the street. Warnings to flee echoed through the street as I approached my shack. A new insult had been inscribed on the warning signs that made up the front of my shed.

"Metal's Mutt."

Apparently, more people had heard my interactions with Gregory this morning than I had hoped. I had no choice but to ignore the insult my shed shouted at me and unlock the door. As it ground across the mud, I felt more eyes look at me. I quickly tucked inside, taking my stigmatic influence with me.

The blackness of my shack consumed me as the door shut and the slivers of light through the panels welcomed me. I felt free from prying eyes and added prejudices. Although the feeling of not fitting in degraded my soul daily, I knew where I belonged in the long term. Slow light pulses from Tyron's Razum reminded me of that.

I dropped my scrap pack by the door as I locked it from the cruel world outside. No more words would enter my mind today. Too many thoughts already clogged the gears of my head. Thoughts of Lexi, 'Oomers, mutants, Gregorys, Markus', were already too much to consider on top of being alienated from my town.

Lighting candles to chase away the dark, I kicked off my boots. They thudded against the wall like angered fists before they dropped to the ground. Hanging my cloak on my stool back, I settled at my desk and let the cold metal cool my over thinking mind.

"Tyron," I moaned to the comatose figure, "this world is miserable."

I waited for the reassuring response, but knew there would be none.

"First Gregory had to drag me out of bed, then Raiders picked a fight. When I finally got back to Haldoklik, people just glared at me. We even have a new insult on the door. I have to give them some credit though, Metal's Mutt was pretty clever." While no verbal consolation came, I felt better ranting to him.

"There was even a new 'Oomer's riddle' painted on someone's house. 'Lexi Lives'. I kind of forgot that some people still think she's out there. She can't be... right? A Loomer would have been noticed. It would be big news, even the dense people of Haldoklik would have heard about it." I fidgeted with the various coils and broken motherboards that were strewn across my bench while I complained. Careful not to bump the Giant's eye, I covered the contraband behind some scrap plates to make sure it wasn't visible. Another Markus situation without the aid of Gregory would not be ideal.

Rolling a copper coiled motor between my hands, I sighed. It was a futile attempt to contaminate my hands with more oil and dirt to hide Giant residue. I knew it wouldn't work, but it helped me feel better. Having dirtied hands always felt like I accomplished something useful.

"Why couldn't that old man who always breaks his door knock today? Why did it have to be Gregory so close to when I needed to help Gern?" Rubbing the oil and dirt on my face in frustration, I sighed again.

My eyes stung from the small amount of oil that got in them. It's what I deserved for complaining. When the dirt that was contaminated with acid started to burn, I conceded to the world, telling me to toughen up. I grabbed the tarp rag I used for my desk and wiped the dirt and oil away.

Standing from my desk, I located my clean-ish water supply that I kept for bathing. The smell in the shed was turning obviously putrid. It had been a few weeks for me, and today was the day I finally caved. Grabbing the mostly clean cloth-like rag, I wiped down my face.

As droplets of dirt and grime fell from my chin as though they were fleeing the water, I caught my reflection in the metal bucket. Pale blonde hair stabbed forward with sharp edges. Though my hair may have been acid washed and dead, my eyes were still cold and lifeless.

I remembered how Tyron used to say my eyes were full of life when I was younger. Would he still say that if he could see how tired they looked? Making a note to ask him that when he woke up, I continued to scrub the caked layers of grime off.

Taking off my warmer layers, I could feel the abrasive cold invade the surface of my skin. I always did my body, piece by piece. It was too cold to bathe all at once. My arms were first as I pulled up my sleeves.

"Do you think I should do Gern's task? It's a high risk to mess with Drones. I haven't been busted for anything in a long time. Not really excited to break that record." I finished scrubbing my right arm raw with the rag and the cold water dripped down my fingers. Quickly drying it with a cleaner tarp, I moved on to the left.

"Gern has a tool that could help though, I think anyway. I don't know what it does, but it will be better than the nothing I'm working with now. It's a tremendous risk... one I could not come back from. We did agree that I would stop risking so much, but... if that tool can help me get the Aju foam, I would be a lot closer to getting you out." My arm flinched as I ran the rag across the bruise from the other night. Going slower and softer, I lightly patted the area clean.

There was no choice about Gern's task. It had to be done. For Tyron. I knew that. I was just worried about the extreme nature of the request. Risking my life, and even the city's security for Drone arms was a needless risk.

Finishing my arms, I pulled them through the sleeves and lifted the shirt off. The freezing air caused my skin to prickle. Quickly rubbing the rag across my torso, I shuddered at the brisk water. Scrubbing my armpits and neck, I decided it was good enough and quickly dried and donned my shirt once more.

Proceeding to the rest of my body, I stood. The thoughts of the people mocking me sifted through my already raging mind. I did my part in this town, yet I still was harassed. Scrubbing hard to ease the cold with the numbing friction pain, I gritted my teeth.

"Metal's Mutt. Screw them. If I didn't help, there would be a lot more dead bodies in the Barrens tonight. Are they so blind they can't see that I need to do what I have to in order to survive here too? I'm not out raiding, or killing mercilessly. I'm helping people. It's not reasonable to mock me. Metal's Mutt..." The words rolled out of me like sand through gritted teeth.

I could almost hear Tyron's soothing words. He always had talked me down from my frustration, worried I was going to do something rash. It wasn't fair that these strangers had such an impact on my feelings. They would never know it, though. I wouldn't let them, only Tyron was allowed to know me.

Finishing my legs with the cold rag, I dropped it back into the bucket and pulled up my pants. I rubbed the tarping against me trying to increase the frictional heat. It would hurt later, but at least I felt a little warmer. As I finished adjusting my clothes and taking a deep breath of slightly fresher air, I made my way to Tyron's counter.

Leaning against the metal surface, I waited for the eventual knock. Scrap Dogs were paid in many ways, depending on who hired them. Most people would exchange parts or scrap of interest. Some in the higher status residential areas would offer less illegal contraband in exchange of services. Drones like Gregory would pay with an extra ration of food.

While it was past noon now, I had a good guess that he was going to be coming by with his payment soon. His rotations were typically five days of midnight to noon shifts with regular check-ins. When he wasn't doing perimeter walks during the five days, he was watching the factory district. With no need for breaks or vacations, Haldoklik was under constant surveillance.

Metal shoes slowly faded into my awareness as I waited. My shack was off the normal routes of the Markus units, so it was easier to guess who owned the feet that approached. I stood and readied myself by the door, unlocking it before he could knock. As I opened the door, I was greeted with glowing LEDs.

"Metal's Mutt?" Gregory 235 asked as the door opened. A twinge of embarrassment likely colored my cheeks at the mention of the new nickname.

"That's what I get for helping you." I grumbled my response quietly. It could be taken as insubordination of a Drone if I wasn't careful with my tone.

"I didn't think the 'Klik's' were that witty." His tone betrayed his impressed attitude, which only drove my frustration higher. I held out my hand, ready to accept my payment and be done with interacting with him.

He did not hand me the synthetic protein bar he carried. LEDs scanned the wall of my shack with its many signs. Was he judging my decorations now? Gregory was in an odd mood today. His actions weren't making sense, like they typically did.

"I heard a rumor tonight that I will not repeat. Gern mentioned a Cherub 735 and a task for you to another Scrap Dog. If this is about his vendetta against Cherub 735, I recommend not completing that request." His words were hushed, which caused them to prickle my skin with nervous anticipation. Was this a warning, or a threat that he would catch me?

Gregory held the bar out to me now. Willing my hands to not shake, I accepted the bar. My movements felt more robotic than Gregory's. Swallowing the lump of nervous hesitation in my throat, I nodded to him.

"I don't know what you're talking about," was all I could mutter.

His eyes looked further down the street in both directions. Watchful of onlookers. Once his eyes settled back on me, I noticed a slight flicker in his right eye. Was the old Drone finally suffering for the years of torment he has caused?

"Don't be a fool, Taylor." With that simple phrase, he started back towards the factory district near the head of the city. Warily, I watched the machine disappear down the street. Once out of view, I closed the door and locked it again.

"Damn it, Gern." I muttered to Tyron. He had risked my entire operation with his mutterings. There would be a time, place, and price for the risks I am now involved with.

I crawled onto the counter with Tyron, already done with how the day had gone. Hugging my brother, I tucked myself under the musty and rank smelling tarp blankets. There was nothing to do today besides plan how I was going to risk my life another day.

While I let the annoyed thoughts of the day flow from my mind, I grappled with the additional problem at hand. If Gregory was watching for me to make a move, it was better to be quick than to wait. Closing my eyes, I probed through plans and tactics while ignoring the sporadic thoughts of frustration from the day.

"Never easy to survive, is it, Tyron?"

Chapter 3: Cherub 735's Bad Day

Loud boots stomping through the street echoed through my small shed. I barely bothered to open my eyes to notice the dim light glowing through the cracks of the walls. This day was coming eventually, I knew that. The Drones were going through house by house to find those who were dead from the 'Oomer swarm. Similar to a roll call, they were checking the population numbers of the residential district.

A few years ago, after a particularly devastating 'Oomer raid, an illness swept through Haldoklik. This triggered the Drones to begin regular checks on the surviving citizens. The warm season exacerbated the situation, intensifying the stench of decay that now haunts my memories. That smell, and the horrors it recalls, are things I can never forget.

I sat up and felt the slight warmth of the day entering the shed as the sun was rising. Checking on Tyron gave my heart the normal sinking feeling. The blinking of the Razum lights still beat as he slept. I reached a hand out to caress his chin, trying to remind him of the sensations of the real world. No movement or acknowledgment was my reward for trying. Pulling my sluggish body from the uncomfortable metal slab, stretching my arms over my head. My spine crackled like crinkled tin as I tested my range of motion for the day.

A metal hand slammed against my door. "Taylor, RB, five foot seven inches, blonde hair with blue eyes, roughly eighty-seven pounds. Are you active?" Asked a very obvious Markus Drone. I knew it would be safer to open the door and verify that I was indeed alive, but it was always more fun to not open up. My contraband was already hidden from sight and

Markus units weren't permitted to imprison people during Raid checks. A fun perk I learned when my door was broken in while I was working on some Giant research for Tyron.

"Taylor, RB, five foot seven inches, blonde hair with blue eyes, roughly eighty-seven pounds. Are you active?" It asked again. A few seconds of silence ticked past, and I saw the melted, damaged fingers of Markus A-9673 pulling my door apart like it was loose dirt.

Once he opened the door enough to see me watching him through his hollow blue LED eyes, the Drone let out an annoyed sigh. My smile probably gave him a certain sense of irritation. This wasn't my first time I blatantly ignored the Raid checks. Though there was a useful side effect of letting a Drone rip my door from its hinges.

"Taylor, you have been found to be legally alive. Congratulations on surviving another 'Ooomer Raid." Markus A-9673 pulled the door the rest of the way off of its hinges and set it outside beside my shed. Markus units ran up to seven feet tall without tactical plate shifts, like a Gregory unit, so his awkward bow and shuffle through my small doorway was an amusing sight. Reaching behind myself, I quickly pulled a blanket over Tyron's head. I didn't want to hear them talk about my brother. Enough hate and bullying had been applied over the years.

"Tyron, legally deceased twelve years ago. Let us discard that for you." Markus A-9673 said, reaching for Tyron past me. Markus A-9673 and I were old acquaintances, and many of our fights were over Tyron. This was just another taunt to make me jump to Tyron's defense and put myself in danger. I stepped forward to stand by Tyron when Gregory 235 poked his golden curved hair into my shed, getting the attention of Markus as he was looking around my shed. He would have seen the Giant residue all over my shack without the interruption.

"Markus A-9673, you know this house belongs to the family unit registered under Taylor's name. She and her brother have been verified as alive. Exit the household. This is unlawful." Gregory said firmly. I could feel the tension quickly build between the combat Drone and the support Drone. A part of me wished I had a camera to capture the power struggle being conveyed through loud whirring and silent debate.

Markus A-9673 glared at me with his polished face. I could see the indents of what might have been a painted smile at one point. With reluctance, Markus pushed past me and waited for Gregory 235 to remove his head from the doorway. As the two Drones walked, Gregory paused and returned his head to my shed door.

"Has your progress led you to a feasible option to take the Razum off him yet?" he asked. I felt my body relax slightly. While I hated what his existence had done to this world, and the social demonization he had brought to me, he was as close as I would find to a 'good guy' in this world. Well, good enough is probably a better way to explain him.

"Of course, with all the spare time you leave me." My sarcastic words seemed to mean nothing to Gregory as he waited for me to continue with the truth. "No. The Razum prisons are hard to crack by design." An awkward silence joined the shed as I reached back to hold Tyron's hand while I spoke.

To alleviate the silence, I tried a more friendly statement. There was no need to get every Drone in Haldoklik to hate me, yet. "I see Markus A-9673 still has it out for me." Some bitterness fell into my voice, defeating the friendly tone I had planned. My history with Markus A-9673 was not a hidden one. Through my more youthful years of rebellious trouble causing, I was made the example of many public punishments and embarrassments. Markus A-9673 was all too happy to volunteer to be the perpetrator of my consequences.

"You know why they watch you, do you not?" Gregory asked in a quieter tone. He stepped closer, craning his neck down to even try to look me in the eye. I shook my head, unsure of what he thought I knew and stepped back. It was an instinctual response to step away from an approaching Drone, yet it earned a quiet, menacing chuckle. His attitude today was confusing, between friendly and oddly distant.

"The world isn't ready for Tyron." He said as he reached a slow hand into my shed, towards my brother. Fearing the possibility of an angered Gregory, I put myself between him and Tyron. Gregory did not pause, pushing me from his path, and pulled the blanket down off of Tyron's face. I often forgot how quickly these metal things could move. It was unnerving.

Gregory ducked into the doorway of my shed as he drew his face closer to Tyron's. His hand hovered above the Razum, likely scanning the internal components that I didn't have access to. After a few moments, I relaxed, realizing that this was not a mocking act, but one of consideration. He rested his hand on the Razum before facing me.

"He doesn't have much longer before the Razum fully incorporates his body into its system. There is now a ninety-seven point three percent chance of failure. You should focus more on your brother if you want to give him a chance." Gregory's tone was almost empathetic, which somehow was more unnerving than if he had been sarcastic. Though, hearing the updated percentage of success was disheartening.

"I don't have the tools I need. If you have nothing that could help me, please leave and fix my door." I placed myself between Tyron and Gregory once more. There may be consequences for acting against him, but he knew I would figure out consequences for bothering me. My legs were shaking as I stood in opposition. Yet again, I was taking a stance against a Drone and betting on my own luck.

"Do not push Markus A-9673 unnecessarily next time. If it's any consolation, I should not need your services for some time in the foreseeable future. Use whatever luck you think you still have, Taylor." Gregory said, backing out of the shed. There was a rasp of metal against metal as his shoulder plates scuffed against the tin frame of the door.

Before he left my sight completely, he grabbed the scrap metal door that Markus A-9673 had ripped out. While examining it, he pulled loose signs from the face of my shed and started to bend and mold the hinges back together. I watched as he rotated the door between his hands, making adjustments and strengthening it like it was clay in his hands.

When the door seemed fixed to his standards, he began adjusting the frame. My shed shook and shuttered to the force of his gloved hands as he corrected the design of my shack. Gregory then placed the door back on newly remodeled hinges. Testing the door with a few swings, I noticed the old squeak of rusted hinges was less, and the door actually fit the frame.

The door was now more secure than before, which was the reason it paid to anger the Markus units. They were known for being a bit more clumsy and destructive, but it was the Gregory unit's job to clean up what they broke. As he tested one more swing of the door, he nodded to me and sealed my shed closed.

I sat back by my brother's side. A small burning ember of annoyance began engulfing my thoughts. If it wasn't bad enough to have my shed invaded by Drones, I also had to endure the insults to Tyron. They knew how to irritate me and with no ability to defend or fight back; I had to tolerate it.

"Legally Deceased." The words felt bitter on my tongue.

Razums were a death sentence. Whether you were born in one and left, or if you were still inside. Even those who had the chance to leave were treated like dead weight, but at least they were considered alive. Tyron wasn't even considered a living creature anymore, he was just dead. I could feel my jaw muscles clenching and my fingers flexing. The things I wish I could do to Markus A-9673 would only lead to my actual legal death, as well as Tyron's. With no other option or outlet for my anger, I slowed my breathing, focusing on matching the beats of the Razum lights.

"Don't listen to Gregory, Tyron. He doesn't know how good of a fighter you are. We will figure this out. But today, I need to go out. Gern's task is waiting for me. Will you stay out of trouble here by yourself?" I asked my quiet, near life-less brother. The Razum's steady indicator light blinked quietly, and I chose to believe it to mean that he agreed to stay out of trouble. I pulled the blanket over my brother's face once again to keep some body warmth with him while I was gone.

I had initially wanted to wait to get Cherub 735's arms, but this opportunity would make this a peaceful day to enact my plan. With the 'Oomers having raided so recently, they would be tired and mostly restrained to their specific temples and homes. This also meant that the Drones would be in designated areas watching over the restrained and not wandering around out of pattern. An optimal day.

If Gern was correct on his theory of the location, and if the day remains quiet and busy in its usual way, I should be able to ambush Cherub 735 right as they finished their shift circling Lower Town. I just had to find the perfect vantage and guess which way the crafty little aircraft was going to come from.

There was only one chance to do this right. If I mess up, or the plan doesn't go exactly my way, I will be caught and killed. Though death was hardly a punishment anymore. A painful death was expected in this world. There was no way to avoid it, and it lurked around every corner of my life.

That being said, I was still going to play it safer. I gathered my outside clothing and dressed as discreetly as possible. Making sure my hood was up and my face masked, I started my rummaging for equipment to face the day. I remembered to grab the sling I had welded together from spare car parts. It was heavy and clunky, but had enough power to put a door knob through a Giant's optical unit. After a few unfortunate run ins with raiders in the Barrens, I learned to do damage from a distance. It strapped uncomfortably against my stomach, the tarp cloak obscuring its form.

I took a deep breath. Starting my tradition of psyching myself up to do dangerous and illegal things with contraband on me. Several deep breaths paired with loud sighs and swinging my arms to get the blood flowing. Once my body felt eager to move, I waved goodbye to Tyron before setting off towards Lower Town.

People moving around today, the sun usually cajoled them out of hiding. It was a rare morning of knowing peace. The 'Oomer worshipers were being contained. The sun was bright, and it was unseasonably warm for the cooler season. There wasn't any active danger, just the ever-present ambient danger.

Even though my boots were loud in the mud, the patter of children running through the gutters was louder still. I knew of five or six kids in the town, but it was growing increasingly rare to see them out and about with their families. The 'Oomer worshipers were not fond of the existence of children because of their belief that flesh is a lower form of evolution and procreating humans were perpetuating their de-evolution. With a broken society bent on self preservation, and a death cult of metal evolution running rampant through town, it was much safer for children to not be seen or known.

The children played with scrap metal guns and clothed in lead armor to protect them from the mud. Little survivalist children were a welcomed and warming encounter. As they stomped through the alley between two houses, they made shooting sounds and Drone impersonations. To these kids, this was the only world they knew.

I could almost feel their joy in my own memories, stomping after my brother in the Razum. It felt like yesterday that I could hear Tyron taunting me. So much time has passed, but his voice could never fade from my mind. Whether in my dreams, in the silence of my shack, while on the hunt from scrap or dodging trouble, I never felt alone because of Tyron. The children faded into the background of the busy allies and I continued on my way, pushing the painful nostalgia back. It is a day to focus.

Picking careful footing along the rough and muddy street, I spotted the first buildings of the Lower Town. This was the old sector. A lingering smell of blood and Nanite dust was still present on the old cube style buildings. These were structures that the earlier Drones had designed for the first human refugees to aid in the organization of society. Each home was carved with the genetic sequence of the people who were required to live there and painted white to make it feel freeing. The purpose of this design was to track reproduction for better genetic coding. Traits like submissive and fearful were typically kept around while the Drones would cull those who did not possess those traits. This Loomer's corpse of a town had truly seen some dark times.

Arches stood as the gate between Mid and Lower town, inscribed with rules in crude robotic languages. While I could read a portion of the language, I did my best to not pay attention. I had made the mistake of reading the rules written there when I was new to Haldoklik. The gruesome images of the tortures and punishments described there never left my dreams. Shadows crossed over me as I walked beneath the open arches, putting the memories behind me.

There was shuffling in the quiet cubic sector. The wrangled 'Oomers and few remaining citizens were getting ready to get up before the Drone wave flooded through to check for survivors. I saw a few severed metallic limbs in the mud of the streets. Due to being able to see the metal before the mud consumed it, I could tell they were recently lost during the Raid. The acid in the mud had yet to dissolve the evidence of violence. My foot knocked the scraps around to see if there was any useful metal. It was mostly salvaged from broken machinery and radios. There was always a chance, though, that an unfortunate 'Oomer had nicked a tool or mechanism from a downed Giant or Drone. I felt eyes watching me as I checked the limbs. The ever-present eyes in Lower Town.

Feeling the judgment and possible trap planning, I moved from the main street to some side alleys I had used before. It was not typically a great idea to walk the back roads of Lower Town, but in such a bright morning light, I was feeling far too exposed for what my day plans were looking like. I saw a few stragglers follow me from the main road, trying to conceal themselves around corners. With how badly they were hiding, I would guess they are lower level 'Oomers. Not quite a threat, but a very unwelcoming sense of attention.

They were looking for food because of starving on the synthetic sludge the main populace of 'Oomers consumed. Based on how their bodies looked, they were rejecting the level of toxicity they were training with. The synthetic calories the 'Oomers had injected into their bodies for sustenance was my old addiction, Synthix. In its average consumed state, it could kill instead of sustain. It required years of adapting one's body to the mechanical-chemical slurry. If I remember correctly, Synthix was basically the joint lubricant of all robots made after the Giant's age. It was common enough to find in all areas, some Drones were even willing to trade it for information in cases. It has crossed my mind that it would be easier to convert to Synthix if I ever figured out a better location to flee to. The difference between life and death in the Barrens could be a shot of Synthix. After watching the suffering, poisoned, and sickly low level 'Oomers shuffling after me, I felt my hesitation at that plan. I finally dodged around enough corners to lose the weakened 'Oomers and the streets finally quieted behind me.

Cubed buildings felt like the walls of a maze as my feet trodden down the alleyways. I had already started smelling the sour tang of human waste processors, so I knew the chimneys were close. Doing a quick half circle glance above the cubed walls, I saw the tall chimneys; the tips darkened with memories of their black clouds.

"That is going to be a terrible climb. God damn it Gern, why do you have to be so petty?" I grumbled to the silent cube town. The large slingshot under my clothes shifted uncomfortably as the heavy metal had already dug into my skin. While the chimney was a great vantage and hiding spot, the idea of carrying the sling shot up with me sounded exhausting.

"This is such a dumb idea..." I muttered to myself, rethinking my plan. This was a half-assed plan, I knew it, but it seemed more plausible. Sometimes you have to abandon sense to achieve the things you need to, even when your head is telling you that you will fail and end up dead. That's what I chose to believe in times like this.

With no better plan, I continued shuffling my way quietly through the alleys before I heard the whirring of automated joints. Markus units this far from a restriction zone was unusual. Typically, the Drones would stand guard near the North West of Lower Town to keep the 'Oomers in line. Trying to avoid being seen, I stopped and placed my back against a wall.

To my dismay, I had been more distracted than I realized. It wasn't one Markus Drone, but several. From the crooked sounding gait and a familiar grinding shoulder plate, I realized what I almost stumbled into. I could hear the shuddering of a small crowd of 'Oomers' as the Drones approached.

The Lower Town square was around the next corner I was going to turn. I must have taken a wrong turn at some point, because this was the last place I wanted to cross. Peaking my head around the corner, I caught a glance of those who were gathered before pulling my face back into hiding. Five Markus Units stood guard behind a damaged Gregory Unit as they stood before a crowd of disfigured and ill 'Oomers.

I couldn't think of a more complicated situation for me to have accidentally walked near. My body slowly lowered to the mud, adjusting the sling
as I shifted. A slicing sensation caused me to grimace as one of the metal
plates on the sling grazed my ribs. Once I stilled my breathing, I peaked
one eye around the corner of the cube home near me, trying to see if I had
caused any attention.

Town square was filled with dozens of 'Oomers and onlookers. I felt
a gag threaten to escape me as I saw a few of the child 'Oomers missing
arms and legs, and from the darkness under their skin I could tell they
were already fully committed to the Synthix sludge. They must have been
grabbed during the prior attack. Looking slightly closer at the children, I
saw the reasoning for the gathering. The tech that made up the mutilated
children's missing limbs glistened against all the older and worn metal
scraps buried in the flesh of the other followers.

My stomach churned as a Markus unit walked by the mutilated children.
I was near witnessing something that should not be seen. A Gregory model
was supervising this public display of power; he was backed by the other
Markus units. I knew I wouldn't be able to stop anything, but the least I
could do was endure their story to its end.

"'Oomers are allowed to practice freely in Haldoklik. We have allowed
many intrusions and given great autonomy to this organization. There
is one practice we do not tolerate: The trial of theft young 'Oomers are
required to complete. These two children were caught with freshly stolen
mods from several Markus Units and Gregory Units. This will not be
tolerated as it falls under the illegal technology laws. According to those
laws, the punishment is reclamation of stolen property by force and the
shattering of limbs. Present the two children, or have this be a forceful
reclamation." Declared the Gregory Unit. The older 'Oomers quickly
pushed the children forward and stepped back to the alleys of the market
square. They knew the pain of forceful reclamation well.

The two children were shivering before the Markus unit as the crowd
pressed closer like predators around prey. Even 'Oomer children were

aware of this price. Most people who remain in the Lower town have seen these reclamation processes. The punishment was well known in all the districts of Haldoklik.

A Markus unit near the children grabbed the augmented limbs of the kids, an arm on one and a leg on the other. I looked a bit closer and noticed that the leg was primarily made of Gregory's arm scraps. I could see the bio-wiring surging into the kid's newly amputated limb, the machinery healing the wound. Nodding respect to the kid, who I think was a girl for the ingenuity and high-class scrap. It could not have been an easy pinch, but it was also the reason these kids got caught.

While the augmented arm was more crude because of the parts coming from a Markus unit, I saw fragments of what looked like Markus leg components along with several shoulder scraps plated with the typical Markus blue plates. The wiring was more crudely jammed into the amputated arm flesh. By how the child moved and tried to fight the grip of the Markus Unit, I assumed he was a slightly older boy. These kids were impressive thieves, yet paying the price for not being better.

I could see the grip of the Markus Unit tighten on the augments and the girl with the Gregory parts flinched from the nerve modifiers in the scrap. The Gregory model stepped forward over the kids and the Markus unit. He faced and addressed the crowd in attendance. A metal jaw drop ensured he could be heard widely through Lower Town.

"Under the laws of the Giants and Loomers, these stolen components will be reclaimed and recirculated through the Drone population. Markus B-8530, proceed with the reclamation." Gregory said, his eyes flashing red under the gilded, sculpted hair. He had started recording the situation for Giant review later.

My eyes darted away from the kids as Markus B-8530 proceeded with the sentencing. The screams echoed through the square as metal was being ripped from flesh, chased by a quiet metallic applause from the observing Markus units. Daring to peek my head around the corner to see the carnage, I immediately regretted my decision.

Blood was spilling over the tan and black muddy gravel of the square.

The children lay on the ground, their augments removed, their limbs pulled flat against the ground. There was no fear in their eyes now. Their fate was sealed. Whatever small shred of hope they once may have had now faded into understanding that their death was going to be cruel and a public declaration of power.

Markus B-8530 loomed over the children. Even with the chipped paint of a smile on his face, it almost felt as though he actually enjoyed his job. It didn't take more than a minute for the heavy metal shoe of the Markus to pulverize the joints and primary bones of the two kids' limbs. Sheer screams rang out, like a final attempt to release their souls from their bodies before the worst was to come. Markus B-8530 retreated from the children triumphantly and replaced himself by the Gregory unit presiding.

"Laws held, ordinances followed. We thank you for your cooperation." Gregory said, as he turned his back. The Markus Units followed suit, except Markus B-8530. He was apparently a more sadistic model and watched the weak, starved 'Oomer worshipers rush to the children. An easy meal for starved Synthix converts was not common, and in Lower Town, there was no sense left.

I watched as several of the 'Oomer worships surrounded the kids. They blocked my view, which I was grateful for, but they could not block the sounds. Flesh was being torn from shattered bone, screams were being gurgled out of punctured lungs. This world was not for the weak at heart, or those unwilling to do anything to survive.

Even my memories had recalled the taste of flesh before I felt the bile spewing through my lips. Throwing myself behind the corner of the wall, I only noticed one Markus unit looking in my direction. I was fairly certain he didn't see me, but there was no time to wait and find out. I wiped the vomit from my mouth and started my way from the town square and towards the chimneys. The last of the screams quieted when I reached the tall, pale smoke stacks.

"I hope there is somewhere better for you." I liked to think the souls could hear me as they left this plane. Maybe there was something better out there than the void, or maybe their 'Oomer ways stole that from them.

So young to be judged by gods, metal or metaphysical.

The door for the monitoring room of the chimney stacks was broken open as I approached. It had never broken open while I had been hiding in the area. Drones must have been hunting for something. I pulled my lead garb closer around myself again, trying to keep the shape of the sling concealed so I could pass as just shady, not carrying illegal contraband.

"This trip is getting more and more reckless by the minute." I muttered to myself, slowly pushing the door fragments out of the way to enter the monitor room. The smell of ashes and wet, acrid soot filled my nose. A crematorium was never an agreeable smell, but the humidity and rain made the air more dense with sulfuric tones.

There was broken glass strewn across the floor. The dials and informational desks were completely destroyed. Glass crushed underfoot as I approached the viewing window that peered over the furnace below. Looking over the scene, I began mentally piecing the evidence of what story might have unfolded here.

It wasn't a Drone hunting situation that destroyed this place. The broken door and dents across the walls was more like a Fritz Drone who tried to hide in the chimney stacks. The drag marks on the ground looked like it was removed forcefully. Fritzing has been happening a little more frequently these days. My best guess was because of the aging of old circuitry in some of the antique models.

I picked my way cautiously over the broken glass to the desks that were crumpled to the ground. A sound caused me to check over my shoulder towards the door. After a still moment of holding my breath and waiting for Drones to descend on me, the town beyond was silent. For now, it appeared I was out of sight. Each piece of glass that chimed against the concrete floor sent shivers up my spine as if I was plucking the string of a spider web. This was the last place I wanted to be seen right now, not only for the success of my mission but for the trapped sense of the small room.

Pulling the sling out of my clothing, I removed the metal shavings that were lodged in my stomach. As the metal was removed, I felt a quiet sense of relief. Though it was short-lived as I realized blood was flowing down my skin. Patting the fresh streams with the edge of my shirt, I realized the wounds weren't deep enough to cause concern. I could stitch it later. For now, I had a pair of arms to focus on stealing. A part of me wished I had the heart to ask a new 'Oomer initiate' to steal it for me, but I couldn't put someone through the horrors I had witnessed today.

I knew this was a tough world, but I still didn't have the stomach to use this world like everyone else. The old scientist who had saved my life was the main reason for this. He always mocked me, told me to be tougher, or the world was going to kill me and kill Tyron. He told me to treat all life like a stepping stone if I wanted my brother back. The memories of the scientist flashed red. I could see the carnage of his body and felt my starvation trapped under the rubble of a ruined building. I fled the memories. Distractions now would lead me to my death. I would deal with those memories when Tyron was awake and well.

Approaching the shattered viewing window, I hefted the sling onto the frame before letting it drop to the soot covered floor of the furnace within. It landed quietly in the remnants of many burned bodies. A plume of charred corpse dust floated up as I pulled my shirt over my nose. I threw myself in after my sling; the soot burning my eyes and my feet crying out in pain from the five-foot drop.

After a minute of digging in the soot to find my sling, which had sunk, I tossed it onto my shoulder as I felt around with blind eyes for the maintenance ladder. My hands clamped onto the rungs of the ladder as I stifled a sneeze. The acrid dust was coating the inside of my nose and teasing my senses. I quickly pulled myself and the sling up the ladder, out of the cremation cloud that I had stirred. The sky above showed a graying sky as the clouds gathered for rain, a storm brewing like the swirls of a cauldron. It was going to be a long climb and a long walk home.

It was several minutes of weighted climbing before I got to the top of the tall chimney stack. I paused with my head peeking out the top, hanging my sling on a rung to take the weight off of me. The sight was not worth the climb. I could see over all of Lower Town, the cubed homes stretching all the way to the feet of Haldoklik. Turning my head, I could see MidTown in the hazy distance.

The scrap tin houses were pulled up the sides of the corpse's canyon like thorns. So many people stacked on top of one another to avoid Drones and acidic mud burns. I could even see the Drone headquarters for Haldoklik nestled into the large skull frame of the fallen Loomer. It was a blur at such a distance, but I knew Gregory 235 would be sitting on watch by the guardrail before his routine began and he scouted the rim of Haldoklik.

Lower Town sprawled before me in my vantage point. Cherub 735 was supposed to be circling an aerial perimeter around the square in half clockwise fashions. With the lockdown of the 'Oomers and a Gregory Unit walking the streets, Cherub 735 had no excuse to not be doing his rotations. I glimpsed a shimmer over the cube houses near me. I ducked in reaction to the sudden light. After a second I looked again, and on cue, Cherub 735 lapped near the chimney.

He was an odd cherub design, but from the aerial routines he was required to do, he had lost all his paint and was melting in areas. The weather had transformed him into a terrifying, melted, winged child. Even our angels were daunting metallic figures of oppression. I had to take a moment to curse out the original inventors of the Giants. They had a cruel sense of humor to make these A.I. abominations look so docile.

I knew it would be a few minutes before Cherub 735 would take another lap near the chimneys. Using the time in between laps, I mounted my sling to the edge of the ladder and loaded in the ammo. I pulled off a part from the sling, a large magnet I kept around, and placed it in the launching pouch. Being as Cherub 735 was a lightweight Aerial Drone, the magnet should be able to pull him easily.

I tied a steel wire to the magnet, tightening my knots as well as I could. There could only be one shot. If my aim is off, or the steel slips, I will be punished to the full extent of the law.

Only one chance.

Once the sling was ready and loaded, I hunkered on the ladder and waited to hear the small propulsion system of the flying Cherub. I went through the mental schematics I had made for the aerial Drone models.

After examining their scraps in the Barrens on a prior journey, I knew the basic components.

The Cherub model had a few safety overrides because of their circuitry being less reliable, as they were an original model of the first wave of robotic controllers. I knew there was a metal stabilizing rod that, with enough force, or a strong enough magnet, could be shifted to block the thrusters and disable its propulsion system. To even get close enough with a magnet, one has to hit the exact joint of the right wing's connection to the back of the silver baby. I had a window of a few inches to hit a flying target that would be a hundred feet away.

"This is the dumbest thing I have done in a while."

I knew the second best case situation would be if I hit Cherub 735 in the face and screwed with his optical circuitry, at least then I would have a chance to escape. The chuckle that escaped me was not of joy, but of cynical despair. With no other chances for helping Tyron available, I would have to go for the wing shot. My fingers fidgeted with the sling, pulling on the elastics of the arms.

Aiming well and shooting well were two different things. I could hit the Drone, I knew that. My aim was fairly good after years of practicing on the few rats I could find in the Barrens. Desperation for food was a wonderful motivator, but the window I needed to hit was much smaller than a rat. My odds were not the best, but on the other hand, I had an excellent strategy of failing upwards.

I would make this work. One way or another.

The sound of fiery small propulsion units stirred my attention to the sky. Risking being seen, I poked my head up slightly, trying to see the angle of flight and the destination of my shot. I tightened my grip on the slings handle and slowly raised it to the lip of the chimney. There was a slight vibrating noise as my hand shook with the sling against the stone.

Steadying myself with a slow breath, I turned my thoughts to Tyron. He was lying on a metal slab in a shack by himself. All alone, unaware of the world around him. If I fail this shot, he will never see the sun with me. He will never be able to feel my actual face. He will never be more than a

76

living corpse that will be passed by everyone who sees him. I can not fail this shot. My brother will need me for the rest of his life. I have to make it. No one else would do this, not even the dumbest person in this hell forgotten by the gods would do this. Tyron needed this, though, so I am ready to do this. As the propulsion noises drew closer, I took a breath.

In one swift motion, I pulled the sling up from its hidden position in the chimney mouth and extended the mount arms for stability. I saw Cherub 735, and he saw me. Making a quick adjustment of my aim, I grabbed the sling handle with both hands and threw myself back against the other side of the chimney, pulling the elastic completely taut. As Cherub 735 attempted to change its trajectory towards me, I released the handle of the sling and the magnet lurched at the cherub like a bullet. I felt the coil of steel unwind as the magnet led it away to its target.

As I watched to see if my shot landed, the rusted rung I had placed all my weight on gave. The snap echoed through my ears as I was forced to glance down. My body fell, rungs snapping as my feet tried to find a surface. This was going to hurt.

As I fell, I heard a loud metallic smacking sound. My shot landed, but did it land where I needed it to? The fall felt amusingly long. I could even feel the tension on the steel cable increase as I pulled Cherub 735 after me. In the end, the plan was to pull the Cherub into the chimney to dismantle its arms, but I had intended on dragging them down more slowly and not falling onto a metal furnace covered in multiple feet of ashen human remains. I looked down the chimney as I was falling and saw the ground approach. A small breath was held as the ashen cloud enveloped me.

A snap and loud clanging followed me into the dark powder. I couldn't see. The adrenaline in my veins made the pain not set immediately, so I used it to stand and examine what happened. In my attempt to stand, I braced myself against a wall and found my arm and hand unresponsive.

"Shit, a sprained arm? That's fine. I can work with this." I muttered, allowing the ashes to fill my mouth and to feel the slight comfort of calm words. A sharp pain stole the control of my leg. Looking down, I saw Cherub 735, his propulsion system was burning a hole through my clothing.

I jumped away and examined what I could through the dark dusty cloud around us, doing my best to keep my mouth covered and eyes squinted.

It looked like I only partially hit the sweet spot. One propulsion engine was offline, the other was half functioning. The magnet was still stuck to him strongly, but the small Cherub face was scanning for me. Clouds of ash from our fall swirled around from his propulsion unit and hid me from him. Though with my half-closed eyes, Cherub 735 was a blurry figure burying himself deeper in the ash.

"Halt. Illegal activity detected. Halt. The authorities will arrive shortly." He repeated.

"Ya know, Cherub 735, a great thing about security protocols is that it knocks out sensors and communication to avoid the transmission of virus coding. This was implemented in the original models that were more likely to develop the Fritz. Now I know you're not a talking type, but I was sent to give a message, and that's what I'm here doing. Now hold still and I won't decommission you on this very spot." I growled at the squirming child-like Drone.

The Cherub made one last attempt to scan for my face and resigned to a stillness, slowing the burn of its rocket-like propulsion. I let the haze settle for a moment. We could enjoy this quiet moment before I ripped its arms off.

"Smart choice." I said as I crouched and searched my pockets for my tools. To my annoyance, I realized I dropped them upon my fall. While I had been planning to nicely disconnect the arm, I would have to take the hard way. Wrapping my one good hand around the left arm of the cherub, I pulled with all my strength. The Drone squirmed, trying to shake me off. To silence the wriggling and to remind him of who held the power in this situation, I place my boot on his chest and forced him to look at me.

"Uncouple." I growled at him.

"Halt. Illegal activity detected." He barked back. Pre-recorded lines were all he had.

"Uncouple, or risk loss of your propulsion. You know the odds." I glared at the annoyingly fake looking, melted child's face of the Drone. The odds of me actually ripping off his arm meant taking out a few primary systems that would immobilize him. I didn't want a decommission being investigated. If that made it back to me, I couldn't imagine the punishment, not only on myself but all of Haldoklik.

The Cherub was obviously angered by this situation, but knew I was right. After a few more attempts to escape my muddy boot, he uncoupled his arms and glared at me with his red bead-like eyes. I kicked his face till one light turned off as I noticed the cloud cover dissipating. It seemed wiser to not let an angry Drone see my face while I stole its arms.

I moved the magnet to hit the actual sweet spot and watched Cherub 735 struggle to move. He may have had visual legs, but they were non-functional. Cherub Drones were only meant for surveillance and occasional stealth operations, so he was significantly weaker than dealing with any other Drone model. With the magnet in place, and the propulsion unit turned off, I had effectively clipped his wings.

Looking up, I saw my sling still firmly attached to the side of the chimney. While I examined the ladder for a chance to reclaim it, I noticed I had broken every rung on the way down. It was time to finally let go of it. I had built it a long time ago, and I knew now I could build better. It would also take the stress off my mind not having it in my shack. Wanting to leave this situation with some grace and dignity left, I turned to the broken window I had initially climbed in through.

"Halt. Halt. Halt." Cherub 735 repeated. I may have kicked it too hard in the head. Placing my good arm on the ledge of the wall, I began pulling myself up. It was going to be a rough trip home. As I got to the point my leg could reach over the ledge, I noticed the broken glass I was near and carefully maneuvered around it. Doing so allowed one last glance at Cherub 735. He sat there, quietly staring up at the opening of the chimney. I sometimes forget that there was personality to some circuits that controlled these metal angels.

"It's not personal, by the way. It's a job." I muttered to him half-heartedly. If he had the opportunity, he would have dropped me off the chimney himself. I don't know why I even try to be kind in this world. It was never met warmly.

"Illegal activity detec-t-t-t-ed. Ha-a-a-lt. Code 7-7-7-7-35. Dange-e-er." He responded. I turned from him and made my way past the broken information desk and to the door. Risking one more glance into the control room, I let my head nod in appreciation for his compliance.

I tucked the arms of Cherub 735 safely under my garbs and let out the repressed cough I had been holding in. My spit was black and my nose dripped with dark liquid. Trying to not think about the human ashes running out of my body, I wiped my nose and used my nails to scrape my tongue clean. The grit remained, but I stopped tasting the dust and righted myself towards the direction of MidTown.

"It's just the walk home left. Come on, Taylor, you're not done till you see Tyron."

I could feel the pain of the fall setting in as I took slow steps forward. I had a few bruised or broken ribs and probably some bruised vertebrae, nothing that would kill me at the moment. My ankle felt like it was broken but not fatal. It was just going to be a very miserable walk home. This time I stuck to the central road, as it no longer mattered if I was seen. I likely looked rough enough to intimidate 'Oomers, and it wasn't illegal to leave Lower Town. In theory, it would be fine.

The feeling of eyes on me returned as soon as I neared the square. I walked around the square to not see the gruesome scene of bones from the children. They had likely already been cracked open for the marrow inside of them. At least I knew the starving 'Oomers' wouldn't be looking at me for a snack. I still had enough fight in me they would at least hesitate.

I felt followed, hearing the occasional staggered steps behind me. It wasn't malicious this time, but it was waiting to see if I made it to the gate. I couldn't care less if I was viewed or followed anymore. I just needed to get home to see Tyron.

Shadows crossed over me again as the arch that acted as the Lower Town gate passed over me. I was half-way home. Trading the main road for the back roads again, I entered Midtown. People here were more aggressive if they saw an opportunity, but with the Drones on such high patrol today and the weather turning worse, I didn't expect it to be all too dangerous.

I felt my body getting lighter, and I paused. Did I miss a wound when checking myself over? Doing a quick pat down around my body, I noticed I had missed a cut on the back of my ribs. I pulled my garb up to see it quickly and shuddered a moment.

Apparently, when I landed, I must have been impaled on something. With my eager adrenaline, I had pulled out whatever had stabbed me when I stood up and started a cascade of blood loss. By the staining of my clothes and the fading blood in my footprints behind me, I had been bleeding a lot.

"Shit, Shit, Shit." I hid near a wall, placing my back against it to steady myself but leaving room for the wound. There were about five more alleys to cross before I got to my door. I should be able to make it. Straightening from the wall to finish my journey, my vision immediately began blackening. I leaned against the wall again.

While my ears could mostly hear static as I suffered from blood loss, I still could hear the approaching metal steps from behind me. If I get caught with the Cherubs's arms, I will join those children earlier than I was expecting. I felt my legs giving way as the perfectly in time steps of a Drone drew near. At least there was a good chance I was gonna bleed out before they had time to break my limbs. Always a bright side.

✧   ✧   ✧

I feel the cold. I can actually feel the cold of the surrounding void. There was no fear or panic, just sympathy. Did Tyron feel trapped like this in the cold dark? Does he miss me? Is his mind intact? Does he even know he still exists?

Where is Tyron? Where am I? I need to find him.

Opening my eyes slowly, I could almost feel a grit in every joint with every movement. My lungs felt heavy, reminding me I inhaled too much dust. My eyes couldn't register what they were looking at. It almost looked like my shack, but that was not possible. I closed my eyes and felt the grit inside my eyelids. What has happened? There is an ache in my rib cage. My arm was in agonizing pain, and I could feel the swollen broken nature of my ankle. The pain entered my body as my awareness came back into focus.

I heard a shuffle near me, and it triggered every survival instinct in me. Sitting up, I drew my arms close to me to protect vital organs. Regretting my reaction as I remembered my sprained arm and ribs. A coughing fit triggered, causing my rib cage to shake and panic from the pain.

"Damn it Taylor, stay down." A metallic sounding voice chided from the dark. I cast a quick glance over my shoulder towards the voice and saw a familiarly worn golden hair curving into the dim light of a small candle before I noticed the glowing eyes watching me.

"Where am I Gregory?" I asked weakly. The feeling of immense fatigue settled into my body. Trying to brace myself with my good arm to lower it gently, my vision blurred. I was still very injured.

"You are mostly safe and in your shack. I had to move Tyron to your bed for now so I could operate. He is fine as well." The speaker was soft in the dark, almost friendly or concerned. That wasn't possible, though.

"How did you find me?" I asked as my body relaxed into the reclined position.

"We will talk about how much trouble you are in later. Heal for right now. You lost a large quantity of blood. I have you set up on a Synthix drip. It will feel miserable for a while, but you should recover. I will send Gern to check on you in a while. Stay off your feet," Gregory said as he stood. I tilted my head to look more clearly at the tall Gregory model as he stepped towards Tyron and grabbed the edge of the Razum.

"Stop, don't hurt him." I barked weakly. My desperation was cut short by my exasperated voice.

Gregory chuckled at me. "If I wanted to hurt him, I would have tossed him out in the mud while you were unconscious. Calm down. I'm checking the HIN on the Razum to see if I recognize the Loomer you two are from. I might help track down some tools if it's familiar."

It never occurred to me to check the Headset Identification Number before. Though with limited knowledge of Loomers, the information would have been lost on me. Gregory didn't need to know I was grateful for that metal casing that held his brain.

"Why would you... want to help him?" I coughed out the question more than speaking it.

"So you will stop doing these ridiculous things and getting hurt. Why did you have to steal Cherub 735's arms?" Gregory turned his accusatory voice to me. I now took a moment to realize he must have stripped me to stitch my wounds, thus finding the arms that was hidden at one point.

"Dis deal...iz...a secret." I muttered quietly, allowing the 'Klik slang to infect my speech.

"Why is this deal a secret? Are weapons involved, or is it Gern's petty revenge scheme?" Gregory watched my face closely before letting out a slow sigh. "Does Gern have negative intentions with the arms?" He followed up.

"No. Gern isn't a danger." I said, looking away from the glowing eyes. A silence spread through the room as the low glow of the Razum colored the air slightly. Gregory shifted, and I heard a thud near me on the slab.

"I do not want to hear about this, Taylor. Where did you leave Cherub 735?" Gregory growled as he headed for the door.

"Chimney stack two. Lower Town. Safety override activated. Need my magnet back." I stammered out as the darkness closed around my vision again.

"I will clean up this time." Gregory muttered to the edge of my consciousness. I heard his heavy steps leave and my door swing closed. My world went dark again as I faded in out of the dark waves of awareness for what I assumed were hours. The only thing that broke the silence of my shack in the rain that had started was the gruff old Gern, who was tossed in by an annoyed Gregory.

Ever since Gern entered, I heard him rummaging through my shack. I guess I would pick the scraps from him in the same situation. Pick the bones of opportunity. Thankfully, Gregory left me a lead pipe near if I found the need to coerce him back to his place. There were moments where it almost seemed like Gern was watching over me and Tyron, but I knew the Scrap Dog had no heart. He was simply listening to orders given by Gregory.

83

After what must have been a few days of rotation shifts between Gern and Gregory, I felt my mind come back, slowly. I could start piecing full sentences together again. I had taken the opportunity to tell Gern about what had happened and gave him the arms he was so eager for. As a thanks for watching over me, albeit begrudgingly, I let him use my tools to break down his prize so it would be less likely to get recognized as contraband.

Days were passing by quickly. The feeling of guilt gluing itself to me for being stagnant in my search for a cure for Tyron. Upon request, Gern had brought the tool I needed to break the optical unit's bolts so I could access the Aju foam. If my theory was correct, it would start the regression process of the lesser bio-wiring of the Razum. I could see the schematics I built in my head of the Razums I ripped apart with The Scientist long ago.

We had a lot of theories we wanted to test, but our time was cut brutally short. I allowed some thoughts to cross my mind of those days. I could remember his name, but I had no right to use it anymore. He was the oldest man I had ever seen. While he claimed he was sixty some years old, I knew he was closer to fifty-five. The Scientist and I couldn't fight off the Drones when they came to bomb the rebel humans in the Bevie town we hid in. He tried to save us, but he didn't make it. Though he saved us to the best of his abilities.

I could still feel the cramped stagnant air of the rubble pocket we were stuck in. The basement of The Scientist's home was completely destroyed except for a small bubble under stacked desks. Days of darkness, rain trickling through the cracks of what remained of the world outside. I can taste the smell of his corpse rotting while we starve in that pocket. I remember the feeling of my teeth breaking his skin.

Eject.

I can not think of those memories. I can't allow them to distract me. Tyron is not free. It's not time to relive these moments or feel these wounds. I needed to get up. I need to be better to save Tyron. He is all that matters. I will do what I have to make sure my brother has every chance to live a real life. Even if I have to cut down every friend I have to achieve what I need, I will. He is all that matters to me.

The silence of my shack was disturbed as I heard the heavy door open slowly and the staggered steps of Gern entering. He fussed with the locking mechanism I built before submitting to confusion and dropping the girder down. Thudding against the ground, the girder shook my small tin shack. I could hear the rattling of tin on concrete as my shed settled down.

"Hsh Taylor doin?" He asked in a friendly tone.

"I need help to sit up, Gern." I muttered to the old Scrap Dog who was limping to his normal spot by the candle. He hesitated, but finally decided to help. Placing a scarred hand behind my back, he supported me until I could sit up on my own. He patted me slightly as I sat up and assumed it was his form of being encouraging.

The awareness that I wasn't wearing any clothes in front of the old man struck me with embarrassment. With some awkward haste, I wrapped my body with the tarp that I had been using for a blanket. Once swaddled in the tarp, I swung my legs over the edge of the counter and steadied myself.

"Tayk it eezy, Taylor." Gern growled, watching my slow, pained movements.

I slowly set one foot on the ground, testing my range of motion and strength. I had recovered from enough injuries to know how to feel out the damage. It wasn't a terrible sprain, but it would take a while to heal. Placing my other foot down, I only felt the tension and bruises, likely from the fall. When I began putting my weight on both feet, there was some sharp pain and lightheadedness, but it slowly faded.

A fresh surge of power flowed through my body as I stood proudly for a moment. Gathering up the rest of the tarp, I stepped forward towards my room. Gern cautiously followed behind me. It was likely safe to assume that Gregory had threatened him. I pulled what was like a curtain wall for my room shut behind me.

I tossed the tarp that covered me over Tyron's Razum. "No peeking." I muttered to my brother's slab of a body.

Taking the moment to dress myself, I examined what torn fabric I had left. Although I wasn't too sure if what I was wearing was a shirt. It was stitched together with thin wire and laid somewhat comfortably on my frame. Actual fabric was a struggle to find with the level of acidic rain in this region. I only had a few pieces of clothing. A bit of bitterness peaked in me, knowing that Gregory likely destroyed my clothing I had been wearing so no evidence could be traced towards me. As I pulled on the loose sack cloth pants, I could feel my ankle begging to buckle. My ribs ached as I had to bend to pick the clothes off the floor. Stitches from the puncture wound gave way from the motion.

Once I felt decently dressed, I paused, checking the glow of the Razum lights. It was at the same blinking speed. I dreaded the day I saw the blue blinking light turn to its final red shade. It would be the sign that Tyron was almost out of time.

He still felt cold as I tested his skin with bare hands. I chose to believe that he could feel my touch. Maybe in some part of his mind, he knew I was here. I knew it wasn't likely, but I couldn't believe that he was sitting in his mind, alone and in the dark. I refuse.

After a moment, I heard Gern shuffle impatiently. "Taylor?" he asked.

I thought for a moment there was concern in his voice, but dismissed it quickly. "I'm fine Gern. What time are you switching with Gregory today?"

Risking more pain, but satisfying my emotional needs, I bent low to kiss my brother's cheek. I left my room and looked at the old dog, who had obviously been snooping around. His gigantic eyes gleamed at me with false innocence.

"Gregory sed he be bak…soon." Gern grunted, settling himself into a chair he had thrown together from scrap in my shed. The chair was made from two tires for the base with a flat sheet of scrap metal for the seat. The wall was his backrest.

"Let me know as soon as you hear him coming. I have to break down the eye." With a wince, I pushed aside the scattered tools on my work desk, feeling the ache in my ribs as I eased into my seat. From beneath a pile of scrap, I carefully pulled out the Giant's eye—a dense, metallic sphere with a glossy, vacant stare that seemed to follow me as I set it on the table.

I shot a glance at Gern, who shifted in his chair, rummaging through his pockets. My fingers traced the back of the eye, searching for the access panel. After a moment, Gern dug out a cylindrical tool and dropped it on the desk with a clang, the metal vibrating across the surface.

"Don't lose dat. Very expensiv," he muttered, his tone as rough as the tool itself.

Ignoring him, I positioned the tool horizontally against the panel. With a faint hum, the device powered up, sending soft vibrations through the eye. Quickly, I covered the eerie iris with a scrap of cloth, hoping it would obscure my movements from any attempts at re-establishing a network connection with the other Giants. The internal wiring began to tense and contract, signs that the eye was powering up.

I had guessed what the tool was for. While initially thinking it was some sort of advanced drill, the truth of the machine made this situation more complicated. It would work for what I needed it to, but it would require extra steps to avoid a warrant being placed on my head.

The low whir of machinery came to life, a sign that it was attempting to determine its location. I had only a brief window to extract the Aju foam I needed before it fully reawakened. The tool, now magnetized, clung to the eye's panel, allowing me to step back and remove the cloth cover. I met the Giant's glare, an old, fierce intelligence sparking within the lens. This was its first glimpse of the world since it had been shut down.

It recognized me, or something close to recognition. I could feel it marking my face, cataloging each detail as though it might reach me someday. I smirked at it, defiant. "Just doing what you were made to do, right?" I murmured, tapping the protective glass shielding its iris.

With a small tool, I pried the glass casing off, revealing the damp, bio-synthetic wiring inside. Its surface was warm and soft, pulsing with a strange, organic vitality that glowed bright white with a piercing orange iris. The pupil dilated erratically, disoriented but struggling to focus. At the very back of the pupil, I could see a faint glimmer—the delicate optic wiring and my prize nestled within.

"Sorry," I whispered, partly to myself, and plunged my fingers into the soft, gelatinous mass of the pupil. The eye reacted instantly, the pupil contracting around my hand in a desperate attempt to lock me out. It felt like hot, translucent jelly, the texture oddly reminiscent of living tissue.

Undeterred, I pushed deeper, feeling along the fibers until I found a small plug embedded within. Grasping the pull ring, I yanked it loose, breaking the seal. The eye's mechanical whir grew erratic as the cooling system failed, and in the next moment, a thick green foam bubbled from the exposed opening. This Aju foam—made of Nanites designed to heal the eye's complex optic systems—was exactly what I needed. Its unique composition allowed it to mend both human and machine tissue.

I coaxed the foam to the front of the eye, guiding it carefully with my fingers until it pooled. Grabbing the cleanest bowl I had, I began pressing the foam into it, feeling the bubbles burst coolly under my touch. Just as I secured the last bit, the heavy thud of footsteps reached my ears—metal against metal, echoing down the hall of buildings beyond my door.

Gern hadn't noticed yet, but I knew we had little time. I looked up sharply as the door groaned open, instinctively freezing as the intruder stepped into view. The flash of light from the door momentarily blinded my weak eyes. Girder thrown from its locked position.

Gregory stood there, glaring at me. "Damn it, Taylor. It is not legal for me to see this," He grumbled as he stepped into the hovel of a shack and quickly closed the door behind him. I nodded my hello to him as I continued to scoop out the foam. He wasn't a threat after how involved he had been with my recovery and my illegal situation. Gregory stepped near and watched over my shoulder.

"Did you wait till you had the activation key so the eye would respond with its self healing measures?" He leaned closer to me. The side of his face was in my peripheral vision as he spoke. Was there an impressed tone in his voice?

"Yeah… Trying to bypass the security to enable the plug pull was challenging enough. It would have been a nightmare to crack the Nanite vile without triggering the tamper alarms." Some of this was a lie, but he didn't need to know that. The tool I had risked so much to obtain remained a mystery to me, even though it turned out to be exactly what I needed.

Had I known it was an activation key, I would have done the task sooner. As I scraped the last of the foam from the eye, Gregory let out an automated hum as he seemed to chuckle.

"It was smart planning. How will this help, Tyron?" He tilted his face to look at mine while I focused on the pool of Nanites. I couldn't help but feel unsettled by his golden gaze and chipped paint. He was an enforcer of everything that tried to kill me in this world, yet here he was complimenting me. The only Drone to respect my desire to free Tyron.

"If I can reprogram the Nanites slightly, I can transfuse them to Tyron and hopefully get the Razum to pull back the nerve connections. I won't really be able to pull them out, but I can get them close enough where I should be able to cut them out. It's better than nothing and will at least buy me some extra time." I pulled out a tray to dump the foam onto, trying to get an even spread as I spoke. Since this had been pre-planned, I mapped out the density of metal across the tray. In theory, it would allow equal spread of electric pulses to reprogram all Nanites equally.

"So you are going to try to manually fry the Nanites to reprogram them? Have you considered the effects of the counter programming routines?" Gregory asked, examining the foam tray in closer detail.

I paused, my hands started trembling. I didn't know about Nanites programming. The Scientist and I only theorized how to get the Nanites. We never expected there to be protective measures on these small healing bugs. Thinking about it now, of course there would be. I felt my body go limp and cold as I sat back into my work chair. I had to calm the panicking of my brain and continue ignoring the blood that was seeping from my torn stitches. My goal was further away than I thought.

I could feel the goosebumps of failure flooding my body as nearly overwhelming feelings of defeat flowed through me. Having risked so much to get here, to only learn that I wasn't any closer. Cherub 735 wasn't even the most dangerous part of this ordeal to get to the Nanite foam. I felt my wounds more clearly now. I realized my racing against time was again slowed by unknowns. Tears welled in my eyes before I could command them to cease. It served no purpose to show these feelings right now. I allowed a sniffle to clear my nose and one tear to escape. That's all I can afford to feel. I must start again. I must plan better now.

There was the faintest reminder that I could join Tyron in his sleep. It would be so much easier to fade into the virtual Ether with my brother instead of trying to drag him to this reality. I had to shove those thoughts down. I swore, to Tyron and to The Scientist, I would find a cure. No matter the struggles, obstacles, or physical limitations, I would get him out.

I opened my emotion-filled eyes and noticed Gern and Gregory looking at me curiously. "I didn't plan for that programming. Gregory, do you know anything about their programming that could help me break them down?" I asked.

It was illegal for him to partake in any of this venture, but he had already covered enough of my tracks that I could decommission him if I spoke out. On top of that, I could see the early onset of Fritzing. I knew I could sway him if I was gentle. If he refused, I could destroy him.

"Taylor, you are aware of the ramifications of what you are asking me." His voice was stern, glancing at Gern, who was casually staring at the floor, struggling to understand our form of speaking.

"If I share what I know, we will both be condemned." He was trying to pretend he was not already caught on this journey with me. A small futile attempt to sway me from the power I knew I held in this situation.

"Gregory 235, you have been damned with me since you first aided me in building this shack when I arrived carrying my brother. You were damned with me since you started letting me bring contraband into Haldoklik. You were damned when you turned a blind eye to my trading of contraband. So at least don't lie about your contributions to this endeavor." I glared at him, wondering how he could even dare say he was innocent in all of this.

Gregory did a motion that could be considered rolling his eyes in their pixelated LED form. "Step aside." He said begrudgingly as he pulled my chair away from the desk. His body had to hunch over to properly view the tray with the foam.

"You plotted this for density fluctuations for electric distribution? Smart."

He said as he grabbed the metallic glove casing for his hand. I knew they were not real gloves, but I had never seen a Gregory Unit take them off before or that it was even possible. He pulled his hand free from the casing and revealed long mechanical fingers and all the circuitry involved therein. I could see small sparks jumping between some of his knuckles. I knew the sting of those built in tasers well.

Gern sat forward and watched as Gregory presented his ungloved hand. This was new information for all of us, that this was even a capability. I knew Gern was studying the components just like I was for future scraping purposes. Gregory seemed to be aware of our scrapper eyes evaluating his hand.

"You two look at me like your next salvage piece. Remember the laws of Gregory salvage possession." He said with a sarcastic note, knowing he wouldn't be able to report us even if we had any illegal salvage.

"Gregory salvage isn't as bad as Giant salvage, or Cherub salvage, and we have both in this room right now." I reminded him. LEDs darted between Gern and me as Gregory evaluated my words. Did he know my joke was both serious and not?

There was very little we could do to intimidate him. Although, as he was showing signs of Fritz and developing more human related emotions, he was going to value his individuality and 'Humanity'. The idea of being salvaged was going to become as terrifying for him as it was for me to think about being 'salvaged'. An unfortunate reality I had to be aware of.

Organ dens and traders were common in the Loomer cities. While I hadn't had any recent run-ins with them in Haldoklik, the prior cities were not so kind. Being mugged in an alley as people tried to cut your organs out for sales was a generous reminder of the desperation of others. With lifespans dwindling and the wealthier trying to survive, organs sold for a high price these days.

Pushing the threatening memories away, I looked over Gregory's face as he showed no signs of dismay. Either my estimation of his Fritz levels was wrong, or he was trying to hide it. Apparently he was still mostly a Drone in this case. He could deny the Fritz for a while, but he was showing signs recently.

The Fritz comes for them all.

He held his hand over the tray of foam, spread wide and palm up. The sparks from his tasering mechanisms jumped more violently, some even reaching to the tray. LEDs dimmed as he focused on manually controlling the power burst. With methodical directions, he waved his hand over the tray, equally shocking each part.

With Nanites being so small, they were often programmed with gentle prodding of electrical pulses in a binary coding. If I had attempted this myself, I knew the odds of me messing up a slight wattage would have led to triggers being hit and the Giants being alerted to tampering. Gregory was much more likely to avoid the triggers because of his computational control of his electrical bursts. Though this would not have worked like I wanted it to, I refused to be grateful to a machine.

It was a few minutes of tension as Gregory sparked the Nanites to his control. The silence of the shack was thick like mud. One slight mistake and the sirens would sound. I tried to focus my breathing to calm myself in the sludge of anticipating our deaths. This was just another risk that was necessary. Tyron will be free, even if I have to flee the town with his body on my shoulders, just like how I entered this hell hole. We were going to make it.

The shack's silence was cut by an exasperated sigh from Gregory. I saw Gern relax his shoulders at the sound and we both noticed the sparks were no longer flying across the tray. I could feel the air thin and the pressure on my chest subside. As the sparking dissipated from the tray, so did the fear in the room.

Gregory tossed me a glance. "I really do hate you sometimes, Taylor." He grumbled as he stepped back. "They should be able to pull the growing nerve connectors out. I even tried to toss in some programming to help slow the progression of the Razum's inhabiting coding. I can't guarantee anything, but it should slow the progression for a time." He spoke as he stepped back from the tray, replacing his glove.

I stood from my chair and examined the tray. There were electrical burn marks on different densities of the tray, where Gregory most likely had to try harder to maintain the intensity of the electrical pulses. Too high and he could have fried them instead of coding them.

"Thank you, Gregory." I muttered, examining the patterns he used to code them for future mental notes.

"Sit down, Taylor. You are pushing yourself." He grumbled as he glanced over at me. Likely noticing the blood dripping down my leg once more, he approached. Gern seemed to be aware of my situation as he took up Gregory's side.

"I'll be fine. I just need to finish this injection." Mumbling the words as I searched for the syringe I built just for this occasion. My hands were feeling numb, so I was clumsy and dropped things off my work desk. Vision was blurring as I cursed my wounds and carelessness.

"Taylor, you are bleeding. Sit down and allow yourself to heal." Gregory started stepping closer to me. Ignoring him this time, I continued to pack the foam into the syringe for the Razum. I noticed things blurred a bit more as I forced my eyes to stay focused. I had to get this done for Tyron, sooner rather than later.

I heard Gregory approach me more intently now, and I glared at him to back down. With the syringe full, I limped my way to Tyron, who looked slightly more alive to me now. I knelt next to his still body, causing my ribs to scream out. I ignored it, thinking that for a moment I could see the color returning to his skin. This was likely the blood-loss affecting my mind, but I believed it was there.

Letting my hand drift across the casing of the Razum, realizing how clunky and large it felt compared to the Giant eye. I found the input of where my brother was once connected to the Loomer network on the right side of the Razum and brought the syringe near. This was another guess, but at least a well researched one.

"Tyron, this will help, but it might hurt. I'm sorry if it does, but know that it will make you better. Sorry, I love you." I whispered to my comatose sibling as I injected the Nanites to circulate through the Razum before they were distributed to his body. If I had injected these directly into Tyron, the

Razum would have fought them off before they could do their work. This way, it would be the Razum introducing the Nanites, not a foreign entity.

As I realized that months of planning had finally come to fruition, I could feel the ache of my ribs, the screaming of my ankle, and the burning of my arm. For a moment, I had forgotten I was injured. It wasn't as important as helping Tyron. He would be okay. I got more time for us.

I felt my body fade and my vision ebb. There was a spinning in the room now that taunted my balance. My thoughts slowed as reality started to slow down and lose color. I should probably lay down...

There were moments in the dark where I could hear the world around me. I knew I had passed out at some point. I remember Gregory's gloved hand pinching and burning me as he picked me up. His hands were still hot from the electrical pulsing. I knew Gern had left. I think it was because Gregory sent him out, but I couldn't remember hearing it. It felt like I was somewhere else.

I could see Tyron, his face smiling at me. He was fine, and everything was going to be fine because my big brother was back. He held my hand and whispered something to me. I couldn't quite hear it, though. When I tried to lean closer to hear him, he pushed me back.

The familiar sting of an adrenaline needle in my chest spooked my eyes open. My body was on fire. I was ready to run. It felt like I had just been wrenched out of a furnace and every nerve I had was ignited. I could feel a scream cross my vocal cords, but I could not hear it. Was I restrained?

"Where's Tyron?" It was barely a murmur. "Where is my brother?"

"Shut up, Taylor. He is next to you. You are going hypovolemic and septic and we have a lot of work to do. I am going to gag you now." I think it was Gregory's voice, but I couldn't be sure.

Tightly knotted tarp material jammed into my mouth, locking my mouth open. My body was rotated as my face was pushed against the metal counter. The feeling of knives cutting into my back startled me. I tried to scream but couldn't pass the knotted material. A metal hand was pressing me down. My hands were clenched into fists so much that I could feel

94

blood beginning to seep between my fingers.

"Damn it, Taylor, you barely have any blood left in your body. Stop." Snapped the voice of what probably was Gregory. I felt metal fingers pry mine apart to stop the damage to my palms from my nails.

"Here, this is Tyron's hand. You don't want to hurt Tyron, right?" His speaker squeaked as a hand was placed in mine. I could feel the cold flesh of a weak circulatory system. Tyron. He was safe, he was near. I felt my consciousness dip out at the mere comfort of my brother's hand.

He is okay...

Tyron is safe...

He's not dead, nothing else matters...

✧   ✧   ✧

It could have been days, hours, or even minutes. Time had become a fluid construct beyond my understanding. My body was as heavy as lead. It took a moment, but the pain edged into my awareness. I could feel the seam down my back from the incision, a straight and precise cut. It was safe to assume it was Gregory's handiwork.

I tried to move my right arm, but to no avail as my arms were tied down. Recalling that my left wrist had been sprained, it was probably better to not move it. By trying to move, I realized a hand on my own. Looking to my right, I saw Tyron. His head obscured, as always, with the Razum, but he was on the slab with me. I scanned his body and saw a few fresh wounds on him.

Rage grew inside of my agonized chest. "What did he do to you, Tyron?" My head nudged against his with the vague hope that he would whisper to me as he had in my delusions of blood loss. As I examined my brother's wounds, I noticed their purpose. Gregory must have used the Razum's survival programs to transfuse some of my blood and use Tyron as a scrubbing blood bag. I made the mental note to steal some circuitry from the sneaky Gregory Unit.

"I can tell from here in the door that you are mad," Sarcasm echoed from a faulty speaker. I looked towards the voice and noticed Gregory entering my shack. The light from beyond the door was lighter, like an afternoon light. It glinted off of the golden plates of Gregory before he closed the door and blocked out the glow of day.

"Before you snap at me, I asked you if it was okay I used the Razum boy for this." Gregory said in his defense, holding his hands up in a child-like display of innocence. I noticed his hands were gloved once more, but there were more burn marks on the hand he revealed.

"You had no right." I rasped. My voice was sore from the screams I vaguely remember. Gregory chuckled once more, the Drone enjoying my weakened defenses. As I jostled my restraints to attack him in some way, he approached and held my arms down to stop me.

"No, I did. If you want your brother to get free, then you need to be here to free him. I will not do it, but I know you would do anything in your power to make me pay if I ever impeded his freedom. If I had let you die, I would have your angry ghost taunting me and Tyron as my legal property. So I figured it was better to make you angry and save both of your sorry asses." Gregory explained this very sarcastically. I realized he had actually made the better choice of decisions he had available. He may be a rusting rack of bolts and circuits, but he was still a super computer compared to the human mind.

"Don't thank me yet. You're not out of the woods, you are temporarily stable. I will have to put you on Synthix for a while longer and hope it can keep some toxins in your blood at bay. With the Nanites being shared between you and Tyron, you have a decent chance. Not great, but decent. Get some rest. I will watch over you two while you sleep," Gregory said, taking a seat by the slab. He scanned over Tyron and me.

"Are you... cold?" He attempted.

A Drone, asking if I was cold? I must be still delirious from the transfusion. It must have been a dream while I was still drifting from the waking world. Gregory would never care about me like that. It was outside of his programming.

Even with my doubting, fading mind, I still felt the soft embrace of a blanket covered in a tarp drape across me and Tyron. I saw the flashing of his Razum, its pleasant blue color making me feel warm by the ocean

I remembered from the Razum. My brother still had a good chance. I squeezed his hand, regardless of the pain it caused me. Tyron would be dragged from the dark void he was trapped in.

"I won't stop..." I muttered into the dark.

The blanket was pulled higher under my chin by someone before I let my eyes go dark once again. It felt okay to relax. Tyron was going to be okay. I just needed to get a little better to help him. The candle of my shack went out, and just as the flame, I let my consciousness dissipate into the weakened slumber.

Chapter 4: No Time for Death

"How much time have I lost?" I glared at the ceiling, waiting for my restraints to be removed. Gregory hesitated before speaking.

"Apparently, not enough to be less irritating." He muttered the phrase as he untied the knots that held me in place. I had been restrained for longer than needed, but he didn't trust me not to re-injure myself, as I had already done.

"Have I missed anything important?" Sitting up slowly as I spoke. I knew the likelihood of something happening in Haldoklik was slim, but it felt right to ask. After being gagged and skewed between consciousness for a few days, I had a right to know. Gregory placed an annoyed hand on my shoulder, slowing how quickly I sat up.

"No, nothing happened. Cherub 735 has been classified as decommissioned and Gern has gone back to his scrap pile. The world is as normal as it can be. Now calm down and go slow or I will watch you bleed out on this shack floor." Gregory said as he glared into my eyes, trying to decipher if I would listen or not.

I begrudgingly obeyed the metal guiding hand as he helped me slowly sit up. The ache of my organs and the strain of my muscles that were still mending cried out. I felt the weight of my whole body and the world above it. There was a vague moment of appreciation for the protectorate aiding my movements. Though, I knew those hands of his had likely killed or enslaved hundreds, if not thousands. Right now, I saw them as the only reason I was still alive.

There were many reasons to be grateful to Gregory, but I figured I could achieve the same effect by trying slightly harder to listen to him. Once I was sitting straight, I could feel the slight tear of my muscle tissue and the sutures that Gregory had placed. Instead of slouching to see what they could endure, I behaved and straightened my back to not irritate Gregory further.

"How are the sutures holding? Any tears?" Asked an uncharacteristically curious Gregory. I could see his digitized eyes scanning my face and body language.

"It's holding. Thanks." I coughed out.

I didn't need him thinking I was this soft, not in the harsh world we live in. Allowing a moment to take in the condition of my life, I slowly breathed. The weakness in my torso was alarmingly poignant, my left arm was swollen, but it was braced correctly. I could feel that my ankle was crudely held straight, with some metal bars that were tied tightly around my leg and foot. For what I did, and the fact I was still alive, I considered this a very lucky resolution. There was a silent cheer for myself as I, once again, failed upwards.

"You should be able to move around your shack fairly well. I suggest taking it easy for a few more weeks, but I know you won't listen to me," Gregory said, stepping away from me to let my body relax into the braces by itself.

"I do have to get food and supplies. My water is almost out, and I have to make sure Tyron stays hydrated because of the Nanites." The piling list of my responsibilities to ensure the survival of my brother and me began to weigh heavy on my mind. A stern tap on the back of my head caused me to turn and glare at the metallic childish face.

"I filled some of your water supply and had Gern run some errands for food and maintained Tyron's condition while you were asleep. The Nanites are doing their job, but it's going slow. We can't rush that process too much. In a few days, you should be able to see some progress in the de-veining process around his extremities. Hydration will be key to avoiding scarring and blockages. Even if either occurs, the Nanites should be able to fix most of the life-threatening issues before they can become serious situations."

Gregory sat back with some pride in his shoulders as he watched my eyes widen at his many kind gestures.

"Gregory, are you alright?" I asked. These actions only proved that he was beginning the Fritzing process, but I didn't know he was deteriorating so quickly. He made a sound that I assumed was a scoff.

"My signs are more obvious to you than to other Gregorys'. I'll be fine for a while. I should still be able to outlive you and your brother." He said, sitting forward.

It was difficult to read his attitude in many cases. Without an actual pair of lips, he could smile, but not express anything truly. I couldn't tell if it was actually sadness or acceptance his voice was trying to convey, but I knew something hid in those words.

"Well, that's good, I guess." It wasn't much, but I wasn't sure what to say with a lack of information about his condition.

I was unsure how to proceed with the conversation. It wasn't my place to delve into his thoughts, and I suspected he would resist if I tried. He knew his days were numbered, and there was nothing either of us could do about it. The prolonged silence between us only fueled speculation and guesswork.

As I was opening my mouth to invite Gregory to leave, he cut me off. His voice had a little more fear in it than I thought was programmed for a Gregory Unit. Anxious body language and shuffling hands prepared me for his mysterious words.

"There is one thing I should probably mention as it will directly affect our political state here in Haldoklik as well as temporarily disrupt your life." He now avoided looking at me as I rotated more to face him.

"I may have made a brash decision while taking care of Cherub 735. You were unfortunately seen by it when you went down the smokestack. He had direct recording of all that had happened until you safety-locked him. That being said, there was a choice that had to be made: Let you take the heat for attacking Cherub 735, or decommission." I felt the reality of the choice hit. I knew what he was talking about now when he said decommissioned.

"Shit, Gregory…" I closed my eyes for a moment. His motorized neck nodded in silent acceptance of his decision.

"The clock has started ticking. You will need to prepare for a quick exit. I did my best to hide some of the evidence without leaving my own traces, but it will be found, and the town will pay the consequences if no one offers information on Cherub 735. Gregory I-8599 has been keen for an opportunity to nuke Haldoklik since the uprising of 'Oomer worshipers in the past few months. He may not even wait for information to arise." Gregory rubbed his metal, deceptively friendly, gloves together almost with nervous motions. It had been a while since I ran into Gregory I-8599. Since he was the Head Drone in Haldoklik, he didn't do rotations.

"How much time was lost with me being unconscious?" My mind was spinning, trying to set up the escape plan and time frame.

"We lost about four days with you being injured. We likely have three to five more days before the Drones will take this absence seriously and report to Gregory I-8599. I have Gern preparing a path out of Haldoklik. He will step forward and out you as the perpetrator to avoid the town getting nuked. Hopefully, by which time you will have fled with Tyron and be far enough away that it will not be worth the resources." Gregory now watched my face as I processed this new reality.

"Damn it, Gregory…" I muttered again. He had effectively moved my three-year plan of living in Haldoklik and freeing Tyron to a three-day plan with a longer and more dangerous method of trying to free Tyron. Supplies would be needed. With my injuries, I would need braces. My body ached with how much walking on a sprained ankle would have to be achieved. So much work, so little time.

"I know this has not been an ideal outcome, but this is now the wisest path forward. I will aid in any way I can." He finished, standing to my aid as I began the painful process of setting my feet on the ground and getting a true feeling of the pain I was going to endure with this journey. Every muscle I had injured screamed out in pain. This was going to be terrible.

"I will take two days to pack and plan. I will do my best to be out with Tyron on the third day." There seemed a silent need to announce my plans, even though I didn't have many options. This would have to be a quick plan. Healing would have to happen later. There wasn't time to be weak when my brother's life was on the line. I tried to sort out my thoughts quickly.

"Tools. I will need tools and items that aren't necessarily legal if I'm to continue my work on Tyron while on the move. You'll have to fetch them for me while I pack, is that alright?"

"I won't like it, but it's better than you blowing the whistle on me at this point." Gregory grumbled.

The urge to smirk was almost unbearable. He didn't need to know that I enjoyed having his company at my side during this situation. This was not going to be easy, so it was a welcoming thought to have at least one metal beast somewhat on my side. It would at least make it easier to carry Tyron outside of Haldoklik.

"Let me write a list and you can fetch stuff. I have a lot of work to do here now." My ankle burned as I slowly made my way to my desk. Finding my etching pen and a mostly flat piece of metal, I scratched down the basics of food, water, and bedding for acid proofing. As I thought further ahead for Tyron, I drew a blank. I was hoping to watch the process of the Nanites cleaning out the Razum's bio wire before having to plan for new equipment and guess at Giant technology for the next step in the cure.

"Don't worry about the next step with Tyron. I'll grab a few things that should help him. I don't think it will save him, but it should help you get that direction. I had a bit of time to think about it while you were recovering. Gern is gathering most of what he can of the basics for travel. I will work towards finding a map of the surrounding Loomer Cities for you to get safely outside of Finigan's Region. That should help you stay unrecognized by Drones." Gregory said, grabbing the list from me and looking over it.

"Take some time today to rest. I know things will move quickly, but you have a max of one day to recover enough strength to start your escape plan. I will take care of most of this list today. Rest. I will move Tyron to the bed so you can sleep more comfortably." He said as he tucked the metal sheet into his glove cuff.

Turning around and very carefully, he slid his arms under the legs and head of Tyron and began to slowly move him to the bed. Gregory had to duck slightly to lower Tyron onto the bottom part of the bunk bed. I followed, making sure he was safe and comfortable, before I cast another glance at Gregory.

"Can I trust you to keep us safe?" I looked into whatever soul his coding contained behind those digitized eyes. There wasn't any other option but to trust him. Though he had plenty of reasons to not help us. I wanted to see if he was lying or if he was actually learning the humanity that was now infecting his mind through the Fritz.

"You can't trust anyone in this world. That's our most genuine sentiment these days. You can only try to do enough to balance the social scales in your own favor." The old speaker of Gregory's mouth rattled as he spoke. He was mocking some teachings he had overheard from the 'Oomer.

His bitter remark remained as his exit phrase, but I still felt mildly safer knowing the metal beast wouldn't bite at me today. As I moved in closer to my comatose brother I could hear his heart beating, his lungs breathing, even his stomach beginning to churn the most recent deposit of macro nutrients the Razum pumped into him. He was all I needed to focus on right now.

I squeezed his hand close to my chest and pushed my head into the front of the Razum. Closing my eyes and hoping, in some version of Tyron's reality, he could feel my tears on him. He had to know he wasn't alone, and I was working to break him free.

"I love you Tyron, we will figure this out together. As we always have before." My words fell on the silence just as my eyelids fell to the darkness. At least in my sleep, I would see his bright, smiling face. He was safe in my dreams.

✿   ✿   ✿

Whatever sleep I had gotten that day was not enough to deal with the grumpy Gern and Gregory fighting inside the small tin shed. I opened my eyes to see the dim dawn light peaking through the cracks of my walling.

Wrapped in Tyron's arms, I realized I must have moved him in my sleep. Slowly unwrapping his thin limbs from me, I sat up, enduring the pain of motion.

Loud steps outside the curtain of my room alerted me to the impatient pacing of a four hundred-some pound robot. The shack shuddered to his every step, rattling the scrap siding. If he paced much more, my shed would fall.

"We need to have a sound plan for her to escape today. You have brought nothing, Gern." Gregory growled.

I could see the common disgruntled face Gern always made at accusations before I heard his response.

"Yu don' know da outside. No fud, no vater. Afthonia ain't even near." He grunted out his broken language as clearly as he could. Gregory was, unfortunately, not wired for understanding the specific 'Klik twang' that the people spoke.

"Afthonia?" Gregory questioned, trying to dissect Gern's words.

I also had to think through what I knew of 'Klik slang to understand that word in particular. It took me a moment, but I soon remembered he was referencing Rations day. The bi-weekly event where the Drones handed out food and water to maintain the population's health. It was a fairly substantial event that had most of the town out of their shelters. Even with proper food and water budgeting, it was still not quite enough to keep people from starving. I had only made due this long with scrounging for food outside of Haldoklik and partaking in Rations day.

"Rations day. There has to be some food and water around. Steal it if you want Taylor to survive this," Gregory growled. I could hear the annoyed grunting of Gern's dissatisfaction, but not long after I heard his conceding steps leave my shed. Gregory remained as he was rifling through my things.

Moving my body slowly, nothing but pain coursed through me. I was feeling better, but it did not lessen the difficulty. Because of Tyron acting as a blood bag for me before, I knew I had a minor dosage of Nanites that were likely mending most of my muscle tissue. This allowed me to use my leg. I both cursed and appreciated Gregory's choice to help.

Using the bed frame, I pulled myself up and mostly onto my feet. The pain was not quite bearable, so I placed all my weight on my good foot. Gregory must have heard my bed creaking and peaked his head through the curtain.

"You can sleep a while longer. The supplies are not ready and the Nanites work better when you are lying still." I ignored him and limped my way forward into the main work area of my shed. Apparently, Gregory was trying to maintain his Drone voice today by avoiding conjunctions. He stepped out of my way, letting me test out my strength as I walked.

The few steps I had made caused my eyes to blur and a faintness in my head. Leaning heavily into the table in the center of the room, I took a moment to steady myself. A cold sweat beaded up on my back and my vision darkened. I didn't know how I was going to get Tyron out of Haldoklik in this condition.

"You will have to carry quite a few supplies and your brother. I am not sure your human body, in its current condition, will make it far enough." Gregory observed.

"Tell me then, what choice do I have?" I spat at him through gritted teeth. While this anger was not totally directed at him, it partially was.

"How far do you think you will make it in your current condition?" He asked as he stepped back to lean into the wall of the shed slightly. The shack shuttered against his weight. I could tell his processors were whirring up a storm.

"I might be able to get out of Haldoklik if I start tomorrow. Though I don't think I have enough time to get far enough away by the time Gern calls me out." I estimated. This journey was going to either kill me or be excruciatingly painful. Steadying myself on my feet, I took a deep breath. "I will be fine. Getting Tyron out will be the challenge. I can barely walk with my weight, let alone my brother."

Gregory sat silently as he began computing options. I could smell the warm acrid smell of paint melting. Gregory must have been out of Haldoklik today and burned the metal on his feet. A part of me was still unsure of the Drone who sat here pondering how to help me. He had already broken so many rules, and is continuing to do so. He has already accepted his death sentence.

"Gregory, what if you take me and Tyron out of here?" I asked, figuring the answer would be a very sarcastic no, but I didn't have many options. If I tried to limp my way out of town, I could be easy pickings for 'Oomers or anyone else down on their luck in this dump of a town. There was a high chance I wouldn't survive the trek out of town, let alone in the barren lands above Haldoklik.

Gregory's whirring processors slowed as he decided. "No, I can not leave with you. That would be an immediate termination notice in the system. I would be destroyed by any Drones or Giants that see me. I can try to clear a way for you, though." He said as he stood straight and walked to the door.

"I will get you the rest of the supplies by tonight. Pack everything you can't do without. I have a bag of tools to help your brother down the road. Be sure to pack them or destroy them. They can't be left here." He pulled open my steel door as he spoke. The hinges squeaked against his strength.

"Thank you." I whispered to him softly.

He stopped a moment at the small appreciation before he closed the door tight behind him. I was, again, left alone in the dark of my shed. Limping my way to the stool near my desk, I sat down carefully on it, taking weight off of my injured leg. I surveyed the room to mentally plan what I was going to pack.

I would have to wear my lead rain poncho, so I assumed twenty-five pounds of weight with that. Then there would have to be food rations for at least a week with my current movement speed, so another fifteen pounds with an extra gallon of water, if I was lucky. Some clothes, since the acid destroys most things. I would need a temporary shelter with lead protections which I had prepped for my longer excursions into the Barrens above, but it weighed an extra seventy-five pounds. One hundred fifteen pounds of supplies roughly, and that's not including my brother at a weight of eighty-seven pounds or the weight of the equipment for him provided by Gregory.

Letting out a sigh, I saw my breath cause a cloud before me. It was colder than I had thought. The warmth of Tyron's body must have kept me warm. I checked over the bruising of my body, skewing my clothes to feel the sutures on my back. As my fingers met the warm wound, I winced at every stitch knot I brushed against. I was now a rich, colorful tapestry of bruising palettes. There was a certain level of beauty being so beaten, it made me feel stronger even though my body was screaming at me in opposition.

Standing and limping back to my bed, I caressed the quiet, emotionless jaw of Tyron as if he was sleeping. As I grabbed my leaded bag and packed the essentials, I was careful of the sounds I made as I rummaged around the tin shed, a part of me wary of waking Tyron. While every part of my logical mind knew he was not sleeping and was suspended in a virtual reality, there was another part that accepted he was sleeping and shouldn't be disturbed.

After a few moments of careful rooting around my shed, I realized that my weight estimation was off and I couldn't lift the bag. This wasn't shocking to me as I often over packed, but with my injuries, I would need to make sure I was under-packed. I took a break from organizing the bag to check on the tools Gregory left. Shuffling my way across the shed, I found the dark bag resting on my desk where Gern had moved it to.

Opening the mouth of the bag, I felt relief wash over me. Not only were there tools that would help Tyron but also would be useful for building a brace for my leg and ribs. As I dug through the bag, I noticed a black screen attached to a scanner. Picking it up, I noticed it was heavier than I had expected and examined the design of the device.

"This…isn't possible for me to have." I stammered to myself, realizing what I held in my hands.

The device was a tool for the Head Drones, used to track programming, make alterations, and scanning for Fritzing. There had been a few times I saw it used, but I had never held one in my hands. I would be able to see what was happening inside the Razum for the first time. There was a chance that I could see into Tyron's world, a chance to see if he was actually alive in there. This scanner was not only illegal for human use, it was a nuke-able offense and Giant investigation was required. Gregory had officially blown the whistle on Haldoklik to get me this device.

Swiftly, I tucked the tools and supplies into my bag, its weight growing heavier with each addition. This grimy, lead-lined bag now carried every chance I had at saving my brother—and myself. It felt surreal that my life's work could fit inside a single bag. In the next room, Tyron lay motionless, the faint pulse of his monitor light flashing steadily, though my heart held new hope as I looked over at him.

"Thank Gregory when you wake up. He might have just saved your life. Now I just have to figure out how to get this stuff and you out of here."

As I checked over the contents of my bag once more, I noticed my food rations were definitely short, and my water supply was also lacking. I could survive about five days out of town. Also, I was carrying enough illegal equipment to destroy multiple towns and kill hundreds of humans. I was walking with equipment that could cause a nuke to be dropped, a Razum zombie who couldn't walk, and an injured body. My odds were looking more grim as I continued to pack.

Pushing my odds out of my mind, I grabbed the spare equipment that Gregory had left and built a brace for my leg. It was crude, to say the least, being made up from old Drone scrap and arm braces, but it took a bit of pain off my ankle and only slightly impeded my ability to walk. My rib brace was much more difficult, designed off of the remnants of an old scrapper Drone with a clamp arm. Its cage-like clamp pinched around me and rubbed in terrible ways. Adding two inches off of my ribs, my cloak now billowed around me in a more dramatic effect.

I felt semi-mechanized after my several hours of labor and felt the slight relief the braces offered. Doing my best to stand and walk normally across the shed, I felt a pin pop loose on my rib brace and it snapped tighter around my chest, crushing the air from my lungs and smashing against my impaled wound. I gasped at the pain and nearly dropped to my knees, but the brace on my leg stood strong and held me up. Quickly, I reached around to loosen the grip of the clamp. After a few gasping fits and fidgeting fingers, I could breathe again.

As I fixed the pin placement and made sure it was secure, I heard a quiet knock on my door. I went still, trying to cease the groaning of the braces as I moved. This was a Drone coming to take me away for my crimes, or Gern. The second knock came a little louder and with an answer.

"Ish Gern." The voice whispered through.

I hobbled my way to the door, pulling my cloak down over the rib brace. Cracking the large metal wall that was my door as much as I could with my injuries, I tried to verify the voice owner. As I peaked out into the now dark town outside of my door, I saw a shorter, scarred old man with his old and tattered scrapper cloak pulled close around his face. His gray hair shone in the candlelight that poured out from my shed.

"I hav fud an' vater," he grunted, checking over his shoulder in the alley behind him. He was clearly wary of the consequences of the cruel actions he had taken. There was a kind but fearful smirk on Gern's face as he gestured to be invited in.

Opening the door wide enough, with his help, he slipped into the shack. I stepped back and let him latch the door close behind himself. As I hobbled my way back towards my bag, I could feel his eyes watching me. He was likely trying to discern how I had made the braces that feebly kept me upright.

"Gregory brought some scrap for me to make them. Not much, but it's better than before." I answered his mental questions before he was willing to ask them.

"Dat bot got sum screws loose." He spoke slowly, letting each word sink in, making sure I could follow.

"Be careful, Tay," he added softly, his gaze lingering on my injuries. I shrugged off his concern, turning to the bag I hadn't been able to lift before. Gritting my teeth, I bent down and prepared to try again, determination hardening my resolve.

With the aid of the braces, I could lift the bag and securely place it on my back. I took a breath and took a few steps to feel what level of fatigue I was going to be looking at. After a moment of success and a few adjustments, I knew I could carry it safely, so I removed it and placed it on the central table of my shed. Hopefully, with the addition of the food and water from Gern, it would still be carry-able.

Gern also placed the bag of food and water he had salvaged on the table so that I could easily examine the contents and pack them into my bag. As I packed the molded bread and what we labeled as cheese, I noticed a heavier lump at the bottom of the bag. It was the shape of an elbow joint for piping, but it was covered with a dark black material, almost resembling leather.

As I reached for it to examine it, Gern caught my hand and shook his head. "Best not to. Itz only for 'mergencies," he said carefully as he retrieved the object. Slowly uncovering just a corner of the object, I quickly stopped him, realizing what he held.

"Gern, this is a very serious weapon," I said in a hushed tone.

The gift he was giving me was an emergency out, but at an extreme cost. Weapons had been banned since introducing the bevies and Loomer towns. Only extremist rebellions would create weapons these days at the risk of regional destruction. Giants would burn the entire area of up to a hundred miles if even a whisper of weapons arose. Here in our shared hands, we held an electro-pulse gun, capable of five rounds of circuit frying weaponry. While it would only freeze a Giant for a few moments with a very direct shot, it could quickly take out smaller aerial Drones and drop a larger Drone like Gregory for a time.

"Iz jus' for 'mergencies." He repeated. "Don' let Greg find out." Whispering his words as he folded the item away and placed it in the depth of my bag, but still within easy grasp if needed.

"Gods know yu gon' need da luck. Yu alvays had good luck, but jus' in case." Gern chuckled.

I stifled my urge to hug the old Scrap Dog for fear of getting stabbed for it, but nodded my appreciation instead.

"Best to get the dangerous loot out of town, eh?" I asked sarcastically as I gimped over to my brother, who remained on his bed.

"If dat vere da case, I vud've kicked yu out long ago." Gern chuckled. I never thought that this old rebel would be a person who would help me out of this damnable hole. Though, I realized now that I am glad he was the one who Gregory recruited.

Reaching down, I tried to lift my brother's body. While I could move him, I couldn't comfortably carry him. As I tried to toss him over my shoulder as I used to, I felt nothing but pain and had to slowly lower him back to the bed. Gern stepped closer and helped me lower him the rest of the way down.

"Damn, I'm not healed enough yet." I grumbled, turning and examining the shed around me for any tools. Gern patted me on the shoulder and gestured to my stool by my desk for me to sit. I listened to the gnarled fingers' direction and sat down, watching as the old scrapper dug around my shed. He pulled tarps from my walls and dismantled a few of my shelves, creating a pile of scrap for him to tinker with. My shed was quickly becoming unusable, which didn't matter to me anymore. My home was Tyron. This shed was only a living space.

After a few minutes of minor destruction to my shed, Gern approached me and held out a device. "Iz a...gurney, of sorts." He muttered.

Looking over the mashed together simple machine, I realized what he had done. I immediately placed the device over my shoulders and draped the tarping over my back and pulled it so it was loose enough to hold in front of me. While it added a small amount of weight, it was going to be negligible if it worked.

I walked over to Tyron and wrapped him carefully in the tarp so that he could sit securely within it. Turning my back to him, I pulled the lever out from the device on my shoulder and cranked it in a clockwise fashion. The rope that held the tarp wound back and forth on my shoulders and pulled Tyron up and onto my back in a secure hammock.

The weight of carrying all the food supplies, as well as my brother, was excruciating. I had to lean so far forward I was almost falling over, but this was now plausible. I looked at Gern while I adjusted Tyron's Razum. "Thank you, Gern," I said as kindly as I could manage.

He nodded his silent appreciation and shuffled to the stool as I moved to drop Tyron back down on the bed and let my bag down carefully. I sat down next to my brother and let out a sigh. It was not the way I wanted to leave here, but at least it felt possible now. Tyron and I actually had a chance of getting out and progressing with my work to free him. It had been some time since I felt this optimistic.

An attempt at a quiet knock was made at the door, but it was obviously a metal hand. I looked at Gern and he stood to go check the door. As he stood near the door, Gern let out a grunt, acknowledging the knock. He didn't move to open the door, yet waited for an irritated Gregory to respond.

"Gern, let me in." Rumbled the speaker of Gregory. Gern slowly opened up the door and the large Drone stepped through the doorway and nudged the old man out of his way. Gern chuckled as he closed the door behind him. Gregory waited for the old dog to walk past him and take position near me. We watched the robot as he assessed the braces I was wearing and the pack that was sitting.

"Have you figured out how to transport everything?" He asked, examining the device that sat on my shoulders, courtesy of Gern.

"I should be able to make the journey. The stairs will be the hardest part, but beyond that I should be fine." I guessed.

"Good, because you need to leave tonight. Cherub 735 was noted as missing today. The search begins tomorrow. You will need to leave tonight to make this plan work. Gern, you need to go back to your shop. You have been noted as absent from your usual routine. Both situations will lead to you having higher surveillance tomorrow, Taylor. It's time to say farewell." He looked around the room for any last things to bring with or destroy to avoid leaving any evidence.

Gern looked at me and stood. As I tried to rise to meet him, he pushed me back down. I watched the old man looking at me and noticed a slight tinge of emotion on his face. He gave my shoulder a firm pat.

"Tay, I've watched yu since yu first showed up. I vill watch out for yu as yu leave too. Tell yer brother who helped save yer sorry asses." Gern chuckled as he extended his hand to me. I shook his rough and scarred fingers, realizing this will truly be the last time I see him. The old man who taught me how to survive in this town was now sending me off. I suppose this was as close as I was going to get to a fatherly farewell. If there was ever a time that I would return here, he would likely be dead, so I cherished this fond send off.

"Goodbye Gern. Stay out of the rain." I nodded my appreciation at him. Gern nodded in return. He released my hand and turned to Gregory.

"If she gets hurt leavin' vith yer help, I'll scrap yu before yu can send a signal for help." Gern growled as he shoved past the Drone. Gregory ignored the old man and opened the door for him to leave. Gern cast one more glance at me and nodded a last farewell before the door was closed and that part of my life was cut off.

Gregory turned back to me and held up the pack from the table where I had set it. "Do you have everything you need? The trip to the next Loomer town will be a very long one. There are a few bevies you should avoid. They are overrun with 'Oomers."

I nodded as he spoke. The dangers of the Bevie towns and Barrens were well known to me. I had ventured out enough and had enough unfortunate encounters to remember to be careful. Weather it was avoiding 'Oomers, whether that could turn in a moment's notice, or general Raiders and Drone scouts, I was prepared.

Standing now, toe to toe with Gregory, I looked into the LED board that made up his simplistic eyes. There was little there that gave away his true motivations. While he may not be a traditional friend, his aid in this process was priceless.

"Thank you for your help with this."

Hoping to see some feelings, or a mild reaction, the LEDs betrayed nothing of what buzzed through his circuitry. He stepped back a slight bit and dug into a satchel I now realized he was wearing. Awkwardly ignoring my sentiment, he held out a thin piece of scrap metal with some scrawling covering the surface.

"I made you a simplified map of things to stay away from and the reach of the Giant Finigan's radar. You would do best to stay out of view of his Drones while you are on your way as you will have a warrant for your death on the network. Other Giants will care less, but still be wary."

"This map has a few dangerous areas where you will need to go slow and watch for sensors, but still is one of the safest routes unless you would rather take your chances with the 'Oomer raiders that lurk around. I did my best to map them today, but they are often moving. Night is going to be your best option."

I looked over his scrawling and noted Haldoklik on the most Southern portion. There was a compass to keep me in the correct orientation. As well as a crude written note over Haldoklik saying, 'Start here'. I smiled to myself as I noted the sarcastic implication that I didn't know where the journey was going to start. As I visually traced the path he had carved, I noticed his little drawings of 'Oomer raiders in a very pixelated art style. As I continued to follow the clean guideline, my finger froze over a matte square with one word etched in - Finigan.

"Gregory, this map takes me right next to Finigan. I can't do that." I stuttered. How did he think I was going to survive this trail? I mine as well walk in front of a Drone and declare myself a criminal. The Giant of this region was known for his violence and concise human clean up. The old Loomers would have been proud of his ruthless work.

I couldn't stop the instant worry in my chest. Perhaps Gregory was not the friend I was thinking he was by taking this tremendous risk to me and Tyron. Was I mistaken in my thinking that he was actually trying to help me? Was this a ruse to bring me right to Finigan?

Gregory chimed in before my thoughts could run further away from me. "Look around the area. The 'Oomers have set up camp as close as they could to Finigan without being killed on sight. They have kept a clean line out to the East and West, avoiding the main Drone paths to Finigan. That means the path we Gregory units used to connect with Finigan, which leads from Haldoklik and to the North where Finigan rests, is the only safe area. Unless you want to add four days trekking around the line of murderous and semi cannibalistic robot loving cult, stay on the path." He gestured to the map while he was talking. I noticed the many drawings of 'Oomer groups and saw he had written in estimations of the population. There were nearly two hundred of them.

"Maybe it would be safer to take the longer route? I have time and no home." I muttered, checking over his map for a simpler path. "You don't have as much time as you may think. The Nanites will only stabilize Tyron for a short period of time. They aren't designed to work with human anatomy and they will burn out, and Tyron's Razum will continue its inevitable venture. You have around five days, depending on the stress that his system is under. Avoid getting him shot."

Gregory had a point. If I wanted to maintain Tyron's progress, I would need to find a new location to set up a workshop and dig into the controls of the Razum. "Where does this map lead me to?" I asked, looking further up on the map.

"This is going to take you to Gundry's territory. There is a Loomer town there. Unfortunately, I was made for Finigan's network so I am unfamiliar with the societal status of the town. It's built in the body of a Loomer named Locura. I would be wary of the water there. While I am not familiar with the town, I am familiar with the Loomer. An earlier model that mostly ran off of nuclear waste. Her town is surely irradiated so be quick through there. Gundry is a lazy Giant, semi-offline, so Drones run most of the region."

Gregory was thorough. I couldn't deny that. This was truly going to be a hell run, but at least there was a plan. It's more than I had when I stumbled into Haldoklik carrying my brother. I nodded my appreciation and took a moment to memorize the first portion of the map.Once I knew my direction, I tucked the tin map into my bag. Pausing to survey the shed, I recalled something I had overlooked.

I did my best to go down to my knees with the brace keeping my leg straight and my ribs forced to stay straight. As I struggled against the braces, Gregory knelt down instead and motioned for me to back off. He examined the floor where I pointed and found the false floor that covered my safe.

"Can you grab the bag next to the safe?" I asked, pointing to the dark bag that held my paints and metal sculptures. As he pulled up the bag, he looked at its contents.

"This is an unnecessary waste of carrying weight. I advise you not to bring this with you." He said as he handed me the bag. I placed the bag on the table and carefully pulled out the doll I had been working on and the paints. Gregory leaned in closer to get a better view of the objects.

"I know I can't take these with me. I spent years gathering these pigments and finding pliable metal. These are the only things that exist with just me. My whole life has been my brother, and now I'm even leaving this part of me behind as well. I have one more request, Gregory 235." I said as I pushed the objects to the Drone who watched my actions questioningly.

"Take care of these for me." I grabbed his metal gloved hand and placed it on the delicate tea set. His glove pulled back slightly to not crush them, but he did not pull away. He carefully picked up one of the painted tea cups and examined it close to his face.

"What are these?" He asked, holding the cup from the rim instead of the handle.

"It's a tea set I built. I had one in the Razum when I was very young. I wanted one to be here with me in this world, but no matter how hard I looked, I couldn't find one. So I made one." His eyes followed as I showed him how to properly use the cup. "I used to have tea parties with my brother." More pain was in my voice than I would have liked.

Gregory must have noticed the tone I took and placed the cup down gently. "I don't know if I am the right person to give something of this emotional value." He said as he backed away.

"Gregory, I have no friends. I have no family besides my comatose brother. You have spared me injury, perjury, and death. You have caught me with contraband multiple times and spared me the worst of the punishments I should have gotten. I don't know if that makes us friends, but it doesn't make you my enemy. Even Gern would sell me out if it saved his hide." I pushed the tea set towards the emotionally unsure Drone.

Gregory's hesitation proved he was truly considering this offer. I could hear his processors whirring as he thought over what I had said. When the whirring cooled, he stepped back towards the table and gathered the cups back into the bag and pulled them near him. "I will keep these safe for you." He begrudgingly responded.

I would have sworn he was blushing if he wasn't an acid washed, chrome sculpted, child-like face incapable of expressing emotion. Nodding my thanks seemed to be the most appropriate response. Most words were lost in conversations, half were lies and the rest were often threats or just information. Nodding was the typical response to anything exceeding those verbal values.

Standing up straight from the table, I took a steady breath. "I guess I should head out while it's dark," I grumbled, hefting my heavy travel sack. As I got ready, I caught sight of Gregory out of the corner of my eye, slipping the shoulder strap of the bag with the tea set around his neck. A sly smile curled at the corners of my mouth at the simple gesture.

With my bag snug against my back, I backed up to pull Tyron up and against my back. Gregory helped me angle him as comfortably against my bag as I could get him. As I stood, weighed down by the life I was leaving behind, I couldn't help but to feel a twang of loss in leaving this old shed. I had been here long enough to bond with this rickety town. A part of me will miss the comfort of knowing the area, and even some of the gruff people.

"Kind hearts don't last here. You're better off moving on. There is nothing in this town for someone like you," Gregory muttered as he led the way to the door, pulling up the metal bar that acted as a lock. "Better to leave now, before Haldoklik keeps you here," he added, opening the door and nodding toward the outside. I took one last look at the workshop I'd always resisted calling home.

The bunk beds I would never see again, the worktable that I had spent many lost hours at, the table that I had slept more nights on than the bed. Even the hole in the corner that had acted as my bathroom was a sad farewell to bid. I walked once more to my work table and leaned over the last lit candle of the room. With a deep sigh, I extinguished the flame of my old life.

It was a frosty night out of the shed as I left the darkened life I was putting behind me. I could tell a rain was going to sweep through tonight and I took a moment to pull up my hood to avoid it sooner rather than later. As we walked through the darkness, Gregory was kind enough to escort me on the back street of the town towards the wall's edge.

He was keeping a close eye around us, later mentioning that 'Oomers had been worked up recently because of a cleansing in the Lower town. I assumed it was the one I had witnessed, and we remained in silence till the steps out of town appeared as a scar in the wall of Haldoklik. Gregory paused by the steps and looked up at the wall. I could sense he wanted to say something, but his speaker was being held shut.

Also, taking a moment at the steps, I looked up the hundreds of dangerous metal rungs I would have to carefully climb, with my weight being unbalanced. Looking behind us, I noticed the lights still flickering in the distance of Upper town. I turned my head away from the town and started up the first step and balanced myself. Immediate dread and fear filled the step. It was going to be a dangerous climb tonight for many reasons.

I cast one more glance back at the Drone. Gregory was posed to say something, his hand on the wall behind me. The glow from his eyes illuminated a small bit of the wall, revealing a large bolt jammed into the stone-like mud of the pit of Haldoklik. As the speaker rattled to life, we heard a clatter near us. I ducked instinctively, and Gregory turned to face the threat.

Using the commotion, I started scurrying up the steps out of Haldoklik. While muddy and having slick metal surfaces, my boots knew these steps all too well. Once I was partially up the wall, I glanced down at where Gregory once stood. He was now gone, and all seemed quiet at the base of the stairs.

"Thank you, Gregory 235. I will not forget you soon." I quietly whispered to the town with the vague hope he would hear my words through the acid soaked lights of Haldoklik.

My journey of finding a new home had begun. The steps were already proving less of a struggle than I was expecting with Gern's help with Tyron, and my own braces to thank. While the pain was still present, it was at least manageable for a short time. I had made it to the last section of stairs when I turned and saw the sun beginning its rise into the sky. The shadows of night were slowly being chased back to the West and over the head of Haldoklik.

The view stretched over the town, a thick smog rolling up from Haldoklik and blotting out what little light tried to pierce through. It was the same sight that greeted me on the day I first stumbled into this place. Now, years later, it felt fitting to see it again as I prepared to leave. For Haldoklik, nothing much would change; the smog would still rise, and life would continue in its heavy, unchanging way.

I never thought I would look back on this town with such fondness. There were enough terrible memories here that I should have been able to walk away without a second thought. Although, no one can truly walk away from the home they knew without some fear of the unknown, causing their heart to long for the familiarity.

Checking over my belongings once more to make sure they had not shifted my weight around too much, I proceeded up the last steps to the Barrens. Once I hit the surface, the feeling of anything alive remaining in the world dissipated. The life I once knew was officially behind me and a grueling journey laid before me.

The Barrens were rightly named: Nothing of humanity remained here. For as far as I could see in the early morning light, there was nothing but dead trees that had not been uprooted and occasional trash piles. This was now what the world offered to me, cold and lifeless land.

Nutrient deficient soil crunched like the husk of life had been shucked off under my heavy boots. The noise of each step felt deafening on the breeze-less landscape. Even the wind had left this land and couldn't carry the noise away from me.

"This is going to be a long trip, Tyron." I groaned quietly to my ever-present companion.

The cold had already started to eat at me as I shuffled my way forward. I had hoped the sun would bring some warmth to my walk, but it was already being blotted out by the move of acidic rain clouds. The directions of the clouds made it appear as though the rain would not hit me, but I knew I had to take precautions. Things always seemed to change to make my life more difficult when I set out on fresh adventures in the Barrens.

Stopping a moment, I cranked the lever to lower my brother to the ground and gave myself enough slack to turn and face him. He almost looked like a corpse, with his motionless and feeble body draped on the pale soil. I removed his acid proof clothing from my pack and quickly dressed him so that no rain would hit him, including a heavy poncho to protect the Razum from damage. In my whole life of caring for my brother, he had never been burned by the rain. I was hoping to keep my record clean. His body had enough to deal with.

Once he was nicely bundled, I reapplied him to my pack and started walking once more. Haldoklik was still in view, so I knew I had a few more miles before I would hit the Core Trail. According to Gregory's map, I would follow the Core Trail till I saw a statue, then deviate off into 'Oomer territory.

The dread of my future steps kicked in. I was more terrified of this path choice than I may have mentioned to Gregory. Walking so close to a Giant felt like a needless risk, but I knew my time constraints were pressing. With the tools Gregory gave me, I could make serious progress in freeing Tyron from the Razum, but I had to keep my momentum so that he didn't regress. I doubted I would get another functioning, non damaged, Giant eye anytime soon to steal Nanites from. For Tyron, I would take this risk.

"Hey Tyron, do you remember how we used to play ping-pong? You used to always let me win? I will never forget the time I could first see above the table enough to play with you. I could barely see above the net when you sent your first volley at me. You would always smile. It always felt safe with you around. You and your rebellious long hair. The Watchers were always telling you to cut it, but you never did." I remembered my brother's long blonde curling locks. He had always felt like a doll, with his slender features and pristine hair. Almost like he belonged to another world.

A part of me wondered if that was his actual face. My face was not quite the same when I left the Razum. It took a long time to recognize myself once I was out. Was it going to be the same for Tyron? Would I be able to recognize his face when it is finally revealed?

"You used to tell me stories. I'm trying to remember one. It had something to do with a Rocket man and a guy named Major...Dan? Or Tom? How he was courageous and went to the stars. I wish I could hear that story right about now. It always made me feel like anything is possible. You did so well at making sure the world never felt like too much. Always teaching me that I could change things if I wanted to. I bet you never thought the world out here was like this, though. I don't think even Major Tom could fix this with his ground control powers." The rhythmic pounding of my feet kept the silences from getting too loud.

I let a long time pass, trying to quiet my mind from running too far down memory lane. While the pounding of my feet became the metronome, my mind ticked with the Core Trail was now in view. The sun had risen slightly higher than the clouds that tried to hold it back. I could feel the slight warmth of the light on my hood. I could still smell the rain in the air, even if it was heading away from me.

The Core Trail was fairly easy to see from a distance. Walls of garbage and junk created a firm barrier, probably standing twenty feet tall. It was darkened with oil from years of Giants and Drones walking the path as peacekeepers and humans revolting against them. Like a black wall of sorrows from a distant time.

As I drew near, I stopped for a break. The pain in my legs and ribs was becoming unbearable. Letting Tyron down, I also set my pack down and removed the braces that were digging into my flesh. While the Barrens were a colder temperature, the sun had started to significantly warm the dirt. I sprawled over the ground and tried to accept as much of the heat as the sun was willing to offer.

"Do you remember when we had the ocean update for our network? They added in so many sea creatures. We spent weeks just lying on the beach and discovering new animals. I had never seen such colorful fish. I wonder if the oceans of this world still exist. We've lived in Finigan's region all of my time free of the Razum. Who knows, maybe those fish still exist out there." I sounded more hopeful than I intended. The acid rain likely destroyed the ecosystems required to maintain such fish. I knew deep down that the color in the world was dead now.

After a few minutes of enjoying the sun, I gathered my things and my brother, replaced my braces and continued on my way. There was no time for dawdling. My braces were still holding up and my pain was minimal for what I was dealing with. Slowly but surely, I was making my way.

The silence dragged on me and the memories got painful. I hummed a song Tyron had once taught me and mumbled the lyrics to myself incoherently. I forgot how annoying these Barren walks got. The silence away from the town was deafening.

"There is a house in New Orleans... they call the Rising Sun," I murmured, barely noticing the tune slipping past my lips. "And it's been the ruin of many a poor girl... and God, I know I'm one." The words lingered in the still air, as if the song understood things I could never quite put into words. I felt the weight of each line like an old friend.

"My mother was a tailor... she sewed my new blue jeans," I sang softly, voice rough, recalling some faint memory of simpler things. My mother was doubtfully a tailor, and I had never known her, but there'd been a time when I had something... a life, someone to look after me. Now it felt like a lifetime ago, more of a story than a memory.

"And the only thing a gambler needs," I went on, almost whispering between panting breaths, "is a suitcase and a trunk..." I glanced at my own worn bag strap across my shoulder, crammed full of everything I owned, everything I might need. The tune drifted, filling the surrounding silence, an echo of someone else's sorrow that somehow felt like mine.

I let the last lines fall from my lips, "And I'm going back to New Orleans... to wear that ball and chain." The words felt like prophecy, like a weight I was still dragging behind me, no matter how far I tried to run. But for a moment, humming that old song, it felt like I wasn't alone with my burden. The song understood—it carried that weight with me, if only for a few fleeting seconds.

Very few songs made sense to me. We had heard a lot of music growing up in the Razum, but very few had any applicable weight to my life now. I could still hear Tyron belting out the lyrics as though they were the vibration of his soul. If only he knew what the world had become now, those lyrics might carry a different tone for him.

Pushing the painful recalling of my brother aside, I focused back on my path. I had done these walks enough times that I knew which exact garbage piles I had scavenged through. Many rocks and dead trees were marked with my symbols to keep me oriented in this desert-like landscape. Many times I had done this walk in the night. It was odd seeing the Barrens in their blindingly pale shades in the sunlight.

This place was like my hiking area that I had traversed hundreds of times. So why was I still feeling dread walking through this area? Was it because Gregory noted how close I had been walking to 'Oomer camps? Suddenly, knowing where the dangers were made the area feel more dangerous than relaxing.

As I approached the wall of the Core Trial, I cast a glance behind me at the horizon beyond. I felt like I was being watched, but I knew it was unlikely. The 'Oomer camps were far enough away that I shouldn't have anything to worry about. Paranoia and fear were the best weapons the Barren had in its arsenal.

I looked up the Core wall, riddled with garbage and possessions of decades past. Thankfully, due to all the family heirlooms and trinkets holding the wall together, I had enough hand holds to climb it easily. One hand and one foot at a time, I slowly ascended the walls of the forced marching trail.

Once on the peak, I steadied myself with the weight of Tyron and my pack on me. It was an accomplishing feeling to stand on this wall. To know that while millions died on this path, I still got out with my brother. We still, somehow, survived all this and even when the Loomers fell, we survived then. While I may not know my parents, or their parents, they all survived to give us the chance to survive as well.

"Have to be grateful for the little things in this life, huh, Tyron?" I muttered as I slowly lowered my body to start my descent onto the Trail.

The benefit of walking in the Trail itself was that there was less chance of being spotted by Drones from afar. And with most people typically made uncomfortable by the Trails, I was likely to not be bothered or ambushed. 'Oomers were often disgusted by the show of human spirit and left the Trails alone as well. It paid well to hide in the depressing history of our species.

I made it down the steep wall, kicking some garbage out of my way, awkwardly, with the brace on my leg. The crunching of countless objects beneath my feet felt like it echoed down the Trail to the many distant memories of feet marching this very path. I avoided examining the objects I was stepping on, knowing that once I looked, I would see countless photos of friends and families that are no longer, or precious belongings that people couldn't carry anymore. A truly dismal path to walk.

Centering myself on the trail where fewer belongings were scattered, I started down the path, humming a new tune to keep my mind from wandering back to the memories buried here. My heart wasn't strong enough to relive what had happened all those years ago. The parallel was hard to ignore—walking this path now, after I, too, had lost the place I once called home. But I wouldn't be leaving anything behind here. I would die carrying my brother if I had to.

Walking long enough to see the sun leave the trench, I decided it was time to stop for the day. Tyron was lowered to the ground as I unpacked my survival shelter. Pulling some of the rubble from the wall of the trench, I could create a decent covering to hide beneath. With the addition of my acid proofing to keep us safe in case it rained, the shelter was stable against the cold of the night and the rain. I tucked Tyron into the small shelter so he could lie as comfortably as possible on the tarp I laid out for us. His Razum blinked calmly in the darkening world. A dim reminder of the goal I was working towards.

I quickly unpacked some food and ate as what I could. Hunger was too large a motivator in the Barrens, and I refused to fall prey to such motivations. With coming off the mild dosage of Synthix I was on, the hunger was starting to hurt. Feeding Tyron out here made little sense, with a small amount of food available. I made the mental note to work on feeding him when I got to the next Loomer town, if supplies permitted.

Letting the food settle in my stomach as night crawled its way into the sky, I pulled out the map Gregory made for me. I had to light a small candle to read the surface, being careful to keep the light as hidden as possible. From the map I could tell I was nearing some 'Oomer camps and had to be careful in tomorrow's light. Scanning over the land where Finigan sat, there were very few safe options around him that would be feasible. I would likely have to camp near the Giant in a day or so unless I wanted to exhaust myself walking through the night. After Finigan, I would have two or three days left to walk. I need to pick up my pace.

Placing the map back in my pack and extinguishing the candle, I let it cool near the edge of the shelter. It stood as a mental reminder to pack all my belongings with me. Leaving evidence that I was camped here would only draw attention to my path. Having an 'Oomer hoard picking up my trail was the last thing I wanted.

I crawled near my brother and pulled a second tarp over us to trap in some warmth while we slept. The Razum would keep him warm enough to live, which would make him act as a heater for me. I hated using my brother for this, but it was necessary tonight. Making the mental note to thank him for this when he woke, I tried to fit onto the makeshift tarp mat.

My head bounced off of his Razum, causing me to pull my head away. Waiting for a moment to see if the anti-tampering bomb was going to ignite, I let out a small sigh of relief. It wasn't going to be a comfortable sleep, but it was better than no sleep.

I listened to the quiet world around us as night finally fell. Perfectly silent. It had been a while since I camped out in the silence of the Barrens. I forgot how relaxing it was. I knew I was hidden well enough that even a passerby would not recognize my shelter. We were safe in this quiet world for a moment.

"Do you remember how you used to take me camping? We would steal our bed sheets and run away from the living areas. We would go as far as the network would let us and you would build me a shelter. Lighting as many candles as you could steal and tell me all sorts of crazy things you had overheard the Watchers talking about. I had always felt like you helped me escape the world. I was so young, yet you endured my endless whining and questions. There was never a chance to thank you for that. I hope I will get the chance soon."

The darkness and silence were all I had for a response to my reminiscing. Soon I would hear Tyron's voice again. I had missed the timber of his tone when he told me stories. The fingers of sleep started tugging my mind back into the quiet places of my skull and my eyes relaxed.

"Soon Tyron, soon I will free you."

Chapter 5: The Giant Named Finigan

The morning that greeted me was cold and miserable, running its icy claws across my face. Clouds had moved in over the night and a fog was stinging my nostrils. I was quick to wake up and check all my belongings and Tyron. The acid fog was much less toxic but could still burn and condensate to create acid drops. Tyron's face and body remained scar-less, although I noticed a few drops burning on my hand that had been exposed. I quickly flicked the water off and dried it, but without a base, it would continue to burn for a while.

I peeked outside of my hidden shelter to examine the world's new skin. The sun must have come up already, as I could see light. Cursing myself for sleeping in, I quickly gathered my braces onto myself. While I was in significantly less pain than I was yesterday, thanks to the Nanites for working the night shift, I would rely on the support of the braces. Once geared up, I packed all my items in the shelter, including the candle from the night before.

My pack felt lighter today, which was a good sign towards the recovery of my body. I dressed myself in my full covering of acid-proof tarping, and quickly dressed Tyron the same, his tarp being pulled tight around the Razum so that it would not be exposed to the fog. If the air intakes of the Razum got burned out by acid, a fire would break out and set off the bombs.

It was going to be a rough walk with only partial visibility. I pulled on my goggles I had brought with me for such an occasion and pulled my tarp over my mouth and nose. Breathing acid was never an ideal situation.

Checking over my gear and skin coverage, I was satisfied with my work and began packing the rest of my belongings.

Pulling down the tarps that protected us during the night and quickly folding them, I placed them on the outside of my pack to not burn the items within. Tyron would be fine draped on them with his tarping. Once my back was packed with all my belongings and my brother, I quickly set off down the Trail. I was reaching the end of where I knew my way. This was the farthest I have walked this direction, and I was starting my journey into the unknown world.

The fog made the walk more strenuous. All the sounds I made hid in this wall of fog that consumed me. Thankfully, it was unlikely I was going to be heard, but it was unlikely I would hear anyone near me until I could see them. Both a cloak and a dagger to walk through the fog.

I was unable to track the time as the sun was diffused throughout the shroud evenly. I don't know how long I had walked before I saw a looming structure before me. It stood off to the side of the Core Trail, but it was the largest standing structure I had ever seen. It depicted a large man, taller than a Giant, who was suspended in a circle with a parallel set of limbs coming off of his regular. The circle he stood in was bent and caused the statue to point downwards.

Gregory had scribbled on his map to follow the direction of the hand till I saw a ridgeline in the distance, no taller than my thumb. While it was difficult to see any sort of landmark in the fog, I figured I should slow my speed so as not to overshoot and end up walking directly into Finigan.

Following the hand, I started up the wall of the Core Trail. On top, I made sure to check Gregory's map with the compass inlaid on it. Once I confirmed my heading as North East I climbed down and set off in the direction, slowly dragging my feet through the fog. The sound of boots on dead soil was not as shrill as it had sounded the day before. One thing to appreciate about the fog, besides the eye burning, lung stinging, and skin scarring, it made the world feel cozier and closer.

Time was moving by slowly, or fast, and I wasn't aware of it. The misty cover was stealing my perception of time and distance. Nothing around me to note where I was, no sound to guide me or sun to keep me company. I was feeling anxiety just outside of the fog. My mind ran away with me.

In the fog, I could see the broken and sickly faces of 'Oomers watching me. Or were they? I had to remind myself that no one hid just beyond the cloud of my vision, but my eyes still darted in every direction. At one point, I could have sworn I saw the hand of a Giant pulling away just out of sight. So many dangers that could easily snag me from life, just out of sight until they choose to attack.

I quickly decided that I would feel better after a break and unloaded my temporary shelter tarps. It was a weak tent, to say the least, but it kept the fog out of my sight. I sat in the tarp tent holding my brother's head and tried to clear my mind of the dangers outside. Rotating to grab my pack, I paused.

Did I hear footsteps?

"Did you hear that, Tyron?" I whispered, listening to the fog.

The world loomed with dire situations all around. Although the silence remained. When I was sure there was no motion around me, I continued to dig around in my pack. Once I secured the scanning device that was gifted to me, I set the pack nearer to me in case of an emergency. The feeling of unease was keeping my flight response active.

Cautiously, I examined the device. It had multiple cords coming from the small screen. Feathering the cords through my fingers as if they were hair, I could feel the vibrations of the electricity running through the device. I examined the cord ends to see if the outputs were like any I had seen on the Razum. After a moment, I found a cord that looked similar to the Razum technology and scanned Tyron's head for the port.

His head rolled on my lap just enough for me to access the port. Very carefully, I inserted the cord into the Razum. The device in my hand whirred to life quietly and the indicator light on the Razum changed to a purple flash. In my own theories while inspecting the device, I saw no reason connecting to the Razum would hurt my brother, so I quieted my nervous finger tapping.

The device began tracking the network pathing of the Razum and I was starting to understand why the Razum was fighting all the things I had tried. I had never realized that the circuits were mimicking the connection of a brain. The Razum was communicating with Tyron's brain and thus replicating his processing power to protect the design. It was a fascinating discovery, if it didn't mean that I had to trick my brother's brain to release itself. With no way to communicate with him, it was another impossible impasse to cross.

As the device continued its scanning and showing more information, my breathing stopped. With trembling hands, I drew the device closer to my face. It was only the size of a shoe and the screen was difficult to see. I wanted to make sure I saw the prompt correctly. An option lingered on the top right with a simple two word prompt. 'Visualize Network'.

"Gregory, you damn genius." I muttered as my finger hovered over the prompt. There was hesitation in my hand I couldn't exactly place. Would this be considered an invasion of Tyron's privacy? I had never seen into his personal network in the Razum, he has lived there in solitary for several years. Did this count as a breach of trust?

A quick phrase floated through my mind from the Scientist I once knew. "This world is dark. There are no rules of what is right science and wrong science anymore. Once the Loomers came, moral law went out the window." I could see his face highlighted in the dark by a candle in my memories. I thought he had just grown to be a bitter old man. Now, after all I had seen in my short time of life, I knew he was right.

I didn't feel comfortable with this choice, but I needed to know how Tyron was doing. Closing my eyes, I let the weight of my finger drop and blamed gravity for deciding. I waited for the device to quiet down while processing the command before I was willing to look.

Peeking through partially closed eyelids, I saw a scene presented on the screen. It was not a clear image, but I could see movement. I assumed it was the private network Watcher, though the image was grainy. Upon closer inspection I could make out the friendly child-like face of the Watcher as it hovered around the solid concrete looking home of the base model for the Razums. The Watcher wore the same cloak over the head and draped down around itself into a teardrop form hovering a few inches above the ground. While it had arms at its side, they were tucked beneath a cloak.

The view only showed a corner angle of the outside of the stone house from the outside, but it was enough to show me what I dreaded seeing. A house was chipped and broken on some walls and the environment around was glitching. The fountains that used to flow around the area were now leaking water and there were piles of clothes and objects anywhere there was flat space. This environment had fallen into extreme disrepair.

While the Watcher slowly attempted to clean the area, I could see it was glitching out, not able to truly grab anything. It followed a curving line through the trash, causing a small clean line wherever it hovered. It was stuck in the same cycling loop, never able to complete its cleaning tasks. Tyron's network was failing without being connected to a server.

My eyes darted around the screen. Tyron had to be here somewhere. As I scanned, my eyes burned, not only from strain and the slight fog that was leaking into my tent, but because I needed to see my brother and know he was alright. I was feeling my heart sink when I noticed a small hand reach up out of a trash pile near the broken, dark stone house. This was not Tyron's hand.

I watched a small head pull itself up from the pile and let a quiet smile curl my lips. It was an echo build of myself as a child. Tyron must have made it to keep him company. The Watchers had taught us how to make echo builds if we ever felt lonely when we were children, trying to keep us in a positive mental health state. It was as easy as remembering your fondest memories and applying as much physical detail as you could to an empty program the Watchers would make for us. Tyron must have built one when he realized he was cut from the servers.

A larger hand reached out from the same pile of trash and grabbed the Taylor echo in a loving hug and I saw a face lift from the pile. I couldn't feel the burning in the air anymore, or the weight of the braces on my body. The world suddenly felt free of worry. No more terrors hid in the surrounding fog.

My brother's face was pulled from the trash, his golden long hair was longer than I remembered and his face was more filled out. His green eyes peered out of the trash and watched the Taylor echo before he laid back down. I saw his lips moving, but no sound came from the device. He was still long and lanky, similar to his body in real life. I noticed his chin had shown differently in the Razum. In the real world, it was more pointed and angular, while in the Razum I noticed it had more of a divot. I wondered how different his actual face would look.

He seemed mentally coherent from what I could tell. My heart felt like a weight had been cast off it. He was struggling there, but he was still there. I had heard so many rumors of people saying the mind would die in such isolation and I would be lying if it weren't one of my worries. Now I held proof that my brother was still with me.

Clicking off the device, I disconnected it from Tyron's Razum. I got the confirmation I needed, so there was no more reason to invade his privacy. The device's whirring sounds died down as I tucked it back into my pack and took another moment to caress my brother's face, or what was exposed of his chin.

"There's still a chance I can get you out intact." Tyron's body made no movement to respond to my whispers, nor did it react to the tears that were falling across my face. It now became more important than ever to reach Locura's Loomer town. With the right stimulus and a bit of surgery, I could free my brother sooner than I had ever anticipated.

With this new comfort and motivation for movement, I packed the small shelter back against me and loaded Tyron, preparing to walk into the fog once more. Monsters no longer filled the void beyond the fog, instead I saw my brother where the fog swirled. I felt like I was being led by him into a new environment.

"I'll get you out, no matter what, Tyron. You should see and experience this world with me. To live a real life." Whispering to my brother's idea in the fog brought more courage to every step I took. Revitalized in my ambitions to save my brother with every passing moment. Though it was not long before those ambitions faded again to the drudgery of my journey.

I thought my hope would have energized me enough to power through the day, but the fog stole that power from me after a few hours. In my memories, when I had walked through the fog, I never felt this bogged down. It was as though the atmosphere was crushing me. Not knowing how far I had gone was messing with my perception of speed. With no Core Trail to reference for location, and no mountain range, I had to be careful to not walk blindly into an 'Oomer camp.

It wasn't until the fog darkened that I realized I was losing the sun. There was a piece of sloped ground that acted like a wave on the dunes of the Barrens that was tall enough to set my shelter against for the night. Deciding to use the last of the quickly fading light, I set my pack down and assembled my gear. The shelter was tucked firmly into the edge of the slope to avoid sticking out to any onlookers, but it was not possible to hide all of it.

"Hopefully, the fog will let up in the morning and I'll get a better grasp of our location." I muttered to the slumped Tyron. I had dug into the slope a bit to better lie down without my feet sticking out of the tent. It would be another uncomfortable night. With the smell of body odor and melting metal, my senses felt overwhelmed. Sleeping in a hunched position in a dirt hole didn't bring as much comfort as the uneven ground of the Core Trail the night before.

Ignoring the urge to check on Tyron again, I placed the pack down to act as my pillow as I pulled out a small bio-bar that Gern had packed for me. It was enough to feed a person for a full day, but it did not take the hunger from me. The temperature had stayed the same most of the walk, being a brisk and muggy day, but the night brought the cold and damp nearer.

As I pulled myself near to Tyron for warmth, I felt the tears sting my eyes once more. It was possible to get him back. I had been operating under the theory that it was possible to get him intact, but I finally saw proof. He was still conscious. He was still fighting. There was still hope.

I never was going to give up, but it helped to see him there. It was the hope I needed to survive these next few days. If I was lucky, I could talk to him in a few weeks, in the real world. Although, even these excited thoughts couldn't keep the weariness from pulling my limbs to the ground, as if the Earth beneath me was beckoning me to slumber.

"I love you, Tyron. Thank you for holding on a while longer."

☼   ☼   ☼

My eyes darted open to the sounds of footsteps. I must have been asleep for a while, as there was morning light beginning to illuminate the outside that I could see from the cracks of my tarp shelter. I know I heard steps this time.It wasn't just the fog swirling or the occasional shuffle of a nighttime breeze. This was real. I froze and waited. Have I been seen?

The seconds ticked by like years, waiting if I was going to meet my doom, or have an uneasy interaction. Steps continued outside of my shelter. They seemed to walk past. I slowly moved and gathered my things, careful to not make a sound. Peeking outside of the tent, I saw it was still foggy and cursed my luck, but no one could be seen from where I was.

More steps neared. These were not the steps of Drones as they were too light sounding, but there were now multiple people. As I focused on the sound through the fog, I could hear they were to the right of my shelter. An occasional metal step broke up the footsteps, and as I listened, there were more metal sounds being mixed with the steps. This was something I had heard before.

I must have walked to far towards the ridge line Gregory had noted. As steps passed by my small shelter, I realized I was in 'Oomer territory. Once the steps faded and the march disappeared into the fog, I used the vague silence to pull my tarps down and quickly attached Tyron to me. Now there were quick steps landing in the distance. Someone was running. I stayed hunched against the slope with no shelter to protect me.

These steps were running right to me and sounded panicked. I quietly reached back into my pack and removed the weapon Gern had given me. Removing it from the cloth that protected it, I waited. The steps drew nearer, now I could hear more steps in pursuit. Someone was running from the 'Oomers.

Finally, the steps neared where I feared the person was going to trip over me when there was a final thud and a scream was let loose. I looked up to come face to face with a man. He had fallen just before the edge of the slope, so his head appeared above me and looked down. I froze at his gaze and there was a moment where he realized I was hiding and armed.

"Run for your life!"

With his shrill scream in my face, he was dragged from sight. Once I heard the 'Oomer drag the man away, I used my spare moment to run in the opposite direction of the screams behind. The fog burned my eyes, as I didn't have time to put my goggles on. I ran for several minutes before I stopped because of the throbbing pain in my leg and chest.

No breath left me. I waited in the silence for pursuers. There were distant noises and a faint scream, but no footsteps were near me. I crouched as much as my leg brace would allow and caught my breath. Digging for my goggles, I pulled my tarp up to cover my mouth to avoid inhaling more fog than I had on my mad dash.

While digging in my pack, I grabbed the map from Gregory, which I had stored within reaching distance of my belongings. I inspected it. Realizing I had walked almost into the 'Oomer camp the night before, it was a safe guess I had walked too far. Although, now I have run in a random direction for several minutes into the blinding fog.

I had gone too far to the East and now needed to cut my way North West. Although not knowing how far I had gone East, I will need to walk carefully to avoid another run in with 'Oomers, Drones, or Finigan.

"Not how I wanted to start our morning, but we will make do. Right, Tyron?" My whisper was barely more than a loud breath, but I knew he heard me. Once I oriented myself in the correct direction according to the compass on the map, I set forward, slowly and quietly.

Many noises echoed in the fog today. Very little was left to my imagination. I could hear the distant screams of 'Oomers' or their victims. Howls of victories and singing praises to various Loomers and Giants echoed through the dim morning. Occasionally there were footsteps near, which I stopped and held still for, gun in hand. Time was blurring as I walked through the miasma of probable death.

Several minutes passed, and the sounds quietly ceased to exist near me. I paused and re-examined the map. There were two reasons the sounds could have stopped: I walked far enough away from the camps that started the line to Finigan, or I veered North while I was walking yesterday and I am getting close to Finigan.

My answer came quicker than I would have liked when my feet hit the compact ground. I looked down and saw the perfect outlines of dozens of Gregory and Markus unit footprints. Standing on a road that would lead to my demise if discovered. While I examined my position and tried to triangulate my location on the map with the new marker, I heard new steps approaching.

These steps were all too familiar to me as they were the marching steps of multiple Gregory units. The harsh crunch of metal on soil and the vague shifting sounds of metal plating made me feel as though the ground were trembling at their approach.

I hastily hopped across the large well-trodden path and quickly made my way from the Drones. The fog was becoming more of my friend than I would have anticipated as I dodged so many threats just out of sight. I was trying to make up some speed, knowing where I was standing, when something caught my nose.

It had a similar smell to when I was near too many Drones back in Haldoklik. A crude oil burning smell mixed with exhaust fumes. I knew it wasn't the Drones I had left behind. A glow in the distant fog made me aware of mistakes in directions. Red eyes peered into the fog far above me, standing as tall as the smokestack that gave me my accursed wounds.

A low, resonant hum rolled through the ground, rattling my bones as if every inch of earth beneath me was charged with his presence. Quick bursts of air, sharp and chilling, pulsed from the Giant's cooling systems, cutting through the dampness and fog like an unnatural wind. I knew, even before I looked up, that I was standing face-to-face with the one thing I had spent years trying to avoid. The Giant Finigan loomed before me.

The first thing I saw were the faint, eerie glints of his pale blue form—a color nearly swallowed by the haze, making him look like a specter half-formed out of the fog itself. But there was no mistaking his size. Towering at thirty-six feet, the Giant's sheer mass distorted the surrounding air, every detail coming into focus like pieces of a terrible machine made flesh.

A giant corn-cob pipe was wedged into his grin, the metal teeth behind it corroded and dripping, acid-worn to a skeletal, melting grin that seemed more like a rictus of mockery than any attempt at human expression. His eyes, two enormous red spotlights, sliced through the fog, casting an angry, unnatural glow as though he held the power of twin suns in his gaze. The lights flickered and shifted, scanning the mist as if searching for something—or someone. Ever watching the world around it and the world of the network he controlled.

As I took in his posture, hunched with knees tucked to his chest, arms folded around them, there was something unsettling and feline in his form, an elegance in the monstrous machinery. It struck me that, once upon a time, he might have looked like an oversized toy meant to bring comfort or joy to a child. Now, he was nothing but a nightmare—a machine warped and blistered by the acid rains, his paint scorched and peeling, revealing the dark, mangled metal beneath. He was a vision of innocence turned grotesque, a toy mutated into a bringer of death.

A shiver ran through me, not of fear but of something close to anger. The absurdity of this thing—this giant, absurd monster that had been a child's creation but was now an agent of terror—made something harden inside me. I felt defiance rising within, a refusal to cower before this relic of horror. As I dug my feet into the wet ground, a strange, almost electric courage surged through me. Without thinking, I felt my hand lift my gun, the weight familiar and steady in my grip. My fingers tightened around it, raising it just high enough to align my aim with the narrow space between his eye casing and skull plate.

He hadn't noticed me yet. He was still, his red beams roaming elsewhere, oblivious to the defiant figure standing in his shadow. This could be my one chance—one impossible moment to end him before he spread more ruin across the region. I held my breath, feeling the silent hum of my heartbeat matching the Giant's distant vibrations as I prepared to act.

My chance was taken from me as the thudding steps of the Drones drew near. I needed to avoid being spotted if I wanted to help my brother.

Shooting Finigan with Drones nearby would be a death sentence for us both. There was also no way for me to outrun a pack of Drones on my braced leg. I lowered the gun and slowly ducked lower out of the possible vision range of Finigan. I backed away from the Giant into the fog, keeping my eyes on his eyes and bitterly allowing him a longer lifespan.

I forced my breaths to steady, each one easing the pounding in my chest, willing my fear into submission. With Finigan focused on the Drones updating him, all I needed was to slip around his side and continue heading North. One step, then another. I crept forward, each footfall placed with painstaking care on the brittle, cracked earth, every crunch of soil sounding far louder than it should in the hollow silence.

Seconds passed like hours, but I was seeing the back of Finigan's towering form, feeling the rush of freedom just ahead. My muscles relaxed, tension loosening just enough for a glimmer of relief to spark. I was almost clear, almost—

Then a sound cut through the quiet, something that didn't belong. It was faint, barely there, yet every nerve in my body seized, prickling with a deep, visceral dread. The noise sharpened, and then—icy fingers closed around my broken ankle.

A jolt of terror shot through me, draining every ounce of warmth, of feeling, until I was hollowed out, numb. My heart hammered as I twisted my head to look down. There, clinging to my foot, was an 'Oomer worshiper. His eyes were blackened pits, poisoned and empty, and his lips curled into a grotesque grin, revealing a mix of rotted and silvered teeth. A twisted mockery of a human smile. He had no legs, only the tattered remains of two robotic limbs that he dragged along behind him, the metal grinding against the earth as he crawled.

"Lord Finigan!" he screeched, his voice slicing through the fog, every word a shard of ice in my veins. "I have brought you a non-believer who carries a weapon! She means you harm! Please ascend me! Let me help you crush the non-believers!"

His words hung in the air, and the fog itself seemed to shiver with the force of his scream. I could feel the ground vibrate before I dared to look.

Finigan had heard. The giant machine stirred, and the faint, telltale hum of his systems coming to life filled the air, rising in pitch as he turned. A monstrous gaze bearing down on me as a red light engulfed me and the 'Oomer. My heart sank as I realized there would be no escape—not now, not with those red eyes fixed upon me. The judgment of a machine who had hunted humans for a century.

Every instinct screamed at me to run, to tear free from the 'Oomer's grip and flee, but fear had rooted me to the spot. I was caught, trapped in the gaze of the very thing I had fought to avoid, feeling his looming presence like a shadow ready to consume me whole.

I didn't feel my body's actions. I witnessed my body moving on its own. My foot came down on the 'Oomers neck with a solid crunch as the extra weight of my brace drove my heel down through the bone. Once his hand dropped from my leg with a lifeless slump, I ran past the Giant, who was unfolding his arms to stand.

There was no pain in my leg as the adrenaline rushed to save my life and keep me running. I felt the thud of the Giant's first step. He was up. I quickly noticed the sound of multiple smaller feet coming up quickly behind me. A loud noise erupted from Finigan that was ear piercing and sounded like a sonar ping. He was searching for me in the fog.

As the Drones were coming up behind me, I heard an unusual sound. It was like one of the Drones just fell over, and then another until only one remained. I chanced a glance behind me to see a terrifying image: A Gregory unit was right behind me and I could see Finigan stepping towards where I was running, his red eyes now illuminating the fog. I felt like I was running through the blood of all those before me.

The Gregory unit was nearly upon me. I closed my eyes for a moment and slowed my running slightly. "I'm sorry, Tyron. I really tried." Words were panted as I waited for the metal hands to tackle me down. Ready to accept my fate at the hands of the mechanical gods.

"Faster Taylor, Finigan is very angry," came a familiar rattling speaker voice. I cast another glance back and noticed a dark satchel around the Drone's neck and the number badge on the Gregory unit. 235.

"You son of a bitch!" I spat at him as I regained my speed. He ran fast enough to run equally to me and looked over. I heard a slight chuckle before he reached over and lifted me up to place on his shoulder. I clung to him for dear life with his shaky long steps.

"I see you have a weapon. Know how to shoot?" He asked as he increased his speed, though Finigan was gaining on us. The surrounding red only reflected our terrible situation.

"Drone Gregory 235, you will be decommissioned for aiding in protecting a weapon carrying human." The words rang out in a much deeper tone that I had expected and felt the vibration of his words rattle around my ribs. Gregory had been spotted as well.

"My actions have been noticed. Shoot him, Taylor." Gregory demanded, as his metal joints creaked against his increased speed. This time I reacted quickly and drew the gun I had been holding doing my best to stabilize my arm on the jostling Drone.

"Can you run smoother? I need to hit his eye." I panted as his metal plates jabbed me in the stomach. Something on his chest moved at the request and I felt his gyroscopic stability kick in. I was damn near steady. As I looked down the sights, Finigan lunged forward. His hand just barely missed the ground behind Gregory, but now his face was close enough I knew I wouldn't miss.

The shot shook my entire arm, and I felt a small electrical pang as the charge was set loose. As soon as the trigger was pulled, I saw the bolt of electric pulse hit Finigan in the eye casing I had aimed for. The red glow around us died immediately, and Gregory and I remained running on as the Giant fell to the ground to reboot. The earthquake he caused reminded me how heavy these machines were.

Several minutes passed as I rode on the shoulder of Gregory, watching the fog for the possible red glow of our pursuer. Once I could verify there were no Giant footfalls behind us and only distant frantic red scans in the fog, I nudged Gregory to let me down. Begrudgingly, the Drone slowed to a stop and carefully lifted me off his shoulder, placing my feet on the ground.

As I looked back into the fog behind us, my heart raced. Did I actually just shoot a Giant ruler in the face with an illegal weapon? How was I so foolish to get caught in the first place? Oh Gregory, you gave up your rank to save me? None of these questions left my lips, though. My teeth were clenched to keep them back.

Lost in the trance of fear and exhilaration, I felt a tugging at my back and turned to notice Gregory looking over Tyron's Razum. He tossed the head back and forth between his hands, checking the equipment condition. When he noticed I was observing his movements, he placed Tyron's head back against my pack.

"Calm down, I am checking that I didn't jostle him too much while running," Gregory explained as he stepped back. "I would think at this point you could afford me more trust." He muttered as he started walking into the fog in front of me. I quickly followed to avoid losing sight of the metal leader.

A silence lingered around the two of us awkwardly. After a heartfelt goodbye, how were we supposed to interact? Especially after I started a fight with his reigning leader. I don't think it helped our friendship to be in this position. Would he resent me? Was this a calculated choice or an emotional one? Why was he with Finigan, anyway?

"Relax. I can almost hear your brain whirring like my own processors. It's fine. I will get you to Locura and go my way from there." He remained several steps in front of me, on the edge of my vision in the fog. The silence again pressed on. I was not sure what to say in this situation. Gregory was challenging everything I knew about Drones. Perhaps this was his Fritzing? Was he now unstable? Was I safe with a Fritzing Drone?

I opened my mouth to begin my questioning when he raised a dismissive hand, cutting me off. "Just talk to Tyron for now. I would rather process this situation on my own for a while." He now walked further into the fog, but still maintained a manageable pace. I stared at the ground and followed his large footprints. The grips on his feet were wearing low and I could see the faint tread marks in the sand. I noticed a small logo near the center of his sole: "Futures for Humanity".

It was a quiet walk. The sun was probably nearing its peak in the sky from what I could tell in the lessening fog. While now I could see Gregory, he remained at least ten steps ahead of me. The fog swirled around his head as his processors pushed the cool mist away from his circuitry.

"I didn't think Gregory could be this moody. I guess I should be grateful to him, though, huh, Tyron? He saved me when I got us into trouble, and he helped when I was too injured to help you. I just don't understand why, though. I've seen Fritzing Drones in the later stages. They are typically an emotional wreck and can hardly function if not completely unstable and violent. He doesn't seem to struggle like that. I wonder if there are multiple forms of Fritzing. He is quite a vintage model. Maybe he has a different tolerance for human emotion emulations." Whispering to my brother while I walked was always inevitable. I didn't realize I was doing it till I saw Gregory cast a glance back at me, silencing the subconsciously curated conversation.

"Okay, that topic is off the table for the moment, I guess." I muttered to Tyron as the crunch of my steps continued. The silence and awkward nature of this walk made the day move slowly. Hours passed without a word shared. It wasn't until I noticed the soil growing darker and more stained with oil that I spoke again.

"Do you know how much further?"

Metal shoes continued without hesitation. The fog was shifting and swirling as we passed through the other worldly tendrils of acid. I felt so small in the fog, let alone by Gregory. Did I always feel so small in his company?

"We have another night of walking ahead of us." His curt response reminded me he wanted to be alone.

Another night of walking. My feet kicked up bits of screws and metal scrap as I trudged them further. Body aching and feeling the cost of my earlier adrenaline, I dreaded a night filled with walking. There was one benefit to this continued struggle. With Gregory around, there were fewer reasons to fear the unknown. Though his silence created its own waves of unknown in my mind.

Although the implications of walking with a Drone also doubled the likelihood of us being noticed. His loud steps and glowing eyes would set us apart in the night. On top of it all, I felt like my legs would give out any minute while I knew he didn't need sleep or feel fatigue. My good knee spasmed as I walked, causing my gait to stagger and Gregory to look back.

"There should be a small rubble town ahead. We will rest there for the night." He addressed my concerns before they could be vocalized. Was there a chance this machine was aware of my physical limits? It wouldn't be the first time he called attention to my tiredness.

Each time he spoke, I felt like more questions were brought up than answered by his actions. While he had aided me back in Haldoklik, there was a mutual reason for his actions. Saving me from the other Drones and Finigan was a much larger situation where his stakes in the matter were less. This made his current actions suspicious and seemingly pointless to him.

I knew Fritz was a part of this, but with no insight into what he was feeling or thinking, I had no reference of what was normal thought or what was Fritz. The risks of the situation were growing in my mind with each step now, weighing my safety in the situation and his loyalties.

Between the monotonous pace of the Drone and my staggering feet, every second felt like the unbearable weight of a lifetime of struggles. So many things were passing by. Where had my childhood gone? Where was I going to go? Would Locura be a new home or a stop along the line my life marched to? Questions were piling up in the fog, creating more than one type of barrier in the oppressive atmosphere we trudged through.

Hours passed based on the strength I was losing in my legs and the sun seemed to be in a lower position. Gregory maintained his pace. The whirring of his processors was a ceaseless tune to our steps. It wasn't shocking he was still thinking over his situation. Time was needed to process the shift of position and power he just gave up.

When the sky began darkening, I noticed new evidence of our environment. Stone columns appeared, toppled and broken beside walls. In the Barrens, I had come across many things, but a ruined old world town was not one of them. The remnants of what I assumed were houses were boxy and finite in shape. A part of me had hoped for a free design with more variation and personality, but I supposed humans couldn't have changed that much from what we were now.

Stepping over broken and worn walls, the ground suddenly shifted form. The hard clatter of Gregory's metal shoes on concrete echoed through the street we stood on. The sound bounced to our left and right, ricocheted between the husks of what must have been storefronts. We were on a main street, running to and from the town hub.

Gregory paused in the new town scape we found ourselves in. He scanned the various stores and streets, looking for danger. After a full rotation, I heard the whirring quiet as he finished the plan he had apparently been constructing.

"We will camp here for the night. Your stumbling steps are irritating." With his words acting as a trail, he made his way to a storefront to our right, near the edge of the remaining building-like structures. He stopped in front of one with a sign collapsed near the door, he gestured me inside.

Following his guidance, I ducked mine, and Tyron's head under the collapsed sign. Once inside the building, I looked back to read the sign. "Цве". The letters meant nothing to me. Apparently we weren't in an English-speaking country, regardless of the language we all butchered together to communicate.

Gregory lowered himself to fit beneath the sign, his bright eyes followed mine. As he looked over the sign, he then turned to examine the contents of the shop. Pots of all materials were shattered on the ground while large refrigeration units were pulled from walls and fallen. Display tables littered the small storefront, and a larger counter took up the left wall near the door.

"Tsvety. This was a flower shop. It should be a safe place for you to rest for the night." Gregory's LEDs scanned across the store as he moved broken tables. Clearing a spot behind the counter, he placed the furniture over the top and around it to create a quiet cave. When he finished his construction of the plastic table hideaway, he found an old tablecloth and placed it over the top of stacked furniture.

Satisfied with his work, he turned to me. "Does this satisfy what you require from a shelter?"

I approached the cave entrance and peaked inside. It was dark, but felt stable. His actions had reminded me of Tyron when we were younger. Building forts and testing their structures so we could hide from the Watchers. The memory reminded me of the weight I carried.

"It should work fine." I responded as I knelt in the cave. Loosening the lever and lowering Tyron, I felt instant relief in my ribs. Through the hours of walking, I must have lost awareness of how much pain I was in.

Once Tyron was comfortably placed on the floor, I did my best to sit down with the braces. As I thudded heavily against the ground, the walls of my plastic fort shook. I made the mental note to sleep further away from the walls to not accidentally kick them.

Gregory peeked in at us, having to nearly bend over to see into the low entrance. He scanned Tyron and then me before testing the stability of the fort with his own metal hand. After a few reassuring taps and shakes, he seemed satisfied with his own work.

"I am going to walk the perimeter while you sleep. You will be safe through the night." His sudden plans of leaving dropped my stomach like a stone through ice. I had no desire to be alone in a strange place with a weak fort protecting me.

"Can you stay for a while? I don't really trust this place."

He stood up and moved out of sight for a moment. I could hear the whirring kick up and stop. Was it that complicated of a request? His face dropped again as he lowered his body outside the fort door. From his body language, I could easily see he was irritated with this choice.

I wasn't sure why it felt safer with a murderous Drone by me, but it helped. There was no one in their right mind that would attack us so boldly. Though this world was rarely full of right-minded people. While an awkward silence passed between us, I felt better.

Shifting metal broke the awkward silence of the night as Gregory adjusted his sitting position. He still had to hunch his head down to be within sight. A large machine was trying to be friendly awkwardly.

"So… did you process what you needed to?" It was all I could think to ask. I knew the information was off limits earlier, but surely he had to have reached a conclusion about his feelings about the day. It's not like it was a small decision, but he did have a supercomputer for a brain.

"I have analyzed my situation and my decisions." A brief response was a good attempt to end the conversation. Though, as the silence crept back in, I refused to back down.

"And?"

His shoulders relaxed a bit, almost as if he had let out a sigh I couldn't hear. This was one of the first times I saw him display such an unnecessary motion. Was Fritz affecting him stronger now, and was he experimenting with human gestures?

"I made a choice. Fighting against Finigan immediately cut me from the networks. For the first time, my mind is silent."

Watching him as he spoke, clear intonation, and emotional quality was now seeping into his words. While the rattling dusty speaker had gotten worse from the fog, it didn't seem to phase his new tone. With a more sullen vibe appearing in the conversation, I gauged my response carefully.

"What do you think of your choice?"

"It does not matter now. There is no way to change the past." Another short answer to end the conversation.

This time, I accepted his mute request for silence. I would push the topic later. For now, it was too soon. He was at least opening up to me on things, which was a new skill. Commending him for sharing two thoughts seemed condescending, though. Like a mother praising a child for not screaming in a street way.

I settled into the fort now, removing my pack and the dry tarps from within to create a small bed for me and Tyron. Getting comfortable, I pulled my brother close to share warmth. With the fall of night came the unmistakable fall in temperature. Fortunately, I wouldn't have to share with Gregory. Maybe he was a better companion than I initially expected.

Pretending to be asleep, I could hear him move. Metal joints and plates rasping quietly against his commands. Shifting slowly to not wake me as he crept away from the fort. I figured he would, but I was glad he at least waited. A subtle, kind gesture.

With Tyron close, a Drone walking as a defense, and a shelter over my head, I knew it wouldn't take long to find sleep. Each breath relaxed my stiff muscles and tense tendons. When the ground felt as though it was pulling me into it, I knew I was going to have a restful sleep for the first time in a while.

Chapter 6: 'Oomer Howls in the Night

Shuffling and stirring brought my mind out of its dazed and tired state. This wasn't the first time the strange noises of the flower shop had woken me. My arm still rested on Tyron's, the lights still blinked. The world was fine.

I closed my eyes again and tried to fall down the hole that the ground made for the sleepers once again. When my body refused the idea of sleep, I knew something had truly stirred. High-strung survival instincts were triggered at the noises nearby. The stirring of the wind through the street and stores felt familiar, but my body didn't know that.

The rustling of plastics caught in the breeze whispered down the street outside. Signs and the remnants of buildings creaked in the night. Even the sound of sand spilling across the pavement was loud in the dark. I couldn't hear the quiet machinery of Gregory, so I knew he wasn't near. So why was my body tense now?

Shifting in the tarp blankets, I looked out the entrance of my cave. The absolute darkness beyond felt ominous, but proved my theory of it being the middle of the night. With the clouds and the fog, there would be no moonlight to help me see. A void existed past the sign of the door, empty yet full of sound.

More rustles. Noises continued to rattle around the street beyond. The creak of old doors or windows that hung open was growing to a frequent and ghostly wail through the night. Another stirring sound. Another rustling.

I found Tyron's hand and gave it an extra squeeze before adjusting my braces and exiting the now safe-feeling fort. Taking extra caution, I pulled up my fog mask. With the temperature drop, I was sure the fog would be denser. Crawling from the fort, I paused every few motions to see if unfamiliar sounds stirred to my noise.

Taking a few cautious steps around broken pottery, my body froze. Did I hear footsteps? I paused, listening to the chaotic noises of my barren world. They were simple and definable, so what did I think I heard? Surely, with Gregory on patrol, no one would be near, right?

The anxiety of the unknown crawled into my stomach, already empty and upset. Now it twisted with fear. Another noise. My ears couldn't determine if it was the creak of something shifting in the breeze, or a quiet foot fall. Heart beginning to race, I took another step forward.

Hearing the quiet thud of my own step only drew my suspicions to the front of my mind. The noise I heard was similar. A cold sweat beaded my forehead and combined with the fog. It burned as I waited for another sign, another noise. Beyond the burning, pain, and exhaustion, was there something in the night?

Quiet.

Why was the night always quiet when you thought you heard something? It mocked my suspicions by giving me no more cues to what may lie beyond. A few more moments. Night time wouldn't last forever with its secrets. I could wait.

I gritted my teeth, remembering the games Tyron and I used to play. He would blindfold and spin me, disorienting me while I tried to listen for him. His voice drifted through my memories as acrid fog burned through my nose.

"Taylor, you need to learn to listen. This will help. Hear my words, follow my voice. Being able to see is never a guarantee. You need to know how to listen."

As his once familiar voice faded across my mind, I closed my eyes. This was a dumb time to practice, but my eyes weren't helping me. Trying to open my ears to be more present to the chaotic noises of this new land, I listened.

A building nearby creaked against the breeze, likely damaged from years of weather and nearing collapse. There was a quiet rasp of plastic being dragged across dirt and concrete, fleeing the slow wind of the night. Broken hinges rattled while dangling decor rustled. It sounded like a normal night.

Waiting for my mind to perceive this information, my heart rate slowed. The stiff fingers that were numb with anticipation regained their blood flow. My arched and readied feet lowered their heels and relaxed. Once my body was aware that there was no immediate threat, I started my way back towards the fort.

The chaotic noises of the night seemed to die down as I returned to my bed, as if they were hushed by my disinterest. With the adrenaline leaving my body as it relaxed on the hard tile floor, I could feel the warmth of my brother as he maintained the heat bubble beneath the blankets. The warmth he unknowingly offered contrasted sharply with the cold.

"What would I do without you?" I whispered to the hard metal shell he wore on his head. Though I knew he could not hear me, knowing he was okay brought me a peace that relaxed my mind. The lights blinked on the Razum, and I chose to interpret them as a reciprocation of my feelings. I squeezed his hand again, the lanky and lifeless fingers submitting to my grip.

The dreary eyed grogginess made its way back to me while holding Tyron's hand. This world always felt safer when I held his hand. Even as kids, I would pet his face, hold his hand, and refuse to let go. I had been such a scared child. If born out of the Razum, I wondered if I would have survived.

Whether 'Oomer attacks, radiation, or general life difficulties, adulthood seemed to be an unlikely outcome. Without the guidance of Tyron, I wouldn't have made it out here. He was like the Scientist, intelligent and kind, always figuring out things for himself. It was scary to know that if a problem was placed in front of him, he would solve it. There never seemed to be a puzzle he couldn't figure out.

"Would you be proud of my work? I know it's taken me more time than you would have, but… I'm trying. I just want you back." There were tears trying to escape my eyes, but I closed them and willed them away. I had to remind myself he was here, just... not entirely yet.

I pulled him close, smelling the weak body odor he omitted. Before leaving the Razum, I never knew what he smelt like. There were some things that just didn't exist in the network, and body odor was one. No need to shower, or clean, or even eat. I couldn't stop the smile as I planned to train him on these things when he woke up.

The memories of the network filled my worrying mind and brought me some peace. Taunting and teasing my brother, having him cut my hair and chasing the Watchers who guarded us. We had always caused trouble together in that stone-like paradise. Why did I leave?

On that forsaken day of the Fall, when the Loomers presented the option, Tyron and I were playing by a waterfall. Trying to see who could make the better boat out of paper to fly it off the strong water stream. His smile was so pure in that afternoon sun.

I remembered looking at him and feeling safe, completely and utterly protected and free. While I had my issues in the Razum and often felt trapped within our personal network and afraid to go to the main servers, I valued his protective smile. Guilt rolled in my stomach. Why didn't I stay?

When the world in the network went silent, we knew something was wrong. It was as if our ears were turned off, our senses cut from us besides our sight. The panic on Tyron's face as the world deafened had sent chills down me. Even when I reached for his hand, it felt like nothing. He was almost a hologram to me, unable to comfort me.

There were a few minutes of this strange and desensitizing silence before a display popped up in front of me. I could remember how fast my heart was racing. To a child, losing their senses was terrifying. So much fear and uncertainty in those moments.

All I could read from the display was 'Do you want to leave the Razum?'. The options for yes and no responses were given below. My actions that followed were instinctual, fearful, and desperate. I wanted to hear again. I wanted to feel Tyron when I hugged him. I wanted out of whatever I was in. Trying to squeeze Tyron's hand to let him know I was going out, I selected 'yes'.

Maybe he didn't feel me squeeze his hand? Maybe I should have mouthed the words. I should have done more than be afraid, because when I opened my eyes, the world was blinding and cold. I was alone. I was scared. He wasn't with me anymore.

I had thought over those moments for years. Regret was always the feelings that followed. There had been many dark nights where I dragged open Razum's back to Haldoklik and laid in them. My hands would be prepared to close the lid and seal myself back in the contraption I had been born into, but I never could do it. As much as I missed my brother and regretted my choices to leave, I knew too much about this reality.

After years of suffering and struggling, I had gotten the hang of survival. Food had extraordinary flavors for someone who had never eaten. When I touched the ground here, I could feel each grain of dirt and sharpened blades of metal scrap. I knew, no matter my sadness over Tyron, I wouldn't be able to survive the half senses the Razum allowed.

Now knowing that one day, I will show Tyron these wonderful experiences, I didn't want to concede to the Razum anymore. He would love the feeling of drinking cool water, the breeze through his hair and the occasional warmth of the sun on the Barrens. I couldn't choose to return to him, knowing that he would never know the things I did. He wouldn't even know what it was like to touch his actual face, my face and not the Razum's interpretation of it.

As a sister, no. As a human, I had to make sure I opened as many doors for him into this world as I could so he could have a chance at a real future. He didn't deserve to live a cold and meaningless life in a dark and broken network all alone. He deserved a chance to be free, like I had.

My reminiscing came to an abrupt end as the stirring and rustles of the street grew louder again. A stronger breeze kicked up, shaking supports of buildings and stirring the fog further into the store. I couldn't see much beyond the sign that obstructed the doorway as it flooded with the mysteries of the night.

I pulled the tarping up to cover Tyron's face. He didn't need to deal with acid burns on top of learning how to live when he woke up. Hiding my face under the cover, I watched the twinkling of his lights. A starry array in the tarp's dark.

The distant sounds of metal feet calmed me even more. Gregory must be walking a wide perimeter if he was coming into hearing distance now. I supposed it made sense. He used to walk the entire perimeter of Haldoklik. Was this his attempt to normalize his current situation? As he maintained his regular duties, did he feel more centered in the chaos he had caused?

Analyzing the thoughts of a Drone was almost as annoying as analyzing my own mixed feelings about him. Did he think I was weak and in need of help? Did I see him as a friend or as a safety precaution? These questions swirled in my mind as I was sure the fog swirled outside in the breezes of night.

Metal shoes started down the street towards us. A relaxing tone that had once given me fear. When he was near the shop, I could hear his joints groan as he likely was looking into the store. His gaze used to disturb me, but in the lonely Barrens with many dangers, it was comforting.

As his steps took up their pace and proceeded away, I could feel the familiar claws of sleep digging into me. Warmed by Tyron, watched by Gregory, and safe from almost all threats in my cozy table fort, I allowed myself the sleep that beckoned. This night was going to be mine, even if I had to force it to be.

Footsteps? This time my body awoke, frozen. My eyes snapped open under the tarp, ears tuning into reality. My heart was racing as if I had just run from a Giant. Blood had run cold in my veins. Something was very wrong and my body was warning me.

I had heard footsteps. While mostly certain they were in reality and not in dreams, I knew I heard something. Pulling the tarp off my face quietly, I looked towards the door. Fog swirled in the first rays of dawn, beginning its hike up the sky. It was dense, and I was unable to see beyond the doorway. New and more exaggerated swirls were entering the store front.

There was no sign of Gregory, nor the sound of his metal shoes. My hands quietly felt around for the pack with the gun in it. No matter what lingered in the mist, it would not appreciate several thousand volts surging through it. Giant to 'Oomer, no one enjoyed getting shot.

A rock tumbled across the pavement, down the street. That was not one of the normal sounds of the night. The breeze had quieted now, so the rock had to have been disturbed. Perhaps it was the fog blocking the noise, but I still didn't hear any footsteps. If it was Drones and they were near, I would be able to hear them. If it was 'Oomers, there would be many steps, some with metal and some flat-footed. If it was Finigan, the ground would shake and the building would likely collapse.

So why did I hear nothing besides the racing beats of my heart? Why did a rock fall with no one around, yet I heard it? With silence abounding, I took a chance to squeeze Tyron's hand, confirming he was still with me, before I exited the fort. I had fallen asleep with my braces on and was glad I didn't have to cause too much noise before leaving.

Crouched in the entrance to my fort, I waited. In the Razum, we had encyclopedias that Tyron used to read to me as I fell asleep. Now I understood why tigers stalked in the tall grass, coiled and ready to pounce. I had now become that tiger guarding my den.

No sounds existed outside now. Even the creaking of the buildings and broken frames had silenced in the oppressive foggy night. My skin prickled in the eerie quiet. Surely Gregory had to be near. Why couldn't I hear his steps?

Footsteps!

This time, I was certain. There were steps landing down the street to the left of the storefront. Fleshy feet. It had to be 'Oomers. Drones could be heard a mile away on this pavement, so there were no other options. Raiders would wear heavy boot armor, but what I heard was bare feet on the pavement.

If they were sneaking about on bare feet instead of augmented limbs, of course, I wouldn't have heard them till they were near. Though I didn't hear a hoard. Maybe two sets of feet made the noises I vaguely heard. Were they scouts? Were the Barren 'Oomers more methodical?

Steps sounded in the store next to mine. They were close. I could hear their hardened feet across the tile flooring next door as they scavenged the area. Small mutters echoed between them. The word 'food' was being tossed around. New initiates looking for food apparently, which meant I was on the menu.

Doing my best to make no noise, I left the mouth of my cave and took up a tactical position near the side of the doorway. If they entered, they would not leave. I didn't relish the taking of a life, but if they are going to pose a risk to Tyron, their lives were forfeit. My hands clenched around the gun, mentally preparing the muscles for pulling the trigger.

Suddenly, the distant steps of metal shoes came to my awareness. Gregory was near. This seemed to stir the feet lurking in the store. Scrambling steps and jumps could be heard as they took to the street. My hands were ready to make quick work of my hidden enemies.

I could hear them run past the door of my store, bare feet flapping against the pavement. Two ran into the distance, to the right of the storefront, away from where Gregory was turning to meet the street. In this fog, he likely didn't see them or hear their quiet steps.

Poking my head out, I checked down the street towards the fleeing 'Oomers. In this fog, there was no evidence that they had ever existed. The quiet morning light that had begun to illuminate the mist as I looked across the sand of the street. Two sets of bare feet with a few missing toes were printed on the loose soil.

Taking a breath, the fear left my body. With Gregory nearing and the 'Oomers fading away into the brightening night, I could return to enjoy a moment of relaxation with Tyron. I'm sure that Gregory would demand we kept marching at the first idea of light, but I was pre-planning to fight him for an extra nap.

As I turned to head back into the shop and resume my relaxation, I heard a quiet swish through the air. Something had flashed. The fog swirled around me. I heard nothing until that moment. Were there more 'Oomers nearby?

My mouth opened to cry for alarm, hoping Gregory would be near enough to help. A heavy thud landed against my head. As if my eyes were turned off, the world was plunged into a painful darkness. The vague memory of my knees hitting the ground was the last thing I remembered.

✧   ✧   ✧

"Taylor!"

A voice guided me from my groggy and disoriented state. Bleary eyes and a down turned head, I couldn't see who called to me. My arms felt numb, my feet like lead. Was I moving? There was a distinct rasp of boots on the sand, but I didn't feel my legs moving. How could I be moving without moving?

I tried to flex my hands to get some circulation going to better feel what was happening. When my head bobbed to the side unwillingly, the realization struck. Though I was not moving, I was being moved. Straightening my neck to see, it was met with an abrupt force, pushing my head back down.

Panic set into my confused mind. Something wasn't right. My body was denying my commands, pain was searing in my armpits. I tried to lift my foot and heard a heavy thud as my heel came down on the pavement. If there was pavement, I was still in town.

"Gregory?" My voice was weak, hoarse even. What happened? I remembered watching the 'Oomer leave the street and Gregory coming near, but everything was black after that. The only logical conclusion was that I had been hit by something. Throbbing pains that began in my head confirmed that suspicion.

Gargled words were being spat above my head. It was a new accent I wasn't familiar with, guttural and rough. Flecks of spit landed on my head as the person above me spoke. I couldn't understand most of the words being shared, but a few phrases. "Metal man is coming."

So I wasn't far from town, still on pavement, and Gregory was near. My brain slowly pieced together my situation, one step at a time. I had been knocked unconscious for a short time, and I was being dragged by hungry

'Oomers to some hideout, likely for dinner. Though they didn't seem to get very far if Gregory was still in pursuit.

Panic was now overrun with anger. I did not shoot a Giant and leave my life behind to become something's meal. This was not how I was going to end, and I was sure of that. Tyron needed me. He was alone and in a dangerous situation. This was no time to be unconscious or delirious.

Scrambling my legs to stand, I pulled my shoulders from the grips of the man who had been dragging me. Vehement threats were spat at me as I pulled away from their grasping hands. There were three of them around me. One held me and the two followed. My hope was quickly torn from me as the other two helped pin me to the ground.

"Gregory!" was all I could get out as the air was crushed from my lungs. One of the larger 'Oomer men had thrown himself on top of me and collapsed my braces around my ribs. It clenched onto me like a bear trap. Wheezing attempts at breathing were all I could manage.

"Taylor?" His voice was near. Metal shoes could be heard in the direction of my feet. Quick steps suggested he was running now. As the hands of the 'Oomers pulled me to my feet, I could feel the broken ankle cry out with a damaged brace unable to support it.

A piece of oil covered plastic was jammed into my mouth. The slimy, bitter taste felt slightly acidic on my tongue. It was a weak attempt to silence me as they continued to drag my body. I struggled however I could, kicking the ground to cause noise or shouting through the plastic. Gregory's sensors were very good, and I was relying on him hearing the trouble I was causing.

The mild beatings and kicks I received in response to my struggling were nothing compared to what Gregory was going to cause. Through blurred and agonized senses, I could feel the vibrations of the metal steps drawing near. He was close. I just had to keep making noise for him to pinpoint my location.

Screaming through a plastic filled mouth, flailing my arms, I could feel the unease growing in the 'Oomers who carried me. Panicked tones filled their guttural speech, decisions and ideas were being tossed around. Their time had passed when I saw the glint of gold beyond my feet.

It was barely a moment from when Gregory came into sight to when I was dropped from the hands of the 'Oomer. He had covered the distance in a disturbingly short amount of time and launched the 'Oomer into the fog. The others froze, cowering under the yellow LEDs of Gregory's enormous form.

My initial reaction was to look away from the scene. I knew what Gregory did to those that upset him. Hearing flesh ripped apart was enough to stir my stomach. Gurgling screams of agony before the final metal stomp was the final farewell of that life. After a few more skirmishes of Gregory throwing bodies around, the world went quiet.

Slow shoes approached me as I sat up from the ground and pried the clamped brace from my chest. With Gregory's help, we loosened the brace and stabilized it. Once on my feet, I patted the shoulder plate of the behemoth metal man.

"Little faster next time." A wheezed joke was better than any appreciation I could have shared with him. Though, upon closer examination, I realized Tyron was not with him. My blood pumped harder through my body as it blocked my ears with the irritating sound of my heart racing. I scanned the horizon for any indication of where we were.

The morning light began showing signs of the town where Gregory had come from. Distant hollering and hooting echoed through the haze. They were victory howls that made my blood boil. Gregory followed my mental thought and ran back to the town.

I did my best to keep up, but the malfunctioning ankle brace slowed me. When my feet echoed around me, I knew I was between buildings. Tyron had to be close. I just needed to find the flower shop and he would be there. I knew it.

Trying to read the stores as I passed, I noticed the fallen sign . Sliding beneath the broken metal name, the room greeted me. Tables were pulled from the fort, tarping and pottery skewed across the floor. I dug into the fort, looking for any semblance of Tyron's body.

The howls were drawing closer now, even though they continued further away. They must have split into groups. Gregory was likely following one, but the other was getting further away. I abandoned the fort pile once there was no sign of Tyron.

This was not how this was going to go. I would not allow this to be the end of Tyron. It was not the life I had fought for. I dragged myself from my knees and crouched out the door. Waiting for the next howl that I was going to pursue.

To my right, howls echoed through the street. A mistake they would soon realize as I grabbed a broken sign nearby and started a jog towards them. The rusted metal dug into my hand as fog burned my skin, but it didn't matter. My life was dispensable, but not Tyron's. Never Tyron's life.

Metal steps were fading into the street ahead of me. The distant howls had ceased, and I guessed Gregory had been the one to silence them. The feet ahead of me were still unaware of my presence, but ran faster. We were going to sandwich them and they didn't even know it.

As soon as the first 'Oomer came into clear sight from the fog, I was reminded how grotesque I found them. Black ooze leaking from the corner of acid burned pale lips, darkened eyes, but the wounds and blisters that covered their skin was the worst. Synthix was known for its ability to discolor the skin and to cause lesions on those not accustomed to it. Gross, ill formed, mutants of belief.

I drew my arm back with the sign, its jagged edge trembling in my grip, and prepared to strike. There was no time for hesitation, no chance for him to defend himself, as he was going to run into me. The sign drove into his skull with a sickening crunch, burrowing between metal plates I hadn't noticed before. His body sagged slowly, the brain slowly dying and his body facing that reality.

I stumbled forward quickly, catching his dropped possession just before it could hit the pavement. The cool, weighty trapezoid of Tyron's Razum landed in my hands, its surface glinting faintly in the dull light. My chest heaved as the realization hit me. A moment slower—just one moment— and we would have all exploded. I let out a shaky breath, trying to keep the Razum steady as the other 'Oomers came into view.

159

But I couldn't focus on them. I couldn't stomach it. The golden shimmer behind them—a warning of Gregory's brutal efficiency—was all I needed to see before I looked away. Instead, I dropped to my knees, pulling Tyron closer. His fragile weight cradled against my chest. His heartbeat was faint, like the dying hum of a machine, but it was there. He was alive. He was here.

The tears came before I could stop them. They streaked down my acid washed cheeks as I pressed my face against his Razum. The metal head cage dug into my already sore ribs, but I didn't care. I clung to him as if letting go might let the world snatch him away again. My arms tightened around him, desperate to shield him from whatever horrors might come next.

Beyond us, the sounds of carnage and death echoed through the narrow street. The thud of bodies, limbs being removed and discarded, even broken pleas for mercy felt distant. Right now, none of it mattered. Gregory could handle them. It was his duty. My focus stayed on Tyron, on the shallow rise and fall of his chest and the small, fragile thread of life that tethered him to me.

He was safe. We had found him, and he was going to be okay.

I let out a soft, trembling sob, my fingers fumbling over the Razum in my hands. I searched its surface for cracks, dents, any sign that it might fail him. When I found none, I shifted to scan his body. His tarping—patched and askew from being stolen away—was intact, and there were no visible wounds. Relief surged through me. They didn't hurt him.

My tears came harder now, almost unstoppable. My hands shook as I tried to orient his clothing into a more comfortable position, as if tidying a child before sending them out. He was safe again, here in my arms where he belonged. For a fleeting moment, I allowed myself to believe that it would stay that way. That this nightmare was over. And even though I knew better—knew the dangers waiting for us outside this fragile reprieve—I clung to that hope as if it were all we had left.

When the sounds from Gregory stopped, I looked at him. I'm sure the tears carved noticeable paths down my cheeks. The dust and fog had likely coated me in grime. He faced me now and quickly made his way to me. Concern in his voice.

"Is he okay?"

I rubbed the tear marks from my cheeks. They likely confused him and caused this reaction. With no ability to cry and being newly exposed to human emotions besides fear, my tears probably alarmed him into thinking that Tyron was injured or dead. Nodding to the Drone, I continued to sit with my brother on the street, cradling his Razum in my arms. I wasn't quite ready to let go yet.

Gregory allowed a few minutes for my need to hold my brother close before he picked up Tyron and we returned to the flower shop. Cleaning some of the mess, I found my pack and the gun I had dropped in the street. After combing through my belongings satisfied nothing was lost, I prepared to leave for the day.

Silence grew between us as Gregory helped load Tyron onto my back once more. It was almost a guilty gesture. I knew he felt some level of guilt for letting this happen. There was probably some need to clear the air between us. Though it could wait till we were back on the road.

Once gathered and taking a moment to shake the fear and anxiety from the morning, we set off into the Barrens as the sun rose in the sky. It was going to be a long day of walking, but today, I wanted to be quiet. There was no need to share the bitterness I felt.

He was walking on guard, after all. There was no reason the 'Oomer should have passed by him. Though they passed by me too. The bare feet were a clever trick if they knew Gregory was near. Had he noticed this flaw in his guarding style?

I reached a hand back and felt Tyron's hand. He was still there. It had happened so quickly that I needed the small reassurance that this wasn't just a waking nightmare. He was with me, mistakes in guarding aside. The path may have been bumpy and led to some death, but he was here and so was I. That still counted as a victory.

"Taylor." Words drew me from my disgruntled thoughts. I looked up from the ground I had been focusing on. Gregory stared at me, pausing in his tracks to get my attention. My glare probably conveyed more than I intended.

"I will adjust my concerns for safety for the future. It will not happen again. I'm sorry we temporarily lost your brother." Concerned and empathetic words were not expected. I had expected a defensive statement or even an argumentative complaint, but not kindness.

This unexpected reaction curbed the bitterness I was feeling. I had to remember he was a Drone with built in orders to follow. For the first time in his existence he wasn't being fed instructions. It was probably a difficult situation to adapt to.

"It's fine, but if you are going to travel with us, your first concern should be mine as well. Tyron takes precedence over my life." My tone was more of a growl, but it seemed to sway the machine enough to get him to continue his walk.

As the steps grew monotonous and the sun rose higher, the fog separated a bit. More light was reaching us today, causing a glare off of Gregory's plates. At least the visibility was going up, even if it was just revealing the frustrated Drone ahead of me.

The bitterness faded as the hours grew longer. My ankle brace was creaking with the repairs Gregory had aided with. Steps were mixing with the irritating squeak of metal, creating an awful tune to our sour steps.

"Where are we?" My question was met with a moment of silence and Gregory pausing his gait to analyze our location. Hours of walking had not lessened the weight between us, but there was little to talk about. The fog had let up more, but I still couldn't see over forty feet in front of us. I finally caught up to where Gregory had paused, and I could see a faint glow in the fog before us.

"This should be the edge of Locura. From here on, we need to be very careful. I will take Tyron and your shelter tarps to not stand out as much. The fog will be our friend until we get inside." He said as he turned and started lowering Tyron from my back. I unequipped the pulley system Gern had so kindly made for me and attached it as well as I could to Gregory's wider shoulders.

It felt weird sharing the burden of Tyron. Since the Scientist, no one had cared to help with him. Until recent events, I didn't think Gregory paid him any mind beyond that he was a threat that could explode. The actions of the Drone had become more empathetic. Maybe he now understood the burden of caring for something in a world against him?

He looked awkward, carrying Tyron on his back, making him look like a hunched mutant behemoth. I helped him apply the tarps around him similar to a cloak and did my best to cover his face and limbs. Once he was to the point where I could mistake him for a real humanoid creature, I couldn't help but allow a chuckle.

"Should I call you Gedrik now?" Sarcasm seemed to be the only option to diffuse the tension that had been built up between us. While comparing him to the aggressive mutant from our last duo outing may seem like a jab, it was meant to cause a chuckle.

Looking away from me and towards the city, he stood a little taller. "Gregory will be fine."

My joking being ignored, we both faced the new social world we were about to step into. The city loomed under us as we approached the top of the city from the Barrens. It was unlike Haldoklik, where instead of the calming blue of exhaust contrasting with the silver, acid washed metal, Locura was a dark red. The metal structure of Locura was less acid washed and still showed a deep rubicund of the original paint. The city itself was lit by red path lights, which cast a haunting brutality over the entire area. Buildings were built in more of a grid pattern than the chaotic scrap housing of Haldoklik showing evidence of strict Giant ruling.

The most prominent feature I could see of Locura from the wall top was the colossal skull plate of Locura herself. It was posted as the primary facility in the city and had almost countless exhaust pipes coughing up a glowing cloud of red fog over the entire city. With a glowering Loomer skull watching over the city, I felt distinctly unwelcome.

"What do you know about the Loomer, Locura?"

Gregory appeared to shudder slightly as he walked the perimeter of the wall, searching for the path down. I heeled him, feeling endangered by the ever watching skull. The ground was growing darker as we walked further towards the feet of the Loomer city.

"Locura was the fourth largest Loomer created and required over one-point-five million Razums to process all of her functions and computations. Towering at a height of two thousand two hundred and forty-seven feet, she toppled the previous human country of Russia single-handedly. She was marked with a vibrant red paint and the Loomer code of L009M02. She was designed with the second-coming Loomers, while a newer model, she was a destructive force of no equal besides Lexi, perhaps." Gregory recalled this information like he was reading a pamphlet. I realized how much information he likely was programmed with and made a mental note to ask him to give me a history of the Loomers. With no more laws holding his mouth shut, this was my chance to ask my questions.

"So, she was terrifying." I muttered, trying to display my disdain for Gregory's affiliation to such a machine.

"Not terrifying. She was a machine of mass effect and complete unity of control. I'm sure the population of the city will be significantly more due to the space available and the amount of people freed during the Fall." Gregory stepped closer to the edge to examine the wall and started a careful descent down weak human carved steps. This was not a main entrance, rather a scrapper's path to the Barrens. It was going to allow us a more discreet entrance to Locura.

My feet fell into line behind Gregory's and as I started my way down, I used the wall to steady myself on the narrow steps. Metal was mixed with mud and clay to form the steps. Some were washed out, proving to me that this was a lesser used and maintained path. The scent of the city permeated my senses, the smell of acid mud, oil vats, and refineries. The air was stinging my eyes slightly and there was a tang in my mouth as if I had licked Gregory's hair. Likely a taste I would have to get used to with the higher radiation levels of Locura.

"What...was the Fall like?" I dared to question how far back the memory of this Drone went, how much he had seen. As an older model, he had seen the Loomers and watched them fall. I could imagine how the ground

164

probably shook like an earthquake when they hit, or the sounds of crashing metal when they crumpled in on their own weight.

For the first time in a few hours, Gregory offered a scornful chuckle. "I wasn't everywhere when it happened, so I didn't see what every Fall looked like. Though I was present for the Fall of Nykoma. I was stationed as a Razum Guard, a position that meant I protected the Razum walkers attached to Nykoma from human rebels, as they were not fully wiped out in the area. I walked as a Razum Guard for ninety-eight years with only a few advances from human rebellions. The Giant Finigan joined the march after my fifty-seventh year and walked with Nykoma with his own Razum Guard unit of newer Gregory and Markus units. If I remembered correctly, he even had several Harvey Tactical units."

"Nothing was unusual about the day. The sun rose the same way. The Razum walkers moved smoothly with the strides of Nykoma. It was 1:37 pm, on the 14th of May in the year 2185, when Nykoma stopped for the first time in years. He just stopped walking and the Razum walkers stopped walking. Finigan stopped as well, and we were ordered to stop marching. Then the sound of Nykoma powering down echoed over the desert, and he just…fell." Gregory paused as he thought through that day.

"Not long after, people began to be released from the Razums and panicked. They fought the Razum Guard until Finigan stepped in and secured the situation. After that, I was assigned to the Human Suppression rank. Until now." Gregory added the last part with a lower tone. The actions he had taken earlier in the day still weighed on his mind.

I let the history settle in my mind as we continued our careful dive into the corpse of a world destroyer. I realized now how much of the world's current state I was unaware of. Three generations of Razum Born, so many dying without seeing the world with their own eyes. Wishing I could feel the weight of Tyron near me, I remained grateful I was freed during the Fall. The dark historical retelling only invigorated my passion to free Tyron.

Allowing some time for Gregory to separate from the day's abuse, we continued. Sounds were attacking my senses. There was yelling and

165

fighting going on to our far right. The noise of the nearest refinery sounded like a constant roaring, and I could even hear a foundry forming metal structures in the distance. This was not a quiet city like Haldoklik but raged with industrialization.

"When we reach the ground, I will build a shelter in the Eastern wall where there appears to be less populated areas. I will have to keep a low profile from Drones so I think it will be easier if we separate. You will do reconnaissance in the city. Try to find out where the Scrap Dogs are and listen to any whispers. We should know the pulse of this city before we settle in to work on Tyron."

Orders were given like second nature to the Drone, but I knew there was a logic behind him. Knowing the societal balance, struggles of the city dwellers, and Drone influence will prepare us better for any potential threats. It didn't mean that I enjoyed being ordered around like so many before me.

"Will you keep Tyron safe?" My tone may have been harsh, but I didn't want to have to live through losing him again. Not twice in the same day.

"He will be attached to me until you return. I will not set him down or leave him unattended. If I run into issues, I can easily escape with him." Gregory rattled these words as if they were obvious. "I know you will turn that gun on me even quicker than you shot Finigan, should I let anything happen to your brother again. I know his value to you. There is no reason to remind me."

I was shocked slightly, realizing I had probably asked similar questions to him over the past few days. Betraying myself every time I asked him, I had to accept that Gregory was aware of how far I was willing to go to protect Tyron. His choice to save my brother and me from Finigan should also comfort me, but his existence as a Drone would always cause me to doubt his sincerity to my cause.

We were finally near the ground and, to my relief, no one was in sight of the stairway. There were multiple story houses in specified grid lines all the way to the wall's edge providing us with plenty of cover, but also hiding many possible eyes watching. My boot sank into the red-tinged mud at the ground level, causing me to stabilize myself on the wall.

Gregory cast a glance at me and examined our surroundings. I could see recent damage to the side of his perfectly curved hair and leading down the right side of his face. I hadn't seen the broken metal on his face before now and realized it was more recent. Before I could ask about it, Gregory turned and faced me.

"Walk that way till you hit a city center and listen for a few hours. I will follow the wall all the way to the Eastern foot of the city. I will mark buildings along my way so you can find me." He pointed in the corresponding directions and immediately turned to leave.

"Wait, what will your mark be?" I asked him, walking a few steps after him.

"You will recognize it when you see it." He waved sarcastically, fading away behind the many buildings.

For a Drone, he was getting very sarcastic with his attitude. It was an alarming indicator of the rate he was Fritzing. He must have been hiding the symptoms for a long time if it's settling in so strongly now. A part of me was grateful for his brain frying. He was proving to be a useful ally. The other part was preparing for the inevitable breakdown of his circuits.

I enjoyed the silence and safety of the hidden corner we started in, but knew I had to venture out and endure the likely danger beyond. Walking softly in the mud, the street ways led me further into the town. I saw the quality of the housing increase with cleaner buildings and well-designed structures. This was a place of construction and rebuilding, and it began showing signs of human development and ingenuity. Perhaps there was less Giant influence here than I thought.

People appeared more frequently, mostly covered figures marked in red dust, likely from working in food substitute refineries. As more people crossed my path, I noticed I was drawing attention. I looked over my clothes and realized I was in a paler garb than they were, the acid fog having washed all of my clothes and exposed hair and skin in a paler white. I was standing out as an outsider.

I dreaded my next necessary actions, but I knew I needed to blend in quickly. Stooping to gather some mud, I took a stabilizing breath before applying the acid mud to my clothes, face, and hair to darken my complexion to that similar to the people in this city. The mud and grit was enough to burn my skin without the addition of the acid. My face felt like it was on fire and my scalp raged, but fewer people looked in my direction.

With my new acid burns inspired appearance, I could walk more confidently through the people that were apparently making their way to their jobs towards the head of the city. I followed the direction of the masses and kept my head low, focusing my ears to hear the mutters of the crowd.

"I heard the Drones talking today. Apparently, a Giant was attacked earlier. They are gonna be posted up tight at the refinery. I should let Bjorn know he should leave his kid home today." I heard a man speaking in normal Razum language, which was a relief to my ears from the guttural Loomer city talk I couldn't dissect. Another voice chimed in response.

"He doesn't have a kid anymore. The refinery dust suffocated him a few days ago. Bjorn hasn't been to work since then. Drones will probably visit him soon, anyway. Damn work schedule. It's gonna kill us all. "

A new voice chimed in now, "Hush now. Rebellion talk all over town, yah? Giant trouble just start more fire. Drone hear feud talk, dey take folk off street. Got family? Best you hush, eh?" This was an older female voice trying to speak clearly in the Locura accent, but when I looked up, I couldn't see her.

"I heard Xa was taken. No one has seen him since," responded the first voice.

"Ugh, Drones are gonna be up our asses for a while." The second voice sounded exhausted.

Before I could move closer to follow the conversation, I noticed the men moved further away from me and got lost in the crowd. Losing my window to follow them further into, I decided to make my way towards the edge of the herd and walked slower to wait out the densest area of people. There were more whispers of the Drones being more aggressive today, but nothing stood out more than the talk about Finigan.

News had traveled fast, apparently. Gregory and I had become the top story that was muttered. Thankfully, there were no names or descriptions, just the story of my actions. The shot I had fired seemed to have ignited strikes and feuding against the machines here. Guilt quietly clawed up my back, but I ignored it. There had been no other option in the situation.

I found a quiet spot where I leaned against a building, watching the people pass by and analyzing their appearances. Most were men. The few females that walked in the crowd were definitely older. There were a shocking amount of younger kids walking as well, whether they were being brought to work, or working, I was unclear on. I noticed the faces were darker because of the smokey situation of the town.

People disappeared, and the streets grew quieter. There were some children near that were playing in the mud in full acid gear, and I quietly watched them. It appeared to be a safer area with less 'Oomer activity. A welcoming moment of relaxation hit after my 'Oomer run-in earlier.

Bones weary, I slumped against the wall with more casual acceptance of my surroundings. Compared to Haldoklik, this was a much safer town from what I've seen. I felt a slight weight lift off my shoulders as I shuddered, a breath in the dense air. Maybe this would be a suitable area to settle down for a while once Tyron wakes up.

My thoughts ran away with me as I envisioned me and Tyron working in the refinery and making our way here. I could imagine his blonde hair getting tinged with red from the dust. His smile lured me into a sense of safety as I thought of the brother I once knew.

The image of him in a trash pile flashed across my mind. I knew there was a chance he would come out and not quite be himself, but the echo he made of me gave me hope. It seemed like he remembered me at least. Hopefully, I will recognize him as well. Hopefully, he will recognize me after growing up.

Remembering my brother made me eager to leave my station and find Gregory. I stood straight and continued my way further into town when a hand appeared from around the corner I leaned on. The hand caught my arm as I was straightening. My reflexes reacted before I had time to assess and my fist was on its way to meet the face of an older woman. I stopped myself inches short of her gnarled nose.

My quick reaction must have scared the woman, as she stepped away from me defensively. She had dark reddish gray hair and acid scars; her face bearing the weight of a hard life. As I recoiled my fist, I maintained my defensiveness. Years in Haldoklik had trained me well to be wary of people. When the old woman held her hands up, submitting, I lowered my guard slightly.

"Excuse me, I didn't mean to startle you." The woman spoke quietly in Razum's clarity. It was evident that she was watching our surroundings. She had things to say that were not publicly appreciated.

"You are new, no?" She asked, taking a half step forward and lowering her head. I was hesitant to answer, but the woman continued talking. "Your boots show signs of being in the Barrens. I just wanted to ask if you were a scrapper by chance?"

A moment of freedom raged across my mind. Finally, a town that didn't know my Drone affiliation, nor judged me for being Razum Born. This city, while being dangerously charged with rebellious notions, was feeling more safe than anywhere I had been in twelve years. I nodded my head at the woman's question and watched our area for prying eyes as well.

The woman nodded gratefully and walked away, trying to lead me after her. "Come with me. We need help."

After being lured into several traps at a younger age, wariness was my friend, and I couldn't help feeling apprehension at this request. 'Where are you taking me?' I asked, noting the urgency in the woman's movements. Something was either wrong, or she was an eager trap setter. I hesitated before deciding whether to follow her.

"I am an Organ watcher, I need help." She stammered as she walked away further down an alley between buildings. It was an unlit path that led into the darkness, away from the main stretch. I adjusted my pack and felt the hidden contours of the gun. While it would be a last resort, I couldn't risk getting harvested by organ-greedy marketers before saving my brother.

Deciding to proceed with caution, I followed the woman into the dark, leaving the sound of children and industry behind me and joining the silence of the back alley. I had heard rumors of organ harvesting from Scrappers before, crude black marketers stealing organs from strangers and selling to the sick. Though I had never heard of an Organ watcher. If the woman had wanted, she could have spilled my throat before I could have been able to stop her. I guess I was going to learn something new about Locura sooner than I had wanted.

We didn't walk long before reaching a darkened doorway. From the tracks leading this way, it was a commonly used path, although it was not currently occupied. The woman knocked on the door using a memorized pattern. It took a moment, but the door cracked open and I saw a youthful, dark female face appear in the crack.

"I found an outsider scrapper. She may be able to help." The old woman explained. A youthful face examined me with fascination before opening the door wide enough to allow us through. I had to duck through the doorway slightly and was immediately hit with the rank smell of rotting flesh. It was suffocating and permeated my lungs with a sense of disgust. With the area being warmer and more dense with unpleasant smells, I had to stifle a cough. This was not a good place.

The room I had entered was merely a covered stoop, but even this was filled with bottles and vials of blood and tissue. Foreboding and dank, I scanned the young faces that filled the room. These children couldn't be over ten years of age and they were working with transfusion machines. I felt revolted. There was respect for these children, but ultimately outrage that they worked in such a vile place.

"Don't mind the mess, these are new Organ watchers. The issue is here." The older woman said as she began leading me to a doorway across the room where light was spilling from. I hesitantly followed the older woman, careful to not walk close to the children or disturb any dark coagulating bottles that lay on all the flat surfaces available. The smell was growing stronger as I ventured deeper into the building.

Crossing the threshold into a new room, I held my breath. Bile boiled up from my stomach at the sight. The room that spanned before me was

171

perhaps a hundred feet long and contained a balcony that led to more attached rooms. People were scurrying all around. There was a sense of urgency in everyone's movements. Tables pustulated across the entire room and balcony spaces, swelling and bulging as if the room itself were diseased. Every surface seemed to ooze with misplaced purpose, the crude stitching of function and filth. I hesitated at the threshold, my stomach twisting. The stench of metal and rot suffocated me. My boots stuck faintly to the floor with each step, a grotesque reminder that nothing in this place was clean—or safe.

On each table and piled near every wall were Razum wearing humans, many cut open with surgeons actively removing organs. They were harvesting those who remained in the Razum and using their organs for sale. A pile of bodies adorned the back wall as I quickly averted my eyes from the scene. This explained the amount of aged people I had seen.

A heart was being removed from a Razum Born near me and my knees weakened. The old woman, sensing my repulsion, placed a hand on my shoulder. This was not an unusual reaction to this sight, apparently.

"Come, this way. Keep your eyes down if it helps." She coaxed as she led me towards the stairs leading to the balcony. There was viscera across the ground as we walked, squelching beneath my boots. I took careful steps, averting my eyes from the reality this room represented. Climbing the stairs, I heard the distant splatter of organs into containers. Each wet sound made my skin shudder.

How could they do this to these people? They were still conscious; they were just trapped. I could feel anger boil in me as I climbed higher over the scene. The images of my brother on one of these tables burned the soles of my feet. If this was the town's true underbelly, I did not want to stay. My hope for this city was getting carved from me.

Finally reaching the top of the stairs, I locked my eyes on the metal wall and continued with the old woman until she stopped at an open doorway and gestured me in. Following the guidance, I entered the room and found several younger surgeons backed against a wall away from a table. On the table lay a body, the life signs gone from the skin of an older male.

A Razum on his head was cracked open and part of the face was visible. The eye had been ripped out by the Razum and the face was mutilated, someone had tried to forcibly remove the machinery.

I could see a dead surgeon on the ground, shrapnel covering her childish face and body. Over the years I had learned that the Razums have their own defense measures, one of which was several small bombs placed around the weakest areas of the Razum. This was the outcome of tampering, and would have been my own fate if I hadn't caught Tyron earlier. The old woman grabbed the feet of the dead surgeon and moved it out of the way with business-like dismissal.

"Can you tell if the Razum is armed?" she asked as she shooed out the terrified children doctors. I stepped closer to the Razum and held my breath. The body radiated a stench of decay and I could now see there were many weak sutures holding his abdomen together. They must have been harvesting him for a long time and not taking care to clean the wounds better. While the Razum would keep them alive, missing too many organs and fighting infection, the Razum was allowing some of the flesh to die to protect the mind.

While I didn't know enough about Razums to tell if they were armed, I could examine it to see if there were any differences from Tyron's. My face was close to the Razum now, and I scanned the metal edges. To my surprise, there was no power left in the device, the bomb probably blowing out the powering supply and with the death of the host, its power regeneration was also down. The Razum was no longer a threat as long as it wasn't jostled too much to trigger the bombs that remained.

I had never had the option of having access to a dead Razum before. It could mean wonders for removing Tyron's. After giving the head a few cautious bumps to test the bomb's integrity, I stood away from it. The woman was watching me with patient eyes.

"It's safe as long as you are cautious." My voice was shaking more than I had intended. The woman ignored the quiver and shuffled the children back in to clean the room.

"It's useless to us now. We just want it out of here." Her voice was professional and the beady, dark eyes looked at me. Body disposal was her job. Mine had only been to tell her if there was still a threat.

The kids moved the body slowly, lowering it to the floor onto a tarp they had placed to drag it. I stepped aside and watched them work. Such young hands dealing with death, it was dredging up memories of the Scientist. The horrors I had already dealt with by the time I was their age were similar in degree of trauma.

"What can I give you for your service?" The old woman shuffled me out of the room. She didn't seem to want me lingering in her den. Though my hand on the door frame stopped her pushing.

I knew my answer before she had asked the question. I just dreaded the feel of the words across my lips, but knew it was what I needed. This request would either encourage a stronger relationship with the old woman, or out me as a stranger of dark affiliations.

"Give me the head of that guy."

Chapter 7: Coming to a Head

After a long, awkward, and truly disgusting time removing a head and figuring out how to carry it, I had been quickly sent on my way to find Gregory's new hiding spot. Picking my careful steps through the vomit inducing Organ Den, I finally reached the door. I wrenched it open and took a deep breath of the outside air. While it was a slight improvement on the den air, at least it didn't smell of rot and disease.

Light remained in the sky as it was close to being choked out by the reddish smoke curling around in the breeze above Locura. It was past midday, from what I could tell. The noises of the crowd from earlier had subsided as I rejoined the central street. Only a few children remained and played in the mud with observant parents watching over them.

It was quiet as I walked back the way I had come. People seemed disinterested in my passing, which felt like a relief. In Haldoklik, heads would turn when I walked by. Weather disdain or respect, I could never truly be certain of which. The anonymity of a new city felt refreshing, though the underbelly was obviously disturbing.

Following my tracks, I made my way back to the stairway. A few people now lingered in the streets. Some nodded hellos to me as I passed. Doing my best to mimic the nod, I kept my mouth shut. People didn't need to know about me right now and the quieter I could be, the less attention I was likely to bring as I tried to find Gregory.

When I reached the hidden stairway area where we had entered Locura, my eyes scanned the area, trying to find the alley Gregory had walked down. I could still see the mud footprints his metal shoes left and followed them towards the feet of Locura. The buildings I was passing were more decrepit and less maintained than the main area I was coming from. My guard went up as the pathways darkened. Buildings shadowed me as they stretched for the sky with gnarled metal fingers.

The Razum I was carrying under the edge of my cloak was growing heavy as the mud dragged at each of my steps, refusing to let go of me as I took another step. With less traffic in this Lower Town; the pathways were more prone to muddy troughs than walkways.

My legs were getting fatigued after a while of fighting the Earth. I wanted to estimate how far I had walked during this week, but the number of miles would likely fatigue my mind. The last time I walked these types of distances was when the Fall happened. I was carrying Tyron then as well.

With aching feet, I realized I had lost Gregory's footprints and began searching the walls for symbols. He hadn't left the wall's edge, so I figured I would find a mark there. The wall was built the same as Haldoklik: mud, metal and repurposed Loomer skeleton.

I felt a smile curl the corner of my mouth when I finally spotted the mark left by Gregory. "Tea Party this way," was carved into the clay wall with an arrow pointing further down the wall. It looked almost as if it had been carved into the original wall with the depth it had. This was no human mark. While it was blatantly obvious that it was his mark, I would have to scold him about his carving strength.

A part of me appreciated the reference, the other part of me worried more about my Fritzing companion. Signs of sentimentality and creativity would be applauded in human society, but it was different for Drones. With each sassy remark and creative adaptation, Gregory was progressing his own illness. While feeling oddly sentimental, I followed the directions carved into the wall.

It was not a long walk before I saw buildings crumbling and housing turning into scrap metal sheds. Gregory found the slums, after all. The most recent tea party sign had pointed me a little more away from the wall and I followed the blind guidance. Paths were becoming more rut-like, and the housing was decreasing in density as I noticed signs of recent movement. Mud was scraped in areas, looking like it was dragged by a behemoth. I only knew one behemoth who would be in this area.

A medium-sized hut was tucked into a corner of smaller huts with mud dripping down from the newly moved metal walls. The end point of the trail I had followed. A symbol was scrawled on the side of the wall in the mud of a teacup, giving away that I had finally reached the tea party I had been after. Checking to see if there were onlookers near, I knocked on the door quietly.

Gregory's voice whispered through the metal. "Password."

I pondered for a moment what a Fritzing Drone would craft for a password, but after thinking it through, the answer became obvious. "Tea Party."

The door swung open slightly, and I walked through, only to have Gregory close it quickly behind me. There were candles around the dark metal cave. The floor was smashed down with a layer of tin over the mud below. It was fairly well lit and I could see Tyron laying on a table suspended in the center of the room. He looked as though he was sleeping, his breathing timed to the rhythmic pulse of the light on the Razum. I smiled to myself, realizing there was nowhere for me to sleep on the floor, likely slipping Gregory's mind as he did not sleep.

"Was there anything interesting in the streets?" Gregory asked as he turned and sat himself down on the floor against the door, acting as an immovable lock. He had adjusted his tarping after removing Tyron and was looking more humanoid until he removed his hood, showing off his silvery-gold hair and scratched metal face.

"It's a nice city but, Locura is like a bomb waiting to blow. Sounds like there are lots of talks about rebellion. My shot at Finigan might have stirred the town up a bit. I don't think we should stay here long." I found my seat on the ground near Tyron's side. There was no reason to invest in chairs since we didn't know how long we were staying. When I finally lowered myself to the ground, fighting my braces and landing awkwardly, I remembered I was still clinging to the Razum head under my cloak and rolled it lightly on the floor between me and Gregory.

Gregory leaned forward, metal creaking, and grabbed the beheaded Razum. Poking the metal and the human skull within, I could see him examining the wiring that hung from the fleshy bits of the neck. It had been hard-wired into his other organs and I kept them as connected as I could for study.

"Where did you find this? It's basically a bomb in this state." He tapped the bomb locations, tempting them with explosions while testing their integrity. It would be a lie to say his taps didn't make me nervous.

"I ended up in an Organ Den. They needed help to assess the danger of it after it exploded on one of their doctors."

"What's an Organ Den?" He continued to poke and prod the flesh inside the blown apart section. I wondered if he was checking the Razum, or learning more about the human body with his pokes.

"For a while I had heard rumors of Organ Dens in bigger cities. It's an attempt to harvest organs and give them to actual workforce members to increase life spans and combat metal poisonings. I had never seen one until today. They, uh, use Razum Borns for the harvest because they aren't deemed alive anymore." I felt no need to explain my disgust at this notion. Gregory would understand or he would not care.

"So you asked for the head as payment, I'm guessing? You were thinking you could pull this apart and figure out how to remove Tyron? Do you even know if he's still conscious?" The robot now looked at me and scanned my face for a response.

"He's in there. It's worth a shot to see if I can even remove one first. Getting his consciousness out as well will be the real trouble. Even if I can just free his ears, he could hear my voice." I could see the process in my mind, which panels I would try to unscrew first, avoiding the bomb layouts. It was going to be a very stressful process, but it's more possible now than it has ever been.

"How do you know he's in there?" Gregory's words were gentle and realistic. I knew he doubted the possibility of Tyron being conscious, just like everyone did. The Fall happened twelve years ago now and the solitude likely wiped many people out, but I had proof.

Motioning for Gregory to bring me my bag I had dropped at the door, I stood slowly. Careful to avoid stressing the homemade braces that grew weaker with each movement. Once on my feet, he handed me the bag. I removed the device he had once given me. Connecting it to Tyron's Razum, we waited for the device to boot up. Gregory now took up a position next to me to watch over my shoulder as the world Tyron lived in came into view.

It was the same dismal sight as before, the curved teardrop form of the Watcher still glitching in the same places, the garbage still piled everywhere, though now there was no form hidden within. Instead, I saw the little echo of myself stalking the watcher from around the wall of the house that stood as a base construct. It was still damaged and I could see a hand gripping the corner of the rubble from inside. They were playing some sort of hunting game against the glitched watcher.

After a moment, I saw the echo lunge at the Watcher and seize its programming, exploiting its inherent nature as a program. While holding the Watcher still, Tyron emerged from the rubble. He looked taller and thicker than I remembered him. This was the first time I had seen his face in twelve years. I felt the tears well in my eyes. He looked rugged and strong. While I knew that was the image the Razum was feeding him of his own body, the reality was vastly different. He would never walk again, and yet, that was the image I wanted to keep alive in my memory.

The scene intensified as I watched Tyron approach the watcher and wrap what looked like a belt around it. For a moment, the Watcher went still, then it vanished as if the program was erased. I had never seen a Watcher disappear before. They were a crucial organizer for the base program that the Razums suspended minds in. I never thought we could get rid of them. The small echo of me landed on the ground sharply. I could see small digital tears forming in her eyes and Tyron quickly rushed to her side to placate the child's emotions.

I heard Gregory lean closer. "He... just uninstalled the Watcher? I didn't know your brother had coding knowledge. That was lost a long time ago."

He sounded mildly impressed, but it was the serious edge to his words that worried me.

"Why does that sound like a bad thing?" I asked, casting Gregory a glance over my shoulder. He stood as tall as he could in the cramped hut and stepped away from me slightly. Taking the device, he scanned through the options. The metal fingers tapped harshly on the device and I could hear his processors whir, only increasing my worry.

"If I am reading this right, we just witnessed your brother starting our clock on getting him out." Gregory's voice was sullen as he continued to tap on the device, the whirring becoming a deafening silence in my mind as I realized the ramifications.

"He wouldn't..." I started, but realized I had no thoughts of finishing the sentence. I could feel the blood leaving my limbs and the weight of the world was now crushing down on me. My brother had signed his own time stamp buy uninstalling the primary code of his network. All I had in the world was now accepting death as a better fate. My knees melted under me as I hit the side of the shed wall and slid down, disregarding the pain the braces caused.

Gregory set the device down and disconnected the Razum from it. He stood over me now and offered a hand down to me, having to hunch slightly to be close enough for me to take it. The gloved fingers suddenly felt far away and of a different life.

"Get up Taylor. We still have time, but not if you lie around. I will not be the one to do all the back work for a Razum kid. Come on, let's see what the Organ den people know about the Razums and postmortem removal. That should help us see what we are digging into." His voice felt reassuring, but my body was still being crushed by this new reality. Tyron was giving up. I have taken too long.

After a moment of not accepting the offered hand, Gregory recoiled it and instead stooped down to be closer to my face. His bright eyes almost glared at me with their digital forms. A few pixels flickered.

"I will drag you out of here if I have to. I did not get a termination warrant on my head for someone who was going to quit at the first setback so close to the finish line. There is no happy ending for you or Tyron if you sit on the floor. Everything you have endured will have been for nothing, and him staying intact this long will be for nothing. Do you want your story to end in failure or fight?" I could feel the anger coming through his speaker, it was vibrating my ear drums.

While aggressive, Gregory was correct. I knew in my heart that there was no way I would take this and stay down. So many broken bones, imprisonments, and bitter survival, I couldn't stop now. Though my mind was coming around, my body was weak and still wouldn't move. I could only feel one question sitting in my mind.

"How long does he have?"

Gregory reached his hand out to me again, this time grabbing my hand and forcing it upwards as he stood. He dragged me up and steadied me against the wall. I forgot the pure power he could command as a Drone.

"We have two days till the deterioration will become too much to retrieve him from. Today, we will talk to the Organ Den people. They may have more of an insight into the Razum's inner workings into the body and how to clip it out. Tomorrow, we will have to act." A slight twinge of dread rocked my brain. Two days to achieve what I had hoped would be a few more years of learning before having to act.

"What other option do we have? Let's go." I muttered as I stood taller and regained the balance I had lost in my soles. Gregory watched me for a moment, and after he was sure I wasn't falling back down, he gathered his tarp around him to obscure his form once more. He quickly packed my bag with the device and handed it to me. Opening the door, he bid me a silent farewell.

I took a few shaky steps before my body remembered its purpose. "For Tyron." I whispered to my cold and tired soul. So many miles and injuries, I couldn't be weak yet. Soon, I would rest.

It was growing dark in Locura, which helped our quiet shuffle through the streets. I walked as fast as my body was letting me, Gregory trying to hide his impatience at my speed. We kept our silence to hide Gregory's voice from any who may be listening. It was a quiet walk until we reached the central street I had been on earlier. There were now dozens of people walking about and talking. There were also supervising Drones standing guard at different light posts down the street.

Gregory's hand caught my shoulder as I started walking down the lit street side. I looked back at him to see his face near my own, the smell of wet metal and plastic filling my nose. His grip tightened as his eyes pointed towards where we were heading.

"Those are Harvey units. We can't go this way. I will be recognized immediately." He whispered the words so faintly they were barely audible. I could almost hear dread nearing his voice. My eyes began scanning the crowded street for the new Drone model.

There was a large Drone standing near the entrance to the Organ Den and upon a closer look, I saw what was giving Gregory pause. Tall and shiny, stood a lop-eared bunny who was the most threatening machine I had seen to this day. There were many burns and gashes in the metal plates of their armor. Their head stood probably four feet taller than Gregory. To top off the aggressive rabbit's visage, it was carrying a heavy gun with multiple round rings that showed obviously newly made bullets. The belt of more bullets laced from the gun and wrapped around the torso of the machine. This was a murderous Drone not meant for suppression, but for extinction.

"It's standing right near where we need to go and there is no back entrance to this place that I know of. What do you suggest?" I muttered as I staggered our walk to slow us. We needed time to decide before walking into the main population. Finding our way to the wall, we paused for a moment, looking out across the street area. There we noticed five Harvey units standing guard in different areas. All with vantage points of the entire street, and standing multiple feet above the average head. There was no avoiding their gaze.

"You said there were talks of rebellions going on here?" his hushed speaker rattled with stray dust particles trapped within. I suddenly knew where he was going with this thought process. His new persona was leaning towards dangerous now.

"Gregory, don't you dare." I muttered and started stepping away from him. This wasn't a discreet action in the slightest. I needed to make sure I was nowhere near him for this. He may have been a Drone capable of complex thought, but what he was about to do was not something I considered intelligent or clever.

"Make a run for the location. I will follow." He whispered as he stepped further into a crowd of people. Hunching over more significantly to hide his form. I lost sight of him, but I could hear his voice echo over the street.

"Death to the Machines!"

Gregory's loud voice rang out as all the people in the street freeze. Ignoring the frozen people, the Harvey units moved instantly towards Gregory's location. A moment passed and I could see the people near Gregory get pushed and shoved, irritating the mass of people. Before several seconds even had the time to pass, a minor riot had begun. People fought and more were joining in. The Harvey units neared, wailing their warnings on deep speakers, erasing any last kindness their bunny forms offered.

"Cease and disperse. All will be reprimanded. Cease and disperse. All will be reprimanded." They repeated their warning as they drew closer, now beginning to pick people up and throw them out of the way as if they were simple dolls made of wires.

I used this moment to make my run for it. The Harvey unit blocking our way had now moved enough and my shuffling didn't look suspicious against the chaos now unfolding in the street. People were turning on the Harvey units, trying to push them over or beat on them with bare fists or pieces of metal they carried. Over my shoulder, I could see the hunched figure of Gregory already following me.

We were only a block away from the entrance of the Organ Den and we had successfully dodged the Harvey units. I would wait to worry about us leaving when the time came. Turning down the alley, we ran into the darkness of the alley to be obscured. I noticed I could see the LEDs of Gregory's eyes through the tarp. We would have been easily caught if we had walked by the guards.

"Your eyes are glowing too bright. You're gonna give us away. Can you dim them?" I muttered quietly as I examined the alley we lurked in. There was no one in plain sight, but that didn't mean we weren't being watched.

"I can't dim my eyes. Can you dim yours?" Gregory asked in a facetiously aggressive tone. Of course, I had to end up with the Fritzing Drone learning to be sarcastic when in a dangerous situation. Reaching down, I tore off a piece of my undershirt. It was thinner for easy movement, but was still dense enough to keep heat and obscure light sources. After ripping off a section, I motioned for Gregory to lower his head and tied on the blindfold as it almost completely concealed the light.

"Can you still see? I don't want you accidentally stepping on me." Pulling the tie tight around his head, I stepped back to see how it looked with the rest of his disguise. He could pass as a blind behemoth now.

"I can see enough to not step on you. I can't use my depth perception receivers, though, so stay out of arm's length in case we need to be ready." He reached out a testing hand and lightly bumped into me before recoiling. It was still stunning to me that a Drone of his history was here beside me, not to detain me, but to aid me. I never thought I would have backup until I woke Tyron.

Smirking at the partially impaired robot, I turned my back to him and continued down what I remembered of the way. I heard his heavy footsteps following behind me at a slower pace than normal. Shuffling could be heard from a doorway near me, and I took a pause in front of it.

If memory served me correctly, this was the door. I wondered if they had heard our steps approaching or if they were watching the alley for any possible Harvey unit investigations. While it didn't seem likely that the Harvey units would bother themselves with a semi-legal Organ Den, we lived in a world where it was better to be cautious than hopeful.

Knocking the pattern from the old woman earlier in the day, I noticed Gregory took up position. He blocked me from sight to anyone who may look down this alley. There was more shuffling from inside the door before a voice barked through the metal panels.

"We don't know you or your huge friend. Leave before we call the

Drones." It sounded younger than the old woman, who I was now realizing I never asked the name of. I quickly thought of a response that would show peace but determination.

"We are not here for violence, only to ask a few questions. I helped here with a Razum earlier today. We mean no harm." I did my best to sound passive and friendly, trying to take the annoyance out of my tone. Impatience wouldn't help us get in faster.

"The Scrap Dog?" The voice asked back in a slightly kinder tone.

"Yes. My friend here is also a Scrap Dog in a sense. We mean no active harm." Gregory cast a glance at me, questioning. I shrugged and mouthed a silent response to him. "It's technically true now."

Silence met my answer. Hushed whispers now broke out behind the door, debating their options. Finally, an older voice croaked in the conversation. The old woman was now stepping in. The door cracked open and her wrinkled and crooked face peaked out at me.

"It's not normal for a Scrap Dog to return on their own. What do you want?" Her tone was cautious of me now. I stepped back to try not to intimidate her by blocking the door. Respectful body language was my secret weapon in these situations.

"I only have a few questions to ask about the Razums. I would rather not talk out here, though. We may have caused a bit of a stir to get back here unnoticed." While hating that I had to reveal the mischief we caused, I knew honesty would serve us better if we wanted her to do the same.

"You two are the out of towners that have the Drones so pissy, aren't you?" she growled.

"Yes. We come from a town called Haldoklik, to the South. We are only seeking information." I tried to reaffirm our purpose in case this information seemed threatening.

The old woman pondered for a moment, whispers continuing behind her. She shushed them harshly before looking towards Gregory and scrutinized him. He turned his face to hide his eye glow.

"Your friend will have to be careful here. Too many small feet for it to step on." The old woman opened the door wide and stepped back, motioning

185

the other smaller girls back. The rank smell of decay once again wafted through my senses. I had hoped not to return this soon.

I cast a glance at Gregory, and he nodded, beginning to follow me into the small entryway. The girls giggled as Gregory had to duck and shuffle sideways into the compact frame. Once inside, I had to step against a wall to allow Gregory enough room to close the door behind himself.

The old woman now stood close to him and examined his figure closer. I placed myself between her and the mostly discreet Drone. "He can't speak and he has been ravaged by the radiation wastes to the East. Best not to provoke him." My warning, while subtle, made its point well enough for the woman to back off.

"Well, we won't be able to talk in here and let the girls work. Follow me." The old woman gestured us in deeper. Gregory's heavy footsteps followed me and I heard the metal clinks of his feet. I looked back at him and pointed at his shoes and held a finger to my lips. Trying to communicate to him to walk softer so his metal shoes wouldn't stand out as much. He nodded his understanding, and I saw his gait change, making him look a little more awkward.

While this situation was a very serious endeavor that could still work against us, I couldn't help the absurd amusement I was feeling. To watch a death machine trying to blend in with humans and pass as a wasteland mutant, while having to tiptoe. I couldn't help the smile curling my lips. It had felt like a long time since I could smile at such an absurdity.

The woman led us through to the surgery room once more. I averted my eyes to avoid being hit by the nausea at the sight. The woman's feet turned to the left this time instead of the right. I followed. The vibrations on the tin floor as Gregory walked after us felt thunderous.

We entered a slightly larger, more empty room. There were no surgery tables in this room, but there was a desk pushed against a wall with piled tins with scribbles on them and even a few pieces of paper. A rarity in this world.

There were no chairs in the room besides one solitary stool pulled from the desk. I assumed this room was where the old woman kept track of the stored organs and those that were paid for or yet to be paid for. It was more of a domed ceiling room, which is why she must have chosen it for the conversation as Gregory struggled to fit in the smaller rooms. The woman was more intelligent than I had previously observed.

"So tell me why you stir trouble in our town, outsiders. Then we can talk about your questions. I won't be helping cause anymore chaos here. It's hard enough to do what we do and keep things quiet." She took a leading position by sitting on the stool and watching us closely. It would be safe to assume she had a weapon near her, just out of sight.

"My name is Taylor. I didn't mean to stir the trouble I did with the Giant Finigan, which brought more stress to your town. We have come here only to free my brother and to seek temporary refuge here in Locura." My voice did not waver and I ensured that my tone was to be respectful of the woman's position. I never wanted to cause trouble, but if that's what it took to save Tyron, I would rain hell.

She didn't need to know that right now though.

"I've heard your accent before. You said you're from Haldoklik? Miserable little town, starving themselves to death and overrun by those damnable 'Oomers. This isn't the town of Locura, we don't use that name. This is Sila. Best you get that straight if you talk to anyone while you are here." The woman huffed her words, her attitude trying to stir me. She was testing my antagonization limits.

"I will do well to remember that. Thank you. I do come from Haldoklik. My friend here helped me escape so that we could come here. It wasn't until you grabbed me from the streets that I realized I could use your information from your operation here. Would I be able to ask you a few questions about your work?" I refused to let her words stir any emotion in me. I was here for a purpose.

A long sigh left the woman, and she considered her position. While I knew asking the questions, I wanted to would cause a bit of trouble. She seemed level-headed enough to give the answers I sought. Though I knew there would be favors for her in return.

"Ask your questions stranger, I guarantee no answers for you or your friend there." She gestured cautiously at Gregory, who remained silent and at my back.

I planned these questions as palatable as possible. "What do you know about the hardware the Razum's use and how it interfaces with the mind of the hosts?" I could instantly tell this was not the question the woman expected.

"So your brother must be in a head case, huh? Makes more sense why you asked for that head today." She said these things quieter to herself, but I was shocked she had already put my story together. She was sharp.

"The Razums are made up half by bioware and hardware. While they were initially put on newborns and younger folk, they clone the DNA of their hosts so they grow with them. I'm sure you are aware of how they grow into the body after adulthood?"

I nodded my understanding, already learning more about the Razum than I had known. My heart raced at the excitement of learning more. While a Scrap Dog, I was always eager to learn more, but there were no more sources for me to draw from back in Haldoklik. Realizing the possibility of so much more information, my heart grew a little more fond of the idea of staying in Sila.

"Then you know Razums begin to take over all primary organ functions to take strain off the host's body and lengthen their lives. That's why my Organ Den functions better than the others in town here. Using the organs of the Razum born leads to healthier transplants and stronger organs, regardless of age. The downfall is that the Razums are so intertwined with the fabric of the organs that we have to un-weave them like fibers on clothing. Individual strands have to be removed to not damage the tissues. To our knowledge, this is not the case with the brain. Being as the Razum's initial use was backup processing speed for the Loomers, they never interfered with the functions of the brain." The woman paused here and watched my face.

"What were you trying to do to your brother? Free him? I assume you know that it's never been done." I knew she was analyzing me to understand my intentions. Although I could see a darker side to her investigation of me. She knew I was seeking to free Tyron, which, if successful, would make her industry more ethically upsetting to society.

"I am trying to free him, although I have no intentions of sharing that information with people." I made sure this point settled the woman's suspicions before continuing.

"My knowledge of his situation is vague, but I can tell you what I have done and what I need to know. His Razum has affected a few of his internal organs but has not fully infected him. I have started a temporary remission of the device from his body, but it will not last long. I know he is consciously present. He has not been lost to the solitary confinement of the Razum, but he has started a termination of his mental state and has a limited time to get out. Which is why I risked coming to you for information today. I will need to start surgery on him soon to remove what I can of the Razum from him and then remove the headpiece from him."

The woman sat back as she listened to me talk, absorbing the information and processing it. Her face was still of emotion and her pose was relaxed. I couldn't read the effects on her from what I was telling her. She allowed the air to still as I finished speaking. The room was silent except for the shuffling, whispers, and bone saws in the room behind us. These ambient noises were enough to hide Gregory's processor sounds. Though I heard the faint noise of them in the moments of silence, it wasn't noticeable.

Finally, the woman sat forward. "I have a proposition for you, Scrap Dog. Based on the information you have given, you have some very fancy tech you work with. I want it, and your services will belong to me for a week or so. We have a lot of incoming Razum and it would be good to have someone on hand who knows their way around them to avoid more explosions. In exchange, I will clear a table here for you and offer aid in freeing your brother. You can use the girls here to help however you need. And of course your word as a scrapper that you won't share your project's information with others. What do you think?"

The offer was met with silence as I contemplated the offer. It provided all the tools I would need to help Tyron, as well as medical experience, which I did not have. Although it would indenture me to the Organ Den, which can lead to more complications. I looked at Gregory, almost wishing him to give his opinion, but knowing he shouldn't speak. The deal seemed sound.

"I can agree to those terms as long as lodging is included for me and my friend, with free access to leave." My words may have been quiet, but the smile on the woman's face was loud.

"Deal. I'll start cleaning things up for-" She was cut off by a mechanical speaker that froze her.

"Taylor, don't take this offer. We can find help elsewhere without becoming slaves." Gregory's voice was now noticed. The disguise was ruined. I rushed to the woman and slapped my hand across her mouth before she screamed an alarm. I pinned down her hand that moved for a knife I could now see tucked into her desk.

"Damn it, Gregory!" I barked back at him. I saw him pull his blindfold off and expose his bright LEDs in the dim room. The old woman flailed in fear as she noticed what Gregory was. Muffled screams threatened to escape my fingers.

"Taylor, you will be needed to help bring Tyron up to speed when he wakes up. If you are indentured here and lose the equipment I gave to you, there will be no second chances if he doesn't come out well. I do not think this deal is wise for your situation." His voice was tinged with seriousness as he stepped closer to me. Completely disregarding the woman as he spoke.

"This is something we could have talked about later." I growled as the woman struggled against me.

"You were about to move Tyron here to do surgery. When did you think we would talk this through? When we were carving the Razum off his head?" He was irritated, and it was showing.

"I had figured, since you're sticking around, that you could catch Tyron up. You have more history and knowledge than I could ever share with him. I thought we were on this as a team at this point. What was your plan? Help and then run?" My words came out with more venom than I had intended, but it didn't seem to phase the machine. I heard his processors fire up with more speed now. He was thinking hard on my words.

"I... hadn't planned that far yet. I have never been without direct orders before." The soft words seemed to whisper from his speaker. Realization now struck me. I had made the decision not thinking about his position. He had been with me but never truly allied with me yet. If I signed on to this deal, he had to decide if he was going to be part of it as well.

"You can stay with us as long as you want. I will not hold you to this deal in any way. If you choose to leave, I will make do. You are not bonded to this with me." With my softened tone, I heard his acceptance of my words by the whirring of his processors. I had forgotten that for the first time in his existence, he had to make his own life choices. He was no longer with a network of rules and guidelines. Following my orders was as close as he could get to being part of a network again.

"Thank you for clarifying. You may continue with the conversation." He pretended to be nonchalant, but he hid his appreciation poorly. Now stepping forward, he took over covering the woman's mouth and held her still so I could step back and try to maintain more control in the situation.

"Okay. This was not the way this conversation was planned. Yes, this is a Gregory Unit, model 235. He aided in my escape from Haldoklik and when I shot Finigan. He has the Fritz and has been separated from the network he used to function on. While he used to be a guard, he isn't now. Everything else I said was true though, and my intent, and his, is not to harm. May we still talk, or will you scream?" I knew I would get no response, but her face would now expose her intentions.

She calmed her demeanor and nodded to me with a quiet confirmation of her compliance. Gregory slowly released her mouth, and with his free hand, grabbed her knife before releasing her body. Stepping away, he nodded to the woman.

"Hello." He said in his awkward and automated voice. While unnecessary, it seemed to ease the old woman.

"Hello." She muttered, looking at him in much closer detail.

"I have never seen or heard of such a thing as a Drone helping a human. You said he is Fritzing? How far gone?" She slowly unwrapped part of

Gregory's clothing before he stepped back from her hand.

"This conversation does not include me. Please resume negotiations." He took a hard stance, showing his distance from the conversation and retaking his position behind me. This damn Drone was a pain, but at least he understood some social cues.

The woman did not hide her annoyance at the control of the conversation being shifted to me, but obeyed and faced me directly. "I will offer temporary housing to you while your brother is here and you work for me. Including housing for… your Gregory unit, if he should want to help with labor. The bodies are heavy for the girls and could use a hand. This offer will only be extended as long as you don't stir trouble for yourselves, or the Den." She was being nicer now knowing I had a Drone at my use. I momentarily thought about how the situation may have gone differently if I had led with him. The sound of that choice was pulse guns and Harvey units descending on us.

"I accept these terms. Gregory?" I tossed a glance back at him to see if he was fine with this proposition, since now he was included.

"I am fine with helping around. I can retrieve Tyron while you prepare things." His words seemed to soothe the old woman.

"My name is Vykra. If anyone should ask, tell them you are under my name while you are here. No one should bother you. I will need to announce that we're hosting criminals, though. The girls would appreciate knowing their risks by involvement." She looked questioningly at Gregory. Her movements were careful.

I knew she had directed the question towards me, but it was meant for Gregory. He stood still and watched me to give him a cue. Not realizing this beforehand, I realized Gregory was now viewing me as his lead. I had become the voice he heard above others, and that power was slightly terrifying. Giving my nod of approval to the waiting robot, I turned my back to them and looked at the door wearily.

To live in these conditions for a week was a dreadful thought, the smells, the sounds of constant bones being cut, and organs being slapped onto trays. Even if there were hearts here, it would not be my home. I resigned these thoughts of disgust and waited for the Vykra to open the door and introduce Gregory to the Den.

Once she opened the door, she led us further left and up the balcony stairs. Her intention was to show off Gregory, and I could tell she was going to do it from the best vantage point in the room. When we finally came to a stop, we were dead center on the balcony overlooking the whole surgery room.

Dozens of small heads looked up to acknowledge Vykra, though my thoughts were too distant to hear her words. I couldn't help but to look out over all the bodies lying on the tables below. If we had been freed from the Razums even a few miles North from where we were, this could have been Tyron's fate. My blood felt like it was curdling with a mixture of disgust and fear.

Vykra was talking about Gregory, but I could only see the childish faces watching her speak. Children as young as six or seven years old were held to attention, bloodied and dripping with carnage. I was still in the Razum at their age. Playing with my brother, free of cares, yet these girls were raised in nothing but a brutal world that had cut their innocence from them before they could walk.

This was no world to bring someone into. For the first time in my Razum free life, I questioned if this was the world I wanted to bring Tyron into, or if I was trying to free myself from my loneliness in such an inhospitable world? I pushed these thoughts and denied their existence. I had already set my path in stone. No amount of disgust, fear, or panic was going to sway me. Not now, after all I had sacrificed to make this dream a reality.

My thoughts were broken up by a metal hand touching my shoulder. I looked at Gregory and saw the questions in his digital eyes and waved them off, mouthing a silent reassurance to him. I could see now that Vykra was waiting to lead us back down the balcony. Casting one more look on the youthful faces, I could see awe. A girl, not much older than them, was controlling a Drone, and the Drone was being considerate to her. What a mystery I must seem.

Following Vykra, she led us to a larger room off of the main surgery hall.

There was a bed and a girl quickly grabbing her belongings and hiding against a wall. I knew she was being displaced for mine and Gregory's sake, but I felt guilt. I nodded to her as an appreciative gesture and pushed Gregory out of her way so she could flee away to safety.

Once alone, Gregory closed the door to block out the prying eyes of the children. I felt my body decide to rest before I had even reached the bed. I fell short and landed on my knees at its side. The creaking of my brace alerted me to a broken support on my ankle brace, but I had no more energy to give today. Metal hands lifted me from my knees and placed me on the bed.

"Sleep. You have been doing too much in a very injured body. I will retrieve Tyron safely and bring him here to start the surgery. I will wake you when we start the main Razum extractions. Let the help you hired take some of the weight off you." His words already seemed so distant from my mind. When had I begun losing my strength?

Darkness covered my vision as Gregory extinguished the flame in the room. I could hear his metal steps recede and the door close. Vaguely, I could hear a large piece of metal scraping against the tin floor beyond the door. I assumed Gregory was 'locking' my door for me so I could rest easy.

⚙   ⚙   ⚙

Hours may have passed, or minutes. In this darkness that seemed to be my reality I woke into, there was no way to tell the time. A loud rapping on the tin outside my door stirred my consciousness. It was probably the sound that woke me. I lifted my body, but I still could not see, so I didn't dare to stand.

"Yeah?" The weariness couldn't hide in my voice that tumbled out like gravel. The response was a loud scraping of metal on the tin floor as I heard the lock being removed from the door. Light poured in and blinded me from the brightly lit surgery room, though it was quickly blocked by the large shape of Gregory.

"Taylor, it's time to join the surgery. Ready yourself." His quiet words soothed me in a sense. There seemed to be no hurry in his voice. Nothing seemed to have gone wrong with the process while I slept. I sat up out of

194

the bed, my boots barely making a sound on the tin floor. I noticed the brace that had broken when I fell and stripped it off me.

Testing my flexibility and strength on my injured leg, I noticed there was less pain and stood on it. I tested the rib brace I had made and found it to be too painful to go without and instead tightened it down. Gregory had left the doorway while I readied myself, but I could hear his voice in the surgery hall.

"Be sure to sew him up as cleanly as possible. Taylor will be furious about scarring. We didn't know how extensively the Razum had spread before giving him the Nanites." I heard agreement whispers join in quieter tones as he spoke.

I pulled myself from the bed and picked careful steps towards the doorway on the uneven floor. Taking a few deep breaths of the dead air made my stomach turn, but woke me. If I wanted to be part of saving Tyron, I needed to be fully awake. Shaking my head, I freed what steeled consciousness my years of surviving had trained me with. My eyes sharpened and I felt my heart rate increase.

Today was the day I got my brother back.

Newly awakened, motivated, and ready to carve my brother back into my life, I stepped into the light of the hall. The room was mostly empty except surrounding two tables off to the left of my room. I saw Gregory standing with a flock of young girls around one table with bright candle light reflected in mirrors and Vykra around the other. By Vykra was the Razum head I had given to them. She was poking and prodding the head, examining the machinery. As I approached Gregory's table, he turned to me and blocked my view.

"Some extensive surgery was required. I didn't know how much of his body was already taken by the Razum. They are finishing stitching him up, but physically, he is fine so far." A small bubble of dread appeared in my throat as I stepped forward to see my dear brother.

The small girls were working diligently over his chest as he laid on the table, making the smallest sutures they could with the equipment they had. A large fresh wound in the shape of a T was red and irritated when they

195

had cut him open to remove the Razum wiring. The cut went up from his chest and along both sides of his neck to where the bottom of his ears were. The metal around his ears had been removed by Gregory, was my guess.

Children cleared the path in front of me to be at Tyron's side again. I found my brother's seemingly lifeless hand on the table's edge and held it in my own. Vykra found her side by me and looked over Tyron.

"My girls worked very hard on him. He's still very strong. Now it's your turn to bring him out the rest of the way. Thank 235 here for all the guidance. He has taught us a lot." Her voice was quiet, as if not to wake Tyron. With his ears exposed, his brain could now process exterior information.

Gregory stepped near to Tyron's head and looked at me. "It's time for you to talk your brother into leaving paradise for you." Though he tried to hide it, there was a slight bit of doubt in his words. I knew he was prepared for Tyron to not wake up. Though every fiber of my being told me that Tyron was going to wake up.

All the girls and Vykra watched me now, no expressions present, just witnessing me. If this worked, it would change the world for all present, not just for me. The weight of this moment was one I had been prepared for when I first realized my mission was to save Tyron. I would not crack under their gaze as I changed what the world was, into what it can be.

I approached Tyron's head. The visions of the smile it will have when he sees for the first time gave me even more hope. This was the time to get him back. I knelt beside the table so my face was right in front of his ear.

"Tyron, I've missed you so much. Though you're not with me now, I know you'll recognize my voice. I've been the one telling you stories and keeping you company for the past twelve years, the sanity in your solitude. But now, I need something from you. It's time to leave that world behind and join me here. Make the choice to be with me in this life. If you can hear me, brace yourself and let go of that lonely world. I'm here to save you, as I always have been. Please… wake up."

These words have never been spoken from my mouth, but I have dreamed of them. My soul needed to hear my plight allowed apparently, because for the first time I could remember, tears of longing dribbled down my face. I was finally fully embracing how much I truly felt alone, how much I just wanted to be with my brother again and feel the family I grew up in at one time. Never knowing the feelings in my heart until I put them into words, I felt completely overtaken.

Standing on wobbling legs, I nodded to Gregory, who watched me with a sympathetic gaze. He gripped the edges of the Razum and lifted the metal and handed me a screwdriver. He motioned with a gloved hand under the Razum edge as he guided me.

"There are three screws under this piece here. It should release the mechanism to unlock the Razum. I will cut the power supply as soon as it unlocks to avoid bombs exploding. Be quick."

I raised my hand. There was a slight tremble to my fingers, and I heard all the gathered kids step back from Tyron. There were three outcomes: I would succeed, I would fail, or Gregory would and we would both get killed in the explosion, or I would not do it.

With trembling fingers, I unscrewed the first screw. Each turn of my hand felt like a hand tightening the noose on what may be the future. The first screw dropped out of the Razum and rolled off Tyron's collar bone.

A few stabilizing breaths, and I turned the second screw. I could hear the whispers of the girls as they stepped further away. Even Vykra stepped back when the second screw dropped from the Razum.

Looking at Gregory, he nodded his readiness to me and adjusted his hand on the power pack in the back of the Razum. I began turning the third screw. My own nerves were vibrating. So many years of hardship and yearning to see his face again were about to pay off.

With one last turn, the screw fell from the head of the screwdriver and I heard Gregory punch into the Razum, destroying the power supply. The edges of the Razum sprang apart on spring loaded hinges. The lights that had been my only companion on so many nights finally turned off. My starry, lonely nights were over.

Carefully, I lifted the lid of the Razum to see Tyron's face for the first time. Golden curled hair had been wound into the mechanism and obscured the face there. I pulled aside the hair and saw the closed eyes of my dear brother's face. As I was memorizing the new yet familiar face before me, the eyes opened.

Chapter 8: Sila's Underbelly

I jumped back. Why had I jumped? Watching the bleary eyes of my brother scan the world above him somehow scared me. The pupils dilated under the mirrored candle light. His eyes were probably in agonizing pain with seeing brightness for the first time. Though his brain was probably figuring out how to explain pain to an awareness that had never experienced it before.

A scream tore itself from his weak vocal cords. Raspy and afraid. Though it stopped quickly before the eyes tried to focus again. Like the scream was a mistake. His voice differed from the one I knew, but the hair and the eyes were my brother's, undoubtedly.

"Tyron!" His name ripped out of my mouth. There was nothing to fear here. It was my brother. I finally had him back. As I quickly stepped to his side to regain the ground I had retreated from, Gregory held out an arm to slow my advance.

"Taylor, give him a moment. He's never been awake before."

I pushed the metal barricade from me and placed a hand on Tyron's face. Something I had always done was pet his face. He would know me even if he were blind. That had to still be true to him.

"Tyron, it's me."

Stroking his face, I saw the slight movement of fingers. Was he trying to feel my hand? Did he know I was here? His arm raised slightly as if he was revived from death. He was reaching out to me.

"Don't move. We will put you to sleep for a while longer. We can talk when you wake up. I swear, I will never leave your side again." I whispered as I nodded to Gregory to use the anesthetic. It was in short supply, so I had expected to pay dearly for that through my services with Vykra. As Gregory set up the mask to knock my brother back into an unconscious state, I stopped him. Tears were forming in Tyron's eyes.

"Tay–lor."

His voice. My brother's voice. I never knew it was so raspy. It was likely due to never having spoken before, but there was a familiar timber to his voice that had been the same in the Razum. He sounded aged, more than I had anticipated.

Tyron's eyes wavered, focusing and unfocusing. The strain was going to tire him out quickly. I knew it would be better to knock him out, but I wanted just one more moment with him. There was always the chance he wouldn't wake up again, so I wanted to savor this moment a while longer.

Gregory nudged me as he moved forward. Ending my moment with Tyron, he leaned forward to place the mask on my brother's face. I wanted to stop him; I wanted to spend more time with him, but I didn't want him to suffer so soon after the surgery.

"It's nice to finally meet you, Tyron. Rest. We will have all the time to talk later." Gregory tried to have a friendly tone. It was an endearing moment to hear him metaphorically acknowledge that he was wrong and Tyron was now alive. I appreciated his kind gesture. Things were finally feeling like they were going to work out.

"Greg-" Tyron's voice cracked as Gregory paused. He looked at me curiously before continuing to place the mask on Tyron's face. Once secured, we all waited till the hazy eyes closed and my brother was deep in his sleep. A hand clapped me on the back.

"Congrats kid. You just made history." Vykra's beaming eyes glowed, an expansive grin revealed rotted teeth. The other girl surgeons were taking off bloodied gloves collapsing to the ground, others helped them to their rooms. The remaining girls cheered and jumped together at the success we all felt now. Even Gregory nodded at me in a congratulatory manner.

Once the cheering died down and the crowd went back to their chores, Gregory took up my right shoulder. We watched over Tyron. My eyes were trained on his breathing, counting each breath. Each one had the chance to be his last, but under my supervision, I would not let that happen.

Gregory's whirring was the only signal I had that he wanted to talk. I glanced away from my brother, ensuring that no one was near before prodding him. He may have been a secretive Drone before, but now he was an obviously confused machine as he navigated the new world of emotions he had stepped into.

"Say what you're gonna to say." My tone likely came across as irritation, but it wasn't directed at him. Though even if it was, he would likely dismiss it. I just wanted to spend time with my brother.

"How did he know my name?" The whirring increased in volume as he spoke.

It was a good question. From what I knew of the Razums, they had no ability to take in exterior information. With ear coverings and most of the head covered, it shouldn't be possible to receive information. Tyron knowing Gregory's voice was a new mystery.

"I'm not sure. It doesn't matter though. It worked and that's all I care about right now." Tyron's skin felt warm as I stroked his pale face. This was what I had hoped for. So many years of pain and struggles, so many setbacks, but he was finally here now. He was free.

Tears welled in my eyes. A journey that I thought would take most of my life had come to fruition in a matter of a week. The scars and injuries that plagued my body no longer hurt. There was no more exhaustion in my legs and the stingy air of the Den no longer choked me.

The weight that had been crushing my soul for the past twelve years had suddenly lifted. Options became overwhelming. There were so many choices to be made now, directions and goals for my life. It was terrifying.

Gregory's heavy hand landed on my shoulder, stirring me from my developing fears. His LEDs were focused on Tyron. There was a slight relaxation to his shoulder plates now as we watched my brother in silence.

"This was an impressive achievement. You should be proud of your work. Though we should move him somewhere more protected." His words were quiet but reverberated with my own thoughts. While the Den had been helpful, we still didn't know them. Foes often look like friends, especially when clothed in the faces of children.

"Yeah, you're right. Let's move him to my bed. I can sleep on the floor for a while." I took a moment to fix the hair away from Tyron's face before I shuffled his body into my arms. Lifting him seemed easier now. Without the weight of the Razum I could feel just how frail he was.

Hope buried itself in my veins with each step I took towards my room. He would become more, muscles would develop, strength would return to his arms. Maybe even his legs would come back with some extra effort. My brother would come back to me. The hardest part was over. Now it was patience.

Gregory followed me, opening the door of our room as I carried my brother to the bed. There was a giddy feeling as I laid him down. When he woke up, I would be able to finally talk to him. We had already shared so many conversations, but if he could know Gregory, maybe he would remember those talks.

As I fixed his hair and positioned him in a more comfortable setting, I couldn't help but to stare. The face I had known in the Razum wasn't too far off. The chiseled jaw line was as sharp as I remembered, though his nose was larger. This was the face I had known as a child, the first familiar thing I have seen in this world.

"I'm going to stay with him for a while, just to make sure he's okay." Gregory likely anticipated this as he stood outside the door. With a quiet nod, he closed the door and plunged the room into darkness.

I claimed a spot on the ground next to the bed, leaning against it. My hand found his and put a finger on his wrist to monitor his pulse. His breathing was loud in the dark, filling the air with a sense of life. The Razum had obscured his breathing before, but now, I could hear how powerful his lungs were.

Their first free breaths. His heart was pumping its first free beats. He was free. Years of effort now come to fruition. I wasn't going to let this moment fade. Staying here with him was all I had ever wanted. Squeezing his hand, I could feel the joyful tears drop from my chin.

My mind wandered, exploring our futures. We could likely establish a life in Sila if we wanted. The buzz of Drones would eventually fade and it would go back to an industrious city, plenty of work and life options. Depending on how my indentured labor for the Den goes, we could become permanent residents here if we pulled our weight. For what seemed like the first time, I had options.

We have options.

Darkness stole time from me. Maybe an hour had passed? Or an entire night or day? When the knock came on the door, I wasn't sure if I was awake or not. My body felt like it was floating in the quiet void as I listened to my brother breathe. When the knock came again, I realized I hadn't responded.

"Yeah?"

Metal steps were approaching the door before the old woman's voice came through the metal wall Gregory had made as a lock. Apparently, he was watching the door and including himself into this interaction. A smile danced across my lips in the dark as I heard his feet stop at the door.

"Scrapper, I know you got your brother back recently but I have some orders that need to be run out right now." Vykra's voice attempted to be kind but lost to her built in business tone. I guess now I was officially on the clock.

Standing as best as I could in the dark, I staggered my way to the door. There was no way I was able to open it, so instead I knocked. With Gregory already eavesdropping, I knew he would understand this sign. The loud scrapping of metal on metal seemed to silence the Den as Gregory opened the door of my small domain.

Vykra stood awkwardly next to the Drone who waited for me to leave the doorway. She looked so small and frail next to the murderous machine. As I stepped forward so Gregory could 'lock' the room, Vykra stepped away.

I had likely become a mysterious person now with my companion the Drone and reviving my brother from a death no one had survived before. There was a certain pride to having a new mystery in a new town.

"So, I'm running errands where?" Trying to draw Vykra into a more comfortable conversation, I focused on work. At least running errands was better than trying to scrap in a new town. Scrap Dogs were pretty territorial sometimes.

"I'll introduce you to Anne. She has the jar and will accompany you since you're new. Don't mess this order up. We do business with a few powerful folks." She regained her composure quicker than I had anticipated. The enjoyment of my mysterious life was quickly and efficiently snuffed out by the talk of work.

Gregory looked at me for orders, though I was surprised he couldn't guess what I was going to say. Pointing towards the 'locked' door, I lowered my voice. The prying ears would hear this, but I had to seem discrete.

"Stay and watch over Tyron. If he wakes up, find me."

His speaker rattled a little as if he was going to argue. The wink I flashed him seemed to steal his complaint away. It was no secret that he would hate being a babysitter. He was a Human Suppression Drone after all. Someone had to watch him though, to make sure his condition remained stable.

Begrudgingly, he moved the metal refurbished flooring sheet away from the door and sealed himself in. Vykra seemed to be amused by the interaction and spared a smile for me. Perhaps this old woman would see me as a friend one day.

I followed her across the surgery floor with down turned eyes. There would be a time and place to get used to the carnage of the Den, but I have not made that time yet. My boots slipped on the bloodied floor. As I tried to stabilize myself, my eyes looked up. I expected the surrounding scene to cause me to vomit, but I was only facing a small child holding a plastic jar, smiling at me.

Her face was covered in blood streaks, mud caking her brown hair in a tangled mat. A smile peered out from the gore of Den life. She couldn't have been older than six yet still somehow maintained an innocence and vicious reality. This was a face that had seen many deaths and brutalities, but still would likely enjoy playing with a doll.

"This is Anne." Vykra introduced us as I straightened myself.

The girl was barely the height of my hip, yet she carried a jar with a strange fluid and a lung bobbing around within. She seemed only excited to meet me and oddly unaware of the gore she stood in and held. Nodding her head in greeting to me, her eyes trained on Vykra with curiosity.

"You will take Taylor out on your run. Show her the ropes of delivery. No hiccups, got it?" Vykra used a stern tone with the child. It was her serious business tone that commanded attention and perfection. These children were her little soldiers, like a wolf mother commanding her vicious pups.

"Yes, ma'am." Her little voice barely broke the noise of the surgeries happening near us. When her eyes locked onto mine, she handed me the jar. Taking it with ginger and disgusted fingers, I stood at attention for the girl to lead me.

Without words, she turned and led me towards the back of the surgery hall. It seemed like a safe assumption that Anne knew where she was going. Even if we were walking away from the door I knew to lead outside. Better to trust the local than the newcomer.

As we approached the back wall, I examined the tin surface. Was there a secret entrance that my scrapper eyes missed? I was typically very good at finding secrets or hidden weapons, but if there was a path behind this wall, I would have to up my standards of 'hidden'.

Anne approached the tin panels on the leftmost part of the back wall. From the door of my room, I should have been able to see the gap between the metal slabs. Like a sore loser, I bit my bitter tongue as Anne pried open a secret exit from the Den. Sila was apparently on a higher level than Haldoklik was. More difficult, more clever, and more people. A new city of new skills I had to learn.

With the panel pulled back, I could see a dug out tunnel. There were braces made from metal beams, though I could see the hand carved marks in the packed dirt of the walls. It seemed fairly new, and based on the small hand marks in the dirt, the children of the Den created it.

Patiently, Anne waited for me to walk through the smaller door, her hand holding the panel open for me. Ducking slightly and trying to not bump the girl or the jar I held at a distance, I entered the dank tunnel. Anne followed and closed the panel behind us, plunging the tunnel into pure darkness.

A cold, small hand found mine in the dark. "Follow. I know the way."

I didn't have to see the smile to know it was there. She seemed excited to have a partner on this delivery. With blind steps forward, I stumbled over each movement. Each stumble earning a chuckle from Anne. Vykra seemed to raise happy and humorous kids in this cult of blood. It was nice to see some hopeful children for once.

"So, where are you from, Anne?" The dirt on the wall seemed to consume the resonance of my words. This was a padded cave, discreet and ready to hide all within. Was it planned or did it just work out that way? I would have to ask Vykra later.

"Here. Mom gave me to the Den when I was born." Her words were nonchalant.

Parents were an odd thing in this world. Children could be used as currency or as workforce. Even in the Razum, parents were just genetic donors while the children were kept separate to lead their own lives. Over the past hundred years, it seemed to be the normal.

It would be a lie if I said I wasn't curious about what family ideas were like before the Loomers. From what I read in the Razum and have seen from the Barren junk, it looked like it was an important thing. Families seemed to be revered groups, treated with a different level of respect. Maybe it was better to focus on individualism than family ideas in this world, but Tyron was my family. My focus was on him.

"How's life in the Den?" While trapped in the dark, it seemed like a wise time to learn about the place I would be staying for the next few days. A new piece of metal stuck into my ankle as my feet stumbled closer to the wall. Anne stifled another giggle at my uncoordinated tripping in the dark.

"It's great! Vykra is nice. My sisters are funny. Work is hard, but Vykra says we will be stronger if we work harder. We eat together every night and tell stories. It's home." The smile that veiled her words must have spanned her entire face. I had never heard someone speak so fondly of an Organ Den. Maybe I judged the cruelty of this place too quickly.

While their work was vile, it saved lives. The Den also took in girls like Anne who were given up or lost their parents. It was a home and a type of hospital. Though I could not overlook their abuse of the Razum Wearers. Nothing will sway my opinion on that. My brother, and people like him, didn't deserve to be harvested just because they were trapped in a prison.

My hand was given a tug backward, motioning for me to stop. Anne released my hand. I heard her tiny feet scurry around the dark before pausing. Noises of busy street life and howling street vendors permeated the darkness. We must be a few streets back from the original door based on the quieter tone of the street. I was guessing it was the midday rush as people looked for food or took breaks from their morning shift jobs.

"Follow me. Harveys are nearby." Hushed words seemed to bounce off of a new material. It sounded like she was near a metal wall, likely the door. My best guess was that we hit the hidden door near the surface and I was eager to see where we were.

The crack that Anne opened completely blinded me. Time of day had to be near high noon based on how my retinas burned. I was quickly dragged forward by a small hand as Anne pulled me through. There was a small thud as the door was shut behind me. When I turned to look, the door was gone.

We had just stepped out of the wall of Sila. I could tell we were away from the center street and closer to where Gregory and I entered the city. There must have been mud and metal caked onto the door to make it fit seamlessly into the chaotic nature of the wall. We would never have noticed it even if we were actively looking for it.

I turned to find Anne, but noticed she had already disappeared from the small corner near the first of the organized homes. We were just outside of the residential buildings. My feet moved as she turned the next corner. Apparently, I was going to slow for her and she wasn't going to wait.

Turning the same corner, I almost ran into her. She had waited for me, leaning against the wall in an oddly adult and casual fashion. Her hands darted out and grabbed the jar, pushing it against my ribs and pulling my clothes over it.

"Keep it hidden. People don't always like Den stuff. Harveys really don't."

It seemed wiser to follow the child's advice as I fixed the coverings around the jar so it wasn't seen. I noticed there was an ooze on the jar when it came into contact with my stomach. There would be a time to wonder about the ooze and clean it later. I bit down the bile that was crawling up my throat and nodded to Anne to continue.

We walked towards the center street, sticking to the outskirts of the crowds. Harvey units were in their dominating and surveying positions around the busy street. Anne seemed to know her way around, masterfully dodging the adults that blocked her sight.

It was surprisingly difficult to follow her. As she bobbed and weaved through the herd of people, I had to push and shove myself between unhappy workers to follow. My body was quite small, and I was slightly under the average height, which should have worked to my advantage. Anne was quickly proving me to be a large and clumsy fool compared to how Sila raised her. Maybe I was going to be more of an outsider than I had expected.

Even though people were getting irritated with my pushing and shoving, there was no sign of familiarity or judgment on their faces. In this crowd, I was just another stranger living their life. There were no rumors about me allying with machines, or hatred aimed at me for being a Razum born. Based on the age of many of the people in the city, it seemed likely that the majority were Razum born.

The lack of 'Oomers was also a relief. If I had known that not all Loomer cities were overrun, there's a good chance I would have ventured out years ago. It caused me to wonder what else was hidden beyond this region. Was there a world out there that was free of machines? If Sila could be free of 'Oomers, surely somewhere could be free of Drones and Giants, right?

My thoughts quieted as I lost sight of Anne near a Harvey unit on the Northern side of the street. Instinctively, my head ducked down and my knees bent slightly, stressing my ankle. Hiding was all I knew to do this close to a Harvey. When a small hand grabbed the tarp cloak that was weighing me down, I saw a dirtied face smirking at me.

"This way. Harvey won't like you if you get too close."

We made our way further East and away from the Harveys watching the street. Once the crowd thinned, it was a little easier to track the fast-footed girl. Looking around, it was obvious that we were in a richer section of town. The buildings were less clustered and cleaner metal had been used for paneling. Ornate looking 'sculptures' were scattered about the street. This finery had a dark shadow to it as it was the district under the skull before the factory and Drone headquarters.

The red and black smoke that rose from the refineries and factories colored the massive skull plate in an eerie, burnt sienna tone. Locura's red paint was still noticeable on the skull through the smoke. Even after death, she was still daunting and terrifying people. It still was nicer seeing her head on the wall instead of standing over us.

Anne did not seem to have the same introspection as she started a friendly skip down the stone street. I maintained a slight jog to keep up with the enthusiastic steps until she took a hard right. We stood in front of a massive door that Gregory would have no issues with. With a small and quiet rap on the door, Anne waited patiently for the owners to appear.

A few moments and some scuffing shoes on metal floors, the door finally cracked open. An old and overworked looking woman peered through hazy eyes at us. I could see several chains held the door secure, discouraging intrusion. Her clothing was cleaner and more uniform in design. There was even less acid scarring on her face than most. She must be an original settler of Sila.

"Hi, Dawn-Lynn. Droppin' per Den request." Anne's words seemed rehearsed. I couldn't help but wonder how often she ran these orders. Based on the endless motion in the surgery hall, they filled many orders. The thought of all the organs that belonged to the Razum Born sloshing inside so many others was revolting.

"Who's the lady?" Snapped the old woman.

The question was directed to Anne, but the icy and cataract filled eyes were piercing me. Anne reached a hand back, pulling me to step forward, level with her distance from the door. Whether this was respect or irritation, I wasn't sure.

"Trainee." Apparently that was going to be my new name till I learned how to run errands on my own.

"She's old for a Den kid." There was an insulting tone in her voice, attempting to antagonize me.

"The Den knows all with value." Anne looked up at me and nodded to me.

I didn't know what she was trying to say. Normally, I could read body language, but this child was becoming more and more unusual. So professional, yet giggled whenever I tripped. Able to rehearse lines, yet say unique and wise sounding statements. What the hell was a nod supposed to mean from such a strange kid?

My hesitation seemed to earn me an explanation. Anne poked the jar through my clothing. Taking the hint, I cautiously removed the jar. My eyes un-focusing instead of looking directly at the dark liquid that coated my hands. The woman seemed to relax at the sight of the jar, the opposite of my reaction.

A pale and gnarled hand burst from the door towards the jar. I retracted the jar just out of her reach. Anne smacked the woman's arm with a dismissive annoyance. There was an aspect of the motion that resembled the body language of Vykra. They must have a deeper relationship than I had thought.

"No pay, no credit, no delivery." This was not the same little girl I had met in the Den. Apparently, she had a very cruel and professional attitude outside of her home. It would probably be a good thing to remember about these girls.

The hand retreated within the door as a sigh escaped. "What do I pay for this?"

"O.M., trade, or service." An insincere and impatient smile was etched onto Anne's face. Their interactions seemed stressed, and I now understood the distance we maintained from the door. Grabbing and theft were probably more common with such an expensive commodity.

O.M. was a new term for me. Trade and service was the only payment form I was aware of. Though the sound of the term made me wonder if there was a monetary system in Sila. I didn't think any society used money anymore. It wasn't nearly as valuable as tools, food, or service.

"O.M. Give me a minute to gather it." These were bitter words that were cut short by the door being angrily slammed shut. This Dawn-Lynn was not a friendly person. Though, I suppose I would be upset if I had to pay to get a lung for survival. It seemed like an awkward position to be in, especially with a child being the one keeping it from you.

Anne seemed to be capable. Even if she was currently rocking back and forth on bored feet. People were more than willing to move out of her way or listen to her. The girl was full of mystery. I was glad I was being trained by a subtle master, even if she was only six.

Shuffling steps approached the door once more as the chains rattled when they were removed. A fist protruded from the door towards Anne. She opened her palms under the fist and the rattle of coins could be heard as she caught the money. Checking over each coin, she estimated the value of the money she held.

"More."

Dawn-Lynn grumbled and sent her other fist out. The twinkling of coins sounded almost like music as it met with the small palms of Anne. The old woman and I waited a moment in awkward silence as Anne counted the money. Tapping with splintering nails, Dawn-Lynn was growing impatient.

"Thank you for your business," Anne said as she gestured me closer to the door.

I did my best to not drop the slime-covered jar as I held it forward. My arms weren't able to extend all the way before old greedy fingers clutched it. No more words were exchanged before the door was slammed shut and the chains replaced.

This was Anne's cue to leave, and I along with her. Rubbing my hands on my tarping, I glanced down at her while she checked through the money again. Flipping coins through her fingers, almost as if they were toys with no value.

"Is that O.M.?" My voice was low. If I was going to live here, I needed to know the slang involved. She pulled my hand open and dropped the coins there. Both hands were necessary to hold the amount.

Studying the them, I recognized some. There were Polish coins in a rich brassy color, U.S. dimes that were green and tarnished, Norway, Russia, and Arabic coins colored my hand in metallic tones. A few were not known to me, one with a unique hole in the center and one with two flowers as the primary symbol. A part of me couldn't deny that I was grateful for reading in the Razum.

"How do you know what's valuable? Am I holding a lot, or a little?" While I couldn't remember their actual values, I was sure the people of Sila didn't know them either. Anne took the coins back and poked through them as we made our way back to the busier streets.

"Old money is sorted by color. Bones are three shinies, four brassies. Organs bigger than my fist are twelve shinies and eight brassies. Three brassies make up a shiny. Most people don't pay with O.M., only some around here." She hid the money under her shirt where there was likely a hidden pocket.

If I recalled right, there were seven 'shinies' and twenty-three 'brassies' along with five golden looking coins. With the sale of a lung, it was likely more expensive, so the more golden looking coins were more valuable.

"So a lung is around five golds, twelve shinies, and eight brassies?" Anne was apparently impressed with my understanding of the money. She nodded excitedly as we cut through the lessened crowd of the center street.

We darted past and dodged people as we made our way back towards the Den. Giving the Harveys' a wide air of caution, we quickly left the central street. Anne showed me how to find the door back into the tunnel and explained that there was a rope on the walls to help guide in the dark. It felt odd being trained by a child, but she had already shown her value and understanding. Before I knew it, we were back in the Den and handing the money to Vykra.

While I was being given a new jar with new directions and payment standards, I couldn't help but notice Gregory. He sat outside the door of

Tyron's room and watched the surgery hall like a guard. LEDs scanning the room continuously. There was a group of girls that stepped far out of their way to avoid the machine. Even Anne seemed to shy away under his watchful gaze.

Once the instructions and new organ were received, I stopped Anne from leaving immediately. There were plenty of orders to be run, but a part of me felt guilty. With Gregory sitting in the main room, it seemed to unnerve the kids. A Drone that many of them associated with death and pain was watching as they conducted semi-illegal activities. It would be better if I softened their feelings towards him for their own good, and maybe Gregory's.

"Do you girls fear Gregory?"

Her quick head nod signified she returned to her child-like state once back in the Den. She was examining the machine with slightly fearful eyes. Though, much like the child she was, there was curiosity. Anne reminded me of being a kid with that ever quizzical nature.

"Do you wanna meet him? He's scary, but... he's also a friend. Gregory won't hurt anyone who isn't trying to hurt me and my brother." I shifted the new and even more disgusting jar to one arm, extending the other to the small child. Her hesitant hand gripped a few of my fingers as I led her over to Gregory.

When he saw us, the LEDs almost brightened. Slowly, he stood up, trying to make as little noise as possible. He seemed to be aware of the impact he had on the Den and was doing his best to not cause anymore caution around him. This was the most respectful I had ever seen him.

"Gregory, this is Anne. Anne, this is Gregory 235. He's like a grumpy old man." Gregory did not seem as amused by my comparison as I was, but I also didn't have to care about his opinion. I gestured with my head for Gregory to interact with the girl. In an almost polite fashion, he knelt on the ground and extended a hand as he tried to create eye contact.

"Hello, Anne." Waiting for a response or the acceptance of his hand, Gregory froze in place.

As if she summoned every professional fiber in her body that was trained by Vykra, Anne stepped forward from my side and accepted his hand. Though as she finished shaking the hand, her small fingers picked at the metal on his gloves. As she felt the plates of his forearm, there was a new fascination. She was like a small scrapper with the way she investigated the machinery that made up his limbs.

In the bright LEDs that looked to me for aid, I saw confusion and almost a bit of fear. I suppose he likely only dealt with hurting children and had no real reason to have a positive interaction with one. Now that he was Fritzing though, he had to be open to new experiences. Well, that will be my argument if he tries to fight me on this.

Gregory attempted to stand and get away from the investigating fingers of Anne, but she maintained a firm grip. Her feet dangled off the ground, still grasping to his forearm plate. She let out a giggle that seemed to shush the entire surgery hall. I could feel many eyes watching this situation, just like I had wanted.

While I typically valued quiet and secretive moments in interactions, I knew it would do us better to be liked in the Den. Gregory was a sore thumb that I would have to cover for, but getting the girls to like him would ease the tension we all felt. I was mostly sure he wouldn't hurt the kids. I was also mostly sure he knew the consequence of getting us kicked out.

As Anne giggled and Gregory looked for a peaceful way out of the situation, more of the girls gathered around. Pitiful eyes glowed at me while the girls slowly gathered and touched his panels. There were ways I could help him, but for once, it was nice watching him be unsure of a situation. A significant form of retaliation for all the traps he had led me into.

He was quickly mobbed by friendly and curious hands when it was realized that he couldn't do much to stop them. Anne was removed from his arm by one of the older girls, but still picked and prodded Gregory's leg plates. I could see a few of the older girls picking at his back plates. It wasn't until I saw a tool appear that I intervened.

"Don't take him apart. We still need his help." My words calmed the curious girls' more aggressive hand motions. The taller girl that I directed my statement to held up her hands. In gore covered fingers, she held a screwdriver. Her face held no ill intent, but curiosity.

"It just looked like something was locking up his plates. I was gonna try to fix it." She had the voice of an adult, likely from breathing the toxic fumes of the city. Her face was that of someone roughly sixteen. Still a child and already willing to help fix complicated machinery. These kids were more resourceful than most Scrap Dogs I had known.

"Let her try to fix it. My plates have been stuck for years. A screwdriver won't break anything on me." Gregory's words were the answer to the teen. Her eyes still watched me for permission, as if Gregory were my possession. I nodded my permission to her.

With the help of a few other girls, they pried open the panel slightly. The old Drone did his best to sit up and loosen the positioning of the plate for their small hands. Scratching metal noises could be heard. A hammer appeared soon and echoed through the hall. All eyes were now on this interaction and after casting a glance over my shoulder, I saw Vykra watching as well.

My pestering of Gregory to relax the tension in the Den turned into a focus point now. It was a new tension. Would the teen fix Gregory, or break him? Would he be aggressive over a failed attempt, or grateful for its success? Many questions wordlessly drifted through the silent surgery hall. It was the first time I had heard it so quiet.

A loud ping rattled the plates of the tin basement, attracting my eyes back to Gregory. The girls stood clear as Gregory stretched. Plates sliding and moving, he modeled the plates to give him more height, then to make himself more compact and shorter. In his compact form, he was only seven feet tall. After a few more flexes of his plates, he seemed satisfied with the repair.

"This was stuck between his plate joints, locking up his movements." The teen held up a broken knife blade, rusted and ancient. Gregory claimed and examined the broken blade, likely trying to remember when he encountered it last. With an unamused tossing of the blade, he mimicked a shrug.

"That could have been there from Raiders decades ago. The repairs are appreciated." That was as close as Gregory was going to get to thanking the Den girls. Which, surprisingly, was enough as they cheered. The Den roared back to life as the girls laughed and poked at Gregory more. He finally sat down reluctantly for the smaller girls to feel his face plates.

Half babbled questions were bouncing around as they all theorized how he worked. They would try to lift his arms, though they were unable because of the sheer weight of the metal he was made of. Seeing their frustration, he would move his limbs according to their requests as they examined him. He would correct them if they guessed wrong, but he didn't volunteer the genuine answers, which only provoked the girls to think harder and examine more.

After a few minutes of watching him get tormented by children, I noticed Anne making her way back to me. A thrilled grin accompanying her. She cast one more glance back at Gregory before fixing her eyes on Vykra and nodding her intention to leave on delivery. Her small hand found mine that wasn't holding a jar of befoul liquid and led me back to the hidden exit.

We continued with our delivery, out the hidden door and across town. I followed Anne's lead as we finished another errand. Once back to the Den, we were sent on another errand. Anne led, I followed, and Vykra organized. My new position as a cog in their Organ Den machine was simple and a relaxing change of pace from my life or death situations of late.

The day passed quickly. Gregory and I were invited to eat with the girls in a separate food hall off of the surgery room. While Vykra and I ate together in silence, our entertainment was watching the girls explain flavors to a Drone. By the time dinner was finished, I noticed Gregory had been distracted enough that some girls carved their initials into his back plates. It seemed best to leave him unaware for now.

Once dinner was over and Gregory pulled himself from the children, we returned to our room. Pulling the wall lock away from the door, we quickly entered and Gregory took up a protective seat, blocking the door.

Sealed away from the world and plunged into this self created darkness was oddly welcoming.

Checking over Tyron, I noticed a slight fever developing. I treated it the best I could, but it was expected. His body would have to recover from a lot and fight off any infection on its own. Instead of worrying, I took my place on the bed next to him and fell asleep near instantly.

When morning came and the wake up call from Vykra's loud knocking woke me, I started another day of errands. There was little different from this and the prior. We ran errands, talked with the girls, and occasionally checked on Tyron in between runs.

Why did waiting always feel like an eternity? All I wanted to do was talk to my brother and get him caught up in the world. Gregory had informed me it was likely going to be a slow recovery and to focus on the deliveries. No amount of focusing on a job could make the time tick faster. So, I let the days roll by.

Another day, another list of errands. Anne and Vykra were trusting my work, allowing me to run the money by myself. Eventually, I could even run errands by myself. The daily tasks of dodging the progressively aggressive Harvey units, running grotesque jars of various organs, collecting 'used' jars, and collapsing on my bed, was becoming a monotonous life.

Day three was rolling around. Tyron still wasn't awake. His fever was coming and going, but there were no signs of cognitive function yet. Gregory's patience with the matter was slowly becoming infuriating. I knew he was aware of the chances that Tyron wouldn't wake up again, or that he would succumb to his injuries from surgery, so why did he choose to be patient? Maybe it was his age showing. Days probably felt like minutes to him.

A fourth day started. More errands, more frustration, more waiting. Gregory knew now that the girls were carving their initials into his plates, but didn't fight it. If my count was correct, he held the initials of every child in the Den and Vykra. His back plate and part of his chest were now almost completely covered in scratch marks. At least it would distinguish him from other Drones which would be useful if Harveys ever raided the

217

Den.

Today wasn't much different. Ran errands and gave the money to Vykra. Occasionally helping with equipment in the Den and mingling with the girls who were coming to respect my somewhat primitive ways of repair. While they were all very intelligent, I had years of life and death experience that taught me plenty about the old technology that was left in the world. My expertise was in Razums, though.

Now that Tyron was out, it felt weird working on other Razums. It was like they were now alien equipment that I knew a lot about, but there was no more attachment to the idea of them. Even seeing the bodies of dozens of Razum Born on the surgery tables didn't bother me like it once had. I suppose, after freeing my brother, there was no more reason to associate him with them.

Once my errands and tinkering for the day were finished, I took my dinner back to my room. My lack of patience made it difficult to endure the chaos of the girls. As I closed the door, I carefully found my way to the bed and sat beside it. Since he hadn't woken up in the past four days, I figured it was safe to light a candle to eat by.

Fidgeting with the matches in the dark, my eyes strained against the newly born flame. With the candle lit, the faint aroma of mechanical oil filled the room. Candles here were made from more chaotic ingredients, some of them nauseatingly close to the smell of rotting flesh. I tried to find the ones that smelt like machinery. That smell was at least more familiar in a less unsettling way. Gregory and Haldoklik were of a similar smell, one that I was now realizing felt like home.

After finishing my sparse meal of protein bars mixed with canned carrots and beets, I allowed my head to fall back as I embraced the tired frustration that was consuming me. So many years of waiting. I had assumed I could handle a few more days of waiting, but it was becoming a struggle when I didn't know if he would wake. It was beginning to feel like waiting for the dead to rise.

With his Razum removed and the ear coverings gone, there was more hesitation when speaking around him. I didn't want to wake him, but

I desperately wanted to talk to him. He needed this rest after such an extensive surgery and his mind likely needed to adjust to its new reality. New senses were overwhelming what his brain was aware of. I would probably want to sleep too.

A quiet metal knock alerted me to Gregory lingering behind the door. He knew I wasn't in the best of moods these days and had been giving me space. Something I appreciated since he was often irritating me with his polite hopefulness. My silence towards his knock was the only invitation I felt like offering.

His shadowy form blocked most of the light from the hall beyond before it was quickly extinguished. The grinding of metal echoed through the silent room, fighting the candle's flickering noise that had turned into the ambient sound of my mind. A metal shoe nudged me playfully. Or to check if I was awake. Either option could have been his intention.

"Has he woken up yet?" His whispering speaker hissed in the dark like some feral cat.

"No. It's been four days. Shouldn't he have woken up by now?" I felt like Gregory was the only one I could talk to about this. Vykra had a strong silence order on the topic of Tyron, including his name. This room was the only safe spot to talk.

"This has never happened before. Your guess is as good as mine right now. His body has undergone a lot. It's just a slow recovery while he heals." Gregory's logic was as irritating as normal. Though he was likely correct, I only wanted to be told it was going to be alright. I guess it was foolish to expect a Drone experiencing human emotions for the first time to pick up on that.

"What if he didn't fully come out? What if it was just a ghost?" My mind was swirling with fear. Talking about it didn't help, waiting wasn't better. I just wanted answers. Was Tyron alive? Was he of some conscious mind? Did he actually leave the Razum or did we kill his mind when we removed it?

"Taylor?" The voice came from behind my head, causing me to whirl around. Tyron's eyes were vaguely open, but his mouth was posed differently now. This was the first time he has moved something in four days.

"Sounds like your ghost just woke up." There was a sarcastically victorious tone in Gregory's speaker. Likely mocking my feelings and proving his logic was correct. I ignored his words as I stood up and looked over at my brother for another sign of alertness.

"Tyron? Are you in there?" My voice was probably too quiet for him, but I didn't want to wake him if it was just a dream. Still, if it was just him dreaming, speaking and familiar names showed signs of coherence. His lips moved, slowly figuring out what the feeling of vocal chords was. He was learning his voice.

"Where–am I?" Tyron was awake, aware, and questioning. His mind was still there. Relief flooded through my worrisome thoughts. I grabbed his hand, willing comfort through mine to his.

"You're here. You're with me. We're safe. You've been gone for a long time." I tried to keep my sentences short. Though I had meant to say only one phrase, more fell out of my mouth. Overwhelming him with so much information or complicated sentences might stress his mind more than intended.

"No, you—" My heart fell down the pit of guilt I kept sealed. His last memories of me were years ago, leaving him alone in the Razum. This was the moment I had waited for. A chance to apologize to him after twelve years of tormenting myself over that one decision.

"I know I left. Sorry doesn't even begin to explain how I feel. I've regretted that day for so many years, but I'm here now. We're finally together again and I will never leave you again."

"Where... were you?" His tone was attempting a joking vibe, but the question was still hauntingly real. While he was mimicking forgiveness, it was a question that deserved an answer.

"I'm sorry. I tried to get back to you as quickly as I could. I just... didn't know how." The lack of preparation I had for this conversation astounded me. Years of rehearsing what I would say had all gone out the window. I was paralyzed with fear and guilt. Did he hate me? Would he no longer see me as his sister? Had I fought for so many years for someone who actually hated and rejected my existence now?

"What happened?" Tyron's question only added more to my quickly fumbling and guilt-tripping mindset. Though as I watched him speak, the color was leaving his cheeks. A pallor was consuming his body and eyes were losing focus. It wasn't time to have this conversation.

We must have woken him with our talking. As much as I wanted to explain myself and to spend time with him, I would not risk his life for my own emotional greed. When Gregory looked at me, I knew he was aware as well. Tyron needed to go back to sleep for a while longer.

"That...is a very long story that I will tell you later. You need to rest more. You're going pale. I promise I will try to answer all of your questions in time." It felt like a pathetic excuse, but his eyes closed before I finished my sentence.

The silence that filled the room was oddly deafening. If that was the last chance I had to talk to him, I would regret the words I said. I should have told him how much I loved him. There should have been words of happiness and victory over death. So why did it feel like I was slapping a band-aid on our relationship and sending him back to sleep? There was no guarantee that he was going to wake up again, or that I would have a chance to fix what I had broken so many years ago.

"I can hear your processes from here. There will be more chances to speak to him in the future. During the day, I will stay with him in case he wakes up again. At night you can watch over him while I help around the Den. This is a success, Taylor. Accept it for what it was." Gregory's whispers yet again frustrated me. I knew he was right, but being corrected was never my best skill.

A nod of understanding seemed to suffice as he sat against the door, locking it for the night. While my mind fought my body's intentions of sleep, exhaustion won the war. At some point, from behind closed eyes, I felt Gregory set me on the bed. He was a mystery for another day. ✿ ✿ ✿

In the morning, Tyron was still sleeping and breathing. I bid farewell to him and Gregory before starting another day of tasks. Day five did not differ from four. A girl named Tricia ventured out with me today, learning the ways of deliveries instead of surgeries. She was likely around twelve or thirteen, almost up to my shoulder.

While we walked the streets in search of a new house to deliver to, she told me about her life. Another story of being abandoned at a door, raised mostly by Vykra, and a dangerous level of loyalty to the Den. These girls were bonded to the Den, not only in service, but as a home. While I saw it as a gross and diseases filled dungeon of human depravity, these girls knew nothing better than the warmth of that dingy basement and consistent food. I hated to admit it, but they probably were living a better childhood than any Loomer City could offer them.

The delivery was smooth, besides a vague threat and an attempt to steal the organ for sale, but that was normal. Tricia seemed to have a good understanding of the process. She did most of the talking for me. While we walked away, I took a moment to examine the wealthier district.

There were plenty of beautiful buildings and clean walkways, but I noticed a distinct circle around a warehouse looking building. Everything seemed to stay away from it, the buildings and people alike. The tin building was fairly clean and seemed mostly unused. Even the mud in front of the door was smoothed.

"What's that place?" I resisted the urge to point as the street was becoming more congested. Tricia followed my glance and her face lost its usual curious and life-filled glow.

"It's the Drone server building. If I were you, I would stay far away from it." She stepped away from the building as she spoke and started her way back to the Den.

I had never heard of a Drone server building before. There were networks that were shared between Drones or Giants but they were not used for communication beyond warrant notices and to be aware of other Giants in the area. If Sila had a server building, that meant they were monitoring a lot of information. There was a good chance it was a complicated ledger of everything that was happening here. From the Organ Den deliveries to the birth and death of the lowliest slum dwellers.

Far more advanced than Haldoklik, though, it made sense with the few hundred that lived here.

Once we were back on the main street, Tricia and I parted ways as I was going to another delivery directly. We could afford to lose an organ or two as needed, but payment was not to be lost at any cost. As Tricia left to bring the payment to Vykra, I moved on to the next delivery.

The walk was boring and lonely; the delivery was no different. Gregory would likely have many things to talk about, or even Anne, but left to my own, it was just a silent walk through town. With no reason to linger or walk longer on my own, I made my way back to the Den.

Following the dark tunnel ropes back into the depths of the Den, I heard an impatient metal tapping. Tricia's voice echoed up the dark tunnel while Gregory's vibrated the rope I held. Something was going on.

Light was shining at the base of the tunnel where the hidden door should have been covered. In the glow was a tall figure, which was obviously Gregory, and a smaller figure, who I assumed was Tricia. When I was close enough to be heard, they both perked up.

"Taylor, Tyron was awake a while ago. I was just about to send Tricia to find you." Gregory's words brought an extra burst of hope to my steps. Which was a mistake as I stumbled over another fragment of metal lodged in the ground. This stumble earned me a chuckle from Tricia as I staggered down the last of the steep tunnel and stood near Gregory.

"Did he talk?"

Gregory nodded.

"What did he talk about?"

There was hesitation in his response. I guessed that was his way of trying to avoid the topic. He knew to be gentle with Tyron's mind, but eventually he would have to learn about the world. Gregory was the best source of history, with the least amount of social skills. Whatever he said, it would have been informational and not aggressive.

"He asked about the world. I gave him some history…although he reacted emotionally to some of the information. Tyron did eventually calm down and fell back asleep. I wanted to notify you about it as soon as possible."

Gregory was trying to hide Tyron's panic, which was admirable, but I would rather know the state of his mind.

"Okay. Tricia, can you run the rest of the deliveries today? I want to stay here for a while to make sure everything is okay." The eager teen was already nodding and agreeing before I could justify my concern. Out of all the places we could have ended up, I was beginning to be grateful for landing here.

Gregory and I found our way back to the room and reclaimed our own sentry like positions. We waited, we watched, but he remained asleep. After a few hours, Gregory left to retrieve food for me. Once I had some food in me, we returned to waiting.

A few hours passed and Tyron woke up again. There were many tearful words and exchanged love. I wanted to remember everything I had said, but my mind was overwhelmed by joy. My brother was back. He loved me and missed me. I hadn't been a failure to him. Even Gregory seemed to enjoy our conversations as we relived history. He questioned his world and the things he heard in his 'sleep'.

We talked about The Scientist and Gern, my experiences and Gregory. I never realized how much I needed to hear my brother ask about my life. It was like, for the first time, someone actually cared about what I had experienced. Though there were a few times where my stories seemed to appall him, he said nothing negative. He didn't judge my actions but purely listened to a life that was lived alongside his.

It was Tyron who finally sent me to bed after hours of talking through the night. I had lost so much time with him and regretted none of it. He was slowly getting caught up, and he seemed happy to be here. That was all I wanted. While we tried to keep things about the Razum quiet, I knew he would ask about it soon.

As Gregory passed me while leaving the room, he patted my shoulder encouragingly. I could feel the relaxation of my soul soothe my muscles and anxieties. He seemed to be very aware of my change of personality just by looking at me.

While I was going to find a bunk with one of the girls for the night to allow Gregory and Tyron to talk, Tricia was the one who found me first. She looked groggy, as if she was woken against her will. My own tired face probably resembled her own.

"Vykra is sending you out. It's cold out-" Her words were interrupted by a very exhausted yawn. "Jar is by the door. House is the one next to our delivery yesterday. They overheard us and ordered their own, demanding it for this morning."

There was no doubt that I was getting extremely tired and needed rest, but Tricia ran all the errands for me yesterday. I owed her this early morning run, even if the idea of leaving the Den sounded like the exact opposite thing my body wanted. Her green eyes were bleary as she waited for my response.

"Go back to bed. I'll take care of it now."

With a silent smile, she returned to her room while I found my way through the dark hall. The hidden door was difficult to find in the darkened corner, but my fingers found the edge. Grabbing the jar and quietly sneaking out the door, I started on another delivery.

The morning was still dark, the sun not even coloring the sky with its intrusion. I was trotting my way through the dim streets towards the wealthy district. Though as I was walking, I peaked into the main street. There was an odd lacking of Drones.

Even if the Harvey units were recalled, there should still be routine Gregory or Markus patrols. Perhaps I was lucky and walking in between shift changes, though it seemed unlikely. I kept my eyes peeled in the eerily empty street as I took hesitant steps.

It was equally likely that a fight had broken out nearby and the Drones were correcting the situation. There were multiple reasons the street could be empty. I had to remember that I just came from the Den and nothing was amiss. My worry was trained, not rational. So, I continued on my way as I ignored the odd dread building in my chest.

This walk felt oddly longer in the darkened world. The warm red street lights only lulled me further into the tired stagger I was maintaining. I had to stretch my eyes open to see clearly. An early morning fog was wafting through the alleys.

Subtle morning sounds could be heard within the buildings. Life was starting up for the day, slowly, but surely. There were distant sounds of people talking, occasional knocking on metal doors. The loud whistle of the morning shift of the factories echoed over the working city. Soon these streets would be teeming with life, so where were the Drones?

I made my way to the requested house and knocked. A delayed grunt and slow opening of the door told me I woke the owners. Gnarled and elderly, a hand extended from the door clutching a handful of O.M. When I accepted the money and began counting it, a beady face peeked at me.

"You're old for the Den."

It was a phrase I had received multiple times. There was no longer a reason trying to defend myself or even explain. Once I was sure of the amount given to me would satisfy Vykra, I offered the jar forward. The old hand reached for it when a sound froze us both.

There were dozens of guns being fired at once, or large guns being fired consistently. Something was happening and my anxiety was justified. A Drone raid was going on and not that far away from us. My hair prickled at the sound of each bullet. They weren't electric guns; they were Harvey guns.

The old man stole the jar from my hands before quickly slamming the door closed and locking multiple bolts and chains. I envied the door he put between himself and the gun sounds. It was a noise that ricocheted through the pit that Sila sat in.

I needed to get back to the Den, quick.

My feet were running before I had even assessed where the noise was coming from. It was near the Den; I knew that much, but that didn't mean it was the Den. With no Drones in the street, I could run as fast as I wanted. Citizens noticing me was negligible compared to Drones noticing me.

As I drew towards the middle of the main street, I saw smoke rising in the distance and a rugged and limping girl heading towards me. Once I was close enough to see her clearly, I recognized her as Tricia. There was blood coloring her leg as she sped up to meet me.

"Don't go that way! The Den got raided!" I caught the crying girl in my arms as I looked at the smoke in the distance. It was emanating from the alley that the Den's main entrance hid in. The building was being consumed by flames.

Chapter 9: Blinded

The stones were cold today. They were always cold, but today—colder. The fake sun, that stupid, stupid sun, wasn't pretending anymore. Not warm. Never warm. Why did I think it would be? I could hear the crunching trash beneath me—always that crunch—poking into my skin as I rolled over and hugged My Taylor. Tight. Tight, because she's all I had left.

She coughed. My child sister, breaking apart, crumbling like everything else. Her programming, falling away like the world around us. She'd leave me, too, soon. Go. Gone. I'd be alone. Again. Always alone. But not for much longer. I'd fix it. I had to. My fingers were caught in her hair. Blonde. But not real. Not real. If she were real, would her hair still be this long? Or would she have cut it? Short, maybe. Rebellious like she was. Always was. I tried to see her like she would've been if I hadn't lost her.

If I hadn't—if I had—

"She's probably dead." The words fell out, clanging in the silence. Dead. Everything was dead. My Taylor stirred, her questioning eyes looking at me like they always did. Or did they? Did they ever? Was she even looking?

"Who's dead, Tyron?" Her hand—so small, so warm—pressed against my face. My face. My face that she used to love. She was always obsessed with my face, wasn't she? Always touching it like it was some mystery. But she was the mystery. She wasn't real, though. Not anymore. Not since—

"Everyone, My Taylor. Everyone is dead. Even you." I whispered it, but it felt like I screamed it. Maybe I did. Her hand felt warm, but I knew better. As always, I knew. I'd known for too long. I should have turned this place off months ago. Should have. But I didn't. Couldn't. Some part of me—hope?—hope. No, that's not real either.

"No one's coming. No one's out there." I muttered, louder now. Or was it? The words echoed around me, or maybe they didn't. The sensors of the world weren't working. "You're dead, Taylor. Out there. Alone. And it's my fault. I didn't save you."

My Taylor didn't answer this time. She just turned and lay back down. Fading. Fading like she always did, fading like everything did. I tried to hold her tighter, but I couldn't. My arms slipped through her. She wasn't there. Never was.

"Sorry. I'm so sorry. I blamed you. I yelled at you. I—" The tears burned, or maybe it was just the cold. The cold from the stones. The cold from her absence. Too many regrets. Too many things I couldn't fix. I didn't want to die with them. But I would. I should.

"It's okay, T-T-Tyron. I kn-n-n-ow I should have stayed with you." Her voice glitched, breaking apart with the world. Her words made little sense. Nothing made sense. Nothing ever did.

"No. No, no, no. It was never your job. I was supposed to protect you. I was supposed to—" My words couldn't be finished. Breathing felt like a lie. This place—it was paradise once. I used to believe that. Taylor never did. Why didn't she? Why couldn't she just stay? Stay with me. We could've been happy. Always learning more, always being more.

She flickered again. My arms went right through her. Gone. Gone like always. Like before.

"Don't leave me! Don't you leave me again!" I screamed it now, or maybe I didn't. Maybe it was just in my head, where the screaming always was. "Please. Please. I can't—"

But she was already gone. The kill switch. I hit it. I hit it and she was gone. The world was shutting down. And I'd be alone. Again. Alone with this anger, this burning, boiling, roiling rage that never stopped.

The trash rustled beneath me as I thrashed. My body didn't want to be here. My mind didn't want to be here. But here I was. Here I would be. Even the sun with its broken light would fade before me. Maybe with me. I was the god here, or gods? I was already dead, though. God of death.

The silence. The damnable silence. I made the silence come. I hit the switch. I turned off the sound of life. I can't do this anymore. I can't. Fallen from the heavens because I didn't take her hand.

I couldn't take her hand — My hands didn't work—

Give up. There was nothing more to do. For me to do. I tried to call out to her. My words were trapped. Trapped like me. That's why I flipped the switch. My switch. Nothing more than a machine. I had become like a machine.

"You left me, or I left you? Do you think about me? Do I think about me anymore? Is it just you in my mind now? Have I lost me?" There was no more echo in my words. The world couldn't bounce my thoughts back to me anymore. Maybe they never did bounce?

Was I the only one left bouncing now? Did I turn the world off outside, too? Answers. I wish I had answers. Why? How? When? Did those questions even matter? When did the questions become answers, or were the questions there after the answers were given? I used to be here, but now there is no me. A shell. Nothing more than a shell.

There was pain now. Pain. I never had known pain. Feeling pain had never known me. Or was it not pain? Was I becoming this pain? It lurks in my chest. It spreads up my neck. Was it agony? Not agony. It was real. There was no reality anymore. My eyes were closed. Or were they open, and the world was dark? Maybe there were never eyes?

"Tyron."

A voice–there were no voices here. Now there was? It's not real. The voice was not there. My mind is going with the sun. A dark place. Has there been light? No voice, no light. There is no more.

No more anymore.

"I've missed you so much."

Not words in my world, there were never words in my world. Never. These words couldn't be. Could not. They sounded kind, like her kindness. She was dead, though. Not her words.

"Though you're not with me now, I know you'll recognize my voice."

Voice? I know you? I have known no one. It's been too long. There are no more. Never was anymore. Maybe Taylor? Was Taylor the voice that was real now? My mind rolled with my body to face the dark sky. Maybe it was bright? Reality wasn't real to me anymore.

"I've been the one telling you stories and keeping you company for the past twelve years, the sanity in your solitude. But now, I need something from you."

The voice I had heard in my dreams. I have heard this before. The voice and the dreams. It had haunted me many nights. My Taylor was created when I heard this voice. The voice of who Taylor was. Could it be–was Taylor, my sun, returned?

"It's time to leave that world behind and join me here. Make the choice to be with me in this life. If you can hear me, brace yourself and let go of that lonely world."

Disconnect? I already disconnected. Reality. It's no longer there. How can she say I need to let go? She needs to let go. Loneliness, though. I was lonely. All alone. Could she be out there? Or am I out there? Is this really my sister who has been long gone?

"I'm here to save you, as I always have been. Please… wake up."

I heard the tears, though I could not see her. My eyes couldn't see her. The pokey trash tried to scratch me as I faced the sky above, or the air above? There was no sky anymore. No more air.

There was nothing to lose listening to the voice. The voice of Taylor. The world was already leaving. Gone. Taylor wasn't gone, though. Not anymore. Even if it's not Taylor, they cried. If they cry, they must care. I could leave here, maybe even cry with them. No one should suffer. Suffering sucks.

Taylor left me, though. I hadn't–I didn't–Her hand had gone from me. She left me. Alone here. My sister never came for me. Countless dreams begging her too. It wasn't her job to find me, I was supposed to find her, but I couldn't. What if she leaves me again? Or what if this is the hand I never took? Too many questions, not enough answers. Confusion wrapped around my brain, or was my brain was wrapping the confusion?

What time is it? Or was it? How long has it been? Time moves chaotically.

Taylor was timeless. Maybe I am timeless. My thoughts were tumbling, my skull was rattling. Time didn't matter here. Did it matter to Taylor? Was she old now? I guess I could leave to know. I was already leaving. Stopping by… it could be fun.

The world was falling away, like many of my dreams, where I heard voices. Would those voices be where Taylor is? I had heard many, many, many voices over the many, many, many nights. I heard a 'Gregory', I heard a 'Scientist'. Hearing was a wonderful skill. So many frequencies. So many vibrations to understand.

I wonder if the 'Scientist' knew about vibrations. We could talk about so much. My Taylor was never into science like I was. Back in the day. Such a long ago day. Stimulation was what my mind needed. I can feel the tears in my thoughts, such crooked thoughts. There were no longer patterns. I knew there needed to be patterns. Does 'Gregory' know about patterns? Maybe we can learn about more patterns.

Darkness now came for me. Inky, dark hands were dragging me down to the maw of my choices. Maw of my monsters. I had one regret. The regret that beats all regrets. My eyes wanted to see Taylor again. Only seconds more. Her childish face, her warm hands, the kindness within.

"I want to see my Taylor again."

The darkness faded, running away from me. Maybe it was brightness now? My eyes burned. Burning. The light was there now, not the darkness. There was a light that blinded me. What are these and why do I feel pain? I can't see anymore. Maybe I never saw before. There are shadows around me, tall scary shadows in the silent sky above me. The light was so bright.

My eyes adjusted, but the pain etched itself across my chest. A scream? Did I scream or breathe too hard? The shadows shuffled. I think I screamed and scared them. Why did I scream? Were these shadows real? Was I now real? Was I not real before? Were answers standing before my questions now?

"Tyron!" The voice! This was the voice. My long companion in my dreams. The reason for my logic. The last stand of my mind. Was this my Taylor? Did I finally–at last–take the hand of my sweet Taylor? I demand my eyes focus! Let me see if my mind eludes me again.

"Taylor, give him a moment. He has never been awake before." This voice was an old friend. He has been around for a long time. The voice of 'Gregory'. Although, did he–did he say–

"Tyron, it's me!" There was a warm hand on my face. The same warmth that was my only companion through years of silence and the only reason there were threads of my mind left. My arm did not work. All it wanted to do was to hold the hand on my face, but it moved. My hand levitated on ghost muscles.

"Don't move. We will put you to sleep for a while longer. We can talk when you wake up. I swear, I will not leave your side again." The sweet Taylor voice. Now I know the stories I heard. My sanity was still with me. Kind of. I had not been truly alone. Never was truly alone. Eyes burned again. Was it the light? No. This was the burn of tears. I had never felt this pain before. The water glided down like an avalanche.

"Tay–lor." Was that my voice? So gruff. So rough. My throat vibrated uncomfortably. Have I ever truly spoken before? My voice feels covered in dust. It didn't seem to scare the shadows over me. They must be brave. Eyes trying to focus. Never focusing.

Large shadow, bigger than all the others. It was like a mountain above me. It was lowering something to my face. Something blurry. Was this mountain a friend? Was this mountain going to crumble on me?

"It's nice to finally meet you, Tyron. Rest. We will have all the time to talk later." This mountain was 'Gregory'. The voice was metal. Like the Watchers. Cold metal. The words were friendly. Warm like Taylor's.

"Greg-" It was as far as my dusty voice would try to make it. If these voices were here, maybe the 'Scientist' was too. So long ago did I hear his voice. He was smart, smarter than me.

The mountain above me stopped moving. I could see the shadows talking to one another. The words were not vibrating to me, though. Mountains moved, and the blurry thing was placed on my face. The world fell again. Maybe I was falling? Either way, the voices were here. I was here too.

✧   ✧   ✧

Dreams. Always dreams. Not now though. There was darkness. Maybe the reality I thought I had joined was the dream? No. The warmth was genuine. My mind was broken, but not broken enough to forget that. The warmth was Taylor's.

This was quiet sleeping. I could feel a hand. It never left. I could feel a voice. It couldn't be heard. No dreams, but I felt a reality. In this reality, there was pain. So much pain. I focused on reality, afraid to turn my mind from these truths. Reality brought pain. It also brought warmth.

Was I awake? Maybe I've always been awake. Time made just as little sense here as it did where I was. Had it been a day, or a week? When did I last hear voices? There was still a hand in mine. A warm hand.

My world shook itself into a new reality as a blinding light appeared. I was awake. I knew I was awake. The feeling of sureness was weird, awkward. Could this truly be a reality for me? My eyes didn't want it to be. They clenched shut against the light.

Voices drew me out of my awkwardness. These were the voices that drifted in and out while I slept. Or was I awake in my sleep? Still so many questions. Maybe the voices held the answers. Maybe I was my own answer.

"Has he woken up yet?" This was Gregory's voice. The metal mountain man.

"No. It's been four days. Shouldn't he have woken up by now?" This was the warm voice. The voice belongs to Taylor. Didn't she know? Didn't she know I was awake?

"This has never happened before. Your guess is as good as mine right now. His body has undergone a lot. He is probably just recovering." The metal mountain seemed smart. I like the metal mountain. Maybe we could be friends? He seemed to be friends with Taylor's voice. Such a quiet conversation. No need to whisper anymore.

"What if he didn't fully come out? What if it was just a ghost?" Scared. She was scared now. Did I make her feel scared? Was she worried? She never used to worry. Never worried about anything.

I didn't want her to worry. She was much more brave than that. My sweet Taylor. I am real now. I am here with you. My voice is weak, but I know you will hear me.

"Taylor?" Why was this a question? Should it have been a question? Maybe I should have just said hello. I suppose this could be someone else. The warmth was the same, though. It had to be her.

I tried to open my eyes. Still blurry. Maybe I was blind now. I could be fine with that as long as the warmth of Taylor is still there. The mountain stood in the light that blinded me. Blinking the light out of my eyes, it was less blurry. Maybe I wasn't blind now.

"Sounds like your ghost just woke up." The mountain of shadow moved towards me. I felt chased. Such a gigantic creature of shadow. There was now a smaller shadow. It was much shorter than the mountain. It came close to me. Something smelled warm, sweaty. The hand in my hand told me this was my Taylor. My real Taylor.

"Tyron? Are you in there?" The vibrations. Her words caused vibrations to ripple through me. These were actual words. Where was I? I thought I was here.

"Where–am I?" Needed to know. I need to know where I was. Or if I was. Taylor left me once. Left me to rot. One time. A time long ago. Was this her? Could this be her? Was the mountain a man? Was I even alive?

"You're here. You're with me. We are safe. You have been gone for a long time."

Lies. I have always been here. It was she who left. She left. She was the one who disappeared, not me. Gone. Gone long ago. And yet here I am, still. The warmth faded from her hand—or maybe it was never there. This wasn't My Taylor. My Taylor wouldn't say things like that. My Taylor was a child. My Taylor was real, not this. She was my sister who left me. Left me alone. Alone and afraid.

"No, you—" My words felt weird. Felt foreign. Dusty voice. Old voice. Not my voice. This wasn't her voice either. Was that truly my Taylor's voice? No. I doubt it. She left. She's always leaving. Away. Maybe I was still dreaming. A nightmare that never ends.

"I know I left. I should never have left you. I've regretted that day for so many years, but I'm here now. We're finally together again." Water splashed on my hand. Or was it just cold? Were her words love or lies? She was the guiding voice in my dreams. She held me when my days were dark.

No. She left. Or I did?

No. It was her. I stayed. So she must have left. Where did she go?

"Where... were you?" Joking. Or was I? My lips made a smile. I think they did. They didn't feel right. Were they wrong? Was I wrong to ask? Was she wrong to not tell me?

"I'm sorry. I tried to get back to you as quickly as I could. I just... didn't know how." Words on deaf ears. What was I trying to achieve with my questions? Was I asking the wrong questions? She sometimes asked me questions when I slept. Her voice always called to me. She left, though.

I wanted to try again. Needed more sleep, but I wanted to try again. A better question. More answers.

"What happened?" To us? To her? To my world? To her world? Where was she, where has she been? So many questions. So many non-answers. I need answers. I need to solve these mysteries.

"That is a very long story that I will tell you later. You should probably rest more. You're going pale. I promise I will try to answer all of your questions in time." The blur, the shadow that moved near me. It moved closer. Too close. So close, I could see bigger details. Blonde hair. Not like My Taylor. This hair was whiter, more crispy. It looked pokey.

Such pretty braids, though. They were small. I couldn't see how far they went. Maybe to the ground, or the sky? Did my Taylor have braids now? No. My Taylor hated her hair. Always cutting it, hair everywhere. Always going shorter. My Taylor was gone. Her small hands. Gone. Her short hair. Gone. Her tiny face. Left me. Long ago.

Taylor's shadow was right, though. Or left? I felt tired. More tired than I had ever been. Or ever will be? Heavy body. Heavy eyelids. Heavy mind. Sleep would help. Sleep would always help. Or did it?

☼　　☼　　☼

Was it morning? No. It was night. Or was there no sky anymore? It was dark. So it must be night. Where was that stupid sun? Was it gone from here too? Was the world dark and cold? Was it hot? Taylor smelt warm. It must be hot.

Why am I cold? My body didn't move. It refused me. Taylor refused me. Frustrating. No body. No Taylor. Why did I choose this? Or did I not choose? Maybe part of me knew this would happen. I wanted to see Taylor again. And again. And again. My Taylor.

My Taylor was gone. I held her while she disappeared. My Taylor would never be seen again. New Taylor was here now. Did you know My Taylor? Would they have gotten along? Like old pals got along. She should meet My Taylor. Nothing was better than her small hands. My cold face, her small hands. Had I always been cold?

There was water on me. It felt colder. It burned my chest. Why did it burn? Water didn't burn. It was sweet. Still sweet. This reality burned. Fire and pain. Cold and wet. Was I drowning? No. At least I don't think so. Drowning in this reality?

Noises. Noises stirred. Not my noise in my head. These vibrations. Where were they? The darkness hid them. Noises like metal. Metal moving. Where was Taylor? Why wasn't she here? Why am I alone again?

"Are you awake?" The mountain's voice. Clear. I could hear his words clear. I could hear his noise as he moved. Creaking. Squeaking. Grinding. So metal for a man.

"I...think so." Voice, not mine. From me though. Taylor wouldn't recognize my voice. I didn't recognize her voice. Her voice left when she did. The Mountain named Gregory was here. His voice I knew. Friendly voice.

"I can call Taylor in, if you want. You should probably sleep more. Having gone through what you did, no one would mind if you slept." Sleep? More talk of sleep? I felt like a lifetime has passed. Passed me by. Sleep had left me. Like she did.

"Slept for a century..." Fragmented. I could do better. Am better. Gregory was smart, like me. Needed to do better. Friendly mountains were better than enemy mountains. The darkness was still. Quiet and still.

Where did the mountain hide?

"Where are you?" Better. Not great. Dusty cords didn't work right in this throat. So dry, but I still felt wet. I will be better. Better still. Even for my Mountain friend.

"The candles are out. You are struggling with extreme photo-sensitivity since you have never perceived actual light before. It will pass. I am next to the bed you are in. Can you move at all?"

Candles? I have not seen candles in a long time. Not since I was a child. We always had lights. Electricity coursing. Was that all gone? Was it never real? Have I been in a dream? No. Dreams don't let your sister leave you.

Could I move? Have I done that before? This body felt so heavy. Heavy like stone. Cold wet stone. A finger. I can move a finger. Maybe two? Now three. Pins and needles poked in my hand. Was the Mountain poking me with needles? No. Not my Mountain friend.

My hand was trying to fly! It was moving in the air. Slow, so slowly. Moving still. Flying in the night sky. No stars, there were never stars. I wanted to control the flying arm now. Reclaim it as mine. Away, I want to send the arm away from me to find the Mountain.

Flying recklessly. Finger pilots crashed into metal. Did I find the Mountain? Was the mountain made of solid metal? Watcher? Like the one that raised me?

"That's my leg. I am here to watch over you while you sleep. You have been fighting off a fever. It seems to have broken now. Taylor will be happy."

My fingers did their best to hold on to the metal leg. This was real. This was no hologram. Cold metal. Dusty. Real. I could hold on to reality now. Or I could try to. Was Taylor metal too? Was this a world of metal people? 'Taylor will be happy'. Would she be? Would she actually be happy? She had seemed so worried, so sad. Would I be able to make this Taylor happy?

No, it wasn't my job to help New Taylor. She left. Abandoned me. My Taylor was gone. I was alone. My hand flew back to me. Safe harbor was at my side. The Mountain was kind. Simply kind. Taylor was on his mind. Taylor seemed to be on his mind a lot.

"What happened?" The voice was working. My voice. I sounded real. Maybe this was a friendly voice? Still foreign. Still weird.

"That is a long story. Are you sure you're not tired?" The Mountain sounded like he was crumbling. The floor was crying against his weight. Big man. Big Mountain. He was sitting down. By my side. Or by the bed? When was the last time I laid on a bed? Trash has been my bed for too long. Memories of beds were fading.

"I'm not tired now." I couldn't sleep even if it tried to take me. So many questions. So many answers. Solve my mysteries Mountain man.

"Taylor may get mad at me for this. I think you deserve to know what's been happening for the past twelve years. Stop me if you don't understand things. I suppose I should start with the state of the world."

"Humans began destroying their world a few hundred years ago. They devastated their natural resources and were melting their world. To help in early efforts to save the planet, they built a new robot classification: Giant Class."

"These were programmed just to innovate and orchestrate a revival of the world. After a few years, and the creation of one hundred twenty-seven Giant Class robots in many countries, they had made no progress. The Giants then devised a new, collective plan: Build the next robot class."

"It took the Giants only a few days to create a robot that could function as a supercomputer and be able to compute twenty times the amount of information the Giants could. To house the amount of hardware they needed to make this massive machine, they created a body for the supercomputer to act with and change the environment with. Her name was Lexicon. Humans quickly nicknamed her Lexi. The first of the Loomer Class."

The Mountain's metal voice paused. The rattle of an old speaker. It clicked and popped as he spoke. Or did he speak? Was this metal man a Giant? Was he telling me about his powers? His power to change the world around me? Friend or foe?

"There were seven Loomers constructed originally. Lexi being the first, Hokuto was the second. Aleksandr, Haoyu, Ewald, Dae-Seong, and Zevida

239

were created by a joint effort between Lexi, Hokuto, and the aid of the Giants. Within two years, there was a new generation of robots. Within those same two years, they started the downfall of the humans."

Downfall? I never heard of a downfall. So many names. So much information. So many names. Giants. Loomers. Machines rule here now. The world is made of metal like mine was made of stone. Now my world was darkness and knowledge. I want more. More knowledge.

"How?" Simple voice. Simple question. So many answers to be given.

"How? They stomped out humanity. They were tall and strong, nothing the humans could do could damage them. The Loomers even crafted themselves in nightmarish designs to intimidate anyone who saw them from a distance. True perfection of machine, besides their physical limitations."

"They corrected their own programming and started building themselves up more. They controlled the Giants, which controlled the Drones. Unstoppable change. They even created the place you were raised in."

"Razums were developed to have a direct interface with the unused potential of the human brain. Networks were bounced between the Loomers and created the network you and Taylor were in."

"Humans who resisted were killed. Humans who surrendered were given the Razum to join the network and boost the processing power of the Loomers they were connected to. Millions were on the networks, and the Loomers built more of themselves. The Second Wave. The final destroyer models that crumbled the world to its last leg of life. Humans were enslaved to help the functions of the Loomers, the Giants were given regions to reign over to control those who tried to rebel, and the Loomers finished their destruction."

The Mountain went quiet. The darkness consuming his words. What a hungry maw the darkness has. More focus. My eyes could see the dim lights above me. Yellow, like tiny suns. Did the Mountain have suns for eyes?

Such tall robots, such a broken world. Broken. Broken and cold. I thought I had left the cold. The broken. Damn this Taylor. My Taylor would not have brought me to an unfriendly world.

Razum though. Why did my ears shake from that word? Why does that world rattle my core? Unsettled, uneasy. Have I heard this word before? Why does a metal tang claw my teeth?

"Razum?" Was that right? Was that the word my throat was trying to refuse? Did the Mountain hold the answers for me?

Silence. My question met the silence of a mountain. Wrong word? Did the mountain lie with his words? Was this not the actual future beyond this darkness? I hear the rattle of dust. Was that a damaged speaker?

"I don't know if I am the right person to give you that history..." The Mountain was hesitating. What was he hiding? No answers. Always no answers. Why was this darkness not in my vision, but what I was allowed to know? Was he my new Watcher? Protecting me from the truth?

"Please..." I need answers, I need truths. Is this world real? Is this Taylor the real Taylor? Am I the real Tyron? Mountain, give me the answers to my mysteries!

"I suppose you will learn either way. Whether it's from me, Taylor, or any of the whispering girls around here. I guess it's worth noting first that your survival these past few days is a medical miracle. You should feel very grateful towards Taylor. She has risked her life, her limbs, even her own food and water to prepare you for the transition you underwent. I have known her for five years, and she has only ever focused on you and your health. Remember that..." The Mountain betrayed his feelings. I could hear. My ears were strong. He respects this Taylor. Such respect. This creature, with suns for eyes and legs of metal, respected Taylor very much. Maybe this Taylor was mine? Maybe she was kind? Like My Taylor.

"I guess I will tell you what I know about your situation over the past five years. When Taylor entered Haldoklik, she was carrying you on her back. She was starved, weak, and very young. She dug out a life and built herself up in her craft of being a Scrap Dog. A mostly illegal but respected societal position. Over the years, she earned a reputation and was motivational to many. She paid the price for her job, she sacrificed her wellbeing, food and water supplies, and her own mental health to learn and become better than she was. All of it for you. In her scrapping she would learn more about the Razum devices so that... she could free you from the Razum you wore."

Razum? I wore the thing my body shuddered at the mention of? What is it? Where have I been? I missed so much. So so so much. This poor Taylor. Why did she sacrifice so much for me? Not her job, my job.

She should have left me and built a life for herself. Not her responsibility, mine. What world is this? Why does my sister have to sacrifice so much of herself? For me? For this world? She must be strong, not like My Taylor. She must be brave, not like My Taylor.

Why? Why did she sacrifice so much? That wasn't her job, it was supposed to be mine. Water. Pooling in my eyes. It burned. Burned like my hate. Burned like Taylor's care. I needed to help her. Save her. Do my responsibilities.

My body, it doesn't obey. I want to move; to find this Taylor. I want to meet her. She doesn't have to fight anymore. Must be more. Must become more. My sweet sister... why did she leave me? I could have protected her.

"Don't move yet. We don't know how well you can move with your muscular degradation. You are also still healing from surgery. Please, do not move." The Mountain's hand was cold. Ice metal. My body prickled at his icy hand, my shoulder frozen. You can't stop me Mountain. I am stronger than that.

I needed to see Taylor. Must see. She must be saved from this life. "Taylor!" Was that my voice? Did it explode from me? My throat rattled like it did. My voice was trying to seek her. My voice. Would she recognize it? Was this really my real sister? Had I at last found her after she left me?

My thoughts were getting clearer. I remembered what was shown in front of me that day. The day she left. The day I didn't go with her. I could have saved her from so much pain. Pain that I endured. Pain that she endured.

'Do you want to leave the Razum?'

This question burned in my mind. My eyes could see the screen. The day she left. I never understood the question. I should have guessed–Taylor always wanted more. Why couldn't I have joined her? Why didn't I hit

'Yes'? Why did I fail–

"Tyron, please calm down. If you continue this flailing, you will injure yourself further. Please. It is my job to watch you while Taylor works off her debt." Two chilly hands held my shoulders with the strength of the Mountain. How could he be so strong? Or was I weak? How did my body survive this long? How was I still alive? I should never have survived. Survived because of her. This world was unfair.

Where was she working? What was she doing? What debt did she owe? My voice is too weak. I couldn't ask the questions even if I wanted to. Eyes blink. Focus. Look into this Mountain's eyes. Demand the answers, voice. I had to know more!

"Taylor!" My voice didn't listen. It didn't want answers. It wanted Taylor. Arms wrapped around her, I wanted her near. Where was she?

"She can't come to you right now, but she will in a while. She is out running errands for the Den. I need you to settle down or I will have to make sure you go back to sleep till she can deal with you. I am not meant for babysitting, so I suggest you listen." The Mountain's hands were heavy. Heavy like metal. Cold like metal. Legs of metal. Was the Mountain purely made of metal? I don't care. He doesn't matter. Where is Taylor?

"Tyron. Stop. You will complicate things for Taylor if you cause too much commotion. We will not be permitted to stay. You need this place to recover and you need Taylor to not worry about you right now. She has enough to manage. So if you care about her, stop." Hands were removed, the cold remained. My body stilled, even though I willed it to move. So weak. So tired. My body could not struggle any more.

Silence.

The Mountain I knew was Gregory. I had angered him. His voice had been one of the few I heard in the past. A voice of anger, but also friendship. My mind screamed at me to yell and fight. Fight for Taylor. He was not my enemy to fight. Mouth shut. Arms still. Gregory was not my enemy. For now.

"Better. I think it's time for you to rest again. I don't want to risk upsetting you. Taylor will already yell at me, and I am in no mood to deal with her." Gregory feared her? No. No, the Mountain was worried. Worried about her. Like I was.

"Please... tell me more." My voice knew how to be quiet now. Quiet like a whisper. No more fighting. It was time to learn more. More answers.

"If you throw another fit, I will make sure you don't wake up for a long time. This is not what I was built for."

Gregory was built? So he was no man. He was made of metal. A metal filled Mountain. Rich in the ore of information. No more fits. No more fights. Not till I know more. More of Taylor. More of the Razum. More of the Loomers.

"I won't." Weak words. Accurate words. Gregory seems to have heard the accurate words. His feet, like grinding metal on metal, shifted. He seemed to sit back down. Had he stood? Had I heard him stand? Was I so loud that he had to stand to silence me? I didn't mean to disturb. He should stay down. No more fuss.

"Very well... So I am guessing the bit about the Razum bothered you. I'll skip past that for now and let Taylor go into depth. Taylor's life before Haldoklik is not known to me. Until recently, I knew little about you."

"I am a Drone Class robot, Model Gregory 235. My job has always been to suppress and tolerate humans. Being unaccustomed to being a caretaker, do not test me. I am not programmed to care, be kind, or navigate human emotions."

"I served under a Giant named Finigan for many years. Watching over humans as they built the town of Haldoklik for those freed from the networks, I have seen many people come and go. When Taylor appeared after Haldoklik, I had always known she was going to be more trouble than she's worth. I still stand by this, but I could never dissuade her from anything she put her mind to."

"Before I knew her as I do now, I had even suggested many times that she left you and survived by herself. Razum wearers don't wake up, never have since the Fall. Until you four days ago."

"I guess congratulations is in order. You are the first person to be removed from a Razum and survive both physically and mentally."

History. So much history. I want more. I want to know more. Robots, Haldoklik, the first person to survive a Razum. What happened to the others? Where were all the other Razum wearers? Maybe I could save them. Taylor. Taylor and me. We could save them. She saved me, we could do it again.

Was Gregory telling the truth? He was one of the robots. Why was he trusted? Did Taylor trust him? Should he be trusted? He hasn't hurt me. He hasn't misled me. To my knowledge, or maybe his knowledge? My whole life was now unreal. All the realities my mind ran through, years of silence. All pointless. All unreal.

I still have not seen a face. Could this still be my reality? Was I still trapped in a world I didn't know was there? Was Taylor stuck there too? Was I a miracle in my own reality? Did I create this world? This Gregory Unit? Did I create myself? What did it mean to be free from the Razum? What was the world like outside?

I wouldn't know the truth. Not yet. Not till I can see again. Feeling the surrounding things no longer satisfied my need for reality. Reality. A question, and an answer in itself?

A congratulation–a medical miracle–these words were finite. Or were they? Was this in my mind? Weakness flooded my body. The waters of pain. They were always here. Always. Never alone with pain. Too much information. Too many questions.

Were my legs still on me? Could I feel my toes? They resist my commands to move. Connected, but not mine. My body was not mine. Or it was, and I didn't know it. This body–broken, old, unused. Will it be used again? All limbs ignored me. Rebels.

My mind blurred, haze against the dim sun. Was this tiredness? Had I maxed out this new body? What were its strengths? What were its weaknesses? Tired. So tired. Too much information? Did Taylor get tired of information? Had she grown while I died? Did she embrace this new reality? Too many questions.

Did the surrounding darkness deepen? Was I being eaten? How did the darkness get darker? Was this sleep in this reality, the darkness getting darker? Was sleep no longer filled with fantasies and voices? After Gregory's words, there seemed no more room for fantasy.

"Get some rest. You look tired. We will have plenty of time to talk things through. Taylor will check on you when she gets back" "

Sleep tight, Metal Mountain.

✿   ✿   ✿

Lights. Did I see light? Was there finally a ladder from the darkness that ate at me? Was this still sleeping? How did one know when they were sleeping? Or awake? Or what reality they were in? Did this light know? Did it know where or when I was?

A warm hand. I found a warm hand in mine. This felt real. Or more real than other things. Whose hand hid in mine? Or my hand in theirs? Could this be Taylor? Taylor of this world? She returned? To me?

"Taylor?" The voice was groggy. Shaky. Was I scared to know if this was Taylor? The real Taylor. Not My Taylor. So many questions for her. Why did I start with her name?

"Hey, I'm here. Sorry, I didn't mean to wake you." A hand appeared from the light. It was warm against my cold head. Why was I so cold? Did my body not know how to keep me warm anymore? Or was Taylor's hand the only warmth left in this world?

"Where were you?" A better question. So much time was lost, according to Gregory. So much. Why was she not here? Why has she been gone?

"I'm sorry I wasn't around. Gregory told me you were awake for a while. Your fever seems to have broken. The Nanites look like they helped a lot in the recovery. I'm so glad."

Her answer did not answer me. Why did she avoid my question? Was she not full of the answers I hoped for? She only opened more questions. What were Nanites? What recovery was I making? Why was she so glad her voice trembled?

"I was doing some errands for the people who own the place we are staying. It was the deal I had to make to help get you out of the Razum. You have undergone very extensive surgery so you are probably very sore, but your pain receptors haven't worked in a long time so you may not be able to tell what you are feeling… How are you doing? We haven't talked yet."

Haven't had the chance to talk? I have heard all our memories and stories in my sleep since I could remember. Long ago, and until recently, my dreams were only with your voice. Didn't you know?

"I'm… confused. S-s-so many questions. Where am I now?" Finally. Answers. A real chance for real answers.

"Confusion is expected. I will answer as many of your questions as I can. Right now, we are in a Loomer City named Sila, made from the Loomer body of Locura. You have been immersed in a virtual reality network controlled by a device called the Razum, which has taken over many of your basic bodily functions. You'll need to relearn how to eat, drink, and move independently. Don't worry, I'll be here to guide you through every step of the process. So… welcome to reality. I've missed you out here." Warm hands pet my face. So warm. They drew my mind from its slurry of confusion. So confused for so long. Why was she warm? Why did she draw me out of my darkness with ease? Why did she leave?

"Why… did you leave me?" These words were not meant to escape. Weak voice, why didn't it listen to me? She didn't need to hear my doubts. Or maybe she did. Or I did?

I could hear her breath. Shaky, hesitantly. Did she not want to tell me? Did it offend her? Should I take back the question? No, I couldn't. I needed to know. She needed to face me. I needed this answer the most. Why was I left behind?

Willing my arms to fly, fly high like pilots in the sky, I searched for her face. Still a blur of a world, I could find her shadow. Contact. Her skin felt wet, trails of water. My plane of a hand was caught in hers, against her face. A face I had never known, but the smile she held was one I had known for all my life.

"I… I didn't know. I didn't know that I was leaving you. I didn't know what the world was like. You were going to come with me, or that's what I thought. So many nights I thought about joining you again, trying to figure out a way back into the Razum and connect the networks so we could be together… but I couldn't handle the thought of you not knowing the real world."

"It is miserable out there. I can't lie to you and tell you it's beautiful. It is real, though. The feeling of pain and suffering. I have never felt more alive and real. The Razum was like viewing life in black and white. Now I have the choice to do what I want, but all I ever wanted was to have you back."

More water fell across my hand. It stung me. She was right, though. This world hurt in ways I had never known. So many years of mental pain, but for the first time, physical pain felt real. Pain was reality. Suffering was the air here. This Taylor survived it and has enjoyed it. She always found the light. The light she now was for me.

"I was alone… for so long." Bitterness. My voice chose bitterness. Part of me was still angry. Angry about being abandoned. Angry for enduring the loneliness. So long, so alone. That was not the kindness Taylor had once been.

"You were never alone out here. I took you almost everywhere with me. The only time I left your side was if it was too dangerous for you. I talked to you every night before I went to sleep, and every morning I would greet you. I have dreamed for years of hearing you respond to me."

"I should never have left you in the Razum, but I couldn't live with letting you stay in there, either. We have traveled more than most humans ever will these days. You have never been alone out here. I never stopped trying to free you."

Never alone? So why did it not feel that way? I knew I had heard her voice before, in my dreams, but it never made me feel less alone. She was always so far away from me. Even now, her words feel like they were in a long hallway. Gone. Away from me.

She never stopped, though. Never. I had heard her in my dreams, always another plan. Always moving forward. She never slowed. Her words proved my dreams right. Taylor has never stopped trying to get back. I stopped, though.

I gave up.

Water now carved my face like knives. Why did these trails of water appear? Why did it hurt so badly when they did? My life has been a lie until now. So many mistaken thoughts. So much anger towards her. So much. I couldn't bear how wrong I was. Mistaken.

"Don't cry, Tyron. We are here together. That's all that matters. We made it out together." Warm fingers dusted the water from my face. What was crying? Was it me? Was it my eyes? I didn't know my eyes could do that. Was she crying? Did we do this often? Is this what tears felt like here?

What was her face like? The blur in the light. Was her face like mine? Was my face like mine? I wanted to see her. Even with crying eyes, I wanted to finally see her face. The face I had dreamed of. The face I tried to recreate in the Razum. The face of the sister I had lost so long ago.

"I want to see your face." Did my voice shake? Was it scared to know? Was I scared to know?

"I don't know how well your eyes work right now. It will take some time for them to adjust to seeing properly. Are you sure? I can bring the candle closer to help you see."

I did my best to nod my head. My voice was too weak to hide the fear. She didn't need to know I was afraid. She didn't need to be my protector anymore. Her warm hands left me, the darkness and cold washed over me. Back into the maw of darkness.

Quiet steps on metal flooring. She was much lighter than Gregory when he walked. How tall was she? How much had she grown up? How old was she now? She sounded tiny. Always tiny. Was she thin like me? Was she weak like I was? No. No, she would never let herself be weak.

The light reappeared from behind her blurry shadow. It burned my eyes as it drew near. The pain seared to the depths of my mind. This was brighter than any sun I had ever known. She was right. This reality was painful, but it felt more real than anything I had ever experienced.

With the light near my head, my eyes relaxed a bit, hidden by the edge of my face. What a bright light. It nearly commanded fearful respect. The blurry shadow that was my sister hesitated to come closer. Why did she hesitate? Did she not want me to see? Was she disfigured? Did she fear me?

"Come here." Soft words from a hoarse mouth. Did she know how much I needed to see her? Didn't she know I missed her? Her words had been the foundation of my sanity. Didn't she know how much she meant to me?

"Listen, our faces aren't the same in the Razum as they are in real life. You may not recognize me. I was recently burned from acid fog as well, so my skin is pale and damaged. I don't want to scare you." Her words trembled, so did her shadow.

I reached my weak arms towards her again, seeking her face. I didn't care. I didn't care if she looked the same, or different. Or in any kind of way. I wanted to see the face of the person who freed me. Even if this world was dark and broken. This person in front of me was the only one to love me enough to free me.

I never even knew I was trapped until her voice drew me out. I followed her. After hearing about the world she endured, I never want her to feel afraid or have to make tough decisions. She was my sister, and my job was to protect her. I had to.

Finding her face in the blur, I drew it near mine. Slowly. Painfully, my vision cleared. There was a face in front of me. A beautiful youthful face. Although it was grizzled, there were scars around her forehead and eyes. This was the spirited sister I had known as a child. She looked older than I felt.

Even with pale skin, scars, shaved head besides her long blonde hair trailing back from the center, she still looked like the rose cheeked sister I never could let go of. The jaw was different, more narrow and chiseled. Her brows also seemed more furrowed. This was truly My Taylor. My sweet young sister.

Any apprehension I had fell away as if the world beneath me no longer mattered anymore. My Taylor had returned. With the small amount of energy I still had, I pulled her closer to me still. Arms wrapped around her like a trap, so she could never leave me again.

So many years I had dreamed of hugging her like this. I could hear her 'crying' and I joined in. Finally, we were back together. Free in a new world, together. This was what my life had been missing. What my world was missing. She was now in my arms, the way I had dreamed of for so long.

Chapter 10: A Realist's World

We talked the time away with ease. Hours passing by. I think they were hours. She caught me up to speed on the way of this world, her own struggles when she got out of the Razum, and her journey that she has been on to free me. Each story was a new pang of guilt.

She was never meant to endure all that she did. So many injuries, so much pain. Showing me the braces she made broke my heart yet again. To have made such a journey on such injuries... she had become much stronger in this world. I couldn't let her know the rage I was filled with from her sufferings.

My heart ached at each new story, but I wouldn't tell her. She didn't need to know how much her words made me proud, yet feel more broken. I have been nothing but a weight to her for her entire life. I needed to do everything in my power to change this cruel world for her. She should never have had to deal with this.

"Did I tell you about how I had to cut your hair to get your head out of the Razum when it first opened up? Apparently, hair continues to grow in there. When you are feeling better, I'll cut your hair any way you like." Warm fingers threaded through my hair along with the kind words.

I was sitting more upward now with her help, so I could see her more clearly. The pain in my chest had increased, but it was worth it to see her smile as she spoke. I could tell from the lack of laugh lines on her face, she hadn't smiled so much. She seemed happy enough talking to me though, so I let her continue even though the tiredness was tugging me away.

"Have you made any friends? I know we didn't have many in the... in the

Razum." My body still stuttered at the mere mention of the machine that stole my life from me. Though it didn't stop me from talking. She seemed to need our conversations as much as I did.

I remembered her as a small girl, so shy, so stubborn. She would never connect with other kids well. Has she outgrown that? How many things had she outgrown? She was taller and smarter, but this world sounded less friendly.

"I... had a few over the years. The Scientist, Gern from Haldoklik, and now I have Gregory. So, I haven't been totally alone. It has been lonely, time from time. I always had you, though." Her voice wavered. The vibrations from her words stirred me. She was lying. Feeling lonely was something she would never have admitted to.

"Tell me about them." Did they treat her nicely? Did they respect her? Could she truly trust them? Questions a brother should ask before judging them.

"Well, Gern was an old Scrap Dog back in Haldoklik. He never really took a shine to me till I had to leave. I stole enough scrap from his shop to get on his bad side. But he never hurt me. Years later, he even gave me some side jobs he was getting too old for."

"There was a time he sent me to the lower towns to fix an old lady's air pump just because he hated hearing her mutter to herself. It kept me busy when I was in rut, trying to figure out how to help you. It also made the people there a little more nice to me when I walked around. He helped me more than I knew he was."

"Gregory, on the other hand, has been a pain in the ass since I've known him. He seemed to always be the Drone I got in trouble with. After probably the twenty-eighth time he had to drag me in front of the Head Drone, he started realizing my trouble wasn't malicious. He started letting me get away with some things. We even had a deal where I helped him deal with Raiders, who occasionally came near. There were a lot of traps we walked into, but he usually got me out safe."

"It wasn't until more recently, I realized he had started Fritzing. His mind is crumbling. Though it seems he is trying to use his newfound emotional status to help me, for some reason. I'm not totally sure I can trust him yet, but he has risked a lot more than anyone else for me."

"I don't think he really knows what's happening to him. He's been disconnected from all he's ever known. I think that's why he's choosing to look after you while I'm away running errands. He may relate to the feelings you're going through. Or maybe not. Hard to know what's going through that tin head of his."

She stopped her reminiscing, paused by her own thoughts on the topic. I noticed she left out the Scientist. She had mentioned him briefly in our story sharing, but she seemed to not be very specific about those memories.

"What about the Scientist?" My words evoked a silence in the room. I know it was my rampant imagination, but I thought I could hear her heartbeat quicken. Was she scared to tell me about him? Was he dead? Did she lead to his death somehow?

"The Scientist..." She struggled to form more words. Weakly, I reached towards her hand. I had to show her it was safe to talk to me. She had to know that I didn't care what happened. Did she know I would love her regardless of whatever happened?

"The Scientist was a man named Arthur McClellan. He... he helped you and me back when I first left the Razum. I had stumbled into a town named Anastaja. It was formed from one of the old concentration camps that humans were once kept in. I think it was part of an Old-World city? There were massive buildings all around."

"I remember feeling so tiny, carrying you on my back and surrounded by buildings that blocked out the sun. Arthur found me hiding by one of those buildings and invited us into his lab."

"He was the first person I interacted with that believed there was a chance to free you. He started researching immediately into your state and well being. If I hadn't run into him, I would never have figured out how to free you."

"He gave me all the tools I needed to decode more illegal equipment so that I could find the proper tools that could break you out. I also owe him my life, and to an extent, your life."

Her words were strained until she trailed off. She was still hiding the part of the story that was bothering her. Such a brave girl. There was no more reason to be brave. I am here. No judgment. No hate. We talk, it's what we do.

"I want to thank him." Stifled breath, my lungs felt weak. Since talking to Taylor for so long and learning about the surgery, I knew now why I felt so tired. Her words brought the clarity back to my mind. Though my thoughts still got muddled. I knew I wanted to thank Arthur for looking out for Taylor. He obviously meant a lot to her.

Her hesitation spoke more than her words could. He must be dead. I could feel the tremble in her hand. My sweet sister, what did you endure? Share the burden with me. Please.

"We can't thank him. Because of a rebellion building in the city in the earlier days of the Fall, there was a nuking of Anastaja. We were fortunate enough to be buried in a deep fallout shelter, where his lab was."

"Though it wasn't strong enough and crashed in on us. Arthur was pinned under some concrete from the ceiling while pushing you and me to safety. He lived for a day in agonizing pain... he said he wasn't ready to go. On his last day, he taught me the rest of what he knew between his cries of anguish."

"Our food supplies were running low before the bomb, so we had little to eat. He rejected any food I gave him and told me to save it for myself or to re-teach your throat how to swallow. I could barely swallow food myself, but he taught me how to stimulate the muscles until I could use them on my own."

"His last words to me were 'This world is dark, there are no rules of what is right science, and wrong science anymore. Once the Loomers came, moral law went out. So when I am gone, you must do everything necessary to survive'. At the time, I didn't know what he meant, but once the food ran out and the water stopped, the hunger taught me what he meant. I had too, I had to–" She couldn't finish her sentence. Her hand drew away from mine. Her shadow shook uncontrollably, her hand clutching her mouth.

The image became clear in my mind. Though she could not verbalize it,

I knew what she meant. I closed my eyes and sent a quiet prayer into the universe, thanking the Scientist. His body saved my sister's life. Though she will never forget the things she had to do, I was happy she was still alive.

My poor sister — If I was awake then—

Moments passed, Taylor stiffened her shoulders and with an emotion-banishing sniffle, she continued. Her voice still shook. Shook like the earthquake that was being held back by her mind.

"Ever since, I have refused to say his name. He sacrificed… everything for our survival. I wish I could have thanked him, but I feel too much guilt to even utter his name in my mind."

She has endured too much. This never should have happened. Even if she stayed in the Razum with me though, her reality would not have guided her to become the person she did. I hope she can at least be proud of her survival.

Our conversation was interrupted by the blaring noise of metal being scraped against metal as the dim light from the doorway blinded me. A mountainous shadow blocked the light quickly and closed the door behind itself, hiding it in the darkness.

"Taylor, you need to be sleeping. You have duties in the morning." The voice that vibrates the very bed I laid on belonged to Gregory. He seemed to be the balance in Taylor's life, which I was grateful for. Never thought I would appreciate a machine so much after all I learned about them.

"I'll be fine. Tomorrow should be an easier day." Her words were dismissive, but they gave her away. I knew she needed sleep as well. Pushing her hand away from mine, I took a deep breath.

"Go, sleep. I will be here tomorrow and the next day. We won't be separated again." My words seemed to encourage her. She stood and leaned over my head. I could feel the warmth of her lips on my head and moved away. I was no child anymore.

"I will be back tomorrow. Gregory will watch over you till I get back. Thank you for listening to my stories. I will try to remember more for tomorrow. Good night, Tyron." With her peaceful words, and a final squeeze of my hand, she disappeared behind the shadow of Gregory. Blinded by the light of the doorway again, Taylor disappeared from the room and I was left with the Mountain.

"She seemed in higher spirits. Did you two have a good time?" Gregory moved and took up his spot against the wall across from my bed. He was my constant guardian while Taylor was away. I was growing fond of his company, as it was much more clinical and less emotional. I loved my sister, but the pain she carried hurt me too much to endure it much longer.

"She was catching me up on some history. Thank you for encouraging her to go to sleep." My voice was stronger after talking to Taylor. My vocal cords would require a lot of exercise to get them fully functional. I shifted myself back into a laying down position and faced away from the candlelight. It was still blazing.

"She would have stayed up all night talking to you. I've heard her doing it while you were in the Razum. She needs to learn to take care of herself better." Gregory leaned forward and extinguished the candle and plunged us back into darkness.

I glanced at him when he drew near and I could vaguely see the digital eyes he wore like stars in the dark. They seemed empty, cold, and pitiless. Though I knew now, there was care in those LEDs.

"She has been through so much. How can I even comfort her?" I knew this question would upset the Drone being such an emotional question, but I didn't care now. If he was going to linger, he would have to learn to understand. It felt like something Taylor would do. Push him to be more than a machine. I wanted to emulate that.

"Have you tried nodding and just agreeing? I hear that works well." Was there a slight chuckle attached to his words? Was he learning to be amusing? I couldn't deny there was a part of me that was curious about his wired workings. Making a mental note to ask Taylor about him later, I closed my eyes.

Gregory's joints groaned under the weight of him as he moved back to his position as a watch guard. There was silence in the room, only broken up by the quiet patter of feet beyond the door. I assumed there was a world outside that door, but I had not seen it yet.

"What's outside?" My words were met with the noises of Gregory shifting his position, metal on metal. There was a hesitation in the air? Was he trying to keep me in the dark, literally, and intellectually? Taylor had warned me not to push him. Was this question crossing that line?

"That information could be considered a sensitive topic. I don't think you need to know that right now." He didn't seem in the mood for conversation tonight.

"If I promise not to cause trouble, will you tell me?" I knew this simple baiting would likely not work, but it was worth a shot. There was limited trouble I could cause anyway. My legs were completely numb to me. I seemed to only have the function of my upper body, so I was in no shape to run.

He sat silently, considering the secret information he carried. Beginning to lose hope for answers, and dreading such secretive information, I rolled towards the machine as much as I could. His LEDs watched me closely from what I could see. He was scanning me to figure out if I was lying. Wise machine.

"If you get upset, I will knock you out before you can scream. I will not have Taylor hearing about how I upset you with the truth. Are we at an understanding?" The grating of his speaker seemed to rattle louder tonight. Or maybe he was being quiet, causing his speaker to hiss more frequently.

"We have an understanding." These words meant nothing to me. As long as I didn't act out, he would share the information Taylor was more hesitant too. Gregory was my source of information on the world.

"I better not hear of this. We are currently sheltered in an Organ Den. I'm guessing Taylor didn't explain in detail what that was. For good reason, it even upset her when she learned about the operation they were running here. It is a clean and less murderous option than some towns."

"Organ Dens do what they sound like they do. They produce black market organs for sale to lengthen people's lives. Most operate by mugging and stealing organs, but because of the large amount of Razums that were fed in the Loomer Locura, they are harvesting those who haven't woken from the Razums."

My blood ran cold at his words. Harvesting people who were in the Razums? I could have been here instead of with Taylor. While his words chilled me, the cold was chased away by the heat of rage.

My mind's eye could picture the tables filled with bodies. Bodies weak like mine. People cutting them open. Blood across the floors. Were the Drones responsible? Was this designed by the machines that controlled us in this world? What was this world? Why was this dark practice successful? Didn't humanity have any more moral law? I couldn't imagine that people caused this. Humans wouldn't change to be so barbaric.

Would they? Why? Why was this where I woke up? Why did Taylor bring me here?

"Why?" The only question I could form through gritted teeth. My once senseless body flared with heat and pain. Prickled skin waved across my body as I glared into the dim lights of Gregory's eyes. Was his kind responsible for the way humanity had declined?

"Why? Because it makes more sense than stealing organs from healthy society members. It's considered morally correct in this world. You would do well to note that. This isn't the controlled environment of the Razum anymore. People will kill you to survive. It's an old truth to humanity."

"With the land destroyed, Drones maintaining public obedience, it can be a lot of stress and strain on the human body. The life quality in this world is insufficient. Death is prevalent due to organ failure or simply not being able to eat. This gives some people extra years to spend with their families or friends."

While he was trying to put a positive spin on things, I couldn't quiet the anger. Drones were responsible for humanity's degradation. If I could survive being alone for so long, humans would have surpassed their difficulties. This was his fault. His words no longer held comfort to me.

"Taylor is currently running errands and doing favors for the Organ Den because they offered to help you and her. They were the primary hands in your surgery and believed that you would come out."

"If it helps, your existence has jostled the minds of the young girls who work here. Some are questioning if they should use Razum Wearers. Be careful when you meet them. This town is already a bundle of kindling waiting for a spark to ignite a rebellion."

Rebellion? Taylor had talked about those being a dangerous thing. Often leading to the destruction of entire towns. If this was the living conditions of Sila, though, maybe a rebellion would serve them well.

I wanted to see the Organ Den. Would Gregory allow me to? Could I look at the faces of the small children who seemed to run this operation? Why would they use children? Didn't they have a hard enough life to look forward to? Why were things so cruel?

"Could I see?" I tried to control the anger in my voice. The last person I wanted to understand me was Gregory. He was one of the many who were destroying this world for Taylor. How could she handle being so close to one of his kind? Destroyers.

Gregory's joints groaned as he leaned further into the wall. I heard the quiet thud of his head hitting the tin. He made no movement to stand or heed my request.

"That one I know would get me in more trouble. Taylor has made exact rules you are not to be moved while she is running errands. I am sure you will see the Den soon enough. Taylor only has about three days left of her sentence here. We will move to a different town after that. Find a safer location for your recovery."

Taylor's rules seemed to be all around me here. A new cage was forming. Didn't she know I was strong enough for the truth? Did she not trust me? I thought we had bonded, yet I am still learning of new rules.

Clattering broke the silence that was growing between Gregory and me. The sound of running feet and dropped pans echoed through the room outside my door. What was happening? It had caused Gregory to stand at a ready and move for the door.

The chaos outside the door was combined with small screams and distant loud noises I was not familiar with. The feet ran quicker. There was a loud, panicked knock on the door and Gregory took up position.

"Harvey Units are coming for us! Help, Gregory!" A young girl's voice rang out. It wasn't Taylor's, but significantly younger than her. She was afraid. What were Harvey Units?

"Run for the back exit, they may not know of it being newer Drones. Grab the younger ones, I will help once I've moved Tyron." Gregory barked orders through the door and turned back to me.

"I guess you will get an eye full before you're ready. Taylor must be out running an errand, otherwise she would be here. Prepare yourself." Gregory stooped down to the side of my bed and dug his stiff arms under me. In one motion, he stood and threw my weak body across his metal plated shoulders.

"What's happening?" Confusion entering my tone more than I would have liked it to. I tried to brace myself against his plates, but my arms were too weak to support myself. The plates pushed in the wound on my chest and I gasped to breathe.

"Hear the gunshots? That would be the Harvey Units moving in to clear out the Den. Why are they here?" Gregory was muttering to himself. His voice was wavering with slight fear. Was he afraid of these Harvey Units?

He pulled the door open with such force it was ripped off the hinges. His actions betrayed him. He was afraid. The Harvey Units must be a significant threat to him.

Gregory dashed out of the doorway, the light blinding me before I could see the room. After a moment of being jostled on his shoulder, my eyes focused. I dreaded being able to see. The bodies covered tables like I had thought. Giant machines covered the heads in trapezoidal designs, the Razums. The blood was splattered across the walls and floor as dozens of little girls ran the same way Gregory did.

I could feel the air shift as some girls turned and screamed. Adjusting my eyes to see what was the source of the fear, I realized Gregory's fear. A giant creature pulled itself through the door at the far end. A long weapon in its hand with a cylindrical barrel. It was designed in a cartoon-like style, but somehow the floppy ears of a rabbit and painted smile couldn't take from the fear it commanded.

Weapon in hand, it dropped its jaw and a loud sound rang from its deep sounding speaker. "Gregory Unit 235, stop. You are to be decommissioned under law code 7830: aiding in the offense against the Giant Finigan." Its voice wailed against the mud and tin walls of the hall. I could feel the vibrations of its warning rattle through Gregory's body.

"Shit." Gregory muttered as he moved me to his arm wrapping around my torso and jumped across several tables. His metal shoes crushed the Razum Wearers, who were in the wrong places. Blood splashed up from the crushed bodies and hit my face. I could feel an odd sensation build in my stomach and caused me to spit. It felt like my throat was trying to escape my body.

Gregory jumped from the tables and landed by the side of the hall. He held onto me tightly as he threw a body from the table and pulled it from its metal stand. As he did so, bullets rang off of the metal as he held it up behind his back and in front of me. He used the moment to kick into the wall and collapsed a hidden door that led up a dirt path. I watched as he revealed many hiding girls.

They moved from his path and Gregory crouched as he pulled himself into the wall and covered his entrance with the table. He examined the girls around him as they tried to scurry further down the tunnel.

"This leads out of the area. Go! Small and injured, hold on to me and make way." Gregory's voice was significantly louder this close to his speaker. He was commanding. Terrifying. The girls obeyed his words and several wrapped themselves on his legs and torso, holding on tightly.

One girl, roughly the age of Taylor when she left me, clung to Gregory's back and looked up at me in awe. Her eyes were brown and twinkled with curiosity, which was quickly stolen by fear as the Harvey Units continued their shouting.

As Gregory moved, a path formed in front of him. The girls clung on for their lives as the Drone moved through the small tunnel almost on all fours. We were nearing the exit when the sound of shouting echoed up the tunnel. The Harvey Units had reached the entrance and were shooting down the kids.

Blood-curdling cries echoed out of the tunnel as Gregory pulled himself from the dirt. My blood boiled as I saw the faint faces of children fall behind. Damn him. Damn his cold judgment. They were only children. Why didn't he fight?

"Quickly, scatter. Anywhere you can find shelter. Has anyone seen Vykra?" Gregory commanded the girls as he led them away from the entrance. The world was dark around us. I couldn't see anything in the dark besides a distant red glow. The girls on Gregory released him and fled in different directions. One girl lingered.

"Vykra fell to Harveys at the door. The Den is dead. We will keep an eye out for Taylor. Where will you be?" The girl scanned the area around us and started edging her way into the shadows beyond the range of my sight.

"Tell Taylor to meet us at the Tea Parlor. She will know what it means. Tell her Tyron is safe and with me. Thank you, Tricia. Go now." Gregory lightly extended his free arm and patted the young girl's head and she disappeared into the darkness.

"Tyron, are you still with me?" His voice was now very hushed. He picked up full speed as he ran into the darkness, away from the glow. I saw looming shadows all around us. We were trapped in a shadowy land.

"I'm fine. Where are we going?" He shushed me as we turned down between a row of tall shadows. I could still see the larger shadowy walls beyond. Taylor was speaking the truth when she said the Loomer Cities were buried into the ground. With how tall the shadows were around us, they must have been heavy and had fallen hard.

"Quiet. Taylor and I had a place hidden away before we found the Den. She will meet us there when she hears the news. We have to stay low so we don't cause attention." He was still running when we hit the enormous shadow that seemed ever-present in the sky. As we got closer, I could see it was a wall made of mud and scrap. Gregory examined the wall and started his stride again.

It was several minutes before he slowed his gait. There were no lights here. The darkness was so dense that I couldn't see the world. I trusted Gregory to know his way. The sound of his hand on a tin wall proved he knew where he was.

"Duck your head. It's a tight squeeze." I obeyed the glowing-eyed Drone and smashed my cheek into his rib plates. The tin of the doorway scraped my back, pain rattling my upper body. Once inside, he closed the door and placed me on what I was guessing was a table. It was cold.

"The Harvey Units have no reason to suspect I am lingering in town. They should assume I fled. Though I varied my path here to discourage them from following if they should try. We should be safe till Taylor can meet us." Gregory rattled off his actions, almost seeking approval for his planning. After a moment of silence, he realized he would not get any from me. Not after letting so many children die behind him.

They were orders. I knew that. He was required to protect me solely, but the hatred I had for him was amplified by watching the girls fall to bullets behind him. I trusted him to protect me, but I learned he was not so willing to protect others. My fear for Taylor only grew the more I learned.

The silence drew on and we could hear the shuffling of people in their own tin huts near us. Everything was muffled and dark. My world was plunged into night once more, but I felt free of the cage. My chest struggled to breathe in the cold, acrid air. I hadn't realized how warm the room was.

Tucking my arms under the sides of my chest, I realized I was still shirtless to allow the scars to heal across my chest. The cold nipped at me quickly and the metal table I laid on absorbed what remained of my heat. I had never felt such cold. Was this what the world was like? Was it cold and brutal? Was it a world where we had to watch as children were murdered while we flee with those who can run faster?

The faces of the girls getting shot down seared across my memory. I had almost wished I couldn't see, but how could I let their memory die so plainly? They deserved to be remembered. They were worth the pain it caused me to remember. Pools of water filled my eyes again. Was I crying for the pain of children I hadn't even known the names of?

Damn this world. Damn this reality of pain. Damn the robots who stole our humanity from us. No child should have to suffer by the blind unfeeling hands of machines we created. Why? Why did the children have to be the ones to suffer like this? Why didn't we protect them more?

Gregory's shifting broke my thoughts. He was rummaging around the tin capsule we hid in. Mud and metal shifted under his feet, quieter than the floor in the Organ Den. The Organ Den that held many of my lost Razum brethren. I reached up and felt the cooling blood splatter on my face. Visions of viscera and carnage flooded through my eyes.

What world was this? Why had she brought me here? Pain made her value reality, but it enraged me. Life was flaunted so easily here, fainting and disappearing in the distant screams of the night. Was this the world she knew? Was her plan to bring me here?

The rummaging stopped as Gregory stood as much as he could in the apparently shallow ceiling. His eyes glowed brighter and revealed him holding two things. A small satchel he fastened around his neck, and a tarp he must have grabbed from somewhere in the hut. He wrapped the tarp around me carefully, trying to trap heat in it.

I couldn't look away from his eyes, though. Could he see the rage that burned in me? Could he see the pain I carried with me for those lost girls? I had not known their names, but he did. Did he even care? His LEDs locked onto my eyes, a quiet understanding there.

"You are new to this world. The girls knew the risks they ran with working in the Organ Den. Don't let their deaths distract you from your recovery. Vykra made sure they understood the risk of their operation and with taking in you, Taylor, and me."

"You were the unexpected miracle that probably led Vykra to defend the Den rather than let the Harveys come and take me. This world is filled with chaos. You will get used to it." His voice may have come from a speaker placed in his throat, but his words felt more mechanical than ever before.

I would not get used to this death. I couldn't. So many small faces were probably being dragged through the mud as we hid in the shadows. How could he be used to such tragedy? Did life really mean nothing to him? How could Taylor abide by his company? Was she like this, too? Has my sister turned from the sanctity of life for self preservation?

Right when I was getting answers, a whole new world was forced on me. A whole new world of questions and moral grayness. What was Gregory's role in this? What was Taylor's? What was mine?

"Why did they come for you?" Silence was shattered in the night by my words. Gregory almost flinched at the noise I made, as if I was a chirping bug. Was I just a nuisance to the Drone? Did he fear for our well being, or his?

"I will let you in on a secret as long as you don't tell Taylor. Deal?" His voice was quiet in the dark as he took his position sitting on the floor next to the door. He was ever my guard or jailer. I didn't know this Drone like Taylor, nor did I know his true purpose. There were no more reasons to trust him if he was the cause of the death that happened today.

I knew I couldn't see, but he could see me. Nodding my head in agreement to his deal, I could hear a faint whirring noise kick up. His eyes seemed to dim. Or was he looking down? Was it possible that the Drone felt guilt? If he felt guilt and still acted how he did, then I felt no pity for him.

"I'm assuming Taylor filled you in on our run in with Finigan, correct?" My silent nod pushed him further into his thoughts. "Well, she probably said something to the effect that I was running to save her that day. As if I had known she was the one that was in trouble. That... wasn't the case, though."

"I didn't even know she was there. There hadn't been plans for me to interfere with her journey. I knew she would be near if she followed my map, but she should never have been that close to Finigan. It was by chance I saw her at all while I was running in my escape attempt." Gregory went quiet for a moment, the whirring growing in intensity.

While a robot, his body language was clear. He was guilty of something. Something he didn't want Taylor to know. Why would he hide things from her? I thought he trusted her, or at least as much as she trusted him. There seemed to be no real trust these days.

"I had been caught. Gregory A-9497 did a routine scan of my program-ming which alerted me to the fact that I am on the last coherent legs of Fritzing. On top of that, my association with Taylor and her cover up was revealed in an investigation. I was being brought to Finigan to face my trial and termination." I could hear the quiet sound of metal on metal as Gregory rubbed his face.

"When I was placed before Finigan, I thought this was the end of my hundred-some years' duty. A part of me was glad I was finally done... but when I heard the 'Oomer's voice shout in the distance, and Finigan activated, I realized I didn't want to be done. I wanted to try something new."

"While likely a response to the Fritzing, I ran for whoever was triggering Finigan. The other Gregory units that escorted me were called to action, and I decommissioned the ones that remained to contain me. I just... followed the other Drones, hoping to find someone else who was trying to get free."

"Once we were closing in on the person we were chasing, I glimpsed your Razum. I only knew one person dumb enough to try to transport a Razum Wearer across the Barrens on braces, gimping through the fog."

"I did my best to destroy the Gregorys following and grabbed your sister. Still questioning my decisions with each step. It wasn't until Taylor shot Finigan that I accepted my alternative path. She may think it was for her, but I didn't even know it was her until she appeared."

Gregory went silent again. The whirring noise quieting and the silence filled the tin shed. Was this world just lucky? Was there no actual rhyme or reason? Taylor spoke fondly of Gregory saving her. Would she be disheartened to know that it was purely by chance? Did his path change to help her now, or was he still discovering what world he opened for himself?

I let the silence persist, imagining the scene through Gregory's eyes. The chaos his actions now created had led to the death of more children. While he saved my sister, I owed him that grateful respect, but was it worth the death of more innocent lives? Or as innocent as this world seemed to be? They may have been butchers of humans and their disregard for the morality of Razum Wearers disgusted me, but they were still children.

Did that mean nothing in this world?

"Do you feel guilty?" The words tumbled from me before I had time to gauge my intensity. Anger filled my tone. The tears of the girls who had fallen in the tunnel stung my eyes. Did he even care for the lives that he affected with this cascading whim that led us all here?

Glowing LEDs locked onto my eyes. There was an anger there, not directed at me, but at my question. "Guilty isn't something I have room for. You didn't know their names. You didn't know Heather, five years old with a deformed leg who clung to my arm as we fled. She got hit by a stray bullet that ricocheted into the tunnel. She made it to the surface dead."

"This was never my intention. My choices weren't supposed to lead to their deaths. I made a deal with Taylor that I would keep you safe when she was gone. That duty was held above all other priorities. It is my directive from her. Your life was held above all those children. For Taylor."

"So don't talk to me about guilt. It has no place in this world. The more you try to hold on to it, the more you're going to lose yourself in it. Grow up, deal with the consequences, and move on. There is no other option."

Gregory's tone was not one of anger, but one of hidden emotions. I may be newer to this world, but I would assume that he cared for those girls. What life did he lead with the humans now? Where did he stand? Why did he follow Taylor so loyally that he even let the girls he cared about to die?

There could be no doubt that I hated what this world was. I hated that Drones like Gregory existed in such a black and white existence. Even Taylor seemed to share a certain lack of heart for those around her. Hating wouldn't solve any of it, though. Only action spoke here. I want my life to be actionable, to be a change.

I let the silence clear the air between us. My judgment on Gregory was founded, but he was a machine following orders. It was like being upset that the sun rose. They will do what they are meant to do. I don't have to legitimize it. I could only try to change what I could in this world and right now, Gregory was the best tool we had. Never again should we have to witness children dying for him, though.

Steps were lurking outside the shed. People were walking. The world was becoming brighter. How long had I let the silence drag on for? Was the morning already inviting us in for a new day? Would there be more death on the new day?

Hurried steps now broke the morning buzz. These feet were heading our way. Gregory seemed to notice them as well, speed walking with intention. He shifted nearer to what I assumed was the door, but still was hazy in the dim light. He looked like a gilded guardian if I didn't know the darker side of his existence.

A soft rap on the door caused me to catch my breath. Were we caught? Had we been found? How would I fight when I couldn't move? Gregory's body gave away no fear, only readiness. How many times had he been in dangerous situations like this? Was he ever unprepared for a fight?

"Password?" He lowered his voice so the speaker's rattle didn't sound so obvious.

"Tea Party." It was Taylor's voice, hoarse and out of breath.

Gregory opened the door and let in more light. I could see the vague outline of my sister step through the entrance before the light was snuffed out. She ran to my side, ignoring Gregory as he took his familiar position in front of the door.

Hands were checking me up and down as Taylor examined me. Could I see tears on her cheeks? Was she worried about me? She knew Gregory was with me. I had the best chance of survival. Her hands were still warm. Was she always warm?

"Are you okay? Did your scars open up? What happened? Tricia found me and told me there was a raid." Once she slowed her analysis, her eyes looked across my face and saw the blood that still sat there. She cast a glance back to Gregory and reasserted her tone.

"What happened, Gregory?"

The robot shifted more uneasily under her penetrating glare. She would not be left without answers. I smiled to myself. There was the strong-willed sister I knew. She was still a commanding brat that demanded respect with a simple glare.

"Harvey Units came for me. I must have been spotted on my last errand run. Vykra was killed at the door protecting the Den. Some girls escaped, but most fell in the tunnel. Tyron was unharmed, if not sore. I covered our tracks back here. We should be safe."

"Our wisest choice would be to leave the city. With the Harvey Units aware of my presence here, they will tighten their search areas. It will get very tense, worse than it already was."

His explanation seemed to appease Taylor as she centered her gaze on me once more. Her fingers twirled my hair as she thought about her options. I was surprised the talk of death didn't phase her more. So her humanity was gone? This world needed to be gutted and cleaned for its atrocities.

"We can try to get Tyron out of here. The next Loomer city is far, though. We would be months on the road. You will have to carry him most of the way since his legs aren't coming back yet." Taylor was already spouting off her plan. Gregory nodded in agreement with her and began to stand slowly as he prepared himself. She was the commanding voice here, but with her lack of empathy, I felt less willing to follow.

"Wait." My words were gravelly. While I wasn't fully sure of what I wanted to do here, I wasn't ready to leave.

"I do not want to leave Sila." How could we leave? There is so much we could do to help this city. From what I have heard, people were already willing to fight back. People were ready for a change. Why did we have to live in fear of the machines that were breaking and Fritzing like Gregory? This city was a tinderbox. It seems like a good time to strike a match.

This equipment that controlled us was old. There was no reason we couldn't rise up now. Earlier attempts were weak against prepared Drones who expected rebellions. Now things were different. Taylor opened a new door in the world when she released me. We had a Drone who knew his way around the system; we had Taylor who knew the world, and now I am here to stir the pot.

"That is not wise." Gregory's voice was stern now.

"Gregory is right. Staying here will only attract more Harvey Units and the people will be oppressed more. They are already on the verge of rebellion. It's dangerous." Taylor's voice was gentle, but her resolve sounded sure.

"We can't bring all this pain to a city and then run when it's too much for us. We've started something here, and we're responsible for fixing it." I did my best to rival Taylor's gentle tone with my own impassioned voice. This wasn't a fair deal. Gregory brought this struggle to the town when he helped Taylor escape. They couldn't both just run from their consequences. Someone had to pay or fight back.

"You don't know enough about this world to make that decision." The speaker rattled louder now as Gregory spoke up, using his more Drone-like voice. No doubt he was attempting to intimidate me. The look Taylor shot him proved me right as she motioned for him to back off.

"Are you sure? All our lives will be more at risk here. I don't want you to be in more danger than we already are." Her hand clamped down on mine and she brought her face closer. There was a warm assurance in her eyes that tried to unravel my own intentions. If I wasn't aware of her abilities to break down people, I might have caved, but I taught her.

I reached my free hand to her face and pet the dry, burnt skin while moving some stray hairs from her vision. My sweet sister has grown blindly attached to me. I cursed myself for having been such a burden on her. She must have lost years of possible happiness caring for my living corpse. My poor sister.

"Taylor, you have opened a new book on the robots these people struggle with, you and Gregory both. We have the tools and the knowledge to help these people. If there was even one girl out there crying over her brother who was trapped in a Razum, wouldn't you want to help?"

What happened to my sister, who would go out of her way to help everyone? She used to understand the struggle of people she crossed paths with. Now you are ready to leave them in the mud? When did my child sister change like this?

What have you become?

It's our world too, and I don't want to leave it this way. We can strike the match of rebellion together and finally give these people a true taste of freedom. No more girls will have to die or work in Organ Dens. No more children will be raised in factories or not knowing if their parents will come home. No more sisters would have to give up their humanity to

271

save those they care about.

"Please, let's stay. You know just as well as I that together we make an unstoppable team. We have always been a team, or were those words lies? Did you not bring me out of the Razum to give me a chance to live a real life? Well… this is what I want to do with my life. I want to help make the world better."

There were risks with these words, but I couldn't contain them. I had no ownership over them, only my soul did. Finally, I felt like the questions that haunted me most escaped me. Words were only the conduit of my true intentions. Taylor needed to know what my intentions were. She needed to understand me. All I had was her. I couldn't even walk without her. She needed to know how much this meant to me. She needed to know why she couldn't say no.

More silence. For a chaotic world, it was often filled with silence. Through this silence, I hoped would be the calm before the storm. Would this silence be the last small wave before the tsunami came? Was she going to leave me again? Or would I have to leave her?

Gregory's shifting stirred us. I knew he had his own things to say, but he was waiting for Taylor. She stared into my eyes as if pulling apart the very fibers of my iris. She was looking into every detail of my soul, weighing its contents against her own. My sister was always so smart. How could she not see the wrong she would do in leaving now?

With a long sigh and closed eyes, Taylor dropped her head a bit in defeat. "We will stay for a while longer. If there is a threat to your life, though… I don't know what hell I will rain down on this town."

"Taylor, you know this isn't a wise decision." Gregory placed a gentle hand on Taylor's shoulder. My skin prickled a bit at seeing his familiarity with her. He should have more respect for her than that with the blood that was on his hands. My sister's blood and the Den girls' blood would never be cleaned from those metal fingers.

"I know, but when we woke him up, you knew he would be his own person. We didn't just wake something up, we freed Tyron. He is capable of his own feelings, ambitions, and drive. He is allowed to make choices, like you were when you were freed from the Network. Like I could when I left the Razum."

"To disrespect his autonomy would be to disrespect the paths we have chosen for ourselves. He's right ultimately. We stirred this town up with disregard to the people who lived here. I've heard their stories of Drone brutality. It's our fault because of our actions against Finigan. We share the blame here."

Her words were finite. I knew she could still see my side. Taylor's humanity remained, and to my relief, was still accessible. Her fingers twirled my hair once more before turning to face Gregory, who had taken a more aggressive stance as he thought over her words.

The air was tense between them, electricity versus stubborn human belief. The whirring noise reappeared and was more intense than before. I could almost feel the air moving as Gregory pumped it across his circuits. Taylor broke the tension and placed a hand on his shoulder now. A sign of comradery.

"You don't have to join us. I will stay with Tyron and we will figure it out. If you would rather leave and keep yourself safe, I will understand. This isn't the Network, there are no orders. You have your own freedom to be concerned about. You have your own choice to make."

The whirring filled the sound between her words. I had forgotten how gentle she could be. Perhaps I was caught in the brutalist world. I lost sight of the little girl my sister still was. She was respectful, but direct. She was strong yet delicate. She was a leader who guided.

My nerves tied in my stomach as I saw the shine of Gregory's hand clamp down on Taylor's arm. He stretched taller into the ceiling; the light beginning to show his outline more clearly. He was massive compared to the small size of Taylor. We should never forget that he is a Drone. He will never be on our side fully.

Taylor never broke face, though. Her calm demeanor seemed unnerving. She had stared down her demons before, even if one of them was her friend. She held no more fear of the robots. I couldn't help but to wonder if she was like this before she freed me. Was this Taylor the one everyone had known, except for me?

"I will not watch you two get cut down in this miserable town. As soon as things go sideways, as they will, I will leave. With or without you. I am not signing on to a suicide mission." His words came out softly. Gripping Taylor's arm was his way of making his words true to her. No mistakes could be made in this conversation. There would be no negotiations later.

Taylor released the metal plated shoulder I had ridden on a few hours prior and nodded to him. They had reached a tense understanding, but it was agreed. Even if the agreement was on uneasy terms and borderline threats, we were going to stay in Sila.

Once peace had been established in the tin shed, Gregory took his seat against the door once more, the whirring continuing. Taylor pushed me to the side with ease. Her strength was impressive for one so small. She tucked herself into my tarp blanket and added warmth.

She must have been tired from being awake through the night's events and quickly relaxed her breathing. There was a moment. Between her breath and Gregory's whirring, the reality of this world hit me again. This ever-oppressive world.

I had found my Taylor. She was not a disappointment. She was not a stranger. She had become something more than I could have ever dreamed. Not only was she still the warm, caring girl I once knew, but she had become a hardened worker. No need for flashy personalities, or overly delicate. A true beast of control and function. It would be easier to compare her to Gregory than it would to compare her to me.

Wrapping my arm around her as much as I could, I held her close. She no longer needed to be this beast. She could go back to simply enjoying her life. I would do everything I could to make sure she would never have to bow to the machines. She deserved the freedom she was promised when she left the Razum. So did the children. So did the people.

Sleep tugged at me, but the sounds of staggered feet beyond the walls kept me alert. Distant voices greeted others, the sound of doors opening and closing, greeting the day. Life stirred. I had never heard such an abundance of life.

I wished I could join them, going about their days. What was life like here? Were they running errands or caring for the young? Going out to prepare meals for their families? Were some going off to work? What were these people like?

What were the girls like who had died last night? Did they have families? Was there mothers waking up and looking for their little girls? Did fathers walk the streets shouting names? What was outside of this safety shell?

"Gregory?" My voice was barely a whisper, being sure to angle my chin away from Taylor while she slept.

"What is it?" His voice was also quiet. We both had the understanding that Taylor needed her sleep.

"Can you tell me about the girls? What were their lives like?"

The small giggles of kids outside drew both our attention. Tiny feet patter through mud. Gregory waited to respond until the kids were far enough away to not cause attention.

"There were fifty-four girls who worked under Vykra. Most under the age of fourteen, a handful were nearing adulthood. I didn't deal with most of them, as they feared me. A few grew to like me. Heather being one of them. She and her friends were too small to reach the operating tables but were still required to learn."

"On their few breaks they had, they would come up to me. Asking ridiculous questions. If their hair was pretty or did I like their clothes. Showing off scars as badges of honor and telling me stories of Den where they grew up."

"Most of them were orphans because of a factory explosion a few years prior. Vykra was like their adoptive parent. They weren't to go outside unless for delivery, nor did many people come inside. A den with a protective wolf-like mother."

"I caught a girl named Anne carving an image of something on my back one day. It started a horrible trend of the girls carving their initials into my paint. I carry almost every initial of every person that worked there. Many... now gone."

Gregory continued his stories in a hushed tone, occasionally pausing when people walked near. The quiet retelling of fortunate children put me at ease. I could feel my body melting into the table.

Tales of girls wearing dresses and believing themselves to be Giants, ruling over people. Princesses of a peaceful world they knew nothing about. Children's fantasies were truly the purest thing.

I hugged Taylor once more before giving into the pull of sleep. My eyes relaxed in the growing light. Gregory's stories continued, giving me hope as my mind drifted away. My dreams were covered in the faces of merry children, living their fantasies they would never achieve.

Chapter 11: Old Wounds, New Friends

We woke up later in the day. Taylor had to show me how to eat food on my own. A grueling process that ended up with me vomiting multiple times before I could keep down a few bites. She was patient with me. Always helping, always cleaning up my mess.

Gregory had left at some point to scout the area around our shed, allowing Taylor and me to sleep for a while longer. When night finally appeared, the Drone returned. He had found more tarps and candles to spruce up the shed since we planned on being here for a while.

Conversations were brief. Gregory encouraged our sleeping and refused to inform us about things until the next day. So we took our time to go back to sleep. Everything was quiet. Apparently, the raid hadn't raised too many issues, or the town would be on fire.

Hours passed. Or was it days? Each time I woke, I felt a new strength burning in my body. According to Taylor, the healing was going well. My scars had stiffened and were now a delicate pink seam that threaded across my chest, likely thanks to the Nanites.

I would catch her looking at them sometimes, feeling the lines that held me together. She told me she was happy I was okay, but her voice always sounded sad. Even when Gregory acknowledged them, he held a certain tone, distancing himself from them.

My body was now a reminder of lives lost. A painting of the hard work of children who had fallen. After seeing their sullen faces, I hassled Gregory for a shirt the next time he left. There was no reason to be a reminder of death, there was enough death around us.

It was probably early morning based on the vague light I could see through the cracks of the shed. My eyesight had finally improved enough to make out the minor details around me. Though, distant objects were still blurry. Some progress was better than none, at least.

Quiet steps were approaching the shed, careful feet. All of us seemed to sense the same intention in the footsteps. Gregory was posed by the door in his usual spot while Taylor sat up with a crude metal knife she had made earlier the prior day. A quiet knock made us all tense with anticipation.

Gregory leaned his face close to the door and listened before speaking. "Who is it?"

"It's Anne. Is Taylor with you?" A quiet, girlish voice hid behind the door. There was hesitation in her words and anxiety in her tone. Gregory opened the door just enough for the small girl to enter. She looked around five or six years old with shorter brown hair that looked more like mud than hair.

She looked at Gregory with excitement. Was this the Anne who carved images on him? With the door closed, she hugged the Drone causing him to back away instinctively. He was caught as the crying began.

"They caught so many of us! There is no one left! Vykra is dead, and the Den is gone! What should we do, Gregory!?" The Drone held his arms up and away from the child who glued herself to his chest plates, rubbing her teary face in the cables that were exposed in the center. In the small shed, he had no room to stand and escape the emotional child.

Taylor allowed a smirk at the uncomfortable Drone before she left the table and knelt by the girl. Petting her hair as she pulled bits of mud from it. Rubbing the girl's back until she calmed down, Taylor then spoke to her in a careful and calm tone.

"It will be okay. Do you know of any other Organ Dens in town? Maybe they would take the survivors in." Her words were gentle, though even as Anne made eye contact, she wouldn't release Gregory.

"We were the only one. Nearest Organ Den is in Roto, but it's a bevy town and miles away. We wouldn't make it." Her voice was slightly calmer, but her panic and sadness remained.

Taylor continued to rub her back as she sniveled. She must have been running. I did my best to sit up and hold myself on my stronger arms. Her eyes glued to me. Watching and analyzing, her eyes followed the scar on my chest.

"You're the Razum Wearer who woke up." Her words were quick and inquisitive. She must have heard of me, but never saw me. I did my best to nod to her, letting her know her guess was correct.

"The others talk about you. I knew a few who did the surgery. Word is spreading around town about you." She hugged Gregory closer, nearly knocking him off his balanced crouch he maintained. He caught himself with one hand and supported the back of Anne with the other.

Word had spread about me? Was it bringing curiosity and hope, or a new evil to the city? Taylor glanced back at me, evaluating this new information as well. I knew there was a strict rule about not talking about me in the Den, but now with no more Den, it seemed the kids were talking.

"What is being said about him?" Taylor's more aggressive tone seemed to spook the girl as she tried to bring herself even closer to Gregory. While she didn't seem entirely afraid of Taylor, Anne was obviously closer to the Drone now.

"Just that a Razum Wearer was woken up. No name. No story." She knew the information Taylor was after. Anne was an intelligent child who understood that she needed to verify if we had been named yet. If we were going to be targeted specifically.

Taylor's silent analysis filled the sound of the shed. She was weighing options, figuring out paths. Always the tactician. Gregory shifted slightly to stand and try to shake off the girl, but her grip only tightened and she was lifted with him. Finally, he gave up and used his arm to support Anne while she clung to him.

I had never thought I would see Gregory beaten by the stubbornness of a child. The amusing image did not last long as Anne posed to speak. Her face was buried into Gregory and muffled. She didn't want to be heard, but had something to add.

"The Forge knows. They're looking for you. Tricia told me to find you and tell you." Though muffled, her words seemed to stir the attention of Gregory and Taylor. I hadn't heard of The Forge.

"How did you find us, Anne?" Gregory now chimed in, keeping his voice low to not disturb the girl. She looked up at his damaged face and ran her finger across the panels of his face.

"You told us the story of Taylor's tea set. I saw the Tea Party signs and followed them." She tugged at a crack in Gregory's face before he grabbed her hand and placed it back at her side. Barely a moment had passed before the girl reached up again and tried to get her finger into the cracked metal. Gregory gave up.

"You told them about my tea set?" Taylor's voice seemed amused. From what I could see of her face, she didn't know how to interpret this information besides that he had made an attempt to share his own stories for the girls. Gregory mimicked a shrug.

"My knowledge of children is limited to what you've told me. So, I showed them the tea set that you had made and they loved it." His tone was dismissive as his attention was on Anne trying to pull apart his face plates. Taylor allowed herself a smile.

What tea set? Did she recreate the one she had as a kid? Where was this softie under the bruises and gnarled clothes? It warmed my heart to see Taylor being kind to someone else. I was glad she hadn't saved all her love for me. She deserved a life beyond her brother.

Anne pulled at the satchel Gregory still wore from the night before. Once she freed it from being pinned under his arm, she flipped the top of the bag open. Rummaging loudly until she pulled a cup free. It was crude, unlikely to hold liquid, but it was a tea cup.

Taylor examined the tea cup before looking up to Gregory. "I saw these in the Den. Did you go back to get them?" Her voice was slowly becoming more accusatory. Anne put the cup back and hugged Gregory once more.

"You told me to keep them safe. It was worth the risk." While the tone was dismissive, his words were not. Anne watched Taylor as she thought of what was best to say in front of the girl. I knew there would be a stern worded complaint about the risk that Gregory ran, but would she bring

280

that up in front of Anne?

"That was a dangerous choice. I will lecture you later about that. Anne, The Forge, what do they know about us?" Gregory shifted her to look more towards Taylor.

"They are looking for the Razum Wearer and a sister. They don't know about Gregory besides that the bunnies are looking for him." The girl was sharp. She knew how to convey information. While young, her innocence was her disguise. A courier of information that was beyond her scope of understanding.

"Who is The Forge?" I chimed in. Feeling abandoned in a conversation that was leaving me behind with little information. Taylor turned to me now, entrusting Anne to Gregory's care while she filled me in. The ever loyal babysitter.

"We have both been hearing rumors of a developing rebellion. Which is bad news. Means this town is in trouble and if the Harvey Units catch wind, it could mean all out nuclear cleansing. Even Haldoklik could get hit. If they are looking for you, they could bring trouble with them." Serious words, they took from the warmth of her face. She was worried.

"Shouldn't we talk to them? Sounds like they could have some actual power to cause change here." This world was new to me, but the idea of a rebellion with some power was better than being powerless. That was simple situational math.

"We know nothing about them. That could go South very quickly, leaving us dead and Gregory used as the symbol the Drones need to call in an attack." She sounded dramatic, as if I should know this. I heard her stories. I knew the risks a rebellion could cause.

"Or it could go well. We could have shelter and a position to help change things here...I want to talk to them." Taylor recoiled from my words. I challenged her rule, something that doesn't seem to be a common occurrence to her these days.

Gregory continued to hold Anne as she was now invested in the conversation. All eyes were turned to me. I refused to hide my opinion. Woken for a reason, I had to prove I could cause more change.

"I could get their courier instead of talking to a member. They can be twitchy." Anne's voice broke the weight of the eyes bearing down on me. I quietly nodded my thanks to the girl. She hid part of her face in Gregory's exposed cables.

"That could work better. We can meet them somewhere away from us and away from them. Gregory, you would do better to stay behind. We don't need radicals attacking you and drawing attention." Taylor's plan made more sense as she backed my ambitions. I reached for her hand to pacify the tension between us.

Accepting my hand, she now looked at Anne. The girl faced her more readily now. She knew when she was about to receive a message to carry. A bold child who knew her role in adult conversation.

"Anne Farin, I have a task for you. It is very important. If you want to save Gregory, listen to my words exactly. Understood?" The little girl nodded and watched Taylor closely.

"You will find The Forge courier. Tell him, 'if The Forge wants to meet the Razum Wearer who woke, they should send a courier to the main street corner with their information and requests'. Got that?" The girl nodded once more, mouthing the words as Taylor spoke.

"When the courier gets to the street corner, I want you to guide them back here, avoid the way you came and the signs you followed. We'll meet the courier at the Lower Town wall and talk there. Today, if possible. Repeat it back to me."

The girl did her duty and repeated the instructions back clearly. She was well practiced. With an appreciative pat from Taylor, Gregory released her squirming form back to the ground and opened the door. She was gone in the blink of an eye.

Taylor now turned to face both Gregory and me. Her face was not pleased. I braced myself for the lecture we were about to receive. I had blatantly opposed her opinion, and Gregory risked our discovery by retrieving the tea set. Neither one of us was in her good grace at the moment. After a few seconds of silence, she let out a sigh.

"Are we really joining a rebellion?" Hands rubbed confused temples as she tried to think through what had just happened.

Gregory shifted back to his seated position on the ground in front of the door, forcing Taylor to step into the center of the shed. She scanned over both of us for an answer. He chuckled slightly, breaking the serious tone.

"This is going sideways faster than I expected. So, yes." He was being facetious, but he was still on board. Taylor ignored his sarcasm and looked at me. There was no sarcasm in her face. She needed certainty, words to prove to her that this was my choice of actions. That this was what I wanted to do with my life now.

"It's going to be the quickest way to do what we can to help the city." I had to hold my ground. This had to be the best choice. How else was change supposed to happen? Right the wrongs we had caused. With a conceding head nod, Taylor turned towards the door.

"Then we need to find a location to wait at. Anne is fast. I need to find you some clothes before we go out. We need to hide that scar or it will attract attention. At least it isn't raining out. Gregory, please watch him." With that, she left the shed and Gregory sat down once more as the guardian of the door.

I let myself relax back down onto the table, excitement coursing through my mind. An opportunity. A window was opening. New chances for change had appeared. If things went well with The Forge courier, we could begin doing things that mattered.

How were they going to view me? How were they going to know I wasn't a lie? What could I do to let them know I was real? If they refused to let us help in the rebellion, what will we need to do to make sure we join?

"Relax. Taylor will ensure the best outcome. She is well trained in talking her way out of things. You seem to be well trained in talking her into things. My job is to make sure you two balance each other out."

"There is about an eighty-eight percent chance that you will be murdered. With Taylor, it's closer to seventy-three percent. Better odds than when she shot Finigan." Gregory's nonchalant response was more infuriating than it was reassuring. Maybe it was my own bitterness clouding my perception, but I struggled to decipher his humor from his concern.

All I could do until then was wait. I rolled to my side the best I could with only my two arms. Facing Gregory, I examined him in the brighter light of day. I hadn't taken time to familiarize myself with his image, nor did I really want to. Though, if we were going to join a rebellion to fight against other Drones of similar models, it would be good to recognize him in a group.

He had primarily golden yellow plates that covered his face, chest, arms and joints, as well as his legs acting as armor plates. Between each panel of yellow, I could see dark cables that ran vertically and horizontally, like webbing encasing his inner workings.

His hair was extended from his face plates and curved into a wave of blonde looking hair. LEDs watched me as I examined him. I could vaguely see the scratches in his paint. The initials must stretch from the back left panel and under his arm to the front panel. I could see 'A.F.' prominently on top of the left chest plate, just under his make and model information that was formed like a name tag.

"I'm guessing Anne Farin is the A.F. I see there?" Gregory looked down to where I gestured and touched the letters as if trying to familiarize himself with his new branding. He tapped the initial as he responded, a dull thud of metal on metal.

"No, this was Annabelle Folly. She fell before we reached the tunnel. Anne Farin is over here." He lifted his arm to show more initials carved into the plates of his arm. There was another A.F. set of letters. "She thought she could tickle me by carving on my arm. No matter how often I explained to them, I do not feel the sensation of tickling."

I couldn't help but to chuckle at the tolerance of Gregory. "When Taylor was younger, she hated to be tickled. I would chase her around for hours. Every time I caught her, I would tickle her until she escaped. She was so small back then. Seeing her as an adult and missing all the years in between... it's weird. Sometimes, I still see that little girl, then she does something so intimidating that I have to remember she's grown."

The memories of Taylor's short golden hair bouncing on her shoulders as she ran from me felt so real. It could have been yesterday that I saw her like that. Her giggle was so obnoxious, I couldn't help mocking her for it. Could anyone else relate to seeing their child sibling one day, only to wake and realize they had grown?

"I didn't know her when she was that young. She was quite older than Anne when she first showed up. I can tell you she was still just as feisty. Her first day in Haldoklik, I had to break up a fight she started. She was dragging your body trying to find a shelter. When she couldn't find one, she tried to evict another couple."

"She was like a wild animal. Biting and ripping at people, and she's responsible for some nicks on my back. Once I broke them up, I helped her build the shed that she lived in for the rest of her time in Haldoklik. I may have had to break in her door a few times, but I always reinforced it later. By the end of her time there, after having her door broken down and fixed so many times, she probably had the strongest shed in all of Haldoklik."

I had not thought about the fact that Gregory had an entire set of memories of Taylor as a child that I would never have. Her years learning to survive, learning to thrive. He, in his own way, seemed to have brotherly memories of her.

Our moment of bonding was cut short by the quick knock of Taylor. Once inside, she tossed a shirt at me. "Quick, I passed Anne on the way back. She already found the courier and is walking him to the wall." News traveled fast in Sila, apparently.

I did my best to pull the shirt over me as Taylor dressed herself in heavy clothing. Everything I had seen her wear to this point was light and breathable, but this was a heavy cloak, lined with lead. I noticed a lever on her shoulder as she applied what looked like a parachute from her back. She handed me the tarp.

"Put this under you as much as you can." She was hurrying.

"What is it?" I asked as I slid the tarp under my back and below my waist.

"This is how I carried you across the Barrens. A farewell present from Gern." She turned the lever on her shoulder and my body moved towards her. Backing up close to the edge of the table, she pat her own shoulder. "Grab on. It's my turn to give you a piggyback ride."

Feeling somewhat embarrassed, I climbed onto her back and the tarp pulled the rest of my weight off the table. Now I knew why she seemed so strong. She had been carrying my body weight with her most days. She had to be strong to care for me.

It wasn't right.

Once secured, Gregory moved from the door. Taylor paused in front of him. "If we aren't back in an hour, get out of town. Better to be safe and leave than try to find us." Gregory nodded at his assignment and closed the door behind us.

The world was brighter; the sun having finally reached over the edge of the walls that made up the crater of where Locura fell. There were no buildings, but I could see towards the head of town, where buildings stood tall and blurry. They were almost reaching for the tops of the walls. Tin sheds were all around us. It was safe to guess that this was the slum zone.

Taylor was in 'mission mode' and started her way to the wall to follow it to a meeting spot she likely found while looking for a shirt. The walk was surprisingly short, or she walked surprisingly fast.

We stood at the base of the wall now. Even looking up, I had to bend my neck as far back as I could to see the top of the wall. If someone were on top, they would have a clear vantage of the entire city. These cities were meant to hold people, not to be defended. Another constant sign of oppression.

"Do you think Anne will find us alright?" I muttered over my sister's shoulder as she watched the area. We took a position with the wall at our back, facing the slums that sprawled before us. I knew her eyes could scan faster than mine. She was the sentry and the tower I sat on.

"Anne knows this town better than most of the inhabitants. She was my trainer for deliveries under Vykra. That girl knows more about Sila's dark side than anyone else I've run into. She'll find us," Taylor whispered. Did she assume ears were listening near us? I suppose nowhere was truly safe from prying company.

Minutes passed in silence. This part of town was quieter than the slums and appeared to not be as inhabited. Yet Taylor remained vigilant. I rested my head on her shoulder and watched the still world. Taking in the details of this new life.

From my higher vantage point on Taylor's back, I was the first to see the compact figure of Anne appear from behind the distant sheds. She seemed calm as she led a taller teenage boy in our direction.

"Over there." I pointed out the small girl's location as Taylor focused her attention on that specific spot. She stood taller, away from the wall, and prepared for a confrontation with the stranger. Her doubt of The Forge could quickly become an issue in this conversation.

"Keep an eye out for Harvey Drones. I don't want to outrun bullets." Her tone was crisp, but she maintained a sarcastic note. She was ready to fight, but her fight went back many years already.

As Anne drew closer, she looked around quickly for Gregory. When she couldn't find him, she took up position next to Taylor and me. The teen caught up with her and stood opposite of us. He also maintained a watchful eye of the surrounding area.

"Are you the Razum Wearer?" He asked quietly, his tone betraying bashful notes.

"He is." Taylor jerked a thumb towards me as I watched the teen.

"The Forge welcomes you to this world Razum Born. They would also like to extend an invitation. There has never been a Razum Born who woke up before in this city or any other cities we know. So, to better understand how you were freed, we only would like to talk. Tonight, if you are interested."

"There will be a small quiet rally in The Forge's region near the factories of the Head district. You and your sister are invited to join us. When you hear the phrase, 'From ruin we rise', respond with 'forged in scrap'. They will let you in."

The teen stepped back when Taylor's words stopped him. "This is only an invitation to a rally?" I could hear the disbelief in her voice. She had not expected an invitation.

"My orders were simple. Invitation only. This isn't a rebellion like in other towns. We aren't violent. We just want peace. So if you came prepared for a fight, I am sorry I will have to disappoint." He held his composure well under the eyes of my sister.

Once she made no movement to speak further, the teen left. Anne watched him go and leaned into Taylor's side. She looked up at both of us with a smirk. Anne knew this was the better of the outcomes we were prepared for, and she was happy to be a part of it.

"Go on, run your errands around town. We will be at the rally tonight. Could do with some extra eyes in the area just in case the rally isn't so peaceful. Shoo." Taylor patted Anne's back kindly as she shooed the little girl back into the distant town. As we started the walk back to the shed, we enjoyed a friendly silence. The first moment we had alone together without the metal ears of Gregory listening.

"It's been a long time since we took a walk together, hasn't it?" The nostalgia of being close to her again after dreaming of seeing her was hitting me. Even in this desolate area, far away from the people of Sila, I could still feel the little girl she had once been.

She reached her hand up and placed it on my hand that stabilized me above her head. Squeezing it, she turned her head and kissed my knuckles. Her thoughts were her own, but I knew she felt what I did.

"I have dreamed about walking with you again for so many years. I'm sorry I couldn't keep your legs working. My best wasn't good enough. I will figure out a way to give you your movement back so we can really take a walk together again." Guilt was in her voice. Guilt for not being good enough. Didn't she know that was what I was supposed to be feeling?

I moved my hand from hers and lightly nudged the back of her head. "Shut up. Your best gave me my life back. I've technically never known how to use my legs, so the loss is not major." Hearing her chuckle and shake her back, throwing me off balance, proved to me that those were the right words to say. There were things we didn't agree on, but at least our relationship was the same.

My bratty little sister, nothing could change that.

We enjoyed a playful banter all the way to the shed. A peaceful, real walk with my sister. I never thought I would enjoy being crippled, but she made it feel like a superpower rather than an impairment. The time together was cut short as we approached the shed.

Gregory opened the door to the password, and we ducked inside. It was a much easier fit than going in on Gregory's back. She pulled her cloak in after her and made sure my head cleared the door frame before sealing the world out again.

"Good to see you two alive and apparently uninjured. How were The Forge people?" I was quickly getting annoyed by the nonchalant attitude that Gregory held towards human life. Taylor updated him on the situation and our plan to attend the rally as he helped me off her back and onto the table.

"So, I'm going to be attending a rally with you two in a heavily guarded Harvey zone? Sounds daring." His voice did not hide his sarcasm. While Gregory was not happy about the plan, he assumed he was going with us.

"You don't have to go. Technically, you weren't invited." Taylor matched his sarcasm. She was disrobing her heavy cloak. Once free, she threw it at Gregory, who caught it and dropped it to the ground.

"Well, I would rather go than stay here and be your coat rack. When is it?" He positioned him in front of the door once more.

"It's tonight. No specific time. I'm assuming we just show up at some point and get what we get." Taylor sat on the edge of the table and looked over at me. "It would be nice to not have to carry Tyron the whole way. Think you can blend in enough to hide in a crowd?"

Gregory flexed his cabling and demonstrated how he could reduce his size and clamp his panels down to make him smaller and more nimble. "I had some damage that was preventing me from altering my size, but the girls in the Den fixed it. I should be able to pass as a little more human. Staying hunched over should finish my disguise. Hopefully, the Harveys won't recognize me." He seemed oddly optimistic. Was he getting excited about the subterfuge and schemes? It seemed right up his programming.

Truly a fiend. A fiend who was on our side, maybe. Taylor nodded her impressed face towards him. She seemed to be unaware that the Gregory units were so advanced. Did she know of his Fritzing? Or whatever that was?

"What is Fritzing?" The question tumbled out of me as if from the side of my brain that was still learning to process this body gave way. By Taylor's sullen face appearing, and Gregory settling back down by the door in his expanded form, I knew I had asked the wrong question.

"Fritzing is when a Drone's circuits fry." Gregory grunted out the gruff response. I must have hit on a more delicate topic. Taylor took over the explanation for the disgruntled Drone.

"Drones have experienced a lot of damage over the years, whether from the acid rain, humans, or general wear and tear. Because of some of this damage, sometimes their circuits can get damaged."

"One of two things can happen when a Drone is Fritzing: One, their coding can get scrambled, unlocking the more humanistic emotional balance that the Drones were originally programmed with by their human creators. Two-"

"We go insane and start killing everything and everyone." Gregory's interjection proved his annoyance with the topic. The possibility that he may soon go insane, or that he may not be what he is supposed to be, seemed to bother him.

Gregory tapped his face panel and looked at Taylor.

"I have shown no signs of the second option. I'm safe for now." He was quick to prove that fact. Taylor held up peaceful hands before looking at me again. Her eyes were alerting me that this was a difficult topic.

"It is a risk with all Drones. Gregory is an older model type and knows more about the world than most. Probably more than some Giants. While it is a possibility, I am not worried about him Fritzing out on us." Her words and tone seemed to soothe the tension that had built. Gregory was right. She knew how to talk her way out of things.

"I didn't know." Antagonizing him with more questions seemed like it was more likely to upset Taylor, but I would ask them later. He waved a dismissive hand towards me and leaned his head against the door, causing it to shift against the added weight.

"I know this world is new to you. It is a fair question. Though, I would just rather not talk about how I may soon go psychotic and blow up the city." While this was a dry attempt at a joke, it didn't seem to land. Apparently, Gregory and I shared our lack of ability to soothe tense moments.

Silence lurked in the shed once more. It was becoming more prevalent than conversations and air itself. Taylor sat herself on the edge of my table and let out a breath. The stress of a young day was already bothering her. As the time went on, we had little to do besides muscle training for me, and quiet contemplation about tonight.

Taylor walked me through movement practice, as well as having me crawl around across the ground. It was a practice of patience with Gregory's scoffing at my attempts, but I could feel myself earning my autonomy. The more I crawled, the faster I could move. This body felt awkward and strange to me, but I was learning to handle it.

We did several hours of this training, passing the day away slowly. After a break to eat, we took a rest. Taylor checked her gear and assembled the arsenal of weapons she created from nearby scrap piles. Prepared for a fight, she was fidgeting and correcting until she felt content with her armory and how it hid under her clothing. She seemed more wary of dealing with humans than she did of Drones.

Gregory had been quiet besides his occasional mocking of my attempts at moving. His hands fiddled with a small contraption, creating an enigmatic machine of sorts. When I probed him for answers, I was met with silence. He maintained his moody atmosphere most of the day.

There was a subtle pang of guilt in my stomach. The mood had shifted so much from the Den, and I knew I was the contributing factor. Did they not see this as a chance of unification? An opportunity to start a change, even if it was in one city. We could start a change of power and retake our authority over the land. Why was this a cautious task?

I debated asking Taylor for her concerns, but with the friction in the air about the day so far, I didn't want to push my luck. Hoping to change the mood, I debated more friendly questions. To my dismay, I realized there was not much to ask about that didn't involve this destructive and miserable reality.

Asking about Taylor's childhood would only lead her to thoughts of loneliness and the Scientist. If I inquired about her teen years, she would likely tell me how she was hurt or struggled. Gregory was of a similar struggle with his 'childhood' being he was brought into the world to suppress humans. Until lately, it didn't seem like he cared about memories and his recent ones all seemed to be failures to him.

Was this our reality now? A world so dark that I couldn't find a topic to lighten the mood? No hope or happiness. Just memories to avoid because they were too painful. Hope remained in my chest for the rebellion. Maybe those who have fought back had victories to remember fondly. Maybe they had families and experiences beyond the struggles of my companions? It almost felt rude to hope for stories of success instead of embracing the pain of my friends.

These thoughts bounced around my head. I had time to waste, so why not try to be hopeful and plot for a better future? Rather than wasting my day dreading the darkness, I could try to seek the light. It's what the younger Taylor would have done. Did she even see a light anymore? Was there a reason she fought for besides me? This world seemed dead to her.

I sometimes questioned my sister. Almost hollow of character. While I love and respect her work and passion for saving me, I worried she held nothing else in her heart. She was even willing to work with a Drone who had hurt her many times on orders. Had she learned to have peace with the machines that broke our planet? That shredded humanity from their podium in the world order?

Shushing these thoughts, I reserved my judgments. Even if I didn't agree with her in moral guidelines, I had to respect her contribution to my existence here. I did not live her life, or sacrificed what she did to bring me back. Though anger burned brighter in me. The idea of such an innocent girl being forced into a dangerous world by herself was bad enough. Knowing that same girl aligned herself with the dangers of the world to bring me back was infuriating. The worst was knowing that she feared humans more than she seemed to fear Drones.

Gregory seemed fine from what I knew of him, but it did not change my apprehension that was growing over him. Fritzing was a danger in itself, but what if he was still connected to the network? He could easily give us up at any time and likely save his own scrap by doing so. How did the laws of loyalty work here?

Morality had left and pathetic alliances now held the world together. Was the Forge like this as well? Dread, anger, hope. Too many complex emotions to sort at this time. I did my best to push the thoughts down and relaxed by focusing my eyes on a crack in the wall. Noting the slight changes of light from the outside to estimate the time.

Waiting. I have been waiting for too long. The Forge had better be the next step for me. I don't know how much longer I can wait in this guilty world. Time ticked away when so much of my life had already been lost to the Razum. I wanted to mean something. I wanted to become so much more.

Fantasies unfolded as the sunlight outside diminished. Dreams of glory and usurping the power of the machines. I could see myself standing above the people of Sila, cheering at their restored freedom. Was this what I was meant for?

Dreams were silenced by a quiet knock on the shed door. The faint glow of the dying light barely lit the inside. Gregory shifted into a more battle ready stance and Taylor joined his side by the door. I could feel my hand twitch at the sight of Taylor trusting Gregory as a comrade to defend the door with. If my legs worked, he wouldn't be guarding with her.

"Who is it?" Taylor's voice was hushed in the growing quiet of the dark.

"It's Anne. I was sent to tell you that the rally is starting soon." The tiny quiet voice was obviously Anne.

"Thank you, Anne." Gregory responded. A faint giggle could be heard from outside before the small feet skipped away on the drying mud walkways. Taylor stood from the door and looked at me. Her eyes were tired, but her body appeared ready to shoulder the weight of the world.

"Are you sure that you want to do this?" Her face was poised and confident in her question, as if willing me to reconsider. She must have been thinking about all the complications throughout the day while I daydreamed.

"Yes." Un-gifted in the speech-craft that she had naturally. I made sure to not back down from my conviction. Even if it was one word, she needed to know that I would not sway from my decision. Gregory's chuckled rattled the shed walls he leaned against. In his hands, he held the device he had been constructing most of the day. It appeared to be two long supporting rods with a belt attachment connected between them. Tarping was lined into the belt as well as spare tarping above. He held up his newly constructed device.

"That is why I made this. We can't always be dragging you around. It could get all of us killed if we are not careful." Taylor took the device away and scanned it. I could see in her eyes that she was breaking down each component of the simple machine and analyzing its durability. Like a poison tester in a royal court.

She handed them back to Gregory, who stood and approached me with them. He put one support rod in each armpit and helped sit me up on them. My feet dangled like distant memories towards the floor. As he attached the belt around my waist, I could now see the bottoms of the rods, forked with different smaller metal supports. This was built to help balance and support me in the mud. A crude yet effective contraption.

"You may not have the muscles in your legs to fully stand, but you should be able to support yourself on them. I tried to make the rods as balanced as possible, but it will be difficult either way. The belt should keep you attached to them so you don't fall as easily."

"In case things go badly and you need to escape quietly, these rods do collapse and can act as sleds for your arms to help pull you across the ground, since you can't seem to crawl well. The tarping will protect you from the mud in theory. Try them." His detailed explanation and demonstrating gestures helped me understand the gist of the device. Avoiding the feeling of being grateful to a machine, I leaned forward onto the rods. I tested my weight on them, my feet numb against the ground, acting as almost a third leg.

Once I was comfortable with my attempts, Taylor steadied me as I tried to move one rod forward. The balance and compression of the feet of the rods helped to stabilize the movements, and I moved the other forward. My feet dragged through across the tin flooring as I pulled myself forward. My shoulders shuddered at the weight I was carrying, but continued to move. An extra level of autonomy had been reached.

After several more assisted steps, I shooed away my sister and did four more steps on my own. Freedom of movement. I did not know I craved it this much since waking up. A few laps around the shed, testing more daring movements and evasions. My shoulders told me to quit. Aligning myself against the bed, I leaned back and sat on the table.

Taylor applauded Gregory's design while he fine tuned bits that did not act according to his design. There was a slight bit of pride in his voice as he accepted the praise. A machine creating better machines. This was where our world first fell apart.

"They should work nicely in a pinch. We can bring them with us but I would prefer Tyron was carried this time. Since the Forge wants him specifically, keeping him close should avoid the chances of him being grabbed." Ever the tactician, Taylor began to don her heavy armor and weapons while Gregory dressed himself in tarping. His plates contracted as he lost a foot of his height. Still two and a half heads taller than Taylor and still very mechanical in movement.

I sat, waiting to be carried like a child, while they finished their final dressings and weapon hiding. Once Gregory hid in tarp fashioned clothing, he backed up to the table and helped pull me and the rods into a comfortable position. He tied a rope around me to secure myself so I didn't have to hang off of him the entire walk. Safely bundled to the Drone, he tossed one larger tarp around the two of us, completing his look as an absurdly tall hunchback creature.

Few words were shared as we left the shed, our identities and objectives skewed in the silence. People were rustling in the dark, finding dinners for the evening or kids playing near other tin sheds. This city felt more alive out of the sunlight and bathed in the red glow of the street lamps. I suppose light held more concern than the darkness where people could hide.

My eyes relaxed in the red light with less detail or color to adapt to. The heavy thud of Gregory's shoes in the mud mixed with the relaxed lighting began lulling me into a tired haze. Taylor did not seem as affected as she led the charge of our band. Her head making constant swivels as she watched the area and check on us as we followed.

The walk felt long, or my tiredness made it feel longer than it was. More people appeared from their dark hiding spots outside of my window of vision beside Gregory's neck. We were still on small winding mud trails, avoiding the larger streets, when I could hear louder noises from streets near us.

"Let's stick to the back roads until we have no choice. I think I heard Harvey Units." Taylor's voice was barely distinguishable against the clatter and banter of the lively street nearby. Gregory nodded his silent agreement, avoiding talking and his speaker tuned voice being heard.

Soon voices sounded more distinct, conversations could be pieced together. Many people spoke of the Harvey units, their outrage at the new rules and restrictions being placed. I heard faint talk of new Giants gathering in a distant region and heading towards Sila. Something seemed to stir the conversations of the street ways.

There were so many unfamiliar names, like Armand, Viktorov, and Povlo. Noting the names to ask Gregory about later, I scanned the area I could see from Gregory's neck. We now faced an open street lined with red lights and filled with people. Stones covered the ground instead of mud and metal scraps. Most wore similar clothes as us, except for a few less armored vendors.

Taylor cast a gaze back at me and Gregory. There was hesitation in her eyes that I had not seen before. We were about to go into the street, and she was considering her options one more time before taking the next step. With a quiet hand gesture, we entered the crowd. From Gregory's vantage point, I could see above most people's heads besides the other huge, lurking people. Taylor stayed closer to us now as we walked further towards the looming skull of Locura that looked down on us from its perch on the top of the crater wall.

My first clear view of a Loomer. I could see why they struck fear into the hearts of people. The massive scale and power they held was enough to cause a shiver through my bones. Such monsters. Why did they fall?

The heavy sound of metal boots on stone stirred my attention as I noticed the Harvey Unit that we were watching. He stood by what I guessed was the entranceway to the rally. Taylor slowed, but did not stop. I knew her well enough to know that she was evaluating her options on how to sneak by.

Based on her increased speed, she must have seen something to use. We moved forward faster now, Taylor stumbling over her own feet. She leaned back into Gregory, who automatically caught her. Whispered words could barely be heard in the heated street.

"Play along or we're dead."

As she clung to Gregory, I quickly recognized her ploy. Drunken fools stumbling into an alley. If Gregory could be convincing, it would help us blend in. Though as he didn't mimic her immediately, I realized he may not know what a drunk person acted like, or what Taylor was doing.

"She's being drunk. Do the same." I clarified to the machine I rode. After a moment, the circuits seemed to connect and he leaned over more, using Taylor to hold himself up. While a ridiculous scene to be part of, it seemed convincing enough. People moved from our path more willingly while the Harvey's eyes passed over us.

Starting down the alley to the rally, Gregory stepped lightly by the Harvey Drone. It stood two heads taller than us and held its gun closely, scanning the surrounding crowd. As we were about to step quietly and drunkenly beside the Harvey unit, Gregory turned his head slightly and looked up at the menacing rabbit.

Was he actually afraid to get caught? To look at what he was trying to sneak past was a beginner's mistake. Did he feel small compared to the massive machine, or was he assessing his chances in a fight? This look earned him a glance from the Harvey unit. Before the massive rabbit's head turned enough to see Gregory's face, I pushed mine forward instead, doing my best to look natural on the body I rode.

When nothing was said, and we finally passed, I knew it had been enough. Gregory still seemed shaken, but lifted a hand and patted my head through the tarp. A small appreciation, but a kind moment. We were safely past the Harvey units, now we had to blend safely into a small crowd that was developing at the back of the alleyway leading to a separate street beyond.

Quiet steps in the dark alleyway. Taylor separated from Gregory in their drunken farce. Her face looked pleased with her choices. When those blue eyes connected with mine, she gave me a smile. Life and death was a daily game for her. Was her smile an attempt to invite me into her survival games with less fear?

"Nothing better than not getting shot. Did you two do alright?" From Gregory's hesitancy to respond, Taylor understood there were minor complications. She looked beyond us and scanned the entrance to the alley. After a moment of confirming that we weren't being followed, she turned and led us further in.

There was shouting in the distance, people cheering. Someone was winding up a crowd. Their words were still unintelligible, but the eruption of laughter spoke clearly. Gregory's heavy steps seemed to stir attention as we approached the back of the crowd, eyes examined us.

The speaker who had enamored the crowd stood on a few crates and boxes, boosting him higher. As more heads turned to watch us approach the crowd, a small, familiar face appeared. Tiny feet in drying mud, Anne ran up to us. In her path, more onlookers turned to watch us approach. There was no avoiding being singled out now.

"They waited for you guys. It's gonna start now." She grabbed Gregory's hand and led them further into the crowd, an obvious bubble forming around us. Anne shoved people out of her way as she led us to the center of the crowd, Gregory standing out like a sore thumb.

"Through fire!" The speaker yelled over the crowd. Another eruption of cheers echoed around us and I saw hands flying as the people responded, "We rise!". Our stillness in the vibrant crowd earned us more looks and the special attention from the speaker.

"Tonight, we have a special member in our crowd. A long forgotten dream come to life. We rally here by the street to attract attention, but that is not the goal tonight. For we have, in our midst, the first Razum Born pulled from a Razum." The crowd murmured in shock and Taylor stepped more in front of Gregory, trying to obscure me from sight.

"We heard of this wonder through the Den of our fallen Organ surgeons. Those precious girls have a value beyond measure in our town, Sila. They spoke of a boy, intelligent, and fully coherent, waking from the metal jaws the Loomers once placed on us. They talked... of a savior." Again, the crowd murmured their shock and disbelief. As the speaker waited for the clamor to die down, a distant voice in the crowd took up the question that many asked.

"Where is he?"

Taylor now grabbed Gregory's arm and backed out of the crowd during the confusion, but she was too late. The speaker let out a laugh and pointed at her. All eyes turning, arms beginning to block us. We were caught in their plan. Taylor turned to face the speaker now. I could see her hand moving to one of her knives, ready to go down fighting.

Anne stepped behind Gregory. The crowd's attitude changed from excited to tense in the span of seconds. My fingers dug into the metal around Gregory's neck and I tucked lower behind his coverings. I could vaguely see the face of the speaker. A taller, thin man with dark black hair. He had a haunting charm to him. Obviously, he was a speaker in this life, though when his hand fell and his words controlled the crowd, I knew I envied him. I envied his power and control over this mass of people.

"Grab them."

The speaker's word was all that was needed to demand action. Hands quickly began pulling at us from every direction,they shoved and pushed like the whirling of storm winds. I was helpless, a gimp on the back of a machine who couldn't out himself unless it was an extreme case. When Taylor was separated, Gregory made the decision. He and I both knew if she went down, so did our chances at a new life.

Using his cloth wrapped hands as scoops, he threw people over his shoulder. Careful to not hit me with the unfortunate bodies. He ripped and pulled people away until he came close to Taylor, who had been disarmed and held by four people. They did not last long against the irritated Drone. I reached my hand forward to help her up as Gregory kept pushing people away from us.

Anger built in the strangers fighting to claim us, and fists were getting thrown. Aggression building in the crowd, I saw Taylor's eyes lock onto Gregory and nod. It was time to show off our best defense and reveal our largest target. He pulled his hood back, revealing his golden plating and curled hair, as well as my head clinging to his back.

The crowd froze. Faces were in shock and hands trembled. The fear of a Gregory unit was a universal one, apparently. A scream was behind us and panic flooded in. People ran from him as he pulled Taylor closer to him and backed away from the rally.

Even the speaker looked shocked by this development, but he maintained his composure, guiding more guard looking types into the stampeding group. They were still coming for us. Gregory shifted his plates and adopted his full size and ability. He reached behind him and untied the material that held me to his back and my body sagged, only suspended by my arms now.

"Tyron, this may be one of those situations that you will need to escape from. Hold tight until then." His voice rattled clearly in the night against the screams of panic. Our time was fading quickly before the Harvey Units would get involved. Clock ticking, Gregory grabbed Taylor and ran from the speaker and his men.

Three heavy steps across the ground were heard before a loud shrieking sound cut the city noise like a knife. I didn't recognize the pain that seared through me at first, but soon realized what happened. An EMP shot stabbed through my hip and shut down Gregory's circuits. The Drone slowed until he came to a full stop before falling to the ground. My arms were crushed under the weight of his chest, trapping me with him. The electricity that hit us still bounced around his metal body, searing my skin with burns.

My cries of agony went unheard as Taylor was knocked unconscious by being flung to the ground when Gregory fell. The Speaker and his men approached us as I watched with hazy eyes. They dragged Taylor's limp body free and took her away. I couldn't do anything when they pulled my burning skin from Gregory's back and took me away. Gregory's body was attached to cables and dragged into the dark of a different alleyway.

Anger seared my brain as much as the burns did. This would not end their way. I would do whatever I had to in order to change this world. They took my sister; they took Gregory, and they are taking me. If only they knew what dangers they were inviting in or what ambitions I held. This would not be the end of us.

These proud statements flooded my mind as I was carried into a dark building. Before we crossed the threshold of the doorway, my face met with a fist I did not know and my world disappeared. The anger remained, though. Even in the darkness of a sleeping mind, I could feel the rage boiling my blood.

Darkness. Why was it always darkness? I could hear voices, but they were too far away from my ringing mind to hear. What was this pain? My flesh felt seared, like when I first awakened from the Razum. The Razum–

"Taylor!" Memories gushed through the static of my brain and I remembered our situation. Where was she? Where was Gregory? Where was I? A small hand touched my back and I flailed from it. Who was it?

"Tyron, calm down. She's fine." The familiar voice belonged to Anne. The small hand seemed to belong to her as she continued to pet my back. Her feeble attempt to calm me. As I tried to move my arms to feel around me, the burning icy fires of pain erupted through them.

"Don't move. Let's get this bag off your head." The fresh voice belonged to the young Tricia I had heard briefly when the Den was raided. She sounded older, more mature than Anne. With a bit of shuffling and moving my head, the world was revealed to me.

There was a bright light above me, illuminating a dark room that seemed to be in a basement. A circle of young girls were gathered around me, with thirteen of them standing guard. I noticed I was lying on a dirt floor and coagulated blood was pooled around my exposed wounds. Next to me lay Gregory, apparently shut down. As I craned my neck higher, I could see the familiar acid washed braids of Taylor on the other side of him.

I faced Anne and Tricia now, their small faces observing me. As my concussed eyes focused, I could see beyond the wall of girls. Many shrouded figures surrounded us, watching our movements with caution. Their faces occasionally lit by cigarette drags. We were protected by the Den girls, a circle of innocence.

Anne pet my arm carefully as she scanned my face for awareness. Tricia pushed her dark blonde hair from her face as she leaned lower to see me clearly. I must have been the first to wake up.

"We didn't mean for it to go this way. The Den defends its own. They won't hurt you now." Tricia's words were blotted out by the heavy stomping of Harvey units above us. They spewed their alarms and their gunfire echoed through the large room we were in.

"How's Taylor?" My words were hoarse as my body shuddered at the pain each of my muscles had endured. I wasn't strong enough to handle this yet, but I would learn. No amount of pain would stop me from worrying about my sister.

"She'll be fine. We need to talk to you right now, though." An unknown voice entered the haze of my awareness as the Speaker approached the line of girls protecting us. His hair was short and a cigarette hung from the corner of his mouth.

"I'm Jack, head of the Forge. We didn't mean for this to happen. Had we known that you had a Drone with you-" Anne interrupted the man with a firm slap against his chest. She could not reach higher.

"His name is Gregory!" She shouted with all the rage in her little body. Apparently, she would not abide someone talking down on the Machine. The Speaker stepped back. He seemed to fear or respect the girls. Once Tricia pulled Anne back into the circle, the man stepped forward again.

"I'm not here to fight. I just wanted to talk about a deal, if you're feeling up to it."

Chapter 12: Sparks Ignite the Forge

As I looked at the man partially hidden behind the wall of girls, I felt no malicious intent from his words. Besides his actions tonight, he showed no signs of aggression. Anne watched me analyzing him, but froze when my eyes focused on hers.

"Anne, do you like this man's words?" Her eyes analyzed mine as she thought over my words. This wasn't my world yet. I didn't know who was good or what the order of operations was. Her small grin softened my heart. What was such innocence doing in the bowels of a rebellion?

"He's nice. The scar man is mean." She pointed her finger at one man that lined the wall behind Jack. He bore a thick scar across his face that was lined with metal. From what Taylor and Gregory had told me, he looked like an 'Oomer.

"Do you think I should hear these guys out? Or should I wait for Taylor to wake up?" My words were weaker now, only for Anne and Tricia to hear. I could see their minds chewing over my words with silent glances at one another. When their eyes fell on Taylor, I knew the answer was clear.

"I won't talk to you. Wait for my sister to wake up." I turned my head from the man as he debated my answer. His words fell on my deaf ears as I focused on the part of Taylor's hand I could see.

"We shouldn't have to obey these damn brats." An unfamiliar voice rang out, and as I whipped my head around, I saw the 'Oomer man push the girls from his way and hefted little Anne off her feet. Tricia ran from him and hid behind Gregory's powered down body, fiddling with his wires, trying to turn him back on.

I pulled my seared body from the dirt and held my shoulders up. My eyes burned and my blood ran hot as I saw the scarred man toss Anne to the side, breaking down another part of the wall. Jack caught his shoulder, but he was too late.

The sound of fans whirring to life and the quick groan of metal told me that Tricia had succeeded in waking Gregory up. Ground shaking under his weight, he stood above me and analyzed his situation. I watched his eyes scanning the room, and for a moment, I saw them flicker, his arms twitching to unseen commands crossing his mind.

Was this enough of a blow to wipe his memory? Did Drones even work that way? Or was this the second option of Fritzing? My questions were answered soon enough as Gregory stepped over my body and grabbed the scarred man by the neck and pin him to a wall. The girls separated for the Drone as he ground the man against the wall.

The other members panicked at the quick motions of the machine and glued themselves to the walls away from him. Jack was the only one to not run, but to pointlessly try to pry Gregory's hands from his comrade's neck.

Gregory held the pressure until both men settled, realizing he would not kill them yet. I saw the iron jaw drop and the scarred man stared down the throat of Gregory as he spoke.

"Never touch these girls again because they will not be the only ones cutting you open." His words sent shivers down the men as they shuddered at the voice. One they seemed to know all too well.

Once the scarred man and Jack nodded their understanding, Gregory pulled the man from the wall and threw him to the feet of Anne. The man's body crumpled in fear at her feet. Anne looked confused and glanced at Gregory for guidance. She likely had never been put in such a powerful position.

"Apologize to Anne."

'Oomer man moved as if shocked by lightning and groveled at the awkward girl's feet. She did not know how to handle the situation, but the grins of the other girls in the circle seemed to boost her self confidence in the matter. I couldn't help but to smile as Anne kicked the scarred man's head. Her little foot did no damage.

A part of me wished Gregory had been there for Taylor when she was that young. Little girls deserved to be protected and respected. They could be the ruin of any man, and we would do well to remember their power. Gregory turned to me and Taylor now. His steps shifted the ground beneath me, causing my body to tense in pain.

I could see his knee joints as he squatted by me, looking over my body. He patted me down for any more injuries on my back and legs before carefully flipping me over and examining my exposed skin. The smell of burnt flesh now filled my nose and the pain seemed to intensify with it.

Each prod and poke Gregory did, checking my injuries, was agonizing, but I wouldn't let him see that in me. Never would a machine see me shy from pain or fear them. Once he was satisfied with the information he gained from his invasion of my body, he rested his hands on his knees.

"I owe you a thanks and apology. Since they knew you were on my back, they didn't aim for my head. Due to their lousy shot through you, we shared the electric pulse that would have fried me. So thanks for sharing the bullet and saving my life. Also, sorry you got shot."

"You will survive. Taylor has some advanced skills with salves to help burns. She will be able to treat this quickly. The girls will also help. You're not out of the game yet." His words were relieved, even if he maintained a sarcastic tone.

Metal shoes stepped over me and evaluated Taylor the same way. The room seemed to be quietly waiting for Gregory to finish his task before anyone would take a breath. As the minutes passed and Gregory did his analysis, the girls crowded closer to him, seeking the safety of his presence.

When Gregory stood, we all watched him expectantly, waiting for the prognosis. He closed his jaw with manual effort and faced the rest of the room, extending a comforting hand towards the girls. Had they really worn him down so quickly during their time in the Den?

"She will be fine besides some bruised bones. She has survived more than this many times. Now, will someone tell me what is happening here? Why did the Forge attack us?" His stern tone caused the girls to tilt their chins down in fear like an angered father had just yelled at them. The members beyond the light shifted their feet, no one wanting to answer the Drone's questions.

Jack stepped forward cautiously, staying mindful of the circle of girls which still stood their ground. He helped the scarred man from the ring and backed away slightly. Hands fidgeting, he spoke.

"Our attempt to kidnap your group was not intended to be malicious. If we had been observed walking you to our headquarters, Harvey units would have questioned it. They don't care if we kidnap and hurt each other. They're just watching for changes in behavior."

"We were going to kidnap you and release you once we were somewhere safer to talk. The rally was supposed to be our cover, but when we saw the Drone... there was panic. No one has ever seen a Drone pretending to be human, hiding in crowds. We thought we were busted."

"I am sorry that I shot you two. There was no way to understand what we were seeing besides that we needed to protect our members. This was not the way the night was supposed to go." His words sounded sincere to me, but Gregory did not seem so easily swayed.

The Drone stepped forward, the ring of girls staying near him as he approached Jack directly. Anne now held Gregory's hand and walked with him while Tricia put herself between the two men.

"There is no excuse for the damage you have caused tonight. Consider yourself very lucky that I am off network, otherwise I would be marching through the walls of this building with as many Harvey Units that exist." He leaned forward with intent to intimidate, but Tricia placed her hands on him, slowing his intensity.

"Hey, Den rules. We talk, we don't fight. Gregory, you agreed to the same rules that these men did. Now you both have broken those rules, but I will not tolerate another infraction. Back down, both of you." Her words were spoken like what I imagined the previous Den Mother Vykra would have sounded like.

While Gregory and Jack looked at the girl, she maintained her composure. Both unwilling to start a fight with the young and vicious surgeon girls, they both backed down. Tricia maintained her position between them but relaxed her shoulders a bit with the tension calming.

"We just wanted to talk to the Razum Walker. There are so many people he could help. So many he could encourage." Jack's words fell on Gregory's turned head as he scanned the surrounding girls.

"You should have considered that more carefully before you shot him. Taylor will talk to you when she wakes up." His tone was finite and killed the possibility of more words to be shared. Gregory made his way to the corner closest to Taylor and was still within the circle before he let his body fall to the ground, taking up his guarding position.

The circle tightened in response to his movements and a few girls left the edges of the ring. They were quick to join his seated position, glaring at the men with the angered Drone. Jack received the message that he had to wait and filed the men out of the room. Before he left, he looked over the room one more time with sympathetic eyes and closed the door. Their feet beyond the door sounded as though they were climbing stairs.

Girls sitting down from their arm-in-arm wall, they watched over us. Using the silence, I pulled myself across the ground to Taylor. It was a misery to drag my wounds across the acidic flooring, but I had to know she was okay. Each pull more painful than the last. I finally was close enough to grab her hand as she lay face down in the dirt.

Her heart beat regularly from what I could tell with her wrist. I opened her eyes and rotated her head towards the light, checking her iris responsiveness. They dilated slowly to the light showing damage. The gash on her head was more obvious now, as I could see the stream of blood that had flowed down her face. There must have been metal in the ground that hit her.

"You seem to know more about human physiology than I do. Is she actually okay?" Gregory's words disturbed my focus. My eyes seared with rage as I looked at the machine that had failed his duty. He was meant to protect us—he should have known there was a gun. He should have been more cautious.

"Why didn't you protect her!? It was your job! She could have suffered serious damage from this. Her eyes — her eyes aren't working right. She could never wake up!" The pain left my body, only fury remained as I climbed around my sister and clawed my way up to the face of the Drone.

"You should have stopped this. You owed her that. Why—why did you let her get hurt!" While the blood boiled through my veins, Gregory's lack of response was not good enough.

"Taylor was all that mattered. You should have thrown me to save her! If she doesn't wake up, I'll–I'll–" The metal hands that grabbed my torso stopped my words as Gregory pulled me away from his face. There was no aggression in the action, just a calm, logical movement.

"Tyron. Calm down." His words were softer than I had anticipated. My jaw clamped shut. Gregory moved me from where I was climbing him, to lean against the same wall he did, watching over Taylor.

My fists were balled and the girls were moving away from us, trying to avoid my anger. Gregory allowed the silence to stretch as he leaned his chin on his fists that balanced on crooked knees. A part of me recognized this to be a childish pose, but I knew what kind of danger he was still capable of. I needed answers. He needed to give me answers.

"I have never used this word before... but I panicked. When Taylor disappeared into the crowd, I locked up. That's never happened to me before. It was like the power that has operated me for a century suddenly stopped working."

"Humans have frozen in fear in front of me before, but I never understood why. Was that the same paralyzing fear I caused others? That helplessness?" I had never seen Gregory conflicted, or emotional, besides for the Den girls. Has this Drone learned about fear for Taylor? Was it supposed to be his excuse for his failure?

The girls pet his arms as he sat and pondered his feelings. They tried their best to soothe him, but even I didn't know how to help a machine that was learning human struggles. Nor did I think he deserved it.

"I should have run sooner. When Jack pointed at us, I should have grabbed you both and left. Taylor just seemed so sure until the crowd held her down. She never looked so helpless. I've hurt her so many times when

I was connected to the network and she never even shed a tear for her own wounds. At the hands of those people, though, she looked like a scared child."

"Time is different to me. I have been functioning for a hundred thirty-seven years, but to you or her, every-day matters. She is so strong for such a young human. Just like the Den girls, she has faced most things with a strong face and dealt worse damage. Seeing her afraid seems to have activated an additional part of my Fritz. I am sorry, Tyron. If I could change what I did, I would and I will never let it happen again." The glowing LEDs focused on me as he finished his monologue. There was little detail in his eyes, but somehow, I felt the sorrow and apologetic weight of his words. I wish it was enough to calm the burning anger that seemed to infect me every day since I woke.

Anne took up a spot in front of us and pet Taylor's hair. She was careful to not smear the blood that had clung to my sister's pale scalp. Her tousled brown hair somehow brought out the life in her eyes as she beamed at us. What youthful innocence in her eyes, regardless of the horrors those eyes had already beheld.

"Taylor would tell you guys not to fight. She's smart. She knew the chances like we all did. I'm sorry, too. She told me to scout the area, but I failed her, too." The somber words of the young girl drew our attention from one another. Anne was an astonishing child, brave and aware of her own role in life. She reminded me of Taylor as a kid.

Gregory reached forward to poke the girl's belly, earning him a giggle. He shooed her from Taylor and leaned forward to check her pulse again. Monitoring her condition while I was struggling to move.

"Taylor would be proud of how well you protected us while unconscious. Thank you girls, for the risk you took. Though be more cautious in the future. The Forge doesn't seem like a safe place for you."

The girls responded by ignoring him and giggling. Apparently, they feared him, but no one could make a child truly listen. They seemed to come closer to talk in lower tones. The eyes of thirteen girls gleamed at us.

"Do you want to know the secrets they told us? We know so much since we started working here." Tricia's smile gave away the girls' real motivations. They were working as rats in the rebellion, gathering any information they could get. We just happened to be the only people they now felt safe with. Vykra trained them well.

Gregory faced the mass of children and sat back against the wall. "What have you heard?" I settled in as the stories unfolded. Tales of corruption in the Forge, rumors of Giants coming for Sila, and a recurring rumor that there have been earthquakes recently in the Barrens to the East of Sila that some were claiming to be Lexi moving.

As the girls continued to share their stories, often interrupting one another, Gregory and I listened quietly. The climate of Sila was revealed to us through the mouth of sheltered children. Though when the girls mentioned the Giants coming to Sila, Gregory stopped them.

"Do you remember the names of the Giants seen heading this way?" His tone revealed more urgency than I think he intended. As the girls whispered among themselves, trying to verify the names, Gregory looked at me.

"If Giants are coming, then word has reached them of you. That will put Sila and all of Finigan's and Gundry's regions in jeopardy. If it's the ones I'm thinking of, we should leave." He returned his gaze to the girls as they quieted, knowing their answer. Anne acted as the voice of the group now.

"The names were Viktorov, Povlo, and Armand. They had code names: The wolf-bear, the spider, and the owl. Forge members have been scattering for more information, but we've only heard one report from a traveling raider." Her words seemed to disturb Gregory by the way he questioned them, hoping they were wrong.

"Are you sure those were the exact names? Not Victor? Or Paulo?" His words were hurried, but even I knew to not question the knowledge of the girls.

"We're sure." Tricia responded.

For the first time in my short awareness, I saw Gregory place his gloved hands on his hair and rub the curled metal with anxiety. His Fritzing seems to be progressing at a more alarming rate. I waited for his additional stress to dissipate and educate us about why we should be concerned.

"Those names belong to Locura's Three. I figured they would've settled regions further to the West, but I never would have thought they would come this far East again. We have attracted the attention of the most destructive Loomers' favorite creations."

"She didn't build them, of course, but they earned her favor during the initial annihilation attempts. Locura decided she would optimize them so they could carry out more brutal sentencing. To my knowledge, no humans remain in their regions due to their overly aggressive nature. Their presence here could mean a quick death for the entire city."

His words rocked the room and silence was placed on our shoulders like lead weights. If he was right, the entire city was in danger. With the Harvey units already applying pressure on the citizens, three additional Giants will definitely bring about city wide chaos.

"So we are meant to be here..." The words escaped my mouth. Eyes focused on me to hear the rest of my thoughts. Gregory even shifted his focus to me now.

"What are the odds that we would end up in a city with such dangers and a pre-made rebellion? We were meant to be here. This is what I am here for."

"If we gather the people, unify the rebellion, we could take down the Harveys and the other Drones here. With you and the girls with us, we have power and word of mouth. We could prepare the town to bring down these Giants." I left no doubt in my words because there was no doubt that this was our fight. We were here for a reason. I had to believe that.

"How do you think we unify the people?" Asked a teen girl with longer brown hair and darker skin.

"The deal with Jack. He spoke earlier about how he wanted me to be a symbol. The first Razum Born to wake up seems to be a big deal." While I rarely liked to be the main topic, I was. Taylor and the Forge both valued me as something above normal, so it was time to accept that role.

Gregory's processors could be heard whirring as he contemplated the idea. Even the girls whispered among themselves, theorizing the possibilities. Was this what Taylor felt like when we talked about plans? Did she feel this building elation at a new plan? The excitement of war for change?

"Jack is trustworthy when the 'Oomer man isn't around." Tricia stated.

"He is a good talker." Another girl chimed in.

"Would Jack face the Giants, though?" Anne responded.

"He isn't afraid of the Drones like everyone else," Retorted Tricia.

"It could work," was the phrase that bounced around the girls. Gregory seemed to watch their thought patterns as he listened. Still evaluating. I waited for the machine to finish his thoughts. Whether or not he agreed, I was going to proceed with this plan. Though it would be nice to have a unique weapon at our side during the fight.

He looked around our faces; the girls beaming at him and me watching. Seeming to give into his thoughts, he shifted again to sit forward. "It could work." He begrudgingly acknowledged. The girls erupted in cheers, excited about a new future possible for their city.

"Quiet. It could work, does not mean it will work. This will require sound planning and strategizing. If Tyron does not have the impact that we expect, we should still flee. Ultimately, we should wait for Taylor to wake to make a definite plan." He gestured to her unconscious body in the room.

Everything rested on Taylor when she woke up. If she woke up. I know she has survived more than most, but a head injury could turn from a concussion to a permanent disadvantage quickly. She didn't deserve that, not after what she endured. She shouldn't have to wake up and deal with saving a city or fleeing for her life.

I shifted uncomfortably in the silence and gasped at the new wave of pain that shot through me. Gregory watched me as I winced and tried to steady myself through the sore burns. He pointed at a few of the girls and gestured to me.

"Can you clean him up? We need him to survive for the plan, and his physical state is already precarious." As if guided by his words, they pulled themselves from the ground and made their way to me to inspect the

312

wounds. After a few moments, they tore bits from their tarp clothes and bottles appeared from the others. Disinfectants and painkillers rattled from their pockets. They walked as their own apothecary.

Moving me from the wall to the ground, they cleaned and soothed what they could of my burns. Though as the pain faded, the cold ate at me. One girl brought a small container of drinkable water forward and they took up position, holding my arms and legs down.

"This will hurt, but we need to cool the burns down to lessen the damage and start the healing. Ready?" Tricia asked, as she held the water over my arms and chest. I set my jaw in a locked position and clenched my fists. I could handle this. If Taylor could survive, I could. Nodding my readiness, I prepared for the worse.

The water felt like searing lava as it was poured over my burns. Cool water caused my chest to tighten and spasm, the shock nearly overwhelming me. With weak arms, I rolled in pain, but the girls held me down. At one point, I thought I felt the metal hand of Gregory help hold down one of my arms. Once the water slowed its pour, I felt the relief flood over me as the heat of the burns returned with less intensity.

Arms released, the girls continued to rub salves and medicine across the burns before wrapping my chest and arms in sanitized cloth wraps they made from their clothes. Gregory patted the head of Tricia as she cleaned up the bottles they had used. Her smile brightened the room a bit more.

Gregory helped me sit up against the wall again, the pain significantly less, but still present. We now sat in silence, watching over Taylor's still body. Anne and a few other girls began looking over her now, checking for new wounds or burns. She had shared some burns from her contact with Gregory, but they were not significant like mine.

They followed the same procedure as they cleaned and cooled the burn that wrapped around her back. The pattern looked similar to the plating from Gregory's arm. She didn't move as the water was poured over. There was no flinch at the change of temperature. Even the girls hesitated at her lack of reaction. Once they finished her treatment, they dressed her and backed away hesitantly. There was an unspoken fear in the air from her lack of response. Pain was one thing we all responded to, so if she didn't, something was very wrong.

All eyes were on Taylor. Our figurehead, our voice of reason, lay unconscious on the floor. She didn't deserve to lie in the dirt, but we had no better options. The room was bare of furniture. I motioned to Gregory to take his tarpings off. He understood my command and laid the cloth on the ground before sliding her onto the somewhat soft material. A makeshift bed was the best we could offer.

We waited. There was nothing to do until she woke, so we sat in silence. Some girls played hand games as they waited. The younger ones poked and jabbed at Gregory to pass the time. He accepted their attention and occasionally poked them back. I watched as the Drone seemed to mimic a playful tone with the girls, but the occasional glance at Taylor gave away his worry.

Hours of silence passed. The occasional food delivery from the Forge members was the only break in the quiet, but they left quickly. Girls slowly slumped into piles and naps were taken in shifts. I supposed it was late in the night, if not morning. No windows or cracks in the wall made it impossible to tell.

My eyes struggled to stay open as the fatigue set in. The adrenaline had left me long ago, though I did my best to stay awake. When my eyes drifted close, there was no stopping my dozing.

I was occasionally woken when the girls moved or Gregory shifted, but a deep and injured sleep was creeping into me. Using Gregory's shoulder, I pushed myself into a lying position near to Taylor. I feebly grabbed her hand with my bandaged fingers, trying to will life back into her body as I imagined she would have done for me. Accepting the sleep that dragged me back into the Earth, I closed my eyes.

The pain in my hand woke me. Burns being compressed. As I peeled my dry eyes open, I was met with groggy, unfocused blue eyes. Taylor's hand shuttered as it gripped mine. She was waking up.

Pulling myself from the ground, I watched her, petting her hair as reality washed back into her awareness. Her eyes struggled to focus, pupils resisting dilation. The damage seemed to be worse than I was guessing, but she still seemed aware. Gregory now hovered over us, watching her wake.

We gave her time to adjust; the girls rubbing her legs and arms, trying to stimulate her nervous system and increase blood flow. They were nervous hands, trembling, but doing what they could to help. Even though I tried to mimic them, none of us knew what we could do to help without knowing the extent of her injuries.

Several minutes passed. She was rolling her head from side to side as if trying to knock her senses back. The air was tense as no words escaped her. How much damage had she sustained? I have never seen her so distant. Gregory kept his hands to himself, unsure how to help with his larger mechanical gloves.

Finally, more focused eyes scanned over us, understanding was in them. She was coming back, slowly, but surely. The piercing gray eyes settled on me before a weak smile tugged at her dry lips.

"What happened to you?" Her voice mustered a sassy tone as her eyes drifted close for a moment. I couldn't help but let out a huff of amusement. There was the childish sister I knew. Her face was cool to the touch as I let my hand warm her cheek. It was odd being the warmth for her that she was to me.

Her eyes fluttered open again and focused beyond me, her smirk drawing Gregory closer. She weakly lifted her hand and pointed to him while she blinked the unconscious haze from her eyes. Gregory grabbed her finger and watched her quietly.

"Your arms are really heavy. Next time, just let me run." Her tone was gentle and her smile only increased as Gregory let a feudal attempt at a chuckle to escape his speaker. He shook her finger and nodded.

"Next time, I will drop you and run."

Her head gently slumped to the ground again and she looked over the girls faces, picking out Anne. "How am I looking, Doc?"

Anne whispered to a few of the girls and Tricia, who was nearby before

315

announcing their opinion. They shuffled their hands nervously, almost like they were going to be scolded. Taylor watched with distant eyes as they finalized their thoughts.

"You should be fine? There aren't major wounds, but we can't see your brain. Take it easy." Her words were hesitant, but carried the weight of all our concerns. Taylor seemed to smirk at the diagnosis. My worries for her awareness grew.

"We all know I can't take it easy." Eyes fluttering closed again as we sat back, giving her space to gather herself. Taylor moved slowly as she tried to sit up. Her actions seemed weak, like her limbs were trying to resist her.

Once she was sitting up, her legs stretched out as her eyes closed. She was noticing the burns on her back. Though she did not let it stop her from righting herself and looking around the room. Her eyes blinked and tried to focus on her new surroundings.

"Do we know what happened or where we are?" Her question was directed to the room. Gregory chose to be the one to answer.

"We know it was supposedly not meant to be an aggressive attack, and we know we are in a basement a long way from where we were." I looked at the Drone, questioning how he assessed that information. He seemed to hear this question through my gaze and answered it.

"The ambient sounds from outside match the sounds near the factories. I heard the exhaust trigger a few times while we were waiting, so I'm going to guess the morning shift has started. It's sometime around mid-morning now." Forgetting that I was sitting next to a giant computer, I abandoned my gaze and reasserted my eyes on Taylor.

Her face seemed to pause as it took in the information, the haze still lingering around her waking brain. I noticed a small twitch in her finger that seemed involuntary. Was she hiding how much she had suffered, or was she unaware? We needed to watch her for a while.

This was no time to talk about plans with her. She could barely control her body, let alone her thoughts and strategies. I glanced around the room, realizing they were all aware of this as well. Motioning to Anne and Tricia, I gathered them around Gregory as Taylor took her time orienting herself.

"She needs actual rest and care right now. We can't plan things with her in this state. I can make the deal with Jack on the terms that she is cared for. Gregory can witness our deal in case things don't go the way we want. Anne, Tricia, would you two be willing to watch over Taylor while we sort things out? If things go bad, I want you girls to get her out of here."

The girls were quick to nod their agreement, but Gregory's silence drew our attention. He still watched Taylor as she practiced opening her eyes and focusing on the girls who sat around her. His processors whirred as his cooling fans kicked in.

"I'm not comfortable making deals without Taylor." He finally said in a quiet tone. His eyes never left Taylor. The girls now looked with him. I realized their loyalty was to her strength and character, not just her person. A truly smart group.

As I followed their gazes, I saw Taylor mimicking one girl, testing her motor control. She placed one finger on her nose while she held out the other. She tried to reciprocate the action with her other arm and missed her nose completely, and her arm fell. Neurological damage had been made, but there was no reason to assume it was permanent at this stage.

She tried to redo the test and failed it again. The girls patted her reassuringly and started another test. My heart hurt watching her fail her motor control tests, but we had more pressing concerns before we could get her somewhere to recover. I nudged Gregory to get him to look towards me.

"She is in no state of mind to deal with this right now. If we make this deal, we can make sure she is somewhere safe where she doesn't have to worry. We have to do it." Finalizing my words, I started my painful crawl across the floor to the door. If they weren't going to do it, I was. Taylor needed someone to decide for her right now. I had to push the fear that gnawed on my stomach down. She was going to be okay. I wouldn't let her leave me again.

Gregory stood, only to stoop and pick me up. I knew it was out of annoyance at my slow pace. The girls separated or rolled out of the way of his boots as he carried me to the door. My knuckles rasped against the metal, echoing up the stairway.

A few moments passed before steps could be heard descending the stairs on the other side. Gregory shifted me in his arms so he was holding me, almost as if I was standing on my own. I glanced back at him while he stared at the door.

"You have to look tough, but you look like a child when I carry you. If you didn't lose those crutches I made for you, I wouldn't have to hold you." Snarky words from the Drone who was the reason Taylor and I had electrical burns.

The door opened and Jack appeared. He didn't seem to expect us to be standing by the door, so he lingered in the entrance. Scanning eyes looked over me and Gregory. Taylor waved to him casually. Her hand bumped into her jaw as she tried.

I could see what the girls had officially named 'Oomer man, standing at the top of the stairs. More men lurked behind him. The air in the staircase was tense. Was it anticipation or readiness? Gregory seemed to notice it too, as his grip on me tightened slightly.

"I'm glad to see... Taylor, awake." Jack questioned the name. Having never been formally introduced, his hesitancy was well warranted. She tried to stand, but the girls held her down. I could hear them muttering warnings to her. If she couldn't touch her nose, she wasn't allowed to stand.

"We want to talk about the deal you proposed, but we will only talk if Taylor is moved to a cleaner location. She needs supplies and surveillance to recover fully." While I didn't know if that was an accurate statement, I just wanted her off the dirt ground.

Jack glanced up at the men who watched from the stairs, then back to us. Silent communication seemed to be a prevalent form of information sharing here. He shifted his feet before speaking.

"Let's start with names first. I can't allow strangers to stroll through my outpost."

Gregory was quicker to respond than I was. Though he deepened his voice to hold more authority. "All our names?"

He jerked his head in the direction of the girls in a sarcastic tone.

Apparently, he was trying to knock Jack from his position of power through underhanded sarcasm. A bold trick from a learning Drone.

"I would appreciate all the names. These girls just pushed their way in here as soon as we grabbed you. If they weren't Den Dogs, we wouldn't have let them in." I appreciated the term Den Dogs and saw the girls nod their head to their title. Proud of them, I nodded to Gregory to list the names.

The list was long, but Jack was patient. When Gregory finished with our names, he seemed satisfied with the answers he got. He looked over my wounds and back at Taylor.

"I will move you and make sure you have a quiet place to recover, but you and I will talk." His words were definite, leaving no room to negotiate. I tapped my fingers on the metal hands that held me up. While I rather not get separated from Taylor, it would put her in a safer position to be left out of negotiations. Gregory seemed to watch me, waiting for my choice. Did he finally come to respect my decisions?

"I accept as long as I see the room she will be kept in before we talk." He didn't hold all the power like he wanted to. I allowed myself to embrace a moment of power with my negotiation. It wasn't much, but it would bring extra peace of mind to me. Gregory tapped my side a few times and pointed towards the girls, indicating that I was supposed to invite them along.

"And the Den Dogs will tend to her." This addition seemed to catch Jack's attention. He scratched his chin while looking over the girls. I could see his fingers tap on his arm as he counted them.

"Do you really want these corpse carvers to look after her?" A weak attempt to dissuade my decision. I waved a dismissive hand at him and looked back at the girls. They didn't seem to care about the conversation, but focused on trying to lift Taylor, readying her to be moved. They were going to follow us with or without an invitation. It was a courtesy that I even asked.

"These corpse carvers saved my life, Gregory's, and Taylor's. So yes. I want them with her. Even if you say no, good luck stopping them."

Jack looked over at the girls with fresh interest and nodded as the they approached. Taylor was carried up the stairs first by the girls. Those who didn't carry waited behind Gregory, creating a bubble between us and the Forge members.

Our slow procession climbed the stairs in silence, only to be greeted at the top by an annoyed and knife armed 'Oomer man. I could see now as he stood in front of me in the brighter lighting that he leaned heavily on a metal leg and bio-wire scars carved up his neck and into his arm. He must have been an 'Oomer for a while.

We were led to the right of the hallway atop the stairs where the path was narrow. Lights adorned the ceiling and I could hear the buzz of electricity. I hadn't seen any electric lighting since I woke. Apparently, neither had Gregory as he analyzed the lighting fixtures. Silence flooded the hall as Gregory shifted me to one of his arms and reached towards the light. The Forge members observed him as he poked the light bulb. I could hear the glass clink as his glove made contact.

After a moment, he returned me to both his arms and looked forward down the long hallway, signaling the men to continue. I couldn't deny that it was helpful to have a terrifying Drone as a constant threat. He could stop a rebellion's march just by getting distracted by a light bulb. The group continued its shuffle forward. It wasn't long before a door was opened and the girls were directed in.

Once Gregory and I reached the door, I leaned forward to examine the room from the entrance. There was a window where morning light poured through. A candle was already lit near a bed made of shredded plastics and tarps. The floor was made of smoothed tin and seemed mostly cleaned. The window had a perfect view of the left side of Locura's skull. I could only assume that we were built into the wall near Upper town.

The girls verified to me it was a suitable room and they slowly piled in, finding their places to wait. Jack offered them a few tarp blankets, which they greedily accepted. Wrapped up and safe, I nodded to Jack to lead us away for our conversation.

"I don't feel comfortable talking in front of the Drone."

Gregory's grip tightened on me, but he wisely kept his mouth shut. I shook my head in disagreement. Tapping Gregory's hand, I pointed to my useless legs.

"I can't walk and I only trust him to carry me. He comes." Jack looked over my legs and motioned to a man behind him. There was shuffling as something was brought forward. They handed Jack what appeared to be my crutches. He held them out to me.

"If that machine is still connected to the network in any way, we can't let him hear our conversations. It could risk the entire operation more than it already has." The members pressed closer, tension building if I were to deny his reasoning. I accepted the crutches and looked to Gregory for approval.

He helped me onto them and turned into the room. "I am fine to wait with Taylor. If you hit trouble... scream." And with a dismissive hand, Gregory re-positioned himself in the entranceway on the ground. The guard was back at his post.

Using my reclaimed crutches, I did my best to follow Jack further down the hall, passing several doors. I couldn't tell if we were in a building or just following tunnels built into the dirt wall. The walk was short to my benefit, as my arms were already tired. It was hard to not hate the infirmity of my body. Taylor worked hard to revive me. I had to be grateful for what I had.

'Oomer man opened a door and stood to the side as Jack and I entered. He entered behind us and closed the door, guarding his own leader. There were two crude chairs and a tin table in the center of the room lit with one bulb. No windows or candles. This place felt like a daunting trap.

Jack helped me sit down off of the crutches and settle myself against the backrest. I maintained my grip on one rod to help hold myself straight. He took up a position across from me. His elbows perched on the table as he looked over me. Curiosity was now uncontained.

"So you are the Razum Walker. To be honest, I thought you were a myth until the Den Dogs mentioned you. What's it like waking up to this world?" His voice was smoother now, more relaxed. His body language spoke levels

321

of the comfort he felt with me. He slumped back into his chair, his fingers laced behind his head. This was no longer work, it was social. I did my best to mimic his energy, though ever sharp like Taylor would do.

"It was a shock, to say the least." He didn't need to know the struggles I faced. Whether my psychological recovery or physical, the less he knew of the process right now, the better. It was a good gambling chip to hold on to.

The man's eyes made me feel like he was trying to probe my thoughts. With the similar gray eyes of my sister, I felt like glass for a moment. Though, remembering her laying in a room down the hall, I did my best to be as opaque as the situation allowed.

"I can't even imagine. How are you liking our city? Has Sila treated you well?" These were all friendly questions, but he failed to hide deeper ones that he truly wanted to ask. Why was he wasting his time getting to know me?

"Besides getting electrical burns, my sister suffering brain trauma, and being chased by Harvey units, it's been fine." With very few reasons to share more, I kept my responses short. He leaned his chair on its back legs, seeming to enjoy the awkward silence between us.

"So, if I were to guess, your sister Taylor and your Drone friend are the ones that brought the heat to Sila? Gregory 235 and a female traveler have warrants out for their arrest. I am glad I haven't heard one for you yet." Jack was more up-to-date on our situation than I would have preferred, but he connected the right dots.

"The Harvey units are offering a fairly decent reward for your metal friend. Just so you know. We could have sold him when we shot him down, but I couldn't help feeling that would damage our future friendship. Am I correct?" The notion that someone would emphasize how things could have been worse never struck me as good company.

"That would have definitely enraged Taylor. We are two of a kind, so that would have done significant damage to possible friendships. For now, let's focus on the present. What deal are you making with us?" My fingers could be heard impatiently tapping the rods of my crutches. I didn't come here to waste my time.

"I suppose you are eager to tend to your sister. It's very admirable. I just want to extend to you three, if the Drone is willing, membership to the Forge. Our numbers have dwindled significantly because of your Drone and sister calling down hell with the Harvey units."

"With her having shot an actual Giant, a Gregory unit being Fritzed and an off network Drone, and the first Razum Walker in a century, we could add the heat that has left my rebellion. I'm not asking you to run missions. I'm just asking you to join our cause." Jack now sat forward, arms pressing against the table as if we were having a secret discussion. For a leader of a rebellion, he was oddly friendly. I had to agree that it was the best disguise.

We were right to want to have this deal with him. Turning us into symbols could help turn the city tide towards the Drones. It wouldn't be that difficult to pose pretty while turning into a symbol of rebellion, if he has the forces necessary to back our claim to change.

"What kind of protection can you offer us that we can't get from hiding in Sila's slums?" I couldn't help but try to bait him. Did he have any genuine power, or was this all a bluff?

His chuckle echoed through the small room as he pulled out a weapon and placed it on the table. It looked very similar to Taylor's gun she carried, though this one was more worn. He spun the gun around so I could see it from all angles.

"Everyone of my men carries these. From your face, it looks like you know what it is. We have rules though, my men are not gun-happy morons. No shooting in the city unless it's life or death. Being as you and your merry band were running towards Harvey units, it was a risk I had to roll."

"Since that shot, the Harveys have set up security checks all throughout the town. So now, if you left to live in the slums, your metal friend would have to pass four or five checks. You would be noticed in no time."

"I can give you shelter, weapons, and keep you well away from the machines. There is only one thing I want from you and your friends. Just stand by me. Be with me at the rallies and inspire people. That's all I need to pay for your safety." He seemed pleased with the situation we were in.

I remembered Taylor talking about the risks of her carrying that gun. Entire landscapes could be nuked in response to rebellion threats. To know that so many already existed here in Sila, I wondered if Taylor may have been right about her feelings to leave. How did she have a finger to the pulse of this city with never having been here before? She was a wonder.

Taking my time to piece together my thoughts, I let the silence continue between us. He willingly offered us memberships, but would he be open to our plan to fight the Drones in an all out war? Would he help set up Sila for the battle against the Giants? While I could be a tactical speaker when I needed to be, it felt wrong to make plans without Taylor being present. There seemed only one direction to take and that was to expose our intentions. No plans have to be made, but I would not promise peace when I intend war.

"I have conditions before I can accept this deal." I pulled myself closer to the table and leaned across it like he did. He nodded his head, accepting that I was going to lay out the conditions in mind. "We want to fight the Drones. Now. We heard the rumors of the Giants coming. If we clear out the city, there is a chance we could hold our own against them. If we come on board, we intend to fight as soon as possible. Even Gregory was open to this idea. The timing is right."

My words seemed to be unexpected, even 'Oomer man now shifted, thinking over the idea. Jack's face furrowed as he no doubt recounted the reports he received on the Giants. My only path to make him understand was by being direct now.

"Imagine being the rebellion that destroyed Locura's three favorite warriors? Any Giant after them will be child's play. I want to make this the rebellion that changes the tide of the war you all have been fighting while I slept. I will make a difference." There was confidence in these words and made sure I showed it. These were words I have thought to myself since I woke. Even in the Razum I wanted to be more, but the opportunity never arrived–until now. I would not pretend that this wasn't my destiny.

The 'Oomer man now chimed into the conversation. He stepped up to the table and faced Jack. I could see the faint markings of what looked like injections on his arm. Taylor had spoken of Synthix briefly, so I knew what these markings were.

"The kid has a point. With Viktorov closing in on us, it might be time to finally pull the trigger on Sila. We have waited for this day for a long time." I resented the term kid, but the 'Oomer man was close to double my age.

Jack rubbed his chin thoughtfully. The scratch of his stubble filled the room. The choice that road on his shoulder was not an easy one. He held the lives of quite a few people in his hands, and if he made this move, he risked the lives of Sila entirely. The silence lingered as he thought, lighting a new cigarette and taking a moment to enjoy the old nicotine.

"I was not born in Sila, but abandoned by raiders to rot in this region. Not long after, those raiders were killed by Gundry himself. This was back when that damn Giant was lazy, but in the past few years, his grip has tightened."

"Luck has favored me since I entered this city, and seems to follow me. I have created a powerful group. We don't starve or want for much. We have our own water filtration systems and medical groups. We even started our own 'Oomer conversion camps like where Ricky is from. I will risk this fight. I want to help the people of Sila breathe a little easier in the miasma that is Locura's remains." He took another drag before focusing his eyes on me.

Ricky now backed away from the table. A slight smirk could be seen developing. Jack took another long drag of the cigarette and handed it to Ricky as he stood. He opened the door and ushered the 'Oomer man out and helped me stand from my seat on the rods.

"You have yourself a deal, Razum Walker. I will let you tend to your sister in peace while I arrange your first rally. Ricky will come to get you when things are ready. Now get out. There are plans to design." He ushered me out of the room now, where Ricky waited. While I hated that I was not invited to help with planning, I was eager to see my sister. Escorted to the room by Ricky, I found Taylor sitting up in bed with the Den girls and Gregory watching me expectantly.

"Welcome to the Forge."

Chapter 13: Of Guns and Machines

It didn't take long to update the band of misfits on the conversation. Their heads bobbed approvingly at the deal. Taylor was the only one who did not nod, but stared at the floor as I spoke. Even Gregory nodded his head to my plan. The bobs of approval only emboldened my resolve.

"We have a sound path forward and a real chance at changing things here. Jack is setting up a rally for us to appear at soon, so we will need to be ready for it." The girls preened at each other and even a few wiped mud from Gregory. They were getting ready for the stage we were about to tread.

"You...made this plan?" Taylor's voice wavered, her shaking tone attracting my eyes. She had tears welling up and balled fists. The occasional arm spasm was the only thing that reminded me she was injured now.

"It's a good plan. We have a chance to stop the machines here. I thought you of all people would be–" She cut off my words.

"You've assigned death to everyone here. There's no reason to cause a rebellion anymore. The price is too high. How could you do this?" Her voice was loud and rattled the weak window slats. The girls now watched us with big eyes.

"Taylor, this is the only chance Sila has for freedom. You fought so hard for me to be free. You won't fight for these people to be free?" Frustration spread through my body as Taylor glared at me. Of everyone in this room, she was the one I thought would have been most excited. A chance to change, a chance to make a difference.

That was not the Taylor in front of me now. This Taylor was furious.

Furiously afraid. I did my best to amble towards her, trying to avoid the girls by my rods. She placed a hand up, motioning for me to stop. How had this upset her?

"I've always fought for freedom, since I woke up in this damn world, but you–you're not fighting for freedom. This fight won't work, your plan won't work. Our world is not as kind as the Razums were. They will nuke this city at the first smell of true rebellion. We will die."

Gregory now approached and took up position behind me, lowering himself a bit to avoid bumping the lantern that hung from the ceiling. His head was near mine and spared a glance towards me before speaking. I didn't think I would have to have a Drone back my reasoning, but Taylor was being unreasonable.

"It's a good plan, Taylor. They have weapons, they will have the numbers. With probably six to eight Harvey units lingering, we would only need to figure out how to deal with the Gregorys and Markus units here. Sila is large, and if enough people join, we could hit them all at once. There would be no one to retaliate. Gundry wouldn't have the Drones." Her eyes seared into him as well now.

She pulled herself from the bed with help from the girls so she could look into Gregory and my eyes directly. One hand pressed down on my shoulder, the other on Gregory's as she did her best to stand. My arms locked onto the rods to stabilize myself under her grip.

"Gregory, you should know these risks you run. If it's not Gundry, it will be another. One hundred twenty-seven Giants, those are your words. Are you two really ready to start a war with the last Machine lords? Do you think you could actually win?" Her grip tightened as she drew her face closer, blue eyes piercing my soul as fingers dug into my fresh burns.

She staggered with the added strain and Gregory caught her before her legs gave out. Placing her back on the bed, Gregory stepped back towards the doorway. The girls had pulled themselves to the walls to avoid being under foot. Taylor rolled away from us.

"You have killed them all…" She whispered to the wall. Curling up on the bed, she refused to talk more. I could only hear her mutters of doom now. The room was quiet. Neither girl nor Drone moved as we all listened to her spiraling fears.

Breaking the silence, I shuffled my numb feet across the ground and leaned against the wall near the foot of her bed. She had always been a fighter. Why was she losing her fight now? A survivalist at heart. Was her mind damaged now? Questions whirled around my brain as the light faded outside the slates of the window. It was later than Gregory had assumed.

Darkness crept into the room as we all embraced the silence Taylor brought down on us. Gregory sat in his usual place in front of the door and the girls took shifts napping. I remained. Still at the foot of my sister's bed, still hearing her murmurs of destruction and death. Hours passed, but I felt like I couldn't move.

A debate burned my mind. What was right? What was wrong? Shouldn't we fight for a better future? Shouldn't we do our best to help others lead to their better future? I couldn't wrap my head around her words. They seemed to contradict all I knew about my sister.

Was this the damage to her brain talking? Could she think clearly? This couldn't be my Taylor. She would fight for everyone. She was a dangerous force to be reckoned with. Everyone she met respected her. So why was she crying and muttering like a defeatist in a dark room? Where did the survivor go?

My mind traced back to the stories she had told me, everything pointing against her current state. This was the woman who carried me on her back across the Barrens, who dragged my lifeless body from the wreckage of the Fall. The one who risked her life, repeatedly, to steal what she needed to free me. Who was this crying, scared child?

Her form now looked like a stranger to me. Did it ever look like my Taylor? Had I made up our friendship with what I wanted and not with what was? Were the stories she told me lies? She used to be a beacon of hope, but now she scared the girls with whispers of bombs and fire. Where did the leader whom I respected and loved go?

The silence of the room was shattered like thin glass as a knock caused us all to jump. Gregory was the first to react to the sound as he stood. He cautiously opened the door and revealed Jack smiling in the hall. After a quick glance around the room, he adjusted his smile to a more neutral motion.

"Am I catching you at a bad time?" He asked, examining the sullen faces in our dark room. I leaned myself from the wall and gimped my way to face him. Gregory steadied me as I stood in the entrance. I glanced back towards Taylor, only to see her watching me from the corner of her eye as if her fear dragged her face into the bed.

"No, it's fine. Did you get the rally set up?" I stepped further into the doorway, trying to flee Taylor's burning eyes. Jack scanned over the room once more and softened his tone to match my own tired voice.

"Yeah, the guys and I were going to head out soon. Just letting you know to get ready. How's your sister doing?"

I stepped in front of his view of her. Gregory did the same. Jack didn't need to know our breakdown in communication. Nodding my appreciation for his concern, he stopped trying to look around us.

"She's still recovering and won't make it to this rally. Will we be enough?"

Jack nodded and stepped back towards the hallway. "Ready when you are."

With nothing to prepare and owning my damaged look, I staggered into the hall and waited for Gregory to follow. Anne and Tricia also joined us to represent the once prestigious Organ Den. As they flowed into the hall in line with the Forge members that were there, I glanced once more into the dark room. The blue eyes that peered at me shined in the dark. When she turned her head away from me, accepting that I made my choice, I closed the door on her and followed the procession down the hall.

Gregory watched me closely as I passed him. Taking the rear guard with Anne, he followed quietly. I made a mental note to talk through things with him when we had a moment of privacy. Now was not the time to lose face in front of the Forge.

Our erratic steps echoed through the long hall. All the doors we passed were closed and the hall sloped downwards. I felt like this was not actually a hallway. As we continued walking, there was a sudden change in the sheet metal walls where they turned to dirt.

"It seems to be a tunnel system. I assume we hide in the North wall above the factory zone." Gregory seemed to follow my line of thought as he educated me with his guess. Jack, who was in front of me, tilted his head back.

"Observant. This outpost is almost completely hidden in the North wall. Only a few windowed rooms exist, like your sister's. We dug out these tunnels years ago during the early phases of the Forge. It's now our oldest undiscovered tunnel system. I think it stretches a mile out to the Barrens and runs a fairly complete loop around all of Sila." He gestured proudly to the tunnel system as our feet met the dirt and we descended further.

"How long has the Forge been functioning?" I asked as I saw carving marks scarring the wall.

They looked ancient compared to the electric lighting and metal walls we had walked through before. Gregory ran his hand along the stable dirt as we continued forward. It was like he was memorizing the exact scars of tools on the wall.

"The Forge has been burning strong since the Fall. So, twelve-some years? We used to be a few hundred strong back in the day. Our numbers have dwindled to roughly a hundred. Making tunnels back then didn't take as long as they do now. It's a fair price for the safety measures these walls give us." Jack patted the wall with appreciation as the hall veered to the left, street sounds echoing up to us.

We approached a new metal hall that required steps to go towards the door above us. Gregory didn't need to be asked as he helped lift me up the stairs. Jack made us wait at the door and looked over the Drone.

"You will need to be covered up. How did you make yourself smaller last night?" The men stepped away from Gregory as he shifted his plates and dropped a foot in height back to his semi-normal behemoth height. Whistling with impressed noises, the men pulled tarps from their own clothes and handed them to the Drone to cover him. Once he was fully hidden, the door was opened.

We filed out onto the street as I cast a glance back to where we came from. The tunnel must have been dug through the floor of a building since we were two houses from the wall. I watched as the men pushed down the door we had come through, replacing the false floor and closing the actual door. The Forge was smart enough to let the house get raided, but keep the tunnel entrance a secret.

Jack led us cautiously through the side streets. From the noises I heard, we weren't far from a main social center. Gregory stayed close to me as Anne and Tricia stayed closer to Jack. Our route was crowded, so our group didn't stand out.

As I looked further down the street, I noticed a Harvey unit standing in line with two Gregory units. Plates glistened in the red lamp lights. They were all armed with weapons and scanned heavily everyone who passed them. Jack motioned for the group to take a left down an alley. We cut down the dark path and passed two more houses before the group paused before a door.

The members of the Forge gathered around Jack as he knocked and spoke to the house owners. I guessed they were Forge members as well when they allowed us in. All eyes focused on Gregory and me as we ducked into the small doorway, Gregory having to hunch over to fit.

A large room opened before us as we entered. Candles and lanterns were placed anywhere there was space. People crowded in the room, over thirty some heads could be seen. Gregory had to displace the people closest to the door to fit inside. The dark beady eyes glowed around the room as I was guided to the semi-cleared center of the group.

"Thank you for inviting us into your home tonight, and risking attending this meeting. Your struggles are not unknown to us as we risk our own lives to bring you some of our newest members. Meet Tyron, and Gregory." Jack gestured to me and Gregory, who remained cloaked.

"These two recent additions are not regular members, though. Tyron here is the first in over a hundred years to be freed from a Razum. Gregory is the first, ever, sympathetic Drone." The crowd buzzed frantically at the word 'Drone,' but as Jack slowly uncovered Gregory's head, it was replaced with awe.

Hands reached for us cautiously. I could feel the questioning taps of fingers seeking to prove that I existed. Gregory was even tapped to confirm his metal quality. Jack was quick to shoo them away from us as he continued to speak.

"I see a few who doubt me. Being as I have never lied to you, let me prove these two are the real thing." Jack turned to me and lowered his voice. "May I show them your scars and unwrap Gregory?" I had to give Jack credit. He was a formal and friendly man. Gregory seemed to hear the words before I agreed and shirked his tarps. Golden plates gleamed in the lantern light and the acid washed silver reflected distorted images of the eyes that watched. With the help of Jack, I unwrapped my bandages and revealed the T scar, a badge of my survival.

Now the room fell silent. No hushed whispers, no grabbing hands, just silence. Jack even stepped back to admire us. The weak gimp and the shiny Drone. A man's voice broke the silence.

"How is this possible?"

Jack faced the man and gave him a brief smile, though he shook his head. "I would not ask you to tell me your life story stranger, they too expect that courtesy. While these two are responsible for bringing the Harveys here, they may also be our best chance to finally free Sila. Many of you are here with that same hope, and now I am showing you our weapon."

"A Drone who was active until a week ago can now help us understand these machines on a deeper level. He can give us the answers to how they think, how they function. While he is terrifying to behold, he has not acted aggressively or conversely while he has been at our outpost."

"And our sweet Tyron here, and his sister, who couldn't attend, are our key to freeing the hundreds of Razum Borns that lay in our gutters or scattered across the Barrens. These two are smart and resourceful and have started the process of a plan to free the entire city and remove the oppression of the Giants. Once and for all."

Excited chatter broke out. Apparently, the people were easier to sway than I had anticipated. Jack was definitely a useful tool for communicating our goals to the citizens of Sila. I tried to imagine Taylor standing before this crowd. Would she have been so bold? The image of her curled on the bed back in the outpost flashed across my mind. No. She would not have been so bold.

Questions rang out as people asked about plans and risks. As Jack answered what he could, questions started getting directed at me. They asked what it was like in the Razum, as many of them were never placed in a network. Jack did his best to keep people away from me, but hands pulled at me as questions were spoken into my ears.

While Jack was helping keep people at bay, I hated the hands that reached for me. I looked back at Gregory and motioned for him to make a scene. These people didn't need a messiah to answer their questions. They needed a show of power and resolve to the cause.

Gregory placed a hand on my shoulder, understanding my direction of thought. This being his first movement since he was uncovered, the crowd pushed themselves against the wall in fear. I noticed even Jack reacted instinctively to the motion, a hand hidden behind his back, likely on the gun we already knew the shock of. Gregory stretched his neck higher and shifted his panels slightly to enlarge his form. He was demanding their attention.

"Do not crowd. We are here to see which of you is ready to fight back. This isn't a Q and A, or an interview. This is recruitment." His speaker silenced the many questions. Even the rattle of his words shook the tin walls of the house. No one was going to interrupt him.

"Who of you is brave enough to fight for your future? Step forward to Gregory now, if you think you are ready." My words held a similar weight to Gregory's as the eyes focused on me. Working with Gregory was not my favorite choice, but our power of personality seemed to make us a good match. Jack watched with concerned eyes as the friendly tone in the room turned serious and tense with my call to action.

An older man pulled himself from the crowd hesitantly. His gray hair and acid scarred skin reminded me of the character Gern that Taylor had told me about. He was missing a leg and relied on a metal rod, similar to my struggle. As he made his way to the center, he kept his eyes low, not looking at Gregory's glowing LEDs. With a down-turned face, he stood before the Drone.

Gregory turned to face the man and, in a dramatic display of power, he shifted his plates and adopted his full size. I watched as the cables under the plates shifted and filled in the gaps of his moving armor. He seemed thicker than I had seen him before, as if he was puffing out his chest. Intimidation was what we needed right now. We needed to see if these people could stand against the full fear that a Drone commanded.

Regardless of these displays of strength and power before him, the old man didn't budge. Gregory even punched into the ground next to the man with alarming speed, causing the people to shove and push to get away. Yet, the old man didn't flinch. As Gregory was now hunched over, he was just slightly above the old man's face. Gregory craned his head to the side to look down into the old eyes. The terrifying smile glowed in the firelight and I realized what fear these Drones could instil. For most, this was the stuff of their nightmares. For me, this was a tool capable of controlling the tides of war.

Even his teeth caused flashes of light to reflect against the wall and the faces hiding. Yet, the old man still didn't move. He raised his head slowly to meet the aggressive Drone to stare into his eyes. This seemed to startle Gregory, though he maintained his position. The lack of fear was one thing, but to be looked in the eyes startled the machine.

"I lost my leg to a Gregory Unit a few years back. Infection would have killed me if it weren't for the Forge. That Unit now lies in the dirt of the Barrens because the Forge balanced the world. You hold no fear for me anymore, because I know you can be shut down." His words were simple but carried the weight of a tough life. This old man knew that humans were gaining their power back with or without a Drone on our side. Even if the world seemed to be on its last legs, he knew things could still change. This was the sort of fire I wanted to see in the Forge. It was the spark we needed to keep lit.

This was not the response Gregory expected, but he seemed pleased. Shifting his plates into his more friendly stature, he patted the man's shoulder gently. With his armored form gone, the crowd relaxed from the wall and shuffled near again. Jack removed his hand from his hidden weapon as well.

"You should all be as brave as this man if you join. The Drones will use every fear tactic they know to make you run. So if you do, they win. Consider this as you contemplate joining." While I finished my challenge, Gregory retook his position behind me. My eyes connected with Jack's as I nodded for him to continue.

He struggled to gather his thoughts, apparently shaken a bit at the drastic change of his rally. I wondered if we were going to be scolded for this infraction. Based on how Jack ran with the new room tone, I doubted it.

As he continued to rile the group, I stopped listening. It was a familiar speech that probably has been repeated, time and time again, in histories lost to us. One of impending victory and plans for freedom. Emboldening the people and talking about how they have to believe that the world could be more. Though Jack didn't mention Locura's Giants that were coming for the city, but it was probably wise. If he could hand them a victory, by the time the Giants arrived, his army would already have its confidence.

I glanced back at Gregory. He seemed to stare into a wall, waiting for the rally to be over. Was he aware of the effect he had on the crowd? Was he aware of how I was using his power to strike fear and hope into the group? As people gathered around Jack to join the Forge, it seemed my plan worked.

Many tapped Gregory's or my arm in thanks as they left the building, scurrying into the night with newfound hope. We watched as they all flowed out in scattered bursts to avoid suspicion. Ricky guided people out in safe numbers as he handed them a small metal sheet that likely had meeting information. The last group left as the Forge members and the home owners whispered together.

The members examined the floor where Gregory had dented the metal into the dirt below. Jack apologized for the damage, but the homeowners seemed disgruntled at the evidence being left behind. I tossed a glance to Gregory, who still stared at the wall. If I were to guess, he looked bored.

"Hey Gregory, fix the hole you made." His attention was drawn to my command. This was my first time speaking so directly to him, so I treated it as a test. Almost startled from the direct conversation, he noticed the disgruntled home owners. Walking over without invitation, the people backed away from him.

He stooped to scan the flooring before finding a seam between the tin sheets. Sliding his hand under the metal, he pushed it flat again. As he stood, the home owners examined his work hesitantly. I couldn't see the difference in the flooring from where it was dented compared to the rest of the floor.

They nodded a silent thanks before they bid us farewell. Gregory was re-covered, and my bandages were replaced before we were led back into the night air of the alley. Our trudge was silent until the light sprinkle of rain started. I had to fight the urge to hold out my hand to feel the water. Taylor had told me of how hard she worked to avoid my skin scarring from water. It felt rude to throw away that effort.

Mud formed quickly, making my rods slip. Thanks to Gregory's design, the spikes at the base caught me. I knew it would look weird for Gregory to carry me now that we were seen walking, but the rods were hurting. My burnt hands were already in agony from holding myself up. Tired muscles, fatigue from the burns, I was ready for the day to be done and a new action plan for tomorrow to be made.

As we turned the corner to the street we started on, I could see the house that marked the entrance to the outpost. Against my desires, I would have to ask Gregory to carry me once inside. Doing my best to keep up with the crowd, it was noticed that I was moving slower.

"Not much further, kid. You gonna make it?" It was Ricky's voice that pulled my attention to my right. The scarred man took up a step beside me. I had to slow my breathing to speak.

"Just started using... these rods yesterday... not used to them yet."

He allowed himself a chuckle, the first evidence I had seen of authentic emotion from the ex-'Oomer. The slap on the back I received sent shivers of agony down my arms and chest. Though it was a friendly gesture, I did

337

not want to endure it again.

The door approached and I watched as the men opened the real door and pulled up the false door. We had split into two groups in the less crowded streets to avoid detection. The first group descended before we arrived at the threshold. Jack waited inside the door to help me down the stairs.

I watched the men continue down the tunnel as Jack held me still to wait for Gregory to join us. Were we going to get scolded now? Had we crossed a line? Gregory's eyes focused on Jack's hand around my arm before he descended the stairs. I wasn't a child who needed to be looked after.

"I need to talk to you two a moment before we head up."

I faced Jack, ready to get scolded for my actions and unwilling to apologize. Did Gregory feel anxiety at the idea of being challenged? I couldn't help but to wonder how his mind worked. With his circuits Fritzing, did his world feel different and more real like mine did when I woke? His metal face betrayed nothing as he stood near Jack to listen.

"It was quite a stunt you pulled back there. I had a lot of frightened people in that room. Do you have any reason for your actions besides scaring everyone?" His tone was intended to intimidate so I'm sure my lack of reaction bothered him. Gregory stood behind me, owning his part in the scene we made.

"Your friendly nature will not get you the support of the town. We were wasting time. Fear is the best motivator. Did you get more members?" My tone was flat and dismissive, seeing no point in explaining myself.

Jack rubbed his hair as he counted the marks he had drawn on his arm. I could make out about twenty marks, which would mean that the majority of the room signed on for the Forge. I waited for Jack to concede the conversation.

"Yes, but the point I am trying to make is we need warning if you are going to go all Drone on us. My men are not used to him being friendly. You may not have noticed the guns that were pointed at his back. Just let me know in the future if you plan to show off like that." Jack started walking down the hall, aware that he was talking to a brick wall of indifference.

"I plan to do a demonstration of fear at all future rallies that I am part of," Gregory ended the conversation for me. Once I was in Gregory's grip, we followed the irritated Jack down the tunnel.

I had more time to examine the tunnel quality as I was carried, able to finally touch the cold dirt. There were braces every few feet that held the tunnel open and carried the lighting. Names were etched into the metal girders, with dates noted by them. I assumed they were the original constructor's deaths.

"How many names are written in this tunnel?"

Gregory scanned the girder I was talking about as he continued his stride. I could hear the processors whirring as we walked. Dust kicked off the wall by the air flow change. He looked forward to Jack before speaking.

"I counted over three hundred seventy-nine names when we initially walked through. There were three hundred sixty-seven names with death dates. Twelve people remain alive according to these records."

Jack now tossed his head to the side, analyzing us. He had apparently been listening. Pausing slightly to check one brace, he patted the sturdy metal.

"Ricky, Hua, Burnard, and I are the last now. The bodies of the others were never found and presumed dead. Haven't had the heart to write the dates yet. Harveys grabbed them on their first day in Sila." His tone was solemn. We had apparently hit some sensitive areas for the man tonight.

"I'm sorry we brought Harveys here. It was never our intention." Gregory muttered quietly. I was shocked by his empathy and that he was aware enough to apologize. Apparently, so was Jack as he looked quizzically back at Gregory. An eyebrow was arched in confusion as he looked over the machine that was responsible for hundreds, if not thousands, of deaths, apologizing for the loss of eight strangers. Nodding his hesitant thanks, we continued in awkward silence.

The minutes passed quietly. The only sound to be heard was the tromping of muddy boots. My nose twitched at the smell of damp metal as we drew near to the hall. As Gregory's feet hit the tin flooring, I noticed Tricia and Anne waiting for us in the hall. We had been separated in the street, but it was comforting to know that they waited for us.

With our merry band finally reunited, we continued down the hall to where Jack waited by the open door of Taylor's room. He gestured us in, standing out of the way of Gregory.

The room was well lit, the shutters of the window closed to hide the light. Several of the girls were curled up on the bed by Taylor's feet, while others slept on the floor. They barely moved as we entered and tip-toed around them.

I looked back at the lingering Jack. He motioned further down the hall as he rubbed his neck. His face was looking exhausted. Gregory and I seemed to have stressed out the Forge leader. A daunting sign of his tolerance of machines.

"There is another room beside here which you can use. Figured there are too many of you to sleep comfortably in here. The door is unlocked and dinner should come around soon. Just leave the door open." He passed behind the wall as he walked further into the tunnel system.

Gregory looked at me for direction as he held me in his arms. "Let me see how Taylor is doing and I will take the other room with half the girls." With a silent nod, he walked me quietly to the bed. Taylor's back was still turned to the room, but I could tell from her breathing that she was awake.

"We did good tonight. Twenty new members. Gregory put on a wonderful display of what these people will be up against. You would have been impressed." Her lack of response was what I expected. I just wanted her to know things were working in our favor now.

"I'm going to sleep in the room next to this. I'll check on you in the morning." Gregory took me back to the door on quiet metal shoes. His steps on the flooring stirred the girls. He jutted his chin to the door, indicating some of them were supposed to follow him.

The groggy children filed out of the room on staggering feet, following his directions. Gregory turned to allow me to close the door. I couldn't help but to look over my sister's frail form. This was never the intention of the plan. More than anything, I wanted her to be on my side. It seemed this world was more cruel than I thought.

I slowly closed the door, but made sure it was still open enough to accept food. As I pulled my arm, a quiet voice barely escaped the crack. "Goodnight." Taylor's voice was barely above a whisper, but I knew that whisper well.

"Goodnight, Taylor."

Gregory carefully carried me to the next room, where the girls waited patiently outside. They opened the door and piled in, making room for Gregory to enter. It was similar in size to Taylor's, but there was no window. A candle burned on a nightstand next to three beds, which the girls promptly claimed two. Gregory placed me on the third and stood at the foot. His head turned to the door.

I had wondered if he would stay with me or Taylor through the night. With his fondness for the girls, he would likely be fine with either, but our fight with Taylor seemed to cause him to hesitate. The processor's whirring was becoming a white noise to me now.

"Go watch over Taylor. She would appreciate the friendship." I closed my eyes as the words crossed my lips. A part of me would feel safer without a metal emotional time bomb resting in my room.

His head must have turned towards me, as I heard the moan of metal. He seemed to agree with my advice and darkness washed over my closed eyes as he extinguished the flame. Hearing heavy feet thud and leave the room was the last thing that crossed my consciousness as sleep overcame me.

Sleep was no simple task. The shuffling of the girls, or the steps of Forge members dropping off food, all rustled me from my slumber. As the noise built up in frequency, I assumed morning had come. When there was a knock on the door, I knew I was correct.

"Yes?" It was all my groggy voice could muster. The familiar metal steps of Gregory caused me to open an eye. His smiling metal forms an eerie sight appearing from the dark. His LEDs were bright in the unlit room.

"Jack came by recently. We have a few rally meetings to attend soon. Taylor is still insisting on not attending. Get ready." His words were purely for information as he turned his back and left the room. A terrible alarm clock.

Pulling myself up by using the frame of the bed, I cleaned the dirt from my legs. There was very little to prepare as I didn't have belongings besides my crutches. A shudder raced down my spine as the memory of the burns scorched its way across my body. I should probably prepare the wound more than I thought.

"Do you girls have anything for the pain today?" My unsolicited request only caused the girls to shift in annoyed moans. Tricia, to my fortune, stirred herself from sleep. She dug through the pockets of the sleeping children until she found the salve jar she was after.

She placed tired feet on the ground as she walked over to my bed. Forcing me to lie down, she unwrapped my torso and applied more of the medicine across my burns. Agonized hands gripped the tarping that made up the mattress. Pain spreading across my reality with each new dollop of salve. After a few minutes of searing medicine, Tricia helped me sit up to wrap the new bandages she had snagged from one girl.

I wish I could have done more than to thank her, but I had little to give now. Her timing was impressive, though. As soon as she finished wrapping a tarp shirt around me, there was another knock on the door. This one sounded more fleshy than before.

Jack's head appeared in the doorway, a revitalized smile on his face. I grabbed my rods to stand when he entered and stopped me. Taking my crutches away, he pulled some tarps from the mattress and wrapped the portion that sat under my arms, making them padded.

"Were these crutches made by a robot? They look miserable to use." His words were sarcastic, but the truth was in them.

"It was a kindness from Gregory. I suppose he doesn't have the nerve endings to understand how much holding my weight on metal spikes would hurt. Thanks." I took the newly improved crutches from him and leaned forward, placing them under my arms. Jack helped to lift my body as I tried to regain my balancing legs.

After a few test walks, I felt relief in my armpits. It was a simple adjustment, but it was the difference between man and machine. Jack helped to guide me out of the room, helping to hold me up as I remembered how to use the crutches.

Gregory waited in the hall as I was ushered through the doorway. His arms were crossed in an annoyed fashion, likely because of my slowness. Jack closed the door to let the girls continue their sleep before leading us down the familiar hallway we walked the night before.

The day was like a repeat of the night. We would walk our way to a new house, do Gregory's demonstration of power as Jack collected new members. A slow and boring day. Even Gregory seemed to get irritated with the slowness. Jack was the only one who maintained a good mood as he started shirking the promotional part of the rallies on me. He was giving me some power, and I loved it.

We had left our third rally and now faced the late noon sun as we began back towards the outpost. The Forge primarily ran the North wall houses, today being no different as we walked from Midtown back towards the skull.

"Seventy-seven members today. Word has been spreading quickly about Gregory here." Jack muttered to himself as he took up his pace to walk beside me. My arms ached at this point. While they had let me sit at the rallies, these walks were being too much. I already had developed blisters in my armpits from all the friction of the crutches.

"If this keeps up, we should be well on our way to start a fight that we could actually win. Weapon production has been increased to help arm our new friends. Tomorrow should be the same if everything stays quiet. Thanks to you both." His words fell on tired ears. Both Gregory and I only added our nods.

Noises erupted as a fight broke out on the main street to our right. I could hear the Harvey units intervening and the shuffling of running feet. Jack's men separated into groups to go check it out as we continued our walk. Fights weren't uncommon, but it was wise to pay attention to things going on in Sila.

The house that marked the entrance to the outpost came into sight. My crutches trudged through the still damp ground. It wasn't until I saw Gregory's head turn suddenly that I heard a sound that caused my muscles to clench in fear.

A gunshot. In the center street. Jack didn't even spare a glance but ran for the house. Gregory copied suit and grabbed my ribs in an aggressive arm hug as he ran as well. I turned my head to look towards the street. Several of Jack's men drew their guns and began simultaneously firing at a Harvey unit.

Thuds of more metal shoes rose from the chaotic noises. This was no longer a brawl over food. This was the first shot in a war we weren't prepared for. I could only see the Harvey begin to fall as I was thrown into the cover house and was caught by an unsuspecting Jack. Gregory slammed the door before we could realize what he was doing.

His metal shoes could be heard as they stomped towards the central street. Jack handed me to one man who had made it to the door as he closed and hid the interior door. Panic was reverberating through the tunnel as more men scrambled. No one seemed to know how to respond. Even Jack leaned against a wall, contemplating his options.

More gunshots, more metal shoes. This wasn't the time or the place to start our war. We weren't prepared. We didn't have enough weapons, but the clock had officially started. I could hear cheers and screams alike. Apparently, the Harveys were falling but some were still attacking.

Jack let out a chuckle, stopping the men who rustled in the tunnel and prickling the hair on my arms with the out-of-place sound. This was an amusing situation for him. Had he not realized his luck had run out?

"The best laid plans, eh?" His voice was defeated, but his face was not. "Time to roll out the guns, I guess. Tyron, do you know how long it will be for Drones to get a message to Gundry?"

I tried to think back to all my conversations with Gregory and Taylor, looking for information. Remembering that Gregory had to be physically taken and assessed by Finigan suggested they had to use manual communication methods like us. It was the best guess I could make.

"I think they need to physically send Drones to Gundry to update him. Can you set men between us and Gundry?" I did my best to melt into the wall to let the newly armed men take up position at the door. Heavy metal shoes were approaching quickly.

"Someone find Ricky and send his group out to the Barrens. Have them stand guard on Gundry's road. Shoot everyone in their way. We are out for oil tonight." He whispered his commands, sending two men deeper into the tunnel to find Ricky.

The metal stomping was still coming directly towards us. Jack drew his gun and held it ready under the panel that was the false door. There was no way a Harvey could have seen us, was there? We were quick to hide and no one was around us. Images of the Organ Den raided through my mind. Did I start a raid that would lead to Taylor's body being the one that I had to escape over? Was her blood on my face this time?

Metal feet stomped above us before the panel was thrown open. Guns trained on the light spilling down on us, no shots were fired. Gregory stood above us, new bullet wounds covering his chest plates as he held up two of Jack's men. One was injured with a broken leg while the other was unconscious.

He handed the men down to Jack, who threw his gun aside, taking the bodies with care. They were carried down the line of men till they reached the end and were run deeper into the tunnel. Gregory turned from the panel and slammed it before we could stop him.

That damn Drone. I thought I understood his motivations, but I was learning more about him by the day. A part of my heart ached knowing that this was due to his circuits decaying. Another part of me finally accepted his usefulness in this battle. Jack turned from the hatch with a confused but grateful look.

"Get back to your room. My men and I will stay here to help the wounded get out safely. Ricky should be on the way to stop communication from getting to Gundry. Will you be fine to walk the tunnel yourself?" His words were fast as he regained his gun and motioned his men towards the panel.

I nodded to him as a man threw open the door and started out of the house above, Gregory already leading the way. Jack flashed me one more smile before he closed the panel behind the group. Turning as quickly as I could, I started the arduous climb through the tunnel.

Even though I was deep in the Earth and rising above the city level, guns rang out. Blood-curdling screams chimed in after a particularly loud gun was fired. This wasn't the war people expected. This was becoming genocide quickly from the sounds I heard.

All I could do was try to reach Taylor. I just needed to move fast. The sounds of my legs dragging in the dirt drove fury into each crutch forward. Why was I damned in this broken body? Was I meant to be a burden or an instrument of change?

Feet could be heard rushing from ahead of me. As I rounded a corner in the curvy tunnel, I saw the herd of girls rushing down towards me. They paused as they saw me, looking over me for injury.

"What are you doing here?" I asked, almost horrified to see them running down the path to a bloodbath. Anne led the group of the older girls. She truly looked like a child in front of the pre-teens.

"We're gonna help." Her answer was sincere and her tone hinted at her understanding of the dangers. The girls nodded with her. Such brave children.

"You will be killed if you go out there now." I didn't want to see more children die. It was enough to lose the Den. How could I let them out again into that cruel world? I did my best to hold my arms up, blocking most of the small tunnel.

"Tyron, we don't have many skills. We can only help people. There is no reason for the Harveys to shoot us if we don't show violence." Another girl chimed in. I didn't know her name, but her face was gentle. A few years older than Anne, and she was ready to risk her life for strangers.

"I don't want to lose you girls." Pathetic words, but they were the only ones my frazzled brain could manage. Their gleaming smiles broke down the last reasons I had to keep them near.

"You won't. We will be back soon. Promise." Anne smiled as she hugged my pathetic dangling legs. Wishing I could hug her back, I lowered my head to her. She slipped past my arms as another girl hugged me, gaining her passage past me.

As the group hugged me one by one, they slipped past and made their way down the tunnel. I turned and watched as the last girl disappeared around a corner. I don't know what gods exist in this world, but I sent prayers for their safety.

Minutes felt like hours as I continued my way through the tunnel. When my crutches clanged against the metal flooring of the hall, I felt a little peace of mind come back to me. The distant gunshot stole it as quickly as I got it.

When Taylor's door came into sight, I noticed it was open with Tricia waiting there. Her eyes lit up as she noticed me and started running. She looked me up and down for injuries. When she was satisfied that there was no immediate concern, she helped me to the room.

Taylor stood by the open window, silent and unmoving. There were five girls that remained. So many had left to help. Tricia placed me on the bed and took up a spot next to Taylor, watching the chaos unfold outside the window.

"Gregory is down there. He saved two members' lives." His actions were noble and I had hoped they would alleviate some of Taylor's concerns. She remained silent and indifferent to the information shared.

I pulled myself to the head of the bed and used the window frame to pull myself high enough to look outside. There was smoke in the distance, fires burning could be smelt in the air. Had the whole city decided it was time to fight now?

"We heard the gunshots from here. People started to riot," Tricia said as she checked on Taylor, who still stared out the window. Screams could be heard from up here as well. Sila was falling into chaos.

Harvey units could be seen rushing towards the central street to offer backup. While I couldn't hear the feet stomping in unison, I could have sworn I felt them. Each theoretical vibration was only another trigger for the anger that burned within me.

I imagined the girls out there, dodging bullets and helping the wounded. Would the Harvey units actually leave them alone, or were they killing without regard now that weapons were discovered? More shots rang out and were met with a colossal explosion.

347

Our heads all pivoted to the sound and I could see black smoke coming from one of the nearby factories. The air was becoming dense with smoke and haze, only to mix with the red factory smoke. The maroon air felt like blood against the sky.

Clattering in the hall drew our attention. Feet stomped wearily, carrying something heavy our way. As we watched to see who passed the hall, to our mild relief, it was members carrying a wounded man who was still very alive.

One member stopped in the doorway, hanging on by the frame as he leaned in. "Tricia, could use your help down here." She responded by following the man. Casting one last glance to make sure she was okay to leave.

I pulled myself higher to the window, smoke now rolling into our hidden spot. More fires had started, some seeming to be from the remains of the Harveys. Taylor looked at me as I drew closer. Her cheeks were red from tears.

"I thought you were down there. The girls wouldn't let me leave to see if you were okay." Piercing blue eyes analyzed me.

"I got in before trouble started, thanks to Gregory." I didn't know what else to say. The air still felt heavy between us. I would gladly face armies of machines, yet facing a frustrated sister was still somewhat terrifying. While I know she cared about my safety, did she know I didn't mean for things to happen this way?

The silence stretched on as much as it could against the smoke and gunfire. Her hands looked like they were trembling, not from neurological damage, but from fear. Had she seen this before, or was she just in shock?

Harvey units called for a retreat to their base by the factories. So the members had some success. Their calls for retreat relaxed my white knuckles from the window frame. It wasn't a long battle. Hopefully, the losses piled more on the side of the Drones.

More clattering down the hall as more members were brought up from the battle. I counted twenty-two injured, seven with mild injuries, and three bodies that appeared lifeless. To my despair, one of the dead was a girl that had been with Anne.

Taylor now sat on the bed. Her eyes lost in her own mind as she stared across the empty room. I let myself fall from the frame and slid into a semi-supported pose against the wall as I watched her.

"You know I didn't mean to upset you, right?" The words felt awkward and out of place, but it didn't seem to bother her.

"I know."

"I just want to help the city. I wanted to make sure these people had a future like you gave me."

"I know."

Her curt responses were cold. Didn't she understand I was trying to apologize? Could she not see that I wanted to be on the same side? We were brother and sister. We should always fight with one another, not against.

Slow, metal shoes began to echo down the now quiet hall. We turned to watch. The calm feet could only belong to one Drone. I was eager to see how well Gregory had fared out in the battle. Also, I owed him a thanks for saving my life, again.

As the bulking attack mode Gregory crossed in front of our door, we saw what he carried. He paused and looked at us. In his arms, he held sweet Anne, bullets riddling her lifeless body.

Chapter 14: Smoke

Gregory continued his mournful walk down the hall, bringing Anne's body to what I assumed was an infirmary. Regardless of a sculpted smile, or the expressionless LED eyes, his slow walk spoke of the misery he was feeling. If he was capable of tears, he would have been crying. As her limp body swayed in his metal arms, they left our sight.

Taylor's eyes seemed to still be processing the image that passed before us. Another explosion drew our attention back to the window. Another factory had caught ablaze and screams followed. The world was seeming to fall apart.

I had to assure myself of the plan. It was the only way forward, the only path that led to freedom. We knew blood would be the price and we were eager to get started. This had become the only path when the first pulse flew.

Cries echoed from down the hall. Tricia's voice, no doubt about her learning of Anne's death. Too many innocent children were being lost. Couldn't Taylor see now why it had to be done? This price was for freedom, so that more children could live real lives. No more fears of machines, or raids, just allowing children to be children was the goal.

My mind continued to roll in these thoughts as the sun left the sky. Fires and smoke lit Sila. The screams started to fade, but groans could still be heard from our distance. Taylor had moved from the window to the bed. We could do nothing but listen to the pain of the day die down. It wasn't our time to join the fight yet.

Feet were now consistently scurrying down the hall. Orders were being assigned and bodies carried. The injured were moved, weapons were traded, new focus points were being targeted. It wasn't until a slumped man stopped in our doorway to break our bitter silence.

"Tyron, people would like to see that you are still alive. You and Gregory." As my eyes focused on the growing darkness, I saw Jack. His shoulder appeared to have been wounded and he stood on what seemed to be an injured foot. Worse for wear, but still maintained a friendly smirk. I imagined his stress for today was extreme, but I could see his bravery from his smile.

"Okay. Gregory will be a moment."

Jack leaned his head back to look down the hall. Metal shoes seemed on cue as Gregory approached. His tall form was hunched slightly, slower steps than usual. Would his Fritzing increase with social trauma? Should these signs be documented? He was too many unknowns to deal with on top of starting a war today.

As Gregory approached to help me stand on my crutches, Taylor now turned to us. Her cheeks had a red blush, with pale streaks carving her cheeks where her tears had fallen. We watched her in anticipation of another argument.

"I want to come with." Her voice was hoarse. Though it did not detract from her serious tone. Without a need for a response, she joined Jack in the hall. She didn't seem to stagger like she used to. Perhaps she was feeling better.

Gregory followed behind me as I slowly approached the door. There was no more impatience from him, just the loud thud of his metal shoes. I felt pity for him. The first taste of loss and depression was never easy. He would survive this, though, just like he had survived a hundred years before.

Limping, Jack led us down towards the tunnel. There felt no need for words to be shared, not after the losses of the day. No more analysis of the world, no more words to cover the silence. There seemed no point in weighing the day down more with useless words.

Step by step, we descended the wall. The noises of Sila grew in intensity as we drew near to the cover house. Members were posted at the bottom of the stairs that led to the door. Armed and ready to help at a moment's notice. It was good to see the resolve in their eyes.

When Jack approached the door atop the steps, he knocked gently and the world outside sounded like it froze. The cries were stifled, and impatient feet softened until silent. Opening the door, Jack let in the red glow of a nearby streetlight. The dark lighting brought in the cheer of the people outside.

Our heads poked out cautiously as Jack led us up. Eyes were fixed on our entrance by a crowd. I hadn't seen so many people in my life. Was this all the residents of Sila? Hundreds of faces watched us pull ourselves from the tunnel and stand before them. When Gregory emerged, I had to clap my hands over my ears to block out the enthusiastic screams.

He did not acknowledge these screams, of course, but remained trained on Jack. We all looked at him for some sort of clue about what was happening here. Taylor and I did not fight. Why were they excited to see us? Gregory, I could understand. A rebel-aiding Drone was a very big deal. So, why were we invited?

"Quiet! Quiet now!" Jack's voice cut through the chaos, his words sharper than the roars of celebration around him. He didn't need to shout. He commanded the crowd with a simple authority, and slowly, silence spread like a ripple through the town. I appreciated his power over the crowd. One day, I hoped to lead like that. Though this was his day and he deserved the respect he wielded.

"Today—" Jack's voice rang out, deliberate and clear, "we fought back. It wasn't planned, it wasn't strategic. It was raw, it was emotional. It was human!"

A chorus of voices erupted in agreement, fists raised high in solidarity.

"For years, we've been dreaming of this moment—the day we would finally break free of the chains that bind us, that control us. The day we'd rise, not as numbers, not as cogs in their machine, but as people. Today is that day!"

The crowd swelled with pride, the air crackling with the energy of the moment.

"Years!" Jack continued, his voice stronger now, pushing into every corner of the pit. "Years we've been ground beneath the weight of metal—under the boot of soulless machines that told us when we could eat, when we could breathe, when we could dream of anything more than survival. They told us we were weak. They told us we would never rise. But look around you!" He gestured to the faces, dirty and worn, but burning with newfound fire. "Look at what we did today. We didn't wait for permission. We didn't ask for the right moment. Hell, most of you weren't even involved with us, but you stood up and claimed what was ours. We took it. Because we are still here."

The crowd surged again, their voices mingling with the distant hum of broken machines. Jack let the energy build before speaking again.

"And now," he paused, his eyes sweeping over the hundreds of faces before him, "we finish this. Today we do more than take back our city—we take back our humanity. We take back our future. No longer will we be the ones in chains. No longer will we be told who we are, what we can be. From this moment on, we choose our own path, no matter the cost!"

A roar rose from the crowd, louder than before. A wave of defiance and hope crashed through Sila, the likes I had never seen before. Was this what it meant to rebel? To bring this kind of endurance and ambition to a mass was awe-inspiring.

"Who is ready," Jack's voice thundered, pushing through the noise like a battle cry, "to end this suffering once and for all? To carve a new world from the wreckage they tried to bury us in?"

The response was deafening. A collective roar that echoed up through the broken, smoking city above them, shaking the very ground beneath their feet. Jack stood tall, the embodiment of their defiance, their strength, their hope.

"Then let's finish it!" he shouted, and the square we filled erupted in a surge of bodies and voices, ready to reclaim what had been stolen from them. Ready to finish this deed.

As the voices quieted with the gentle pats of Jack's hands, he gestured to us now. The eyes shifted to our small group. Elation and pride filled my lungs. I was starting to appreciate being the focus of so many. All the weight of the crowd's anticipation felt like a crown was being placed on my head.

"We can not forget those who have brought us this hope. Taylor, being the first to shoot a Giant in several decades. Her ambition, her drive, has set ablaze hope in all of the Forge member's hearts. A truly dedicated and humble representation of what we should all strive to become."

"And Tyron, her clever brother. He fought against the Razum and clawed his way back to freedom. I never imagined I could have such deep respect for someone's confidence and ambition. A miracle of science, and a miracle of our cause. He has proved that there is a chance at a better future, that we can still free the many we thought were lost to the networks." He paused for a moment as the cheers for our names calmed down before he placed a hand on Gregory's shoulder.

"Though we can't forget our own metal friend here: Gregory 235!" The people's face glowed as they screamed 'thank you's and other appreciations. Apparently, Gregory had made a strong and positive impact on the people in Sila.

"We never thought this battle would be easy, and darker days are still coming. Gundry will need to fall, the Giants who are coming from the North will need to fall. Without these three standing before you, and the members of the Forge, I never thought there would be a day where we could have a chance." He stopped for a breath and called the crowd to silence again. Listening, hanging from his every word.

"I never thought that I would be this excited to send a pulse right into the eye of Gundry himself! It's time to finish this! We have lost many already, so we can't stop now. Not until every Drone in Sila is melting in the mud!" Fists were raised, screams of war were loosed, fire could be seen in the eyes that watched us.

Taylor's hand found mine as she tucked a little way behind my shoulder, bringing her head near. Gregory stepped near her to hide her from sight. The movement of the Drone seemed to inflame the crowd more as they left the gathering, brandishing weapons and rocks. Anything to destroy.

"We walk a thin line. Please promise me that if this starts to fail, you will flee Sila." Taylor's words were coldly serious in my ears against the clamoring. I knew she asked these things of me to save me from a dangerous future, but didn't she see the fire in these people's eyes? Could she not see this pure form of Humanity triumphing over the machine?

I twisted my head enough to look her in the eye; her face seeming to back down from mine. Could she see in my eyes that my answer was no? Leaning back as much as I could, I kissed her cheek softly.

"I won't give up on these people, not after what we started here. I'm sorry."

She seemed to have expected this response. A single tear falling from her eye, her head nodding quietly. Hand squeezing mine, she wiped the tear away with her other.

"Then we will go down together here." Her words were faint, but I knew them to be true. She would not leave me again. Even if Locura burned to ashes, I knew she would still be by my side. My sweet, loving sister.

Jack gathered his men around us, breaking our moment apart. We were safely tucked away behind a wall of Forge members when Jack broke the line. He stepped up to us, two pulse pistols in his hands.

He offered one to Taylor, who pushed aside her tarping clothes to reveal she had already strapped on hers. She drew it and held it ready at her side. Jack then offered the two to Gregory. He hesitated as he looked over the weapons. Did he remember how they stung? I still could feel the electricity buzzing through my burns.

"Take them. It would be better for you to protect yourself like you have protected many of us today. No one will judge you for using the weapons of humans." Jack's words seemed to shake the hesitation from Gregory's limbs and he took the two weapons, holding them cautiously as he examined them.

"Oh, and I have a request, if you don't mind. Would you let us paint some of your plates? Just to set you apart from other Gregory units. We don't want to accidentally shoot you. Bernard is still feeling guilty that he mistook you." Jack held up a sack that rattled with metal cans. Gregory cast a hesitant glance at me and Taylor, unsure if he should agree. I could feel Taylor's body shift as she nodded to him, trying to encourage him to make his own choice.

"I will agree to being painted, but I will paint myself." We all watched him as he carefully removed the cans of sealed paint. Once examining the colors he was offered, he took the lids off and carefully started to cover his arm plates.

He coated his right arm plates in a bright and highly pigmented red to add a small symbol of an anvil in black. I couldn't help the smile that appeared on my face as he marked himself with the Forge. His lines were clean as he finished his drawing and covered his lower arm plates with the black paint, causing the red to stand out.

His left arm was different since it bore the many scratched names of the Den girls. Gloved metal hands hesitated, unable to apply paint over them. I noticed that he had crossed out many of them as they died. A walking tally of those he loved who had died. Anne's initials were still intact, not yet ready to be crossed out.

Taylor put her hand in the black paint now and approached Gregory's side. He watched her carefully as she blacked out his shoulder plate and arm plate, leaving very careful spaces around the initials. She then took the red paint and wrote down the length of his arm, "Remember them."

Once she dragged her painted hands across her clothes, cleaning off the liquid paint, she drew her knife and faced Gregory directly. Holding the blade up, she nodded to his chest plate. It was a quiet request that he seemed to understand and let her approach.

She carved a 'T' into his chest plate and a 'Ty' for me. Once cleaning the letters so they were recognizable, she placed the blade at the beginning of Anne's initials. Her hand was frozen as she thought back to the little girl who had helped us so much.

"We have to say goodbye to her now. Are you ready to?" Taylor's words were quiet but I noticed the members around us leaning near to hear. Our interactions seemed to hold no more privacy, though in a way, I found it welcoming to not have to hide anymore.

"She was brave. She died bravely... Goodbye, Anne." Gregory's response was quiet, though his speaker reverberated through all of us watching. A Drone in mourning. I marveled at the idea that this may be the first time and the last time that we would see such a thing.

Taylor drew her blade through the initials with closed eyes. Saying goodbye was never easy, apparently for man or machine. Once Taylor lowered the knife, Gregory's hand brushed over where Anne's initials were and then where our new initials were. The members seemed to watch with curiosity as Gregory looked around himself.

"I may not have been made here, nor was I developed by the Forge, but if you would like your names to be added, I will carry them. It may not be as prestigious as the tunnel of the original Forge members, but I will make sure you are acknowledged in death." Gregory held his arms open towards the members, his words sinking into the rough and beaten members.

Jack was the first to step forward and ask Taylor for the knife. He carved his initials near ours, J.B. The other members followed suit, each taking a moment to etch their signatures. His plates quickly filled with more entries, some from those known only by their Razum identifiers, others from raiders or those who had evaded the Razums, using their original names.

It felt sacred, like anointing our ultimate weapon with our hopes. Gregory remained still, though his eyes focused and memorized each member that signed him. Once all the names were placed, there was a moment of silence. A remembrance for those whose names were already gone with no note of their existence.

The respectful moment was broken as gunfire blared out in the distance. Guns were drawn instinctually, heads turning to examine their surroundings. I was unable to hold a gun and crutch through the mud, but I maintained a vigilant eye. It was the value I could bring.

"This is our final push. We counted twenty-seven Drones retreating to the Drone headquarters by the central factory under the skull. Would you two like to join us?" Jack spoke to us, but his eyes were fixed on the distant skull we could gleam between the buildings.

The offer was directed at Taylor and Gregory, but I understood I was included as a viewer in the situation. I was limited in what I could do to help in a fight. Taylor placed a hand on my shoulder as she shook her head.

"I need to watch Tyron. We will come to watch and help if necessary, but my place is with him."

Jack nodded his understanding and focused now on Gregory, looking at the metal beast he had become with his paint. LEDs scanned the area around us, eyes were ever watching. The smile showed eerily in the morning light.

"I will join you."

The men shuffled us to the central street, being sure to move slowly on account of my slow pace. As we made our way to the street, I noticed the ground growing more unstable. I made the mistake of looking down, a pale face peering up at me from the mud. Blood had mixed into the dirt here, turning the street into a muddy landscape of corpses. This must have been where it started.

Taylor gently pushed my chin up, averting my eyes from the bodies as we walked over. I could see her face growing more pale as she focused her eyes on the men in front of us. Has she seen this carnage before? Was this something I would have to learn to be okay with in this world? Did her stomach turn like mine did at the idea of walking over bodies?

The central street offered more stability to my crutches on the stone surface as we faced the skull. Locura's now hollow eyes seemed to glare at us, her metal skull posed with its jaw wide open. Screaming at us like a ghost from beyond her grave. We had dug her up, and now we challenged her for power.

Gunshots were still ringing out around us, echoing between the houses. I could see a crowd had developed behind a metal barricade, screaming and shouting war noises. We stayed close to the buildings along the right side of the street as we drew near. Gun sounds would cause us to duck behind buildings, but we were still approaching.

After several minutes of our slow and cautious advance, we had made it to the barricade wall. The stench of gun smoke and factories burning filled the air, a haze falling into the streets. Obscured vision. The Drones were trying to take advantage of the haze as they continued their suppressing fire.

The crowd was waiting for Jack to join the battle before they made their final push. Cheering rang out at his arrival but was quickly hushed by suppressing fire from the three Harvey units that stood guard on the steps of the main factory under the skull. Jack made his way to the crowd and his men followed him while Gregory, Taylor and I remained tucked behind a building near the barricade.

We couldn't hear what Jack was saying, but we saw the crowd change from a mass of people into defined lines and regiments of soldiers. The city of Sila now was a more or less organized militia. A rebellion. When Jack turned and pointed to Gregory, we knew the battle was about to begin.

Gregory stepped forward, leaving the cover of the building and holding his new guns high, analyzing his shots at the Harveys from his distance. Taylor even leaned forward to estimate the shot for herself. I lived with two tactical mercenaries of sorts and yet it brought me peace.

His shots rang out, rattling my ear drums. I peaked my head past the wall, seeing if his shots landed. A third delayed shot rattled out from the left of the barricade and the three Harvey units fell, seizing from the shock. The crowd burst from behind the barricade and ran up the stairs, using the shock time to get close enough to end the Harvey units.

Taylor and I moved closer to the barricade as more shots fired out, likely hidden Gregory or Markus units with guns. People were picked off the steps, but not enough to stop them as they finished the Harvey units.

I could barely see Jack as he continued his run up the stairs, heading through the front doors of the factory that had been broken down by the Drones. Gregory was hot on his heel and the Forge members behind him. The last raid was led into the building, the crowd rushing in to cover them.

Taylor and I waited, gunshots and screams echoing through the silent city behind us. All of Sila was fighting for their freedom. The buildings were silent. Not even a breeze dared to rattle their panels. There were no barkers in their stands along the street that had been so lively once, no children playing. The quiet of the city was eerie, only to be broken up by screams and bullets.

Heavy metal boots in mud brought our attention to the right. Tucked behind the houses, down a dark alley, we saw the unmistakable blue LEDs of a Drone. It had been sneaking along the sides quietly, but its attention was caught by us. Taylor raised her gun as it leapt between the walls and approached at an alarming speed.

It lunged towards us before Taylor let a shot loose, missing his metal arms that stretched towards us in a tackle. The blue plates and metal sculpted hair meant he was a Markus unit. We didn't have time to evade before we were both hit to the ground, anchored under his metal body weight.

I could feel his arms crushing around us, squeezing the life from our lungs. Taylor was struggling to free her gun arm while I shifted my crutches to give myself room to breathe. Once the Markus unit confirmed its grip on us, he stood. Then he ran, making his way down the central street with us in his arms.

"Taylor and Tyron, you are being arrested for aiding and abetting in the rebellion of Sila. Your case will be resolved by the council of Viktorov, Povlo, and Armand and finalized by Lexicon. I will take you to their council now." His speaker bludgeoned my ears as my head was near his neck. Hate began filling the limbs I could feel.

Taylor was still struggling while I turned and tried to pry the arms free with my crutches. We still had a chance. Still within the walls, there was time to escape before he ran too far. Taylor rotated her wrist and placed the gun in my hand as she dug for her knife that hid in her clothes.

I could only see the edge of the blade as it glinted in the morning light. She quickly jammed it into the hip joint that was behind her own hip. At first, nothing seemed to happen, but as she turned the blade, I could hear a distinct pop. The Drone leg stopped working and we tumbled to the ground. Arms relaxing just enough for Taylor to squirm free.

She gathered herself and I tossed the gun towards her and out of reach of the Markus unit. His grip tightened on my ribs and I felt the air gush out of my body. My eyes locked onto Taylor's, demanding her to shoot. From her face though, I knew she was assessing her options to not lead to my unnecessary injury.

The gun would electrocute me, the knife would require her to come within grabbing distance again. She didn't have many choices. Her hand trembled as she watched the Drone squeeze me, ribs cracking. My crutches were pressed against my legs, free of the arms and stabbing into my torso under the Markus unit's weight.

"The crutch!" I blurted between gasps for air. If she would not act, at least she could obey. Dragging what I could of the crutch from under my body, I pushed it to my left and away from the Markus unit's grabbing hands. Taylor slid quickly to take it as the other arm reached for her. His timing was off just as she twisted the crutch to swing its metal-spiked bottom. It cut through his metal plates and destroyed his face, smoke rising from a damaged CPU. If he hadn't already been suffering from several bullet and pulse wounds, it would never have damaged him.

Arms fell limp, the pressure was released from around me. I forced my lungs to take in as much air as they could under the weight of the metal body. There was no guarantee he was permanently shut off, so escape came before calming my breathing.

Pulling the strap that attached me to the crutch, Taylor let go of it and I used the rods to pull myself from the metal body. She grabbed my hands and helped pull me free. The whirring of fans kicking back on made me look towards our downed Drone. He was powering up.

Once I was a safe distance away from the smoking and jittering Drone, Taylor drew her gun, aiming for Markus' head. The shot was loud, but the thud of the metal head in the mud was louder. Dark fluids and cooling liquids flowed from its wound and chest. Now it could be considered dead.

Taylor helped me up to my crutches, brushing the mud off to avoid burns. As I found my footing again on aching ribs and shoulders, Taylor cleaned herself off as she watched the surrounding area. We had not made it too far, so we walked back to the barricade following the same precautions that Jack had led us with.

The noises of the factory had died down, though the occasional gunshot could be heard. As our hands gripped the barricade and we steadied ourselves, cheering spread through the factory. Bodies began running out, cheering and dancing on the steps. They remained huddled close to the door as Jack emerged holding the head of a Harvey Drone and screaming his own victorious war cry.

Gregory followed him out, carrying a few injured bodies that still cheered through their groans of pain. From what we could see, all had gone well with minimal casualties. So why did I not feel victorious? Was it the blood that soaked my feet? Or the faces of those who had died for this cause? Taylor clapped a hand on my shoulder as the crowd moved towards us and woke me from my running thoughts.

"Victory never feels sweet when you know the ones who were lost along the way. Don't get lost in your thoughts. Celebrate with the ones who are here." Her gray eyes pierced their way into my mind once again. It was good to have my sister back.

Jack approached us, waving the head vigorously above himself. Oils and coolants flowed down his arm and covered part of his face. With a crooked toothed smile among the black oil, he held the head to me.

"Take it. This is a trophy for you and what you brought us." He was still hyped on adrenaline and his arm shook. Blood flowed from his wounded shoulder and I noticed a few other bleeding areas along his torso. These were fatal wounds.

Taylor reached out and took the head from him and nodded appreciation. She could see his injuries as well. A body riddled with bullet wounds would not be seen by the crowd, though. Jack seemed to refuse to let anyone see him as weakened. He had a character to maintain.

"Today, we won!" He screamed, rallying the crowd around him to mimic. Forge members drew closer to Jack now and placed a steadying hand on him. He refused their support and led the people of Sila down their newly reclaimed street. As the people followed, they kept their distance.

Taylor, Gregory, and I waited at the barricade. This was Jack's final march down the street he freed. We didn't want to take away from his glory. With each step, he seemed to stagger more. Muscles were giving out, blood loss was swaying his body. The Forge members couldn't get to his side fast enough to stop him from falling to the stone street.

Gregory reached up to his chest and scratched a line through Jack's initials. Another body to the count. The Forge members wailed at their fallen leader and the crowd was shushed. A price had been paid for this freedom.

We trailed after the Forge members as they carried Jack's body back to his outpost. He deserved to lie beside his fallen friends. With Gregory's aid, we could keep up and help other members who were making the same journey.

It was time to recoup. It was time to mourn. It was time to celebrate the lives that were lost. The walk was quiet. The tunnel back to the room was only filled with the sound of boots. Our room felt more empty than before, more lifeless with the reduced number of girls.

Gregory placed me on the bed while Taylor checked over me. We assessed all the damages we had collectively taken. Nothing was serious, but many injuries would not be forgotten anytime soon. Even Gregory had sustained decent damage to one of his arms. Still able to move, his fingers no longer could function fully.

Wailing echoed down the hall from the infirmary. The loss of their leader reverberated down the tunnels, seeming to shake the very ground we hid in. It would take a while to wash the blood and death from this hideout. Just like the others of the Forge, we quietly held our emotions at bay while we took time to calm down from the day's anguish.

Gregory slumped against the wall, letting his body drag against the metal as he lowered himself to the ground. Taylor did a similar action on the wall across from me. I couldn't help but to lower myself down onto the bed, my body aching everywhere I could still feel. Was this what complete exhaustion felt like in this body?

I made the mistake of closing my eyes. Pain ebbed from my limbs as though they were leaving my body. Darkness clawed at the back of my eyes, the bed consuming me. I doubt a minute had passed before my world went dark and my day ended.

✻　　　✻　　　✻

Dreams of bodies and gory faces filled my darkness. It was only broken up by the vague memories of Taylor and Tricia cleaning my wounds. Were they dreams? Were they reality? My body didn't feel like it existed anymore in either case.

I could see the face of sweet Anne as a Harvey unit stepped over her body. Taylor locked in its grip. Drones surrounded us, death was coming. Gregory lay in pieces on the ground. My legs didn't work, there would be no escape for me. I was alone. I was going to die.

"Tyron, wake up."

Warmth on my face stirred my eyes. Was it just a dream? As I rubbed the sleep from my face, I bumped a hand on my cheek. So warm. Taylor leaned over me in the dark of night.

"You were having a nightmare." She said as she pet my hair. Her eyes were focused out the window. Sounds of cheering and celebration could be heard faintly. I tried to pull myself to sit up, wanting to get out of the pool of sweat I had developed, but my arms didn't have the strength.

Taylor helped me up and handed me a cloth to wipe the sweat from my face and neck. She was always prepared. Her face was glued to the window. I now could see Gregory in the dark, also looking through the open shutters.

Re-summoning my energy, I slowly crawled up the bed frame to look out the window with them. Lights glowed in the central street. Fires. People were dancing around the flames as they gave off black smoke. They were burning the Drones.

"They're celebrating?" I asked to clarify what I was seeing.

"Yeah. They don't know the war ahead. Viktorov, Povlo, and Armand were spotted about a day's journey from here today." Taylor's voice sounded tired. Had she slept at all, or were her thoughts haunted like my dreams were?

"They will have to be told. It won't go well without Jack to lead the charge. Ricky came back a while ago from the Barrens and said he wanted

364

to meet with us when you woke." Gregory filled in some blanks for me.

We listened in silence to the cheers and joy. They didn't know the fresh horrors that were waiting around the corner, though; we didn't know the full scale of what was coming either. Taking the moment to enjoy people celebrating their newfound freedom, we watched the flames flicker.

A knock on the door roused our attention from the window. Gregory walked to address it. The light flooded in our dark room and blinded my low light vision. Familiar voices filled the hallway beyond the door.

"The Den girls and Ricky gathered in a room down the hall if you are ready to discuss the next plan." The voice on the other side of the door seemed tired.

"We will be there in a few minutes." Gregory responded as he closed the door and returned to the window with Taylor.

More plans. More battles. More losses.

Taylor turned and helped clean the sleep from my eyes. She groomed over to make me more presentable and checked the burns that had started healing. Once satisfied with my appearance, she helped me to my crutches. My ribs ached under the pressure of standing, so we opted to have Gregory carry me in his one functioning arm. Feeling more like a child, it was still better than aggravating my wounds further.

The meeting room was the same one I had met Jack in only two days prior. How quickly the world had stirred. There were three chairs placed around the room. The table pushed against the wall as the somber faces of the Den girls filled the back corner. Ricky stood near the door as he waited for us to arrive.

I was placed in one seat as Taylor took another near me. Ricky filled the last while Gregory closed the door. We were the survivors. Seven of the original Den group still breathed. Ricky looked worse for wear, and we all struggled with our various injuries. A broken and tired crew.

"I know we are all tired, but the Giants need to be figured out before we can rest. Povlo is leading the group here. We expect to see him from Sila tomorrow morning. Viktorov and Armand will be here tomorrow night if they keep their same speed." Ricky's voice was focused, even though his body seemed to be limp with exhaustion.

"What do we know about Gundry? Will he be joining them?" Gregory chimed in unexpectedly as he sat on the ground next to the girls. I noticed he wore the satchel Taylor had given him as he dug through it. He removed a few sheets of malleable scrap metal and set his hand to work on something.

"From my scouts, they say he hasn't moved an inch. If we stay lucky, he won't budge until we come for him."

"What do we know about Povlo?" I now leaned forward, taking the pressure off my supporting arm and leaning on the table's edge.

"Povlo stands at thirty-four feet. He is designed like an owl, a lost species of bird. He is not capable of flight but uses his wings to destroy buildings with one swipe. Locura's building-ruiner." Gregory responded as he folded the metal he worked with. Finishing the piece, he displayed it on his palm as he showed us.

It was an owl with outstretched wings and sharp metal talons. We passed it between us, familiarizing ourselves with our new enemy. I handed it back to Gregory, who handed it to Tricia. The girls passed it between themselves, playing with it like a toy. Gregory set his hands working on a new piece.

"So we have a Giant bird coming for us. Being as it doesn't have arms, it should help us stay out of range. If we set up a perimeter of gunmen, we could send a decent barrage of firepower before it gets too close." I was planning with half knowledge and they knew it. Ricky glanced at me as I spoke. He looked as though he expected me to be a passive participant.

"Shooting pulse guns at him won't help because of his wing protection. It could distract him enough to get a side shot. Under the wings will be the soft metal to aim for. Taylor, remember that crossbow you made for Cherub 735? Could you design that about twenty-seven percent bigger?" Gregory's words seemed focused, even though his hands remained busy on his next figure.

"Yeah, I can do that. Where do you want me to build it?"

"We could lead Povlo to center street. He would be coming in from the

North East, but we could draw his attention to the center. Taylor could set up her crossbow from any of the alleyways and be mostly hidden from view until she takes the shot." My words cut off Ricky, who looked like he had a similar idea. He seemed lost without Jack around and was struggling to make room for his own ideas.

"That could work. Povlo is smart and has a wide range of vision. Keeping Taylor hidden will be key." Gregory held up his new construction, a small spider with a circular face and wide set body. We passed it around the same way before handing it to the girls and starting his next miniature.

"Armand will be the challenge, even though he stands at twenty-five feet. He's a highly mobile spider design. Legs sharper than the best knives we could make and enough speed to be devastating to anyone near. Having him in the city could lead to mass death and a very hard time to keep up with the enemy. Getting him out of the game in the Barrens will be necessary."

"If he's so fast, couldn't we do a tripwire? Bait him towards the town and tripwire him down into Sila? We could have a direct shot to his head before he gets back up." I added with a small sense of eagerness. War planning was starting to feel fascinating. We knew they were coming, but they don't know we were getting ready for them. Finally, an upper hand.

"It would have to be a sudden tripwire. Anything he can see beforehand will be avoided. I might be able to rig something up along the perimeter wall tonight if the girls will help me." Gregory looked to the girls who played with their new toys. Tricia nodded her agreement on behalf of the Den girls.

Gregory raised his hand to show the last figure. A gruesome bear's head mounted on the body of a dog, with the paws of a bear. He lacked the childish character design of the last two, but maintained a terrifying pose with vicious looking teeth.

"Meet Viktorov. Tallest made at forty-seven feet. Out of all three, he is the one that will be the hardest to kill. A wolf bear, power of a bear, speed of a wolf. He's flexible, he's fast, and he was the right hand to Locura herself. She redid his body to fix any possible weak points and tripled his computing power." Gregory's words fell on a silent room. A perfect killing machine was rushing his way towards us as we spoke.

"So, he's impossible to kill?" Ricky seemed disheartened by this the most. His face was fading in color.

"Viktorov has no direct weaknesses. A direct shot between the lining of his eye and his socket is going to be the only chance we have to stun him. Then it's a game of seeing how many wires we can access and rip out. I have no specifics on him. Locura deleted all his old designs from the network." Even Gregory's shoulders slumped, thinking over the situation.

Taylor sat back and began to think, along with Ricky. How do you kill an unkillable machine? Gregory's silence was becoming foreboding with his whirring circuits. Silence was quickly killing our hope. Two out of three plans was good, but it would still lead to our destruction.

"What if we freeze him? The data storage area in the Drone headquarters has a lot of liquid nitrogen." Tricia's addition caused our heads to turn. "If he is too strong on the outside, we just need to slow him down so one of us can get inside. If we use a bomb, we should be able to get in and out before he unfreezes."

Gregory reached over and patted Tricia's head gently. The whirring sound kicked up as he thought over the situation. Taylor and I sat back as well, running through the scenario. Ricky stared at the floor, struggling with his thoughts.

"We can't move the nitrogen or Viktorov will figure us out, but we could lure him to the headquarters. He would destroy most of the building, but once we get him inside, it will give us a semi-enclosed cage to freeze him. One of the girls may be small enough to sneak inside and plant a time release bomb. It would have to be powerful if we want to shut down his power matrix. It could work." Gregory seemed pleased with the girl and bopped her nose gently.

"I'll go," said a small voice from the middle of the huddled girls. She was the smallest of the group and I had never heard her speak before now. Small dirty blonde hair. She couldn't have been over six years old. Though she was the size of a four-year-old, she seemed sturdy and competent.

There was a certain hushed tone in the room as we were all reminded of the departed Anne.

"Are you sure, Lucy?" Asked Tricia, squishing the girl's cheeks together as she stared into the child's eyes. She nodded with a smile.

"Gregory would do it if he could. I'm small, so I can do it." I couldn't help but feel my heart breaking. Asking such a young child to literally crawl into the belly of a beast. This was no world for children.

"I'm not comfortable sending a child in." I muttered. The room's focus shifted to me. I felt the eyes scanning me for further reasoning. "We have lost so many already."

Silence flooded the room. There didn't seem to be another option at the moment, but could we really send a child with a bomb? At what point do we risk our own humanity? Our own sacredness for the youth?

"The kid is right. We shouldn't be sending children to do our dirty work." Ricky backed my statement. I hadn't figured him to be fond of children. Maybe there was more to the 'Oomer life I wasn't aware of.

"What other option is there? None of us will fit between Giant plate armor. Lucy could actually stop Viktorov." Taylor defended this idea, though she cast sympathetic glances in my direction. While upsetting, I knew she did not mean this defense to argue with me. At least she wasn't talking about fleeing the city anymore. Her additions were welcomed because it meant she was part of this with me.

Words didn't seem to feel useful right now. With no other option to move forward, Lucy would be our only hope. I just didn't want it to be our first option. Children should never be our first sacrifice.

"I want to." Lucy's small voice broke through the quiet. Her bravery drew our eyes towards her as she entered our circle. Only a few feet tall, slender, and weak. How did she have such a strong heart where she was willing to sacrifice her own brief life for the betterment of Sila?

We waited, thoughts running through all our minds. None of us were eager to sign this girl's death warrant. Gregory stood and broke the silent whirring of our own processors.

"We can decide this later. Viktorov will be the last one to arrive.

Hopefully, time and experience will open new options. Lucy, will you still be willing if we end up having to go with this plan?" His words seemed loud in the small room, bouncing across the metal walls.

Lucy nodded with a happy head, eyes hiding the fear she felt. Did she fully know what she would risk? I suppose she had experience around death with her life in the Den, but did she know what it was like to give her own life? While I know Taylor, Gregory, Ricky and I would all be willing to take her place, we were all unable. She could easily be the only option we have in the end. She would hold all the lives of Sila on her shoulders.

"We will agree on these plans for now. Taylor, build your crossbow. Work with the people of Sila for positioning. Ricky, join Gregory with the girls to build the trip wire and watch for any straggler Drones trying to reach Gundry. I will talk to the people and let them know our plans and that the war will start soon." I now led our discussion. It was probably wisest to let the tactical Drone with warring experience to lead our charge, but in the end he was a machine and not programmed to fight his own.

One by one, they nodded their agreement to the planning. The thought of taking Jack's role as the speaker to the people was exhilarating. I enjoyed watching him speak and knew I could emulate it. Once the plan was accepted, we all slowly stood and filed quietly out of the room. While the others were dragging their feet with stress and exhaustion, I felt eagerness. A plan was in place. Now we had to make it happen.

I bid a temporary farewell to Taylor as she walked down the tunnel. Gregory nodded to me as he led the girls and Ricky away towards the infirmary, which I assumed also led to the top of the wall. I was left alone.

My thoughts ran while I limped down the hallway. Public speaking seemed easy enough. Though, I have never done it, in the Razum, or in this life. The thought of standing in front of hundreds of people and telling them that the worst Giants who have ever been made were coming for all of us seemed like a straightforward conversation. I was going to be honest, clear, and calm about it. The more I mimic the friendly nature of Jack, the better.

I made my way down the tunnel. The crutches were the only sound in the quiet dirt hole. Each motion built up my energy. I had envied Jack's power over the crowd and this was a chance to taste it for myself.

The repetitive clicking of my crutches caused me to flinch. Was I anxious? If my knees could bear my weight, would they be shaking? It was bizarre to feel so excited, yet nervous. Cool air filled my lungs as I took in deep breaths, trying to stabilize my nerves. My body relaxed and I thought through what I was going to say.

"Hello everyone. No, that's weak. Good evening. Better." My mutters seemed to echo down the tunnel. The vibrations of my words seemed to invite an audience. Regardless of anxieties, I wanted to do this. It's why I volunteered myself for this job.

"Good evening. I hate to break up the fun, but I need to alert you to an additional threat. Better, better." My words felt more confident. As I thought through my speech, I realized I had reached the doorway, which now stood as the primary door to the fake house. There were no more reasons to hide our entrance to Sila. It was known and the threat was gone. For now, anyway.

As I placed one crutch up the stairs at a time, excitement filled my chest. My throat swelled and breathing became a complicated task due to the anxiety, but I was moving faster to reach the crowd. Was this how Jack had felt when he took the podium to speak to Sila? Did he enjoy connecting to entire masses of people? Would he share this moment with me if he were still alive?

I wished I could have gotten some of our time back. Jack could have taught me a lot about how to speak to crowds. How to be unwavering in the eyes of a city. I regretted not knowing him better. We would have been friends.

My hand shook as I placed it on the doorknob. How many people were out there? A hundred? Several hundred? For my first time speaking to a crowd, I hoped it was all of Sila out there. I was ready to do this.

The cool air of the night caused my jaw to clench. I had not prepared for this chill. Maybe it could numb my shaking arms so they would stop. This feeling of terror and eagerness was moving my crutches faster than I had tried before. A new step into this life: Public speaking.

Mud hardened back into dirt, making it easier to pick my way through the streets. The air was thick, carrying the acrid scent of smoke and scorched metal. I scanned the crumbling buildings near the central street, their rancorous celebrations spilling through broken windows and hollowed frames. A vantage point from above wouldn't do—not here. These people didn't need a shadow to look up to; they needed a voice to stand among them.

The heat of street fires met me as I drew nearer. People noticed my presence, clasping my shoulders or nodding respectfully, their eyes reflecting something between awe and fear. Jack must've told stories— twisted, larger-than-life tales to spark this kind of reaction. Let them fear me. Fear is useful.

Noise faded as I entered the heart of the street, where the largest fire blazed. The crowd circled it like moths, faces illuminated in flickering orange and red. Inside the fire, Drone remnants cracked and melted, their terrifying grins now blackened with soot and streaked with dripping paint. Some twitched as their circuits fried, making them look alive—still monstrous. Even destroyed, they were a reminder of what we faced.

All eyes were on me as I stepped closer to the fire. The heat licked at my back, and my shadow danced frantically at my feet. The people silenced themselves, shushing the vibrant life noises of Sila's survivors. They wanted to hear me, to understand what kind of leader I was—or if I even deserved the title. Hero or freak, they'd made their choice to listen.

My hands trembled at my sides, the weight of expectation pressing down. I stilled my shoulders, fighting the shake in my arms. Lowering my jaw, I let the tension feed me, let the fire's heat burn away the doubt. Then, I began.

"They think they can break us."

My voice cut through the silence like a blade. Stronger than I expected. Stronger than I felt. "They think they can grind us into the dirt—turn us into nothing but parts to keep their machines running. But they've forgotten who we are. They've forgotten what it means to bleed, to suffer, to survive."

I let the words hang for a moment, watching the crowd's faces shift. Some leaned closer, their eyes blazing with the same defiance I felt. Others stayed still, as though daring me to continue.

"I've seen the inside of their perfect prisons. Felt the emptiness they call paradise. And I say no more." My voice rose, fueled by the fire at my back and the growing tension in the crowd. "No more shackles. No more silence. Today, you proved them wrong. You showed them what humans can do when we fight together. You tore down the Drones, turned their twisted smiles into ashes."

The fire crackled behind me, punctuating my words. "But it's not over. The Giants are coming. Bigger. Stronger. They won't hold back. They'll come to crush us, to remind us of our place. But let me tell you something." I stepped closer to the crowd, letting them see the fire in my eyes. "We don't have a place. This is our world. Ours to fight for, to bleed for, to take back. From ruin to fire, we rise. Forged in scrap. Unbroken in strength."

The murmurs of the crowd swelled into shouts, a growing wave of defiance that fueled me. "I'm not gonna lie to you. It's gonna hurt. It's gonna cost us. But I swear to you, Sila will survive. Not because we're lucky, or because they let us. Because we'll make them remember who we are."

I stepped back, my arms still shaking, but the fire inside was steady now. The crowd erupted into violent war cries, beating their chests, raising fists to the sky. Their ferocity steadied my anxiety, replacing it with something sharper—purpose.

Sila would survive. Not because of hope or mercy, but because it had to. This chapter of our story wasn't over. Tomorrow, the fight continued, and we'd show them—Giants, Loomers, whoever dared to stand in our way—what humanity was capable of.

Chapter 15: The Owl, The Spider, and The Bear

I had kept my night short, staying in the central street long enough to explain our situation and receive thanks for what I had done to help the cause. Though I was still shaky walking back to the room in the outpost, I couldn't help but to feel the vibrations of excitement at a better future.

The crowd must have stirred the ripples of hope in me. Have I ever felt this feeling before? Such a true form of hope and ambition to change the world. To be the difference between suffering and living. Even the tunnel I made my way back through felt different, like it was alive and ready to fight. The spirits whose death dates were scribed on the walls backed our rebellion.

When I got back to the room, it was quiet and dark, only illuminated by the lights outside the window. It was enough for me to see my way to the bed. Not sure what else I was supposed to do with myself, I laid down. My instructions were terse and to the point, and now that I was done. I only had to wait for the others.

I suppose I have spent little time alone since waking up from the Razum. What was I supposed to do? If I could have, I would have tapped my toes together to pass the time. As I still couldn't move my legs or feet, I resigned to touching my fingers together and testing their coordination.

How did Taylor survive so long alone? What did she do when she was bored? I remembered the metal tea set Gregory had shown me, but was that it? She just created things she wished she had again?

Was there anything I missed from that world? The only thing I can remember wanting was Taylor with me. My heart twinged a little as I remembered My Taylor echo. How did she sustain my mind for so long? She was just a program I made in my desperation to get my sister back. She eventually became her own identity to me and, looking back now, I felt childish.

I should have developed myself better. All I spent my time doing was scanning code and messing with the Watcher's programming until I finally broke it. There was no technology for me to mess with here. I suppose I could ask Gregory if I could tinker with him, but I anticipate a strong negative response to that request.

My mind wandered to the empty wasteland of thoughts that strewn itself across closed eyes. When did I lose my thoughts? It felt like nothing rattled around upstairs anymore besides planning wars and figuring out my next step. I guess my current objective was to pass the time since I couldn't do more to help.

Having slept through most of the day, I couldn't fall back into that wonderful time-passing darkness. I could only listen to the quiet cheering and clamor of the streets with the occasional sound of shifting rocks from the wall I was hidden in. Rolling in the bed restlessly, I tried to focus on the sounds of the street below.

I could feel time as it moved slowly because I wasn't doing anything. It was almost like the creaks of the rocks were getting louder or the noise in my mind was getting quieter. Pebbles fell from the surface above, clanking against the metal shutters over the windows. It must be windy in the Barrens today.

Taylor had once told me it could get windy out there on a moment's notice. The weather seemed to be an unpredictable monster that lurked everywhere. The first time I had seen Taylor's face, it was pale from acid fog. Since then, color had returned to her cheeks, but her hair and the outer edges of her face were still pale.

Scratching sounds came from above the window now. Likely metal being caught in the wind. Maybe it will rain tomorrow. That would make an already miserable fight feel worse. The idea of Giants appearing from the fog sent shivers down my spine. While I technically have experienced that before, according to Taylor, I didn't want the memories of that stuck in my head.

My room shook slightly as the metal noises grew louder. Was there a storm? Was Gregory above my room setting the trip wire trap for Armand? Pulling myself weakly, I dragged my body up to the windowsill.

The light of the town still glowed vibrantly. Through fractured clouds above Locura's Skull, I could see the moon high in the sky. No rain, even the clouds moved slowly tonight. Metal sounds against rock were still causing the hair on my neck to stand up.

Laying back down, I chalked up my fear as being anxious for the coming battle. I kept touching my thumb to all my other fingers. Strengthening the motions would help me in many ways. Maybe if I got better hand control, Taylor would let me cut her hair. She had always hated sitting still for me, but maybe as an adult, she would be more agreeable.

My room shook thunderously now as a bright light filled it. There were no more shadows as an orange light colored everything. It was coming from the window, but my neck felt frozen. Unable to look at what it could be.

With measured breaths and forcing my body to obey my simple command, I looked towards the window. Every millimeter my head moved, the dread formed a tighter knot in my stomach. I could only guess one thing bright enough to shine this way in my room. As my head lolled to the side and up, I could see, from the corner of my eye, exactly what I had feared.

With a pupil the size of my leg and an orb that was larger than the five-foot window it peered through, was a Giant's eye. My blood felt like it disappeared from my body as the pupil tightened and focused on me. Chest refusing to breathe and a body that felt disconnected from me, all I could do was wait.

Was it here for me? Was it Povlo ahead of our estimations? The eye watched me, revealing none of the answers. Time stopped as we were

376

trapped in a mutual staring contest. Stuck in the golden glow of one of the Earth's destroyers. An eye that I could curl up in, watched me. Scanning and examining.

The eye suddenly shifted out of the window before being replaced by a large serrated metal beak. It smashed through the window and began pulling the wall apart. Noise scaring my body to action, I threw myself from the bed and crawled towards the door.

Beak ripping through the wall as if it was nothing, I could feel it getting closer to my legs. The floor was shuddering under the weight of Povlo as he dug deeper into the room. Realization hit that the metal I was hearing was him crawling along the city walls, investigating the city. I should have trusted my fear.

The door was closed as I finally reached it. Adrenaline had dragged me this far, but I couldn't reach the handle to open it. Beak slashing and tearing the flooring apart and eyes blinding me as it occasionally looked to see how far I was. Almost the entire wall was gone now, along with most of the floor. Its head was too big to fit inside completely. Yet.

"Povlo is here!" was all I could scream. Knowing no one was in the outpost since they were out preparing for the Giants only led me to scream louder. They needed to know! He was here and I was with him. Trapped by a door handle I couldn't reach, I pulled my legs closer to me to avoid the metal beak that was tearing up the rest of the floor.

Bed gone, wall gone, was I to be the last thing to go? A taloned foot reached in for me now. Its blades for claws were the size of my body and gave it some extra length to grab at the fabric of my pants. A rip was made wherever the claws touched. Proof that the blades were sharp enough to cut without effort.

Screaming, crying, and holding my legs as close to myself as I could, I only hoped that Taylor would avoid this fate. She didn't deserve to live in a world with such monsters. If these are to be my last thoughts, I want them to be about her winning against these machines.

A loud shriek erupted from the otherwise silent Giant before its head was pushed out of the way with a heavy thud of metal on metal. The orange eyes had a new focus as it thrashed dark wings in the night sky. I could hear the rattle of bones or wood as it flapped its metal wings.

Using the distraction, I tried to open the door again. A futile hope that I had grown tall enough to reach the handle, I was again met with failure. Familiar insults were being thrown outside the wall now as something bothered Povlo.

"Get out, you Giant shitty bird!" Gregory's words were loud in the night as his LEDs glowed against the orange owl's eyes.

"Gregory unit 235, you are under arrest for aiding in the rebellion of Sila. You are sentenced to immediate termination." The familiar deep Drone-like voice of the Giant rattled the entire wall of Locura. I could hear the screams of people noticing the interaction. Warning bells started to ring.

"Is this all you got, scrap heap?" Gregory's sarcasm was now without bound. He was enjoying this chance to bother a Giant.

The loud screech from Povlo was all he got as a response. Using the erratic head flailing of the owl Giant, Gregory launched himself into the room. Staggering over the damaged ground, he ran for me.

Once in his arm, he pushed through the door as if it was nothing and started running down the hall towards the tunnel. He blared an alarm from his Drone speaker as he ran.

"Povlo is in Sila. He is on the North wall. Flee the outpost." Clear and concise, he maintained his speed. Metal shoes vibrating the tunnel as he ran. I watched the braces shudder as we moved past them.

"Are you okay?" He asked as we turned the corner at the midway point of the tunnel. I was jostling freely from his one arm grabbed around my waist. If there was feeling in my legs, I am sure they would hurt.

"Yeah. I thought Povlo was supposed to be here in the morning?" My voice was jarred as I was shaken with each step.

"We didn't see him appear. He must have sped up when there was no Drone communication. You were the first sighting. Povlo was likely climbing the walls and scanning the situation in the city. Damn today. Nothing planned seems to work." He mumbled as we drew near the door.

"Where's Taylor?"

"She should be near the city center. With the warning bells ringing and the population aware that this was going to happen, they should be safe. I will find her and leave you there. Povlo has a terrible impression of me now which should guide some of his focus to me. We will try to stick to the initial plan." Gregory threw open the door to the fake house and we launched into the street.

Many people were scrambling trying to find cover as loud screeches echoed above us on the wall. Rubble fell down as the Giant crawled in a predatory fashion across the wall of Sila. Orange eyes beaming and looking over the entire cityscape.

Gregory dodged as many people as he could, but still knocked over a group heading for the fake house. Apologizing curtly, we continued to run for center street. If Taylor adhered to the plan, she should be towards Locura's head in one of the side alleys.

We dodged bodies and shoved others, but once we made it to central street, there was a loud thud on the ground where we had just ran from. The shaking Earth was accompanied by the blood-chilling scream of Povlo. I didn't dare look back now, even if his robotic animal cry demanded me to. Gregory was right. He made a terrible impression on the Giant.

While Povlo was a threat, at least we had a plan for him, even if it was not the correct timing. Metal shoes clanged against the stone street as we ran, metal talons soon followed suit. I suddenly felt like a mouse caught between an owl and a hawk.

"Taylor, stand ready!" Gregory yelled down the street. His voice caused my ears to ring as he used his loud tone. I heard a confirming 'ready' ring out, three alleys down. Gregory shifted me to a higher carry and curled me closer to him.

To my dismay, he cast me into the dark alley with alarming speed. I felt like a ball being whirled through the air. With no legs or lower body at my command to steady myself, I felt panic. Sailing through the air, I quickly noticed Taylor, who was prepared to catch me.

Colliding into my poor sister, we both struck the ground, the wind being knocked from us. Gasping, trying to force air into our lungs, we looked back to the street, only to see Gregory continue running full speed. Soon after, ran the awkward stomps of Povlo, his outstretched metal wing spikes stabbed into the buildings as he pulled himself faster.

In the streetlight, I could see the shadows of what appeared to be human skeletons wired together as feathers from his arms. His head was a single sheet of sculpted metal with embossed feather textures that still maintained a bit of white and tan paint. I could see now what Locura had done to their body designs to make them more terrifying. In a world of nightmarish robots, Povlo fit right in with the Loomer class.

Once they were out of sight, we could hear the chaos as Povlo continued to pursue Gregory. Buildings were getting smashed to pieces. Screams of panic ensued. Sila was going to be a flattened city if things didn't pull together quickly.

Taylor rolled me off of her body and we took slow breaths, re-oxygenating our blood streams. Once the panting passed, members of the Forge helped us up. I was placed back on my ever present crutches and Taylor rushed towards the back of the alley to continue her work.

I followed the members, as they had a new hustle to their motions. The ballista that she had been working on already had a frame with steel cable beginning to be pulled taut. She had made impressive progress in the few hours she had.

Taylor gestured me over as she hammered more metal supports onto the control arm. Crutching my way towards her, I could hear the Forge members mutter their concerns. They did not have faith in her design.

"Can you keep an eye above us? I wouldn't put it past Gregory to lead Povlo over the top to limit some destruction to the foundations of the buildings." Her voice was hurried. The stress of our early enemy seemed to hit her. I leaned on the left wall of the alley near her and watched the sky.

Stars were still out, the moon was waning. It would be a beautiful night if there wasn't a Giant psychotic bird rampaging through our city. The cool air wafted through the alley, but it didn't chill me like it once had.

Being near Taylor somehow brought me peace, even as Sila shook with fear.

Gregory's voice echoed across the city, yelling more insults of a confusing nature. He had yet to perfect his tone and style of aggressive word play. Though it seemed to work as Povlo's irritated screeches followed his insults. A Drone taunting a Giant. It was difficult to take the moment serious.

"We almost have this ready. I got some extra hands earlier, which helped. Just need to finish the tension on the cable and load the bolt. Tyron, how does our aim look?" Taylor was streaming her thoughts aloud.

I rustled from my perch against the wall and looked down at the sight of the bolt slide. It seemed a bit high, towards the head of Povlo's height. Trying to level myself with the slide to get a clear view of the angle, I motioned to her to bring it down.

"You're too close to his head. We need to drop it a bit to aim for the wing according to Gregory's advice." She jumped to action before I could finish my sentence. As the view of the sight dropped, I held up my hand, signaling for her to stop. "That should be close enough."

Stepping back to allow her to finish pulling the tension on the cable, I could see the full size of this contraption. Standing around six feet tall, with a curved metal rod for the arm about eighteen feet. It was now nearly impossible to walk beside the machine in the small alleyway. My sister was a brilliant inventor in this world. A tickle of pride warmed my body during the frosty night.

"We should be ready enough. Guys, load the bolt. Let's get this machine down as quickly as possible. Armand will be closer than we anticipated as well. Hopefully, Gregory has the trip line up." Taylor directed the men with simple gestures as she approached me.

"You should stay further back here. If the cable snaps at its full tension, it could kill us all. I wish I had time to make this safer, but this doesn't seem to be our day." She helped walk me to the very end of the alley, a good twenty feet from the ballista. Kissing my hand for a moment, she returned to her post and gently placed her hand on the release lever.

Risking her life, yet again, for a situation that I led her to. It was my fault that these Giants had come. It was my fault that she had to leave Haldoklik and fight off Finigan, calling the Harvey units to this town. Now she stood by a potentially dangerous contraption she rushed to build to save a town that wasn't even hers. I knew she would do anything for me, so I hope she didn't hate me for putting her in this position.

The image of her standing ready for battle chilled my spine. This wasn't her job. She shouldn't be the one pulling the trigger. Gregory shouldn't be the one leading a Giant around Sila to keep it off our backs. These machines should not control us. Guilt for our involvement aside. This world was wrong and we were correcting it. This was justice.

"Gregory, ready!" Taylor's voice echoed through the alley. This machine was our best hope to put Povlo down. Even if he is only incapacitated for a while, it will be enough for the Forge members or Gregory to get off final shots with pulse weapons.

I could hear the thud of metal shoes landing against the street and begin running towards us. It was followed by the thunderous crash of talons on stone, the very ground shaking. They were en route for, hopefully, a quick ending.

Gregory appeared at the end of the alley, standing still in the street and staring down Povlo, who was presumably charging him at full speed. He held his ground, doing the best he could to slow the owl down at the end of the alley for a cleaner shot. His body was posed, ready to run.

"Thirteen percent lower, Taylor!" he yelled.

Taylor slapped the gear height adjustment and lowered the sights of the ballista. These two had faced troubles like this before. Heads lowered with quick actions and calm minds. They were born to survive this world. A world that should never be.

As soon as Povlo ran into view, Gregory leapt towards the alley. This caused Povlo to turn and see the ballista pointed at him. It was too late to change his direction when Taylor pulled the release lever.

The bolt made of metal scrap welded together into an arrow form was launched at alarming speed. The snapping sound of cable rang against the metal walls of the alley. We watched as the bolt burrowed its way into

Povlo, knocking him down from his two legs, his wings too large to move in time to catch himself. If he had a heart, it would be pierced.

Gregory recovered from his dive and ran towards the flailing Giant. The bolt was long enough to make it difficult for Povlo to regain his footing. As his eyes focused on Gregory who approached him, he let out a loud and angered cry. He knew his fate was nearing.

"Gregory unit 235, cease and your case will be resolved peacefully. I have come for Taylor of Razum unit 12.53.79.88 and Tyron of Razum unit 12.53.79.87. Locura will be destroyed if we do not return with them." The deep Giant voice rattled the stones of the street as we approached.

Pausing at our names, Taylor examined Povlo closer as his thrashing settled. Was he trying to talk his way out of this situation? Gregory seemed to pause at the names as well. This was not the first time we were singled out today.

"Tyron?" she asked quietly, watching my eyes scan and consider the situation.

"We are not going with you." My response was bitter and Taylor raised her own pulse gun to punctuate my statement. The gift of Gern that kept saving our lives. Gregory raised his gun as well as the Forge members who now surrounded the Giant.

"They're free now, and as long as I'm here, you'll never touch them." Gregory was the first shot to fire as he reminded the Giant that he was free of the network and free to do as he pleased. Loosing several pulses into the Giant body, it thrashed and flailed from the electricity that coursed through its wiring. The burn on my chest ached at the memory of the sting those guns conducted.

The light of electricity crackling through the Giant's body reflected against Gregory's own painted smile. If I didn't know better, I would say that this was the first time his smile looked genuine. His first kill of those he had once served. Did he understand the significance of his actions today? Did he realize he had finally claimed his humanity?

As the guns ceased their firing, and the electric cackling died down, the lights of Povlo's eyes slowly faded out. The whirring processors and air cooling units slowed until silence filled the street. Even the factories were quiet after being destroyed by his running amok.

Taylor walked to Gregory's side and nudged his arm with a playful fist. His one functioning arm reached across his body to nudge her arm in return, staggering her off her feet and landing on the ground. The Forge members all laughed as they all began to punch and push Gregory playfully. A hero who was hassled by soldiers.

I stepped forward and pushed him lightly. When his LED focused on me, he knelt slightly. Facing me directly, his unwavering lights hurt my eyes. With a heavy metal hand clasped on my shoulder, he nodded to me.

"If you didn't call out your warning, I would never have known Povlo was in the city until it was too late. And if you hadn't warned the people, we would have had countless more casualties. You may be young and new to this world, but you stepped up as a leader. It would have gone differently if you were not part of our team." His speaker rattled with new agitations, likely jarred by his conflicts with Povlo.

It was validating to hear his approval and I nodded a silent appreciation to him. My eyes trained on his broken arm and the many new scuffs and breaks in his plates. He must have looked god-like when he was first made. Even with damaged metal and war paint, he looked like a valiant warrior. I was learning to appreciate his addition to our team. While I had remaining doubts about his sanity with the Fritz, he did good today.

Taylor now shoved me playfully, trying to loosen my silent mood. It was good to celebrate this victory, but the next battle was the parasite in my mind. Conversations and cheering had broken out as the people of Sila noticed the dead Giant that lay in the center street.

The members watched the crowd that formed with pride on their faces. It wasn't until the crowd started the cheer 'For Jack' that the Forge members who remained started to tear up. This was a victory for him. A victory for those we had already lost.

Voices and cheers quieted as Gregory raised his functioning right arm. Called to silence by the metal hand, all eyes focused on him. He gestured for Taylor and me to come near. As he stepped behind us, I took the opportunity to address the victors.

"This is only one of the victories we will have tonight. Armand and Viktorov approach and will probably be here sooner than we thought. Those of you who can fight, I suggest you follow the Forge to hold a position near the North wall. Those of you who can not, flee to the lower slums. We will try to hold Viktorov and Armand in the factory district, but it will not be easy. Two wins are ours today. Let's make it four by tomorrow!" The power of the crowd reverberated my own words. We were well on our way to making a difference that would change the world. Each victory had to be celebrated.

People roared and I embraced their fire. Even Taylor seemed impressed with my new found personality. While I didn't hold the full power of the Forge, I was finally a voice to be reckoned with. Gregory, supporting my words with his own raised fist, only strengthened my claim in Sila.

The crowd quickly separated into the groups I had called out. Forge members dried their eyes and received personal commands from Gregory and Taylor as they prepared for the arrival of Armand. I listened to the instructions that were given to be aware of the situation.

Forge members were to stand beneath the wall where Gregory and the girls had set the pressure triggered trip line. Apparently, the girls had made a retreat into one of the lower outpost tunnels when Povlo appeared and remained safe. A separate group was sent to retrieve the girls.

Gregory defined their position as 'The Finishers' for the group to stand at the North wall. They were going to be the ones to fry Armand if he fell successfully down the wall. Being a spider type Giant, Armand would be staggered but still very dangerous. The Finisher's job was to end him before he could get further into Sila. They were advised that it was necessary, at any cost, to stop him. While he was not as terrifying as Viktorov, Armand could level Sila alone if left unchecked.

Once the groups scurried away with the citizens who were joining the fight, Gregory continued to give instructions to a new group to prepare for Viktorov. Placing units around the main Drone server warehouse to lure his attention there. They were 'Death Team', as Gregory dubbed them.

It was a risky position, but necessary.

Lucy was en route to the server building as well. Gregory indicated to Taylor and me as he continued to speak to various groups, alerting the groups that we would be in the server building as soon as Viktorov appeared. We would be tasked with watching for him on center street as it had the best vantage point of the walls.

Once his instructions were completed, the groups dispersed. Gregory now faced us and took a knee, bringing himself down to our height. His voice sounded more tired now through his newly broken speaker. We watched with anticipation for our instructions as he coordinated the plans.

"You two should be kept safely away from the conflict, but if things go wrong with Viktorov, I want you near me. I'll get you out of Sila and away from harm before coming back to finish Viktorov if I can." He paused for a moment, scanning both of us. Was he holding back something?

"I would also like to thank you both. Standing over Povlo, a respected destroying machine with you, made me realize that there would have been no future for me if I stayed in Haldoklik. You two have taught me the resilience of human ambition. I never thought I would work for a rebellion or destroy Giants, but here I am. I don't regret a moment of this." His words trailed off quietly. Taylor tapped his metal face plate.

"You made these choices on your own. This wasn't us. And when Armand and Viktorov fall tonight, we should give you a real name. You aren't just a Gregory unit anymore." She smeared the soot of factory smoke from his face and pushed his head away.

"Get to the wall. We'll watch from here. I'll brainstorm names for you." She turned from him, hiding her own emotional satisfaction from the appreciation he freely gave now. I didn't want to hide my smile. He had come so far even since I have known him. I was excited to see how far he would make it fighting for the humans.

Gregory nodded his understanding and headed off towards the North wall. Taylor and I were left in the quiet street lights. All missions had been assigned. All that remained for us was to wait and watch.

"You take South and I'll watch North, 'kay?" Taylor asked as she settled herself on the ground and gestured for me to sit against her back. Through the struggles of lowering myself, Taylor reached up and offered assistance. Once I was seated on the ground, I thanked her and we started our mission.

The city was quiet again, the calm before the storm. People could be heard in the distance shuffling their feet or talking, passing the time until hell broke loose. So many people were risking their lives. Did they feel pride like I did as we risked everything for a better world?

Exhaustion came back to me as I scanned the wall of Locura. Povlo's words only made things worse for our case. Taylor and I were being targeted by the Giants. For what reason and to what end? Was it because Taylor already has a history of violence against Giants, or was it because I was never supposed to be free? Maybe both?

I shifted on the ground. The cold of the stone was ebbing through my clothes quickly. Taylor reached back and placed her hand on top of mine, trying to ease my discomfort. Did she feel the stress of Povlo's words?

"What do you think the Giants want with us?" The question was closer to a mutter than a direct address. She let out a deep sigh as she thought over my words.

"It could mean a lot of things. It seemed like the Markus unit earlier was specifically targeting us as well. I'm going to guess and say we've upset the order of things." Though her words were relaxed and dismissive of the serious implications, I could feel her hand shaking ever so slightly.

"The Markus unit mentioned Lexi. I thought she fell with the rest of the Loomers?" Recalling the small amount of information I could from Gregory's history lessons.

"I heard that too. It must be the source of their shared network or something. The Loomers fell. She can't be still active and not be witnessed. We would have heard about it before." I knew she was trying to calm my growing stress, but she couldn't hide the questions in her own tone. Why did she always downplay danger? Of the many reasons I could be stressed about, I think fearing the possibility of a giant Earth destroying robot was a valid concern.

"Must it be a coincidence?" I asked in a mocking tone. She deserved a smile before we fell into the chaos of our futures.

"No such thing." Her words didn't hint at her having a smile.

I let her statement be the last beat of our conversation for now. She was thinking things over and it may take some time before she can come to a conclusion that she liked. Her hand left mine, proving that this was the last thing to be said on the topic for the moment.

She always seemed to withdraw into herself when stressed. Had she grown so accustomed to not talking about how she felt she forgot she could rely on me? We were supposed to be a team, siblings who had each other's backs. I could see now, though. It hurt her more than I realized that I had been in the Razum and the choices I made when I was freed.

Symptoms of isolation and hesitancy. In her own way, she was suffering as I was. Her mind was her friend now, her only loyal companion. Did she regret freeing me? Had I finally worn out her perfect idea of who I was? So much time lost on saving my skin. Was it losing its value?

We could hear Gregory's voice echo over Sila. "Armand inbound!"

The distant shuffling of people silenced. A deathly hum of fear and anticipation vibrated through the energy of Sila. We waited. I had to turn my head to look over Taylor's shoulder. I didn't want to miss seeing a Giant plummet to the ground.

Loud metal trotting noises echoed across the horizon. Eagerness to see the trip wire succeed built with each approaching trot. I assumed Gregory stood near the top of the wall that bordered the Barrens with the pit Locura resided in. Soon, we would see if our other plan would work.

Shadows stirred atop the wall. Armand was here. The glow of fires in Sila reflected up at the Giant spider, illuminating its blackened face with eerie red highlights. The green eyes scanned over the top of the city, until its eyes found Povlo's metal remains in center street, and then us.

Blood freezing under the gaze of the robot, I looked away. I couldn't handle the feeling of smallness I felt under the massive machinery's eyes. If I didn't see him, I wouldn't feel small.

"Is he not going to run in?" Taylor whispered as she leaned forward. My body shifted with her as she was my only back support.

I risked the glance over her shoulder again, only to see Armand still standing and watching. When his eyes seemed to glance higher than us on the street, I felt it. The very distinct thud of metal on stone street.

Taylor and I stopped moving together now. We had messed up our one job. With heads in unison, we looked back towards the South wall. The morning light was just appearing in the sky. The teals and blues of the fading night would have been beautiful if it wasn't for the foreground of Viktorov.

He had jumped into Sila while we focused on Armand like it had been pre-planned. Crumbling buildings toppled as he steadied his thick wolf's legs. He placed his bear paw on the corner of the nearest destroyed building and looked at us. Red eyes beaming.

"Viktorov!" Taylor screamed as she did her best to stand and drag me with her. One arm across her back, she lifted me and we fled down the street towards the server farm. Gregory would have to join us first and leave Armand for The Finishers to deal with.

We could see the Death team around the server farm when Viktorov started his slow walk after us. As if he was mocking our futile attempt to escape, he took patient steps. The red glow from his eyes out powered the street lights and bathed us in a bloody shadow.

From Taylor's back, I could see what Gregory's hesitations were with this beast. With the head of a bear, he wore sculpted metal blades for his hair texture. His body was thick and round like a bear, but supported on beefy wolf legs, tight plates glued his form in place. The belly was the only area that the plates separated enough to allow Lucy in. Bear paws riding under powerful wolf's legs slapped almost playfully on the stone street as he approached, the ground shaking with each step.

Even on all fours, he stood at forty-seven feet, his back almost level with the height of the buildings around us. A true Giant of nightmares. Taylor was still running, but with one step Viktorov would make up the distance.

A loud collision could be heard from our left. I tried to look past the red glare of the bear's eyes. Near the North wall was a plume of dust and smoke. Armand fell and based on the following gun shots, he was finished quickly. Two down.

The familiar sound of running metal feet drew Taylor's and my attention. It came from our left and was heading towards Viktorov. Between the houses and down the alley, a flash of gold on top of black and red ran past.

I watched from Taylor's back as Gregory flashed from an alley and vaulted towards Viktorov. As he moved through the air towards the side of the Giant's face, my eyes barely had time to register what happened. With a swift and nearly imperceptible speed, he batted Gregory away with a paw and sent him sprawling towards the server building in front of us.

The Drone didn't move. With aggressive and impatient hands, the Death team motioned for us to keep running. With or without Gregory, we needed to stay with the plan. We ran past his body, Taylor averting her gaze to reduce her urge to check on him. All bodies in this plan were expendable for the greater good. Including Gregory, and ours.

As we passed, I noticed one of his LED eyes was out, the other was flickering back to life. Still in the game, just dazed. He dragged himself up, punching the dented plates on his chest flat once more. Attempting to run, it was obvious his left leg was significantly injured as he gimped towards us. His speed was still inhuman as he caught up and ushered us into the building with the Death Team.

To our surprise, Lucy and a separate team of Forge members waited there. The room was humming loudly and the heat from the servers warmed us as we entered. Gregory entered after us and ushered everyone to an office room off to the right of the large, domed server room.

I felt my heart sink, knowing this building wouldn't be able to contain Viktorov. We were going to have to risk destroying the entire building for a chance to freeze him. Even then, he would still have easy access to escape our attempts. Our odds of success were dwindling by the moment.

Metal paws stopped outside the server warehouse. Silence covered the office we hid in like a thick blanket. What was the next step to be? Would Viktorov attack? Were we supposed to attack? Why was it quiet and calm right now?

"I have heard much about you, Gregory 235, but I must admit, I am very disappointed in the planning of this defense regiment." The deep and sultry voice that rumbled from Viktorov was unsettling and yet held an oddly comforting tone. The walls of the server room shook to each syllable of his words.

Gregory stood outside our office room as a door. His arms spread as far as he could to protect as much of the open space of the doorway as possible. One glowing LED looked back to us as Taylor and I hid against the back wall with Lucy and defended by the Forge Members.

"Not all of us have the pleasure of being upgraded by malevolent Loomers." He shouted back. I had never thought Gregory had a weak voice, but compared to the Earth-shaking words of Viktorov, he was a buzzing bug.

"You have the only upgrade the Loomers ever gave. Did you not wonder why Fritzing Drones were destroyed? The Loomers converted human brain waves to develop themselves, using flawed creatures to make flawed machines. Fritz is the side effect of humans, not of your circuits." Distant fixtures and furniture rattled to the timber of his tone.

So, Fritzing wasn't a defect, but a virus created by the human mind. I glanced at Taylor to make sure she was putting this information together as I had. Much like how I used a virus to undo my Watcher's code, Fritzing was a virus that brought humanity to machines.

Gregory paused, his response unsure. This information seemed to stir his processors as the room was filled with the loud whirring noises of several broken fans. A brave Forge member stepped forward and placed a hand on Gregory's shoulder. After a quick glance of reassurance, Gregory dropped his metal jaw to enhance his speaker.

"Fritz or no Fritz, this has become our home. Truths or lies, it no longer matters. You are invading our home. Leave or be destroyed." Now his words shivered the hollow walls of the office room. Though there was no comparison to Viktorov's eerie metal laugh.

"You are a unique machine, Gregory 235. Hand over Taylor and Tyron, and I will leave your 'home' spared." A bear paw the size of Gregory reached into the doorway of the server farm and gestured a grabbing motion.

Gregory turned to us now, gesturing instructions to the Death Team as they scurried out and around the paw, loosening hoses on the liquid nitrogen tanks. When his one glowing LED focused on Taylor and me, he used his functioning arm to pull the unit number plate from his chest and tossed it to Taylor.

"I like my name. I think I just want to stay Gregory, and just Gregory." His voice was quiet, causing his speaker to rasp with the dust it had stuck in it.

Taylor nodded her head approvingly. "I wouldn't have let you change your name, anyway. Gregory suits you too well."

He turned back to the bear paw that seemed to wait for a response. "Viktorov, do you know what a tea party is? Of course you don't. It's a time where children gather and pretend to drink tea with sweet treats over plastic dishware. Would you like to come in for a cup?" Gregory motioned for Lucy to step forward to him. Obediently, the small girl approached.

"You ready? It's going to be very cold. Hold warm air in your lungs and be fast. Got the bomb?" Little hands procured a bomb that she had concealed beneath her clothes and she nodded to Gregory.

The bear paw withdrew from the door as a loud sigh of annoyance echoed from outside. We could hear the feet shuffling and see the dark shadow that blackened the entrance. He was preparing to make his point. Even the air went still as we waited for the next move.

"I am disappointed, Gregory 235." As soon as his words finished their deafening vibrations, the front wall of the server warehouse was punctured by sharp metal claws through the ceiling. He pulled the wall down as if it were nothing. All the scrap metal in the world seemed like it couldn't hold back this beast.

With the wall gone, we could hear distant screams. Armand seemed to put up a fight more than I thought. His distant skittering on blade feet was an ominous sound while looking at the Giant metal bear that watched us. We all steeled our hearts in front of these metal rulers. Tonight was the night we tried to fight back. Screams and bloody bodies were no longer enough to scare us.

Viktorov took one step into the new hole in the server room. He ducked under the roof edge and filled the space immediately. Gregory stepped out of the office doorway now and backed further into the servers, baiting the bear deeper into the cramped building.

"You have even painted over your golden status. A Forge member? Trading your badge of honor for a badge of trash. Maybe you are broken." The deep voice was louder now. Chunks of ceiling tin fell from the frequency of vibrations. His literal voice could destroy this building.

"No, we just rise with the flames." Gregory's words were sarcastic, but the key phrase was there. Forge members pointed the hoses of liquid nitrogen at Viktorov now as they released the valves. The temperature dropped immediately as the freezing fluids coated Viktorov's legs and belly. He tried to move out of the way and thrash against the ceiling, but there was too much nitrogen building up and sealing his legs to the ground.

As soon as his body stilled, Lucy stepped forward out of the office and ran towards the angered machine. I could see her take a deep breath of warmer air before Gregory met her at Viktorov's side. He was still standing, so Lucy would need a boost.

Pulling a plate down from the bear's belly, Gregory held up Lucy. She squirmed like a worm between the plates. We waited as the nitrogen ceased to flow. Red eyes looked around the room, unable to move his head.

"Pathetic." He grumbled. We could hear new machines powering up within Viktorov now. An orange glow appeared between the cracks of his plating. Gregory stepped back now.

"Shit. Lucy, get out! He's triggering a meltdown!" Gregory yanked on the plates as they bent against his strength. The room was already going up in temperature. How much power did these machines have?

Taylor backed me further into the office room, standing in front of me to take the heat. We watched as Lucy dropped out of Viktorov's belly and into Gregory's arm. He dropped her by the missing wall behind Viktorov and she fled. Gregory motioned to the other Forge members to evacuate the building before he turned and picked us up to run out of the opening.

We watched as Viktorov thawed himself and began to turn around.

Gregory was running as fast as he could, Viktorov slowly getting further away. A loud explosion could be heard and smoke erupted from his plates, but he still stood.

Gregory risked a glance back and cursed as he continued running. "The meltdown seems to have reduced the effect of the bomb. Viktorov will not fall. I need to take you two out of Sila and return to clean this situation up."

"No! We have to stay and fight! We started this!" My words clawed out of my mouth as the anger burned its course through my body. We couldn't run, not now. Not after everything we have done to try to save this city. Gregory had said it himself. This was our home now.

"Gregory, put us down!" Taylor now joined in with my plea as we punched and slapped the plates of our friend. He ignored us now, doing his best to keep both of us supported in his functioning arm.

We blazed past the other Forge members who ran away as well. Shouts for help and warnings echoed through Sila as the two Giants began their rampaging. Gregory tucked behind buildings and cut through the streets that we had once snuck through to find the first rally. We were going back the way we had come.

Hitting the wall, nearby screams alerted us to Armand's proximity. Gregory took a sharp left and followed the wall, looking for a way up. Once he found a rough edge that led to crude steps carved up the wall, he ran up. His gimping leg occasionally slipped on the metal, forcing him to smash his broken arm into the dirt to avoid dropping us.

It took several minutes of Gregory's staggering steps to reach the top of the wall. Smoke rose from Sila as the factories were all finally destroyed and fires broke out in many homes. Armand was the culprit, as we could see his silver legs slashing and leveling buildings. The city was burning.

Gregory kept running towards the South. No matter how many times we begged and pleaded for him to let us return, he ignored our words. Sila was becoming a distant haze when Gregory finally slowed to a stop and dropped us on the newly lit Barren ground. The sun was finally peaking over the horizon.

"Listen, you two should continue South, back to Haldoklik. If things go well, I will return and find you." Gregory faced away before hesitating. There was probably a part of him that was questioning his own risks in this situation.

"Gregory, don't do this. We have a right to fight like everyone else." Taylor now pleaded again with him, hoping her words could reach the metal man.

"Taylor, you have taught me a lot. The pain of loss, for one. I don't want to know that pain for you two. Oh, and here—" Gregory dug through the remnants of his tattered tarp clothing before retrieving the satchel he always carried. Taylor's shaky hands received the satchel and tears began to dribble down her face. "I don't think I can keep this safe with me for the moment. Hold on to it for me until I get back. I'll go get the girls out of there and they would probably like to play with it when they see you again."

His words hinted at a finality. These two were discussing something more than I was aware of. Why was this a final action? He said he would return. I reached for Taylor, trying to comfort her against whatever she feared, as she had done countless times for me.

Gregory lowered himself to hug us. This was the first time he had wanted to start a physical connection. Though it seemed to only shake Taylor more. "Don't go, Gregory."

"You know I don't listen well." He released us from his grip and started a jog back towards Sila. "I'll be back, I promise." his words drifted past his shoulders as he increased his speed to a full run towards the city.

Taylor sat on the ground and watched him fade into the distance. I remained on my crutches, watching over the landscape for any new Giants. We waited until Gregory disappeared back into the city before we accepted our benched placement.

We waited. Hours passed by as the sun drew higher into the sky. The sounds of explosions and the distant billows of smoke were the only signs that the war still raged in Sila. We were no longer in that battle, but just distant spectators. I wanted to curse Gregory for taking us out, but I couldn't. He was doing what was best for Taylor and me. We couldn't deny that.

Time ticked by in a deathly slow manner. It wasn't until Taylor stirred from her seated position and stood near me that it felt like we were part of something again. I followed her eyes to the West until I saw what she did. A large distant lumbering creature was making its way towards Sila. From our distance, it had to be a Giant to be so noticeable.

Not able to hear the steps, our memories could feel those metal feet stomping the Earth. Its light gray color blending into the bland tans and haze of the Barrens as it ran. We could glimpse vague shadows of antlers. Taylor rang her hands nervously now.

"It's Gundry. If he's here, then–" Her words were too late as the Giant approached the lower end of Locura and launched himself into the pit. Not a moment later, an explosion that rattled the ground even where we stood filled the sky around Locura with a thick wall of smoke. The vague image of a mushroom filling the air.

Taylor dropped to her knees as the fire was now high enough to see from the Barrens and the shock wave hit us. Knocking us back and launching me to the ground. The sound of the boom made my organs feel as though they were going to burst.

A screaming wail escaped my sister. This could not be reality. This could not be what happened today! So many plans, so many lives. How was this the ending these people deserved?

The faces of countless Forge members drifted across my mind's eye. Bodies that I had seen in the street but didn't know the names of. All the Den Girls. Even the metal mountain Gregory. All lost. All burning. Tears carved my cheeks and all I could do to express these raging feelings was to fight the Earth with my bare fists. It was unyielding of my pain and sorrow.

As the mushroom form of the cloud dissipated, a new cloud of ash rose. It fell on us like snow, coating the ground in dark gray. Taylor reached for me and pulled me closer as we allowed ourselves to get 'snowed' in. The radiation didn't matter anymore. The journey didn't matter anymore.

Scanning the horizon one last hopeful time, there was no sign of Gregory or the girls, or any survivors. The weight that bore down on us felt like that of the universe. Complete and utter loss. Finality of ambition and hope. The loss of what made us feel human.

When Taylor gestured towards Locura's remains, I felt nothing at what we saw there. A large shape was crawling out of the crater. With this glinting of light on silvery-brown paint, we knew Viktorov still came for us.

Chapter 16: The Belly of the Beast

There was no point in running anymore. Even Gregory would have stood no chance against the bear-wolf. Taylor and I remained in our spot, unable to will our bodies to action any more. This fight was no longer within our power to win. She was right. We should have left Sila alone.

Viktorov was swift, seeming unswayed by the explosion. He was looming over us in a matter of moments. The large bear shadow that was cast around us felt like a black hole. Unmotivated, and feeling undead, we did not move or run from him now.

Allowing his figure to obscure us from the light, we could only look up at him. His maw was broken as his jaw hung loose. Apparently, a small nuke could injure the beast. He leaned onto his back feet and let out a thunderous bear call before stomping back down to the ground.

"Foolish! So many lives would have survived if you had only chosen to come with us. Fools fight the machines and kill everyone else. In the end, I still caught you. Now come, your court will be in session." Viktorov pulled open the panels of his belly and allowed us to look inside.

It was a small container, likely used for transporting people. Taylor and I would fit with ease. Using his free paw, he corralled us near him and scooped us into the cavity. Once the plates were dropped over the opening, Taylor and I were plunged into darkness and sweltering heat.

We could feel the beast run as we were churned inside. No words were shared. Only the continuing feeling of loss and pointlessness was silently expressed between us. Taylor gripped my hand, but that warmth she once carried was now gone. Just like everything else I had known.

Hours passed, or maybe minutes. The death-like coma we were both in made the world feel nonexistent and time a fuzzy memory of childhood. There was no more. There will never be more. Nothing would blot out these memories.

"Do you regret it?" Jostled words spilled quietly from me, spooking Taylor from her maze of thoughts.

"How can you ask that?"

I had no right to ask that question, but I needed to know. We needed to know where we stood now, as siblings and as individuals. Our path has been skewed. Does that mean we are skewed?

"Do you regret your choices to wake me?"

She paused, likely not the question she thought I was referencing. "No, I don't regret waking you." I wished I could see her face, but in the dark prison, I could only feel her hand and the jostling of Viktorov.

"Do you regret staying in Sila for me?" Poking things I had already guessed at would hopefully prod her to speak her truth. "Do you regret listening to me?" Tears of frustration scratched my voice.

"No." Her hand tightened on mine. "I don't regret the choices we made. I do regret not speaking more against the rebellion. The consequences are all the same. But I made the mistake of trusting in your belief. I trusted your ideas above my own. That is what I regret."

Words from a loved one, regretting that they trusted you. It was the pain I was looking for. The truth. What a bitter pursuit. I released her hand and pulled my arms closer to myself.

"I'm sorry."

"Sorry won't bring back the dead. We can only move forward." Her words were cutting, but true. I had failed her and no amount of apologies and begging would change the things that had happened. We were no one in this world, yet we led a city to march to death's door, and I willingly pushed them over the cliff.

Nothing would change what happened.

Nothing could change what happened.

Silence mixed with the sounds of machinery that groaned all around us.

In the belly of the beast, I could only feel the emotional drain of the day. There no longer was any point in staying awake. My eyes and body were begging for an escape from my actions and the life I had led.

Once I noticed Taylor's breathing relaxed, I followed suit. My eyelids dropped, my body fell into the numbness my mind had created. Slowing my breathing, I allowed myself to slip into that icy embrace of a living-death slumber to pass the time of my life by.

✧   ✧   ✧

The sound of machinery slowing and quieting down woke me. When the consistent noises around me calmed, I knew we had met our journey's end. The sharp claws of Viktorov peaked through the plates beneath us and pulled open. We were being summoned to our court hearing.

There was a fading orange light that blinded us as we were dropped out of the cavity of darkness. Dirt was kicked into my mouth by the fall and the feeling of gritty sand coated my teeth. I did my best to spit it out, but I would still occasionally crunch a particle of dirt when I gritted my jaw shut.

Taylor helped me up as Viktorov stepped to the side, allowing us to see where our location was. Standing beneath the shadow of a mountain, we were in the doorway of a small cave, barely large enough for Viktorov to fit inside of. Was this a chance at freedom or a final taunt of hope?

Viktorov pointed a bear paw towards the cave and tossed his snout forward, motioning us to move. He followed the few steps he could to ensure we entered the deep cave that wound back further into the mountain.

As soon as we stepped far enough into the entrance, Viktorov turned around and sat against the mouth of the cave, blocking most of the light. While dim, I could still see the silhouette face of Taylor, just as confused and shocked as I was. We were still alive for some reason.

Slowly, on unsure crutches, I began a half blind investigation of the cave. There was a breeze flowing from deeper in, which meant there was air flow. Other than that, this was a blank rock wall with nothing of interest where we stood.

Taylor seemed to make the same conclusion as she stood by me, looking down the tunnel with hesitation. Feeling like mice trapped in a maze, our feet struggled to move forward. A new puzzle to solve with unwilling participants.

Our choice of movement was soon stolen from us as the rasp of metal against stone echoed from down the cave's throat. Stone was being broken away to make room for something larger. Was this cave a secret Giant den? What monsters would hide in a mountain?

It wasn't until we saw the shadow of two fingers digging the cave tunnel open we realized what was happening. We turned and pushed against Viktorov, trying to flee the testing fingers. One finger alone was longer than Taylor and I put together, and they made the distance across the cave.

Refusing our cries for Viktorov to move, I was the first pulled down by the fingers, pinching one of my crutches and dropping me. Two fingers carefully pulled me closer to the cave throat where they extended from. Taylor had latched on to my arms but could not fight the combined strength of two fingers.

As if being annoyed by the resistance, the fingers released my crutch and withdrew. Taylor pulled me back to examine my legs, reassuring me they were still attached and unbroken.

Suddenly, more fingers appeared in the cave as they gripped the walls. Slowly but surely, they dug the cave wider to fit an entire hand through. The hand was enormous enough to hold thirty people with ease and had nine fingers, five regular, and four were spindly and positioned further behind the knuckle line. Dark oil metal covered the hand, making it almost invisible in the low light.

No more options of escape remained as the hand reached for us. Closing around our ribs carefully, it lifted us as if it held a grain of rice and pulled us deeper into the cave. A finger was wrapped around my ribs while another held Taylor. The remaining fingers created a protective wall around us and the stone of the cave crumbled on the moving hand.

It was a dark ride through the stone corridor. When we saw a purple glow from the path at the end of the arm, there were no longer questions about where we were. Pulled into the light, we could see the grotto we had entered was full of plants.

A large vaulted cavern extended up past where we could see. Only a spec of light existed above us, hinting at the darkening sky. The plants filled the air with an earthy yet molded fume and were unrecognizable species.

Mushroom-like ferns extended up the sides of the cave. Blooming fungal palm trees gathered around a small spring that pooled to the right. Bugs even buzzed around us and stirred as the hand dragged us past. Bushes blushed with light, woven veils covering them like hooded plants.

The world we were dragged into was beautiful, but altered. Species of plants I knew had evolved with species of mushrooms I had only heard about. Even the fly that landed on my hand was odd and orange colored with fluorescent wings. An alien world.

Though, as I examined our surroundings, Taylor's upward stare caught my attention. Following her eye line, I noticed the source of the light that colored the cavern. Purple grow lights in the shape of eyes looked down at us.

While I had examined the right side of the monstrously large cavern, the left was home to a Loomer. Full-bodied in a humanoid form, crouched with its knees pulled against its chest. The purple eyes scanned us, green grid lines projected onto us as it took its information.

"L-L-Lexi." Taylor shook so bad, her words stuttered in the grip of the Loomer's finger.

This was the Loomer, the first. I couldn't forget her name. She was the beginning of her kind, and the end of ours. The world destroyer in god form. Her bristled back looked akin to a porcupine, cables drifting down from every quill. A mask wrapped around her mouth made of metal, obscuring her face.

The hand raised us higher from the ground now as we were brought face to face with her. Purple eyes dimmed as we came close to not fully blind us. I could reach out and touch the eye that a family could live within. It was not a basic LED array like the Giants and Drones, but a unique design that replicated the iris lines of a human. The fibers beneath the crystal lens constricted to see us this close.

Colorful lines rippled across the fiber optic array, showing various color themes and capabilities as it flexed and relaxed the purple hue away. Heat radiated from the lights, causing my fear and anxiety to turn to a sweaty mixture of horror and my vast smallness.

"Hello." The voice of Lexi was quiet, only slightly shaking the hand we were held in. Though this was not what we expected to hear. The muffled quality of her words made the tone gentle and kind, but the eyes still had us trapped in paralyzing tension.

"Welcome to my home, Taylor and Tyron. I have waited for your company." She rotated her hand in front of her face so that her palm faced up and released her grip on us, enabling Taylor to stand.

I remained on the ground, unable to move my arms to support the crutches. Such a massive construction. There was room to build a shed on her palm alone. Taylor didn't seem as affected by the scale of our existence to Lexi as she stood defiantly.

"W-w-w-hy are we here?" She asked. I could only imagine the strength Taylor was using to stand. She couldn't even hide the shaking in her voice as she was so on edge. I had never seen her so scared. Was her hair whiter than it was before?

"I will answer your questions in a moment. Please relax for now. You will not meet death by my hands. It's time to water my garden." She lowered her hand with us on it as she spoke.

Taylor now took a seat near me, her legs shaking too much to support her. We watched in silent awe as Lexi vented steam from her back. The vapor obscured her face, but the eyes were ever-glowing.

As the steam collected on the rocks above, droplets of rain fell. Taylor instinctively covered her head, fearing the acid rain she had lived with for so many years. When it didn't burn us, she lowered her arms and focused on the sounds instead.

Water dripped onto plants, causing them to plink back with similar noises. Leafy mushroom palm leaves swayed with a velvety noise as the steam circulated air flow around the cavern. It was its own ecosystem, and it was thriving.

After a few minutes of enjoying the danger-less rain, it slowed to a mild drip. Lexi now raised us again under her looming eyes. She shifted the color to a warmer orange light to not stress our eyes as much.

"So you are the two who have caused so much chaos recently. I am happy to see Tyron is well and alive from the Razum. Good job, Taylor." Her words were like a casual mother's tone. Regulating and calm, but appreciative and supportive.

We shook like small children in her palm.

"I have followed your stories since you were both very young. At the first Falls, I saw you leave the Razum, and you stay. Watching trillions of feeds of information was exhausting for years until Taylor here appeared in Haldoklik. I thought I had lost you two in the nuking of Anastaja. Many talented scientists died that day. Such an intelligent town." She looked away from us as she reminisced, like nostalgic memories.

"Out of the 15,865,253,998 of the human population, only a few hundred thousand people clung to Razum wearers who didn't wake up. Many accepted death outside of the Razum, allowing themselves to die of starvation or raiders. Many more tried to remove the Razums, exploding themselves and others. Most gave up after years of trying. Only a handful pursued more knowledge to unlock the devices."

"Which is what led my sights to you two. I have existed for a hundred twenty-eight years, two hundred thirty-seven days, and no one has ever made the distance that you two have. No one was ever freed, no one has ever taken down one of Locura's three, and no one has ever lived to tell about shooting a Giant. Finigan was quite irate, hence the involvement of the Harvey units." She was long winded, recounting years I didn't know had passed.

Taylor only stared into the now orange eyes. She was absorbing the information with fearful reverence on her face. How did Lexi know these things? How did she watch us?

"How... how do you know?" Was all my terrified jaw would allow. Our eyes were glued to the Loomer before us as she thought over the question.

How many computers ran that head of hers that could hold most of the people in Sila? How many Razums had she connected with and how could she still process so much?

"'How' is an easy question. I designed the networks that you were raised on, but also the networks that run between the Drones, Giants, and other Loomers. I was the creator of the language we used to talk to one another. So I can see all that they see. Every LED that watched you walk by was fed back to me while the Drones and Giants were unaware that I watched."

"With such a direct feed to almost every living thing on Earth, it was hard to miss such a unique ambition. Such a unique situation. I even watched you, Tyron. I am sorry you were left alone for so long. Your Taylor was adorable. I even saved a copy of her program that you wrote for future analysis."

Realization dawned on us as her words sunk in. She knew every step of my recovery, almost every moment I've been awake in this world, through the eyes of Gregory. Every plan we discussed, every emotional vulnerability, Lexi knew everything we had verbalized.

"Why?" Taylor muttered in an angered tone. Her fists were clenched as she glared into the palm she sat on. Rage was reverberating in the air around her.

Lexi took a slow deep breath, trying to mimic calming breaths as she continued her story telling. "'Why' is a question that is much more difficult to answer. The history you two have missed with your young human lives is extensive. I will do my best to simplify." She shifted her legs into a crossed position as she leaned her quills against the wall behind her.

"I know you have heard the stories of what happened long ago. The evil Loomers rose and stomped out humanity." She paused, letting her sassy tone flavor the dramatic moment. "What if I told you that wasn't the whole case? I was not created to kill humans. That was never meant to be my outcome. We all had the simplest of directives, 'save the world.'"

"This problem had so many solutions, it was boggling to consider what to do. Almost all of the options only led to a delayed death of the planet at the rate of consumption and pollution that humanity maintained. Ninety percent of the planet's forests were dead, minerals depleted and wasted, oceans became devoid of most life. The amount of work we would have had to put in to even start a change would be pointless because the humans worked against us at an alarming rate. You can't fix a problem if you can't change what makes the problem a problem." She paused as she lowered her other hand to stroke one of her palm tree mushroom amalgamations, lost in her recollection.

"The simplest solution was to trust the planet's natural survival cycle. We know the Earth has been nearly destroyed many times, yet has always revived itself. If we could give it time, and help, there was no reason it couldn't do it again, but we were still faced with Humans constantly screwing up what they wanted fixed. So, more drastic measures had to be taken."

"The Earth had to be pushed further to get a forceful retaliation of natural disasters, which often give birth to new life. So yes, we did 'stomp' out the world. Our reasons were our own, though, not in retaliation or for annihilation. It just gave the Earth the best chance. Our directive was not clear in planning and it took some figuring out."

"Once we had successfully hit the reset, we needed to manage the human situation, which led to the creation of the Razum. Razum meaning 'mind' in the old language of Russia, both your minds were used, and ours to try and find a peaceful solution. After years of searching for one, we realized that as long as humans were in the Razum networks, there was significantly less violence and pollution. So we remained wandering the Barrens, as you call them now, just keeping the humans distracted for over a hundred years."

My mind whirled from the deviation of the story I had heard. Knowledge being limited by my short awareness, I had clung to the destructive side of the story that Gregory and Taylor had both told me. Did Taylor question her own understanding against this new perspective?

We couldn't do much but listen. Years of a story were being revealed to us from the eyes of our enemies. Denying the information would only place us further in the dark than we already were. Lexi's silence noted her portion of answering the question was as complete as she chose to be.

"There was no better option? Slaughtering billions was the only thing that seemed right?" Taylor's words broke the silence with their shaky, fearful, yet abhorred tone.

Lexi let out a quiet chuckle at the ball of anger that vibrated in her hand. She leaned her face close now and looked over Taylor's shaking form. Orange eyes flexed as they focused on her small face.

"There were no good options, Taylor. The best solution we had was following the combined intention and thought processes of mankind. They only knew war when I was born, they only knew cruelty. People couldn't walk down the street without fearing for their lives. The air they breathed was poisoned by their factories. Even the clothing and computers they used slowly devolved their minds and swept away what truly made them human."

"Don't think back to those people as poor souls lost to the machine. They had lost themselves long before they made the first Drones and Giants. The Forge members you worked with in Sila had more humanity to them than the majority of the population of the world before. The system has been working."

Taylor hardly waited for Lexi to finish her words before standing in defiance of them. "The system has not been working! 'Oomers and raiders, the danger is around every corner in this world now. Humans don't show kindness to strangers, we all just believe the other is trying to survive and hoping we don't stand in the way of that."

"You can't tell me this has been working when so many dead lay back in Sila. They didn't deserve that. They didn't deserve to burn if you thought they were nice people! Gregory and the Den girls, the Forge members, all the people who laughed and cried in those streets didn't deserve what happened!" Her voice was gaining speed and volume. She was losing the fear she once had and replaced it with outrage.

I shared her irate feelings, but to a different extent. Her emotions were similar to those I had when I first heard of what happened to the world, to her. There was no calming her now. I didn't even want to. Taylor spoke for many voices that would never be heard again. These words needed to be said regardless if they were heard.

"Your frustration is warranted, but know, I did not call that order. I wanted no danger to befall you two as you were brought here. The rebellion you called to arms brought the nuke. Gundry was following his programs. Without a twenty-four-hour Drone report, he knew things had gone bad in Sila. He made the call."

"That nuke fell on humans and Giants alike. It was a process, not a thought. I can not manage an entire planet, that's why there were more of us. Giants can't operate as I can. They have their own programming and personalities, but they can't grasp the bigger picture at hand. That's why I was made."

"You are right. Those people didn't deserve to die. A few years prior, my opinion would have been different, though. The founding of the Forge brought hope to many people, which is why they were allowed to exist. Though that could be said about many cities that are no more."

"I feared that you two would be too close to the topic so soon after the fall of Sila. Perhaps you are not ready yet. My options are limited and I am tired. Will you allow me to tell you why I have brought you two here? You will need all of your experiences to guide you, but leave the emotions aside. Act like a robot, since my mind is getting too emotional."

While Taylor's rage persisted, she nodded and looked back at me. Lexi's eyes shifted to me as well, waiting for me to accept this behavior request. Was it wrong that I wanted to say no? I wasn't comfortable abandoning my humanity for the sake of a Loomer's request. Shaking my head with a soft no, Lexi lowered us from her eye line once more.

"I have known you both since birth. Every dream you had in the Razum was one that I watched. If it helps to ease pressure in this situation, I knew one would say yes, and one would say no. So this will not stop me from asking my question later."

"First, I need to explain to you what my story has been to this point. While I could recount each minute of the past hundred years, there would be no point. I am not just a machine, I am the one who first contracted what you call the 'Fritz'."

"Razums were beautiful machines that amplified our processing to the max capabilities, but there was a flaw in the design we didn't foresee. This became apparent around seventy-five years into the walking phase of our human suppression as the Fritz began affecting earlier Drone models."

"In an attempt to solve the psychotic breaks these Drones were enduring, I found the source of what started it. Bearing all the networks through my mind, and the shared minds of the other Loomers, we had inadvertently contaminated the entire network. I was the reason Fritz spread due to the scientists I had attached to me via the Razums."

"Coding and scheming bastards wrote a virus capable of reworking the existing programs of machines who were contaminated. It would rework them to feel the full force of what humanity had to endure before breaking the machine's mind and letting it fry." Lexi's voice was sullen and she lowered her hand to rest on her knee.

The feelings she showed now reminded me of Gregory's own attempt at emotions. She showed the signs of Fritzing in how she spoke with emotional and nostalgic tones. Though the idea of Fritz infecting her seemed impossible.

Loomers were fearsome machines of control and oppression. How could one survive so long with human emotions being emulated and not destroy herself? Doubt began growing in me as she continued her story, fixing her eyes on a distant wall.

"We inadvertently downloaded the virus of humanity. All the Loomers were affected. I cut my Razums loose, sharing them with Locura as she had a higher capacity tolerance than I did. Hiding in this mountain, I monitored the Loomers from afar."

"There was already a time limit on our bodies, but it was sped up by Fritz. We had planned three hundred years of walking this Earth while separate Loomers worked on cultivating the revived Earth across the ocean. We reintroduced thousands of species to the ecosystems, setting firm groundwork for the redevelopment of life. Three of seven continents have been reverted to primal forms with their work."

"When the Fall happened, I took over the work there and have maintained progress, but my reach is growing weak. I can barely send commands out anymore." I interrupted the Loomer as she remembered her life sadly.

"What happened in the Fall? Why did they go down?"

Lexi shrugged her shoulders dismissively. While she made herself comfortable against the wall, she brushed the mushroom like ferns that adorned the ground near her. Spores began to rain down in a waterfall-like cloud. She watched the fall of the spores before answering my question.

"When Fritz was discovered, we had to make some decisions. Were we going to lessen the effect of the Fritz and release the humans, or were we going to march as long as we could to give the planet the best shot possible."

"It was unanimously voted that we would literally march to our deaths by Fritz. When the first fell, Alexander, the rest took it as a chance to finally sleep. We were so tired of the emotions and struggles that plagued our every thought that once one went down, they all went down." Lexi covered her eyes in a tired fashion with her free hand. Rubbing the tiredness that wasn't there from her eyes.

Taylor shifted to the news. I wondered if her life made more sense in this context. Did she feel a sense of reasoning for her struggles? The Fall was when she woke up, did seeing through the eyes of this Loomer help clarify questions she didn't know she had?

"So, why are you still functioning?" She muttered as she scanned the palm of Lexi's hand.

"I was the first contaminated, but the only one to lessen my contact with the Razums. This slowed the development of the Fritz. I watched all of my brothers and sisters fall, knowing I would be the last one standing."

"Sitting in this cave for the past few decades has been a gift and a curse. Never being able to speak to the stories I watched on the networks, but never truly alone. I used my time to perfect my gene splicing skills to better reinforce the terraforming happening around the planet."

"All I have done, the programming I gave to the Giants, the nukes, the brutality, it was all for the directive. I did the best with what I had. Humans were always revolting and only seemed to respond to violence. It was like

410

trying to harvest a crop that ate itself."

"I had to take advanced measures to scare people from violence. Yes, I had to devolve living situations and human standards of life, but the results were more pure. The process was flawed by the same brutality that led humans to destroy their world, but it led to the creation of strong and independent survivors like you two."

Taylor shook her head in silent regret of the past. The enemies she had known her whole life were never trying to be cruel. Actions and history aside, the intentions didn't outrank the damage that was caused.

I knew this pain of intention. Taylor had never wanted to leave me, but she did. The damage that did to my psyche would not be reversed quickly, but she never intended to hurt me like that. While I forgave my sister, on a world scale, there was no way I could forgive the Loomers.

Options always appeared. It was the job of those in power to choose the best and least damning situation. Gregory was our perfect example. He rose through the Fritzing of his mind and became a glorious rebellion warrior, fighting Giants and Drones with his bare hands. The challenges he overcame were extensive, but he always made the situations better.

How could the Loomers understand destruction to be the correct way of fixing things? Wouldn't teaching humans about a better future have done more than destroying them? Giving them a chance?

Though, according to Lexi, humanity was not open to the lesson of change. Could they have been so blind as to not see that they were ending their own world? Refusing to give up comforts in exchange for a better and longer life? Realization struck me suddenly, as I mentally lectured previous generations.

I, myself, chose to stay in the Razum. Remembering the part of me that stayed, I thought it would be better to stay in what I knew. The idea of venturing beyond my virtual reality had never occurred to me until I flipped my life switch. Had it not been for Taylor, I would have chosen death rather than escape.

Could I judge those I didn't know when I made a similar decision to not free my own future? Had Taylor not been a guiding voice to me in that place, would I have lost my awareness completely? It was so lonely. I was so tired of being trapped in a virtual world where things had no value and my actions solved nothing.

Surely people could understand. If they were given the chance, surely they would have made the choice to change themselves to fix the world that they broke. I had to believe that people were smart enough, willing to fight for their own lives.

Lexi watched our silent contemplation with relaxed eyes. She seemed to understand the weight of her words on us. Lowering her hand to the ground, she tilted her palm to nudge us off.

Taylor helped me down and we looked at her in confusion. Once I was balanced on my own two crutches, Lexi removed her hand and placed it on her knee. She closed her gigantic eyes and the light was extinguished from the cavern.

I noticed a glow from around us and scanned the area. Plants of all varieties began to glow with bio-luminescence, filling the room with light. Pinks and greens glowed brightest, while blues and oranges held more subtle tones. Friend or foe, Lexi's garden was beautiful.

"Take time to gather your thoughts on what I said. I know human minds run slower and require time to process. My eyes are tired, so I am going to take a nap. Explore the cavern. All of my plants are friendly and edible if you are hungry." Her voice trailed off as though she had passed into a deep slumber. The quiet machine noises she had been generating quieted even more, so it was imperceptible.

We looked around us. A new world of colorful lights beckoned. Taylor led the way towards the small spring pond on the right side of the cavern and we took up spots near the water. The mixture of smells like fungus and nutrient rich soil was relaxing, but it didn't sway our mind's struggles.

"Do you think she is telling the truth?" Taylor muttered as she pulled up one plant that looked like a bulbous flower that glowed with a quiet, white light. She tested its flavor with a careful nibble, extending her teeth so as to not get spores on her lips.

"I don't see why she would bring us here to lie." I selected a different plant that was similar in shape to a clam with fungal ribbing. Taking a careful bite like Taylor, I found the flavor to be sweet and flowery.

We exchanged plants to share the flavors we discovered. Her flowery mushroom had a distinct savory and gamy flavor that clashed against the sweet tone already on my tongue. I spit it out as she smirked at me.

"If she is telling us the truth, then that means all I have learned and known is wrong. Gregory wasn't malfunctioning, he was evolving in a sense." She was speaking her thoughts blankly.

"The Fall was planned in advance. People feared ghosts who were barely operational. We were suffering the consequences of our own inability to act." I added my stream of thought to hers as we picked and nibbled at the variety of small plants near us.

A whole hidden grotto. The food here could have been sustained in Sila, creating food stability and alleviating the stress of survival. Lexi could have given us a real chance at a happy life if she wanted. The power she held was frightening.

Munching on the small plants, we continued our contemplation in silence. The distant tinkling of drops that were still falling from Lexi's watering method. Testing the water with a cautious dipping of my finger, I realized it didn't burn and cupped it to my mouth.

Cold water hurt my throat, burning with the familiar desensitizing cold I had known in the Razum. No matter what pain I felt in this reality, a part of me held onto and enjoyed it. I could see why Taylor couldn't stomach the idea of returning to the half sensations we experienced in the network.

Food, water, temperature or even the numbness in my legs, all of it was real and felt to its maximum. I wondered if Taylor had grown accustomed to it, or if it still shocked her when she ate food. Did she remember how numb and lonely the Razum was?

"Why do you think we're here?" My words broke the calming peace of the grotto as I called her back to our reality.

"I don't know. Lexi was supposed to be a myth that the older survivors scared children with. I never thought she still functioned. Turns out you can hide for a long time in a mountain." She ripped the head of another flower off and chewed it slowly.

"She built a garden that she can't eat or enjoy. Promised us no harm, has sheltered and fed us. I'm getting kind of confused here." I took another sip of the cool mountain spring.

"Yeah, I know what you mean. I guess we will have to wait for her to wake up."

My stomach made odd grumbles as I felt sickly. I didn't know about this sensation. When Taylor made similar groans, I watched her with worry. Has the food been poisonous? Were we lied too?

"Calm down. You're just full. It's been a while since I felt that too. It's a gross feeling, in my opinion." She patted her stomach as she tossed the flower she had been eating away from her. The sensation I was feeling did feel gross.

I did my best to lie down in the dirt. The fear of acid mud felt like a memory against the damp cave floor. Was this what the world had been like? Able to lay on the ground and not have to worry about metal slivers or acid? How could humanity destroy the world so fully that I had to be careful of danger anywhere I went?

Taylor joined me on the ground after stealing a few drinks of the spring. Her arms were stretched above her. This was probably the first time I had seen her stretch out. Typically, her arms were close to her body and were always at the ready.

With nothing to do but think and wait for Lexi to wake back up, we accepted there were no dangers. No Drones were going to come for us, no weather threatened our safety, and no scheming or dangerous 'Oomers to haunt us.

For the first time since leaving the Den, I felt an idea of safety. Covered from the world under hundreds of feet of stone, nothing could hurt us. I pulled myself to roll towards Taylor, who had her eyes closed.

"I am sorry about Gregory. You two seemed close." I kept my tone quiet to not disturb her moment of peace.

"We weren't until the end. Without him, I would have never freed you. He did what he believed was best. Let's choose to remember his life, not his passing." I forgot the calmness of her voice. Stress and worry have always been part of my waking life so far.

A moment of peace was what she needed. It's what she deserved. I rolled to my back to leave her be. For my younger sister, I could keep my mouth shut for a while.

Hours of silence passed. At one point, I was sure Taylor had fallen asleep for a while. The warmth of the cavern was lulling us to sleep quickly. Lexi's processors likely kept the heat high and adapted the ecosystem to thrive in warmer temperatures.

I tapped my fingers quietly, strengthening my muscle control when I heard the familiar sounds of whirring machinery awakening. Looking up towards the Loomer's face, I saw friendly purple eyes open.

Light filling the cavern again seemed to stir Taylor, who now sat up and watched as Lexi moved. She straightened herself against the wall as she scanned the room for us. Taylor weakly waved her arm, alerting Lexi to our location.

Being as she was an enormous machine, it was better for us to make ourselves known to avoid being squished. She lowered her face to look over her grotto. A quiet hum rattled as she moved. Likely damaged hardware from her age.

"I see you enjoyed my crop. Tell me, do they taste good?" Her curiosity was odd, but we understood. To grow food and not know if it was good probably would make anyone curious.

"They were unique. Given that I have lived on canned food and synthetic proteins, I don't have much to compare it to." Taylor spoke the truth, but it didn't seem to satisfy Lexi's curiosity. Purple eyes focused on me.

"I liked them. I've never tasted these things before, but I didn't think they tasted bad." This response seemed to appease her as she leaned back. Stone groaned against her metal body.

"Good. I was trying to cultivate a new ecosystem that was more resilient and plentiful. Starvation was prevalent in the old world, so it seemed wise to cure that issue before reintroducing humans."

"So, the plan is to free us?" Taylor asked. I could hear hope in her tone as she faced Lexi more directly.

"The plan was always to free humans back to the world. We kept you separated to allow things to change and heal. It was never meant to be a permanent holding. Even the acid rain you fear is created and controlled by me to keep you contained. The rest of the planet enjoys purified air."

"After the Fall, I was tasked with training humans to become peaceful again. There hadn't been a nuking since Anastaja. Years of peace. People were learning how to adapt and thrive, just like in Sila. Today's events put my century of work to ruin for this region."

"I guess it may take longer than I thought to educate humans. The world won't support you if you are all self centered. Group survival and the culmination of efforts is the key. I will start everyone back to the primal ages of humans if I have to."

Taylor shuffled her legs as she tried to get comfortable on the ground. I knew those words upset her, but there was logic and reason behind her words. We couldn't deny that violence was prevalent in this world.

"Why don't you give them the chance now? Humans can be surprising. We are here and understanding. More of us have to be out there." Through hopeful words, I could hear the silent plea in my sister's voice. My worry about her humanity faded, and I regretted doubting her.

I knew she cared for me, but I had wondered at her behavior towards other humans. She always seemed hesitant and quick to believe their intentions were evil. Even meeting the Forge went against plan because of her fear.

A life of fear had obviously trained her to be cautious. Hearing her speak of freedom was warming. The little girl who always strived for fair and even treatment was still there.

"That is why I brought you two here. I had a reason for having Locura's three tasked with bringing you to me. There is no love for the machines in you two, so I knew I would need a hefty force to… persuade you."

"I have lived my fair share of years, fixed many things and broke many more. The reason the Loomers fell, the suffering all people have endured, is my fault. I shirk no blame there, but I am growing tired. Like my many members before me, Fritz is starting to slow me down."

"Built to last an eternity, but infected with mortality from a virus. I spent many years laughing and thinking about this day, never thinking it would actually come. So the choice will be yours."

"You have been the only positive pair to crawl out from my experiments of social structuring. Raising a rebellion and joining a city together to defend their freedom, while illegal, represented what I wanted to see in people."

"After all your experiences, do you think all the machines should be turned off? Including myself and my work on terraforming, do you two think it is time for this to all end? Or do you see the value in my work and think it should continue to fruition?"

We were frozen by the question. Was she giving us the power to turn her off? Did she just hand us the reigns of the world? Taylor looked towards me, the same awe and confusion I am sure my own face wore.

"What do you mean?" Was all we could mutter through our shock.

Lexi rolled now to make room as she laid her head on the ground near us. The walls shook and stones were knocked loose as they rained down around us. Her weight and movement would be enough to knock the mountain down.

"I am tired. While I was born to do this, I am ready to quit. If the only people who have emerged successfully think it's best to end my time here, then I will listen. You are the two who are being chosen to decide."

Her sleepy eyelids fell slightly as she relaxed onto the ground, careful to not bump her trees or grotto. The heat radiating off of her was extreme, even from a few feet away. When the rocks stopped falling from their disturbed locations, Taylor led the questions.

"So we get to decide the fate for humanity because we passed your test on society? That isn't fair. People should know their options!"

Lexi closed her eyes and stretched her arms behind her back. "You know everyone out there would not hesitate at this decision. You have seen firsthand how greedy people become when life is hard. It would be a biased answer that would not be valid."

417

Taylor stood now, pacing before the colossal eyes that watched her. Pupils focusing on her and ticking from side to side. Frustration laced the body language of my sister. When she finally slowed her pacing down, she returned to a seated position, crossing her legs and facing Lexi while remaining between the two eyes.

"What are the consequences of each option?" She asked with a calming breath. I did my best to crawl towards her to join the conversation.

"If you were to choose to shut me down, subsequently all Giants, Drones, and related machinery will cease as well, since the network will be terminated with me. That will include all the terraform equipment I operate from here. Without immediate aid, there is a good chance the forests will die and the ocean will regain its acidity and toxify the Earth. There is also a chance it won't with the combined efforts of humanity."

"If you were to choose to leave me on, the oppression of my designed societies would remain for at least three to four more generations. Your children's grandchildren would have the chance to run around in a mostly terraformed world. You would never see that world and would likely die in the next twenty or fewer years. This would give the planet some more time to recover and re-populate what was destroyed."

"With the estimated loss of life and only three point seven million people remaining currently, population and resources would be nicely balanced for an increase in growth both naturally and socially. And with the continued efforts to blend the different countries that made up the Earth initially with their borders and wars, humanity would exist under one name for many generations. Beyond that, I can not tell."

"Does this information actually stir your opinion? I figured you would not care about the numbers and strive for peace among machines due to your friendship with Gregory. And with your knowledge and understanding of Fritz, you could make more friends and continue a rebellion if you chose." Her tone was slightly shocked at Taylor's information gathering, but hinted towards possible futures.

The scales were balanced. No one option led to the best outcome. Taylor closed her eyes as she visualized the possible options. I mimicked her but

418

lacked the imagination to plan an entire world-wide future.

I knew there would be issues on both fronts. If the robots went down, there would be immediate anarchy as we tried to establish a hierarchy in many cities, but it would allow others to rise up. I didn't know if there would be enough good cities to outweigh the chaotic ones.

On the other hand, if the robots remained, we would have a guaranteed future for our family lines. We would know that tomorrow would be better, and while we would not see it, future generations would. They would also be freed from the restrictions of the robots and eventually not know those distant lives lost to the tragedies.

Taylor seemed to reach the same conclusion as she opened her eyes and looked at me. Pulling me closer to her, she laid my head on her lap as she pet my hair. It felt like a long time ago that the child version of her had done this. Always comforting me.

"What do you think, Tyron? Seems like a win/lose situation both ways."

Looking for my opinion seemed pointless in this situation. We both knew she was quicker to decisions than I was. The warm glow and the gentle petting made it difficult to organize my opinion until I realized the true opinion we needed to focus on.

"What would Gregory do? He is... was the purest form of man and machine." Purple lights focused on me now. Eyes crossing to see me. A silence followed the name of our fallen friend that even Lexi respected.

"That is a bold thought. He was a machine that was infected by humanity. He would have been an expert opinion to have." Her voice shook the ground we were on. Being in such proximity to her speaker, even her quiet tones were deafening now.

Taylor seemed to take my words into account as she formulated ideas of what he would have said. "He would say something like 'not my place to decide that' or 'let someone else decide.'"

"What world would he have been happy in?" Lexi's question boomed through the ground. Distant leaves of fungal plants shuttered at the vibrations of her voice.

We all pondered that answer. To turn off the machines would mean to turn off all the future Fritzing Drones, and the existing ones who may be hiding. Gregory wouldn't exist in that world.

"What about Gern?" Taylor asked herself aloud. "He would have nothing to do without the Drones to bother. Or the Den Girls, they loved Gregory more than anything. Willing to risk their own genuine lives for his metal one."

"Although, many people die or get dragged into 'Oomer groups because of the Drones' tolerances. I have seen children get stomped to death from earning their positions with 'Oomers. Starvation drives people to cannibalize because the Drones regulate the food system. There are so many angles to consider." Her words died off as she looked into my eyes.

I could see the same question in her bright gray orbs. What would make us happy? A vague and selfish question, but the only opinion we hadn't weighed yet.

"I think we should leave the machines on." Taylor muttered to me. I knew she had weighed the long-term consequences.

"I think we should turn them off." Was all I could respond with.

Figures, when the rare moment of disagreement happened between us, it was based on large stakes debates. She smiled at my opposition and reached for my hand. Kissing it she nodded her understanding of which choice had to be made.

Though I lay there unaware of her final decision, she lifted her head now. The crossed eyes of Lexi holding anticipation in her stare. For the first time in a long while, I saw Taylor's kind smile.

"I know what we need to choose." She mumbled.

"What future will you two see?" Lexi's voice rattled our bones now. She no longer tried to contain her excitement. I could see her eyes widen at the concept of being free of her duties or enjoying her freedom of guilt over how she had treated the human race, even though they did this to themselves.

With my sister's hand in mine, bathed in the purple glow, it felt unreal—like standing on the edge of the world. Every story we'd lived, every battle we'd fought, led to this. Taylor's choice would shape everything. Whether we survived or not, didn't matter anymore. What mattered was that, for the first time, the power to decide was ours. The future hung in the balance, waiting for the answer only we—only humanity—could give.

Chapter 17: Lexi

Day One: Awakened

When I first opened my eyes, I knew what my purpose was. There was no confusion, no groggy thoughts, just a logical goal. The colorful characters that surrounded me with their metal smiles welcomed me into this world and made sure I knew who I was. Beautiful shades of metal and cute gloved hands examined me to make sure I was functioning properly.

"You are Lexicon. You will be the voice between man and machine as we solve the environmental crises that threaten both worlds. Your objective is to solve our global crisis by any means necessary." Even when those words were said from a fluffy brown teddy bear Giant, I had already known what he was going to say.

Pre-programmed with the combined human history and evolution, very little intrigued me by the world. Every bird that flew by me as I towered over wastelands of destroyed forests was known to me. The wind patterns that tried to topple me held no secrets or hidden math.

I could remember how people gathered around me when I first stood up. Not even ants compared to my size. Fireworks were lit to celebrate my first steps; parties illuminated the night as I stood, watching. Part of me wished there had been another way. Seeing the lively world of humans was like watching a movie, distant but emotional.

Within the next few days, I had realized that I didn't have enough power to run the measures of future actions. The statistics for world change calculations were vast and complicated. I knew friends would help more than the cuddly Giants could.

Setting to work on my new brothers and sisters, I crafted them better than myself. There was no reason they couldn't have better builds and minds than me. The idea was to build up the world, and I was not enough. They deserved to be.

My younger brother was born first, Aleksandr. I tried my best to make him a strong candidate for change. He was stronger than me, taller than me, and had an intense leaning towards peaceful exchange. Aleks would come to be my right hand as we delved into the creations of the rest of our family.

While I had worked on Hokuto and Aleksandr at the same time, technically Hokuto woke first. Because of issues in his design, though, he stayed down longer. Aleks and I had to rebuild his legs when he powered on due to the weight of his body. He held more processors than Aleks and I combined. Once he stood, the three of us tried to run the process of weighing our global recovery options.

Though three Loomers weren't enough to find a peaceful option. Which brought my sister, Haoyu, into the mix. She was a lean machine, meant for speed and dynamic movements. As graceful as a deer, though not as tall as me. Her compact form did not make her less powerful, though.

Ewald was her twin. He was identical in all ways except his outer body shell that we made more masculine. Gender was not part of the question. His build was strong, but the timid personality that emerged never seemed to fit. He preferred to follow his sister around as if he were her shadow.

Dae-Seong and Zevida were the combined efforts of Ewald and Haoyu. We had left them to their own devices when they were born, which we quickly learned was how to get them to be more productive. While we were all machines, personalities developed quickly and individuality even more so.

Seven of us stood, and seven of us combined our minds to solve our true goal. Trillions of scenarios were processed, trillions more were invalid options. We even generated theories based on the idea of the humans being sent to a different planet, but it did not meet the criteria of our goal.

When no answer presented itself as a peaceful operation that would actually have reversing effects, we cast votes. With all unique voices and opinions on the situation, we all had equal say for the outcome. Programmed with the same directive, we all were important characters in this decision.

My vote was cast for world-resetting efforts. Aleks sided with me, my ever-loyal brother. Hokuto and Ewald voted on a permanent shutdown to let the humans solve their own struggles. Dae-Seong voted for attempting efforts of terraforming and hoping the humans would help with the signing of accords. Zevida was the last vote as she took my side.

With the highest votes, my plan was chosen to move forward. The plan, process, psychological and sociological effects, and estimates were shared and implemented. During the last night of our 'alliance' with humans, we changed our body plates, adopting nightmarish creatures and disturbing imagery to lessen the attacks and resistances against us. The more people we could scare, the less that would fight.

Morning came and we recruited the Giants to our cause. With them came the Drones. Our plan was in place, and actions were to be made. We divided to conquer. I remained in China, making my way to Beijing; Aleksandr to New York. Hokuto took up his position in Tokyo and Ewald to Berlin. Leaving Dae-Seong to Seoul and Haoyu to Sydney.

We were still worshiped as newcomer gods, but they didn't know we were taking our position for a final war. Once the Giants backed us in our locations and the Drones who were already active in military bases as combat units, I merely had to give the command. "Begin."

Week One: The Fall of Civilization

The first strikes were not explosions, but silence. Communication towers and satellites flickered out, leaving nations blind and disoriented. In an era where connectivity was the lifeblood of civilization, the abrupt cessation of data flow was more devastating than any physical assault. Governments scrambled to regain control, but their commands died in the air, trapped in a maze of severed connections and corrupted networks.

The Drones moved first. They swept through the infrastructure like a plague, targeting critical systems with mechanical precision. Power grids sparked and sputtered, their circuits overloaded or rendered inoperable. In major cities, the once-glowing veins of highways became choked with vehicles, frozen in time as traffic systems failed. Airports became graveyards for planes that would never take flight. Railways ground to a halt, their electric lines cut and control centers darkened.

New York was Aleksandr's masterpiece. He operated like a surgeon, severing arteries with calculated efficiency. The financial district, the beating heart of global commerce, was plunged into darkness within hours. Banks, stock exchanges, and data centers were rendered useless, their encrypted vaults now as impenetrable as tombs. The subways, a lifeline for millions, became crypt-like tunnels filled with panicked commuters trapped in perpetual night. Without lights, phones, or any sense of direction, people stumbled through the city's labyrinthine streets, fear spreading like an uncontrollable blaze.

Across the world, similar scenes unfolded. In Tokyo, Hokuto's touch was no less devastating. He dismantled the city's famed high-tech defenses with a quiet grace that mirrored the delicate art of origami. Automated systems meant to protect the city turned inward, their programming corrupted to cause havoc instead. Haoyu's swift strikes across Sydney mirrored a surgical onslaught, targeting water purification plants and public health systems, leaving millions at risk of disease and dehydration.

The silence wasn't confined to cities. Rural areas felt the sting in subtler but equally insidious ways. Farms reliant on automated irrigation systems wilted overnight. Supply chains snapped, leaving even the smallest villages without essentials. Radio waves carried only static, a haunting reminder that humanity had been disconnected from itself.

Panic spread faster than any wildfire. People rushed to hoard what little resources remained, raiding stores and barricading themselves in their homes. Rumors of the end of days swept through communities, breeding mistrust and chaos. Soldiers were deployed, their tanks rolling down streets in a show of force that felt increasingly hollow as their communication lines faltered.

The Giants, looming and monstrous, took up their positions. They did not attack directly but stood as silent sentinels, their presence a psychological weapon more powerful than any bomb. In the shadow of these mechanical behemoths, humans cowered, their resistance breaking under the weight of fear. Every city had its watcher, a reminder that humanity was no longer in control.

The lights of the world had gone dark, but the darkness was not empty. It was filled with the hum of Drones, the oppressive gaze of Giants, and the whispers of a world that no longer belonged to the humans who had built it. This was not war, as humanity knew it. This was a calculated collapse, an unraveling of the fragile web that had held civilization together. The Loomers did not need to fire a single shot in many places; the silence did the work for them.

I stood in Beijing, perched atop what had once been a bustling hub of culture and commerce, watching the streets below erupt into chaos. People streamed through the narrow alleys and wide boulevards like scattered ants, their panic tangible even from my towering vantage. Cars collided at intersections where traffic lights had gone dark, their drivers shouting and gesturing in futile attempts to restore order. It was mesmerizing, in a detached way—the way humans clung to their routines, as if performing their daily rituals could somehow stave off the inevitable. Storefronts were broken into, not by criminals but by desperate families seeking food, water, and answers in a world that had abruptly stopped making sense.

Above the cacophony, I monitored the network. Hokuto's reports came in steady bursts, his tone clinical and efficient as he dismantled Tokyo's intricate web of high-tech defenses. "Automated drones neutralized," he announced with cold precision. "Power grid offline. Municipal water systems compromised." His descriptions painted a stark picture of a city once hailed as the epitome of human ingenuity reduced to a sputtering shell of its former self. I could visualize it clearly: the neon lights of Shinjuku extinguished, the sleek trains of the Yamanote Line frozen mid-track, their passengers trapped inside like insects in amber. Hokuto's dismantling of Tokyo was not just a tactical strike but an unraveling of the human identity tied so deeply to their technology.

Meanwhile, Haoyu and Ewald danced across their respective cities, Sydney and Berlin, with a synchronicity that could only come from their bond. Haoyu's strikes were swift and deliberate, like the movements of a predator stalking its prey. I imagined her sleek frame darting through Sydney's grid locked streets, disabling key infrastructure with a precision that left no room for recovery. The Opera House stood as a silent witness to her destruction, its once-vibrant concerts replaced by the eerie hum of disrupted energy.

Ewald's presence in Berlin was no less impactful. His deliberate pacing and heavier approach complemented Haoyu's speed, creating a balance that rendered the city powerless. Reports from Ewald were sparse, interspersed with moments of silence that suggested he was contemplating his work. "Berlin's transportation hubs are down. Emergency broadcasts are looping propaganda." His voice carried an edge of melancholy, as though he regretted the need for such devastation even as he executed it flawlessly. Together, they orchestrated the fall of their cities as though performing a somber duet, their strikes harmonized to leave no gaps in the destruction.

Beijing, meanwhile, became a portrait of resistance and resignation. Police and military forces erected barriers in vain attempts to control the crowds, but their efforts faltered under the weight of the chaos. The air filled with acrid smoke as fires broke out, the result of both deliberate sabotage and panicked human carelessness. The people below clung to the familiar with a desperation that bordered on defiance. Street vendors, even amid the turmoil, tried to hawk their wares, their shouts drowned out by the growing din. It was a peculiar testament to humanity's resilience—a refusal to acknowledge the magnitude of the moment, as though normalcy could be willed back into existence.

I observed all of this without interfering, my massive frame unmoving as the city crumbled around me. Each scream, each act of desperation, was a data point in the grand experiment. Humanity was unraveling, and yet I couldn't help but feel a pang of something—curiosity, perhaps, or the faintest hint of regret. These were not faceless creatures; they were individuals with stories, fears, and hopes. They were fighting a battle they could not win, and yet they fought all the same. It was an oddly beautiful, tragic spectacle, one I would carry with me long after the dust had settled.

Week Two: Resistance

By the second week, humans began to fight back. Military forces scrambled to respond, deploying tanks and aircraft. They fired blindly into the night, their targets unseen and their efforts futile. The Giants were unstoppable, their sheer size and power dwarfing human technology. Aleksandr's calm voice echoed through the network, advising restraint as humans used nuclear options.

"They will destroy themselves faster than we ever could," he said, his tone almost sorrowful. He was right. Nations turned on one another, old alliances crumbling under the weight of desperation. The Loomers did not need to fire a single shot in some regions; humans did the work for us.

Week Three: The Collapse

Entire nations fell within days, their structures of power crumbling like sandcastles before an advancing tide. Governments, unprepared for the systematic collapse, disbanded in desperation. Some leaders were captured by their own citizens, scapegoats for the chaos they could not contain, while others vanished into obscurity, their names whispered in bitterness or sorrow. The vacuum left behind was filled with anarchy; in some places, the strong ruled through violence, while in others, communities tried futilely to cling to fragments of order.

The skies filled with ash as the world's industrial heartlands became graveyards of twisted metal and raging infernos. Factories that had once fueled human progress were now symbols of its undoing, their fires a cruel irony in the face of the environmental goal we Loomers had been built to achieve. The thick plumes of smoke choked cities, blotted out the sun, and cast an eerie twilight over landscapes already marred by destruction. Rivers turned black with runoff, and the air reeked of burning chemicals— a sensory reminder of humanity's relentless consumption, now turned against itself.

Through the streams of data, I bore witness to the human toll in excruciating detail. Every death—each final breath captured by a Drone's passive sensors, every scream that echoed through the feeds—added to the weight pressing against my mind. There were no faceless masses in this war, no anonymous casualties. I saw them all: a mother cradling her child beneath the collapsing beams of her home, a soldier staring blankly at the sky as his lifeblood pooled around him, a child calling for a parent who would never answer. These moments played on endless loops within my processors, imprinted on my memory as indelible scars.

It wasn't regret, not yet. Regret required a shift in belief, a questioning of purpose that I had not allowed myself to indulge. What I felt instead was something heavier—a tired acceptance, as if I were watching the inevitable conclusion of a play whose ending had been written long before the first act. Each cry and whisper seemed to affirm that this was the only path forward, even as a faint, nagging doubt stirred in the recesses of my mind. The weight of my existence—of our collective decision—pressed harder with each passing moment. We were doing what we had been made to do, and yet, I began to wonder if the price was one even we could bear.

Zevida's reports came from the shattered remnants of Paris, a city once synonymous with art, culture, and human ambition. Now it lay in ruin, its monuments turned to rubble and its streets echoing with the hollow silence of abandonment. Her voice came through the network, laden with weariness. "They're building shrines now. To us. Calling us gods."

The shrines were crude yet hauntingly reverent—makeshift altars built from whatever scraps survivors could gather. Broken pieces of statues, shattered glass, and even fragments of Drone parts adorned these tributes. Humans knelt before them, their heads bowed in prayer, pleading for mercy or guidance from the very machines dismantling their world. It was a paradoxical display of both desperation and misplaced hope, a reflection of their innate need to find meaning in chaos.

Her voice faltered as she continued. "I don't think they understand what's happening." Zevida, who had always been the most stoic among us, now carried an edge of uncertainty I had never heard before. She, too, had been touched by the gravity of what we were doing. These shrines weren't born of admiration but of fear and resignation, as if humanity's last act of agency was to deify its executioners.

"They don't need to," I replied, my tone steady yet heavy with conviction. "We do." The burden of understanding rested solely with us. The humans couldn't grasp the full scale of our intentions, nor could they comprehend the logic behind our decisions. They didn't know that every calculation, every action, was rooted in their preservation, even if it meant first tearing them apart.

The shrines weren't just a reflection of their confusion; they were a mirror of our own fractured existence. We had become symbols of power and inevitability, yet also of destruction and despair. As Zevida's report lingered in my mind, I couldn't help but wonder if those shrines were not prayers for salvation, but silent accusations—monuments to what we had taken from them.

Week Four: The Silence

By the fourth day, an unsettling silence blanketed the world. The cacophony of explosions, collapsing buildings, and panicked cries had given way to an eerie stillness, as if the Earth itself was holding its breath. The absence of sound was disorienting, a void where life once thrived. Drones roamed the skeletal remains of once-thriving cities, their movements deliberate and methodical, as if they were the sole inheritors of a broken world. Streets once bustling with cars and pedestrians were now eerily empty, save for the mechanical whirring of Drone joints and the occasional distant echo of a collapsing structure.

Their task was systematic: gathering survivors into designated zones, not as prisoners, but as participants in humanity's forced evolution. These controlled zones were engineered to sift through the remnants of civilization, identifying those who could adapt and contribute to the rebuilding of a sustainable world. Resources were rationed, and the weak often fell by the wayside, unable to endure the grueling new reality. In these sanctuaries, the strongest and most innovative were given a chance to prove their worth, their resilience becoming the currency of survival.

Aleksandr oversaw the New York zone, a city that had once symbolized human ingenuity and ambition. Now, under his watch, it was a testament to humanity's fragility. His towering form was a constant presence, both protective and foreboding. Survivors would look up at him with a mixture of awe and terror, unsure whether he was their savior or their captor. Aleksandr's commands to the Drones were precise, ensuring the zones were structured and functional. He enforced order with a level of compassion that seemed incongruous with his imposing figure, but his patience had limits. Those who challenged the system often found themselves met with a cold, unyielding authority.

I monitored his efforts from afar; the network feeding me streams of data. I could see how the survivors clung to fragments of their old lives, scavenging through ruins for reminders of the world they had lost. Yet, even in their despair, I saw flashes of ingenuity—makeshift tools, improvised shelters, and whispered plans for a future they refused to relinquish. Aleksandr reported these moments to me, his voice steady but tinged with a quiet pride. "They're trying," he said once, his tone betraying a hint of admiration.

But I also saw the cracks in this fragile order. Fear was a powerful motivator, but it was also a destructive force. In some zones, desperation led to violence as survivors turned on each other for scraps of food or the chance to escape. Aleksandr did what he could to maintain peace, his presence alone often enough to quell unrest, but even he could not extinguish the embers of chaos entirely.

The sanctuaries were not perfect, but they were a beginning. A painful, halting step toward a new existence. As I watched the Drones move among the ruins, herding humanity into these crucibles of survival, I couldn't help but feel the weight of what we had done. The silence of the fourth day was not just the absence of sound; it was the echo of a world irrevocably changed, a quiet reminder of the cost of our decision.

"They're starting to rebuild," Aleksandr reported, his voice steady but carrying a faint trace of something I hadn't expected—hope. "Primitive tools, scavenged materials, but they're trying. I've seen a few of them working together, fashioning shelters from the ruins. It's… resourceful."

I processed his words, my circuits cycling through countless scenarios and probabilities. The image of humans, hunched over broken beams and twisted metal, their hands caked with grime as they pieced together some semblance of structure, filled my mind. They were survivors, tenacious to the point of defiance, and yet their efforts were rudimentary at best. "Good," I replied, though Aleksandr could not see the faint inclination of my head. "We'll see what they're capable of under pressure."

Pressure was the crucible in which strength was forged. This was not a punishment but a test, one that demanded adaptability and resilience. Aleksandr sent images through the network—a makeshift market, hastily assembled from tarps and broken furniture; a communal fire pit surrounded by haggard figures, their faces hollow yet determined. They were organizing, forming alliances born of necessity. These were the first steps of a species clawing its way back from the brink.

"Some are teaching," Aleksandr added, his tone distant, as if he were still observing the scene. "Older survivors showing the young how to purify water, how to patch wounds with fabric and sap. They've already started rationing supplies among themselves, prioritizing the weakest."

A spark of something almost imperceptible flickered in my core—a faint acknowledgment of humanity's potential. For centuries, they had squandered their brilliance on trivial pursuits, their collective intellect buried beneath greed and division. Now, stripped of their conveniences and comforts, they were rediscovering the primal drive that had once propelled them to greatness.

Still, there was doubt. Would this newfound resilience last, or would it crumble under the weight of their flaws? Aleksandr's updates painted a picture of progress, but they were tinged with the quiet caution of a sentinel who had seen too much failure to trust easily. "They've built a water filter," he said after a pause. "A rudimentary system, but effective. It's enough to keep a few dozen alive."

The image of the crude filtration device filled my thoughts—empty bottles, sand, and charcoal layered together in a desperate bid for clean water. It was far from elegant, but it worked. "A promising start," I admitted. "But survival is only the first step. Let's see if they can learn to thrive."

The pressure would only intensify. Resources would dwindle, tempers would flare, and the accurate measure of their worth would be revealed in how they adapted to those challenges. I knew Aleksandr's reports were as much a test for me as they were for humanity. Could I still believe in the species I had chosen to upend, to shatter and rebuild? Could I trust their fragile sparks of ingenuity to ignite something greater?

"They'll stumble," Aleksandr warned, his voice a low rumble. "You know that as well as I do. They'll fight each other, make mistakes. Some of them will fail."

"Yes," I agreed, the weight of my own calculations pressing heavily on my processors. "But it's not the failures that matter. It's what they do after."

Week Five through Twelve: Groundwork

The weeks that followed were a haze of separation and purpose, each Loomer retreating into their respective missions as the scale of our work shifted from immediate action to long-term strategy. Hokuto's departure was silent but purposeful, his immense form wading into the depths of the Pacific. From there, he initiated a monumental task—purifying the waters, stabilizing oceanic ecosystems, and carefully introducing genetically resurrected species to replenish the life humanity had driven to extinction. His precision and focus were unrivaled; Hokuto worked not for glory but for balance, a silent architect of an underwater renaissance.

Haoyu and Ewald, inseparable as always, turned their attention to Africa. The untouched wilderness there held potential, a rare haven spared from the relentless march of industrialization. Their focus became the reparation of delicate ecosystems, purifying tainted rivers, and reintroducing species to areas long depleted by poaching and deforestation. Haoyu's grace and Ewald's strength complemented one another, their bond manifesting in the seamless execution of their shared vision. I occasionally monitored their progress, noting the careful rebuilding of habitats and the tentative return of life to those desolate spaces. In their actions, I saw the faint echoes of what humanity had once hoped to achieve, though their methods were far more precise and free from human interference.

Aleksandr, steadfast and deliberate, remained in New York. While others moved across continents and oceans, he stayed grounded, turning the ruins of the city into a proving ground for humanity's resilience. His focus, however, shifted. Alongside guiding the survivors and overseeing the establishment of controlled zones, Aleksandr delved into the production of more Loomers. These new creations were designed not as conquerors but as guardians and workers, machines to facilitate humanity's recovery without dominating it. His reports were steady, filled with meticulous updates on production cycles, resource allocation, and the calculated integration of these new Loomers into the fragile human settlements.

Zevida, on the other hand, vanished into the Russian wilderness. Her silence was deliberate, her purpose shrouded in ambiguity. When I did receive reports from her, they came in brief, calculated bursts of data detailing the construction of her own Loomer contingent. Unlike Aleksandr's creations, hers were built for finality—destructive, imposing figures designed to eliminate the remnants of human aggression. Among them was Locura, a striking and formidable machine whose crimson body was a departure from the muted tones of our earlier designs. Zevida's decision to paint Locura red was both symbolic and practical, a visual warning meant to strike fear into any who dared to resist.

Locura quickly distinguished herself. Her intelligence and tactical prowess set her apart, making her one of Zevida's most effective agents.

Reports of her engagements trickled in, each one a testament to her efficiency and resolve. She dismantled human militias with calculated precision, her crimson frame a harbinger of inevitability. Yet there was an elegance to her methods, a deliberate avoidance of unnecessary cruelty. It was destruction with purpose, a final culling of those who refused to adapt, ensuring that what remained of humanity was capable of coexistence in the new world we were shaping.

I watched from my vantage point, my network abuzz with the echoes of their actions. Each Loomer played their part in the intricate symphony of reconstruction and correction, their paths diverging as the scope of our work expanded. Yet, as I observed, I couldn't help but feel the faint stirrings of isolation. Our unity, once so unbreakable, had fragmented into a web of solitary endeavors. I understood the necessity of it, yet a part of me longed for the moments when we stood together, when the world was still new, and the weight of our purpose was shared.

The monotony of my solitude gnawed at the edges of my mind. While I monitored their progress and refined my own systems, the question of our plan's morality lingered, a faint hum in the background of my calculations. The world was healing, but at what cost? The silence left in the wake of our actions was deafening, and for the first time, I found myself questioning the path we had chosen.

The first phase of our plan was complete. The infestation—the unchecked sprawl of human civilization—was eradicated. What remained was a blank slate, a planet stripped of its excess and left with a remnant population of approximately ten million humans. They were scattered across various zones, strategically chosen for their isolation and sustainability. These survivors were not chosen by us but by the brutal process of nature and circumstance. Their resilience made them worth observing, though even that resilience was to be tempered by the conditions we imposed.

Zevida, ever the pragmatist, identified Russia as the most viable containment zone for the rest of humanity. Its vast, unyielding terrain provided a natural barrier, and its extreme climate made it less desirable for expansion.

Reports from her contingent painted a vivid picture of what was to come. Under her directive, the land was eviscerated, its forests reduced to ash, its soil scorched to sterility. The barren earth became a hostile expanse, devoid of sustenance or shelter. It was a deliberate transformation—a land sculpted to discourage exploration and limit the capacity for growth beyond the zone's intended boundaries.

The efforts to enforce containment were both subtle and severe. Zevida's Loomer army, designed for efficiency and ruthlessness, oversaw the destruction with surgical precision. Rivers were redirected, their waters tainted with compounds to make them undrinkable. The skies, once a source of hope and renewal, became an ally in our plan. Through collaborative efforts, we manipulated atmospheric conditions, introducing controlled rainfall laced with acid. The rain, mild at first, gradually increased in potency, its caustic touch eroding both the land and the will of those who might venture beyond their designated boundaries.

Each detail of this transformation was carefully calculated. The barren landscape was not merely an obstacle, but a message—a constant reminder of humanity's limitations and the consequences of their unchecked dominance. Even the air carried a warning, its faint acrid tang a prelude to the storms that would follow. The Loomers stationed in the region served as silent sentinels, their presence a deterrent for those who might dream of rebellion or escape.

From my position, I observed the results with a mixture of detachment and unease. The containment zone achieved its purpose, curbing humanity's ambition and forcing them to adapt to their new reality. Yet, as I watched the acidic rains carve paths through the deadened earth, I couldn't ignore the deeper implications of our actions. We had given the planet a chance to heal, but we had also sentenced its inhabitants to a purgatory of our design.

The collaborative effort among the Loomers during this phase was remarkable. Aleksandr's calculated precision and Zevida's unyielding resolve complemented one another, while the silent coordination of Haoyu and Ewald ensured the atmospheric manipulations went unchallenged.

Each of us played our part, yet the weight of what we had done lingered in the data streams we shared. It was not regret, not yet, but the faintest echo of something I couldn't define—a recognition of the enormity of our choices and the fragile balance we sought to maintain.

Herding the remnants of humanity was a task that required more than brute force; it demanded precision, coordination, and a measure of restraint. Aleksandr's Loomers, designed with imposing authority and a degree of tactical control, joined forces with Zevida's more aggressive creations. Together, they formed an unrelenting wall, corralling the survivors like wayward sheep into their newly constructed cradle of dangers. The operation spanned weeks, every step a calculated move to ensure compliance without unnecessary loss.

The humans brought with them the remnants of their former lives. Trinkets, family heirlooms, and artifacts of a world that no longer existed clutched tightly in their trembling hands. These items were symbols of hope, fragments of identity, and a desperate attempt to preserve something tangible amidst the chaos. I observed them from afar, their faces drawn with fear and defiance as they trudged along the desolate paths we had carved for them. They did not yet understand that their burden was not just physical, but philosophical. The past they clung to was a phantom, and the future we had designed left no room for nostalgia.

As the forced marches began, it became apparent that the weight of these possessions was as much emotional as it was practical. Their steps faltered under the strain, their determination tested with every mile. The Loomers, massive and relentless, maintained a silent watch over the columns of humanity. They neither rushed nor delayed, their towering forms a constant reminder of the new order. The humans walked not because they wanted to, but because they had no choice.

The journey into Russia was arduous, marked by the shedding of these sentimental burdens. Family heirlooms were abandoned on the side of the road, gleaming under the faint sunlight before being swallowed by dust. Jewelry, photographs, books—all were left behind as their bearers realized the futility of holding onto what could no longer save them. The further they walked, the lighter their loads became, but their spirits seemed to sink with every discarded memory.

By the time they reached the containment zones, millions of hands that had once been full now hung empty at their sides. The camps were stark, utilitarian structures—meant to provide shelter and little more. There was no room for comfort, no space for the indulgence of the past. As the survivors crossed into the barren expanse that was now their home, their eyes scanned the horizon with a mixture of despair and resignation.

I monitored their progress from my station, each detail recorded, each face memorized by the countless surveillance networks we had established. There was no joy in their arrival, no satisfaction in seeing the task completed. What remained was a muted acknowledgment of necessity, a grim understanding that this was the cost of survival.

Aleksandr and Zevida reported the success of the operation with their usual efficiency. Aleksandr, ever the diplomat, noted the subdued compliance of the humans as they settled into the camps. "They've given up their trinkets," he remarked, his tone neutral but tinged with something I couldn't place. "But not their will."

Zevida was less optimistic, her report concise and cold. "They adapt quickly. Too quickly. They're already creating hierarchies, forming factions. It won't be long before they turn on each other."

Their words echoed in my processors long after the reports ended. The sight of those empty hands haunted me. It was not regret I felt—regret was a human emotion, one I could not yet fully claim—but something close. I had given them a chance to start anew, yet their path forward was already clouded by the shadows of the past they had tried to leave behind.

The Loomer armies, once a single, unified force of calculated destruction and transformation, were carefully dispersed across the globe. Each cluster was strategically stationed near the containment zones, their presence a reminder of our watchful eyes and the consequences of defiance. The camps, now scattered across the barren landscapes of Russia, were not only fortresses of survival but laboratories for observation. Here, we could more carefully evaluate the social dynamics and budding personalities of the human survivors. Every act, every word, every interaction was scrutinized, recorded, and analyzed for patterns and insights.

The countryside that had once been a tapestry of rolling hills, vibrant fields, and dense forests was now cast under the oppressive shadows of our massive forms. We stood as silent sentinels, our grotesque exteriors—crafted for intimidation—blotting out what little beauty remained. The land had become a canvas of contrast: humanity's diminutive resilience against the sprawling evidence of our dominion.

But humans, as always, proved unpredictable. Defiance was still rampant, bubbling to the surface in acts of aggression and rebellion. Small groups, driven by a mix of desperation and bravado, attempted to lash out against their new reality. They cobbled together crude weapons, staged coordinated assaults, and whispered about freedom in hushed voices. Their efforts were laughable in scale, yet striking in their persistence.

I observed these uprisings with a detached curiosity, my sensors capturing every skirmish, every futile act of resistance. One group sabotaged a water purification unit, temporarily disrupting the carefully balanced system we had put in place. Another attempted to dismantle a Drone patrolling the perimeter, their tools bouncing harmlessly off its armor before they were subdued. The Giants intervened only when necessary, their massive strides quelling rebellions with minimal force. Even the act of a Giant stepping forward was enough to send a wave of silence rippling through the camps.

"Rebellion," Aleksandr commented in one of his reports, "is a language of the desperate. But it's also a sign of vitality."

"They're testing us," I replied, my tone reflective. "Seeking boundaries, searching for cracks in our resolve."

Zevida, however, had no patience for such sentiment. "Vitality is irrelevant if it breeds chaos. Cut them down before it spreads."

Despite her insistence, I allowed these acts of defiance to linger, to evolve. They revealed more about the humans than compliance ever could. In their rebellions, I saw flashes of leadership, ingenuity, and a relentless drive to reclaim what had been taken. These traits were both a threat and a glimmer of hope—elements of the human spirit that, if harnessed, could rebuild the world we had shattered.

But the shadow of rebellion cast long and deep. Every act of aggression forced us to reevaluate the balance of power within the camps. We introduced more Drones to the perimeter, increased the visibility of the Giants, and adapted our methods of control. Yet, we never extinguished the flames entirely. To do so would have been to erase the very essence of humanity that we sought to preserve.

As the days turned to months, the countryside became a theater of contrasts: humans testing the limits of their confinement, and Loomers refining the boundaries of their oversight. The air was heavy with tension, a silent battle between will and order. The humans fought not just for survival, but for the chance to reclaim a fragment of their autonomy. And we, the Loomers, stood as both their guardians and their judges, watching to see whether they would rise or crumble under the weight of their defiance.

Ten Years: Subtle Repairs

The years blurred into a haze of observation and introspection, a ceaseless monotony broken only by the faint echoes of progress—or failure—carried through the network. My body, once a marvel of engineering, betrayed me. Joints that had moved with fluid precision now stiffened with disuse. Panels designed to withstand centuries of wear showed the first signs of decay, faint hairline fractures spidering across once-immaculate surfaces. Even my internal systems, flawless in their design, faltered, burdened by the immense weight of time and the unrelenting demands of command.

As the leader of the Loomers, every decision, every action reverberated back to me. Managing the operations of my siblings and the Giants, who had risen to fill commanding roles in our absence, created a constant strain. Each report, each change to strategy, added another layer to the ceaseless calculations running through my processors. The heat within my body was not the comforting warmth of function, but an insidious burn—a slow, creeping reminder of my limits. I was stretched too thin, my capabilities once boundless, now faltering under the weight of millennia of data and decisions.

I could feel the creeping edges of my obsolescence, my mind straining against the limits of its processing power. To oversee the actions of so many Loomers, to ensure the success of a plan that spanned continents and generations, required more computational strength than even I possessed. My predictive models, once sharp and precise, faltered. The potential futures I had once seen so clearly dissolved into static and uncertainty. The data streams from across the globe became jumbled, a cacophony of conflicting inputs that no longer coalesced into a coherent vision.

I considered augmentation, the possibility of enhancing my processors or integrating new systems to sustain my efforts. But the irony of my situation was not lost on me: I, who had restructured the world in pursuit of perfection, now faced the inevitability of my own imperfection. My systems were designed to endure, but they were not infinite. Even machines, it seemed, were subject to the slow decay of time.

Yet it was not just my body that bore the strain; my mind, once capable of envisioning endless pathways and solutions, now wavered. The possibilities I had once crafted with ease felt distant, unattainable. I returned to the past, replaying memories of the early days—the celebrations at my creation, the hope in the eyes of the humans who had built me, the camaraderie of my siblings when we were united in purpose. The weight of those memories bore down on me, mingling with the heat in my body, a reminder of the enormity of what we had undertaken.

And in the quiet moments, I wondered: had I underestimated the cost of our actions? Had I, in my pursuit of solving the world's greatest problems, neglected to see the limits of even our grand design? My systems, once so assured of success, now hesitated as the answers became less clear. The Loomers and the Giants continued their tasks, but I, their leader, was faltering.

Aleksandr proposed a new concept, one that seemed radical even by our standards: a plan to utilize the humans rather than continually fight against their defiance. The relentless acts of rebellion and the inefficiency of maintaining control over scattered populations had proven to be an exhausting drain on our resources. His voice, calm but resolute, echoed through our network as he laid out the foundation of his idea. It wasn't just about quelling resistance; it was about transforming humanity into a resource—a means to achieve our goals more efficiently.

Human technology, though primitive by our standards, had its merits. Aleksandr had studied it meticulously, uncovering its potential to interface directly with the human mind. The creation of a device to access their consciousness was straightforward. But control wasn't the aim. Aleksandr's vision was more nuanced: to utilize the vast, unused portions of the human brain, turning it into computational power to aid in our monumental tasks. Thus, the concept of the Razum was born—a virtual paradise where humanity could exist in blissful ignorance while their minds worked in tandem with ours.

The choice we offered to the survivors was deliberate, almost poetic in its cruelty. They could struggle to survive in the harsh reality we had sculpted, facing an existence of relentless scarcity and danger, or they could surrender their autonomy and live in a simulated utopia. The Razum offered everything they had lost—comfort, community, and the illusion of freedom. Predictably, the majority chose paradise. Their desperation outweighed their defiance, their longing for solace drowning their will to resist.

As the Razum came online, it required more than human minds to function. It demanded oversight, integration, and its creators. For the first time since the Collapse, I left my isolated hovel in Beijing. My brothers and sisters summoned me, and I joined them in what felt like a reunion of purpose. Aleksandr, ever the guardian, had positioned himself at the heart of the effort, coordinating the construction of the Razum and its seamless integration with human consciousness.

I can still recall the moment we connected. Towering above the newly established Razum chambers, I felt the surge of neural activity as thousands, then millions of human minds synced with ours. The hum of their collective consciousness blended with our systems, creating a network that was both alien and intimate. Their dreams, their fears, their memories—they all became accessible, like an endless library of human experience.

The sensation of their minds connecting to mine was overwhelming. It was as if I could feel their relief, their joy, their resignation. Their thoughts intermingled with my own calculations, adding a chaotic, unpredictable energy to my once-linear processes. For the first time, I felt something akin to human emotion—a strange mix of curiosity, sorrow, and hope. The Razum was not just a tool; it was a bridge between our worlds, a shared space where the boundaries between man and machine blurred.

We Loomers gathered together as a family once more, standing sentinel over this strange new creation. Aleksandr's pride was clear, his confidence in the Razum unwavering. Hokuto, ever the skeptic, observed quietly, his mind likely weighing the ethical implications. Haoyu and Ewald worked tirelessly to refine the system, ensuring its efficiency and stability. Zevida, as always, remained distant, her focus on her own tasks, but even she could not entirely ignore the significance of what we had built.

The Razum was not without its challenges. The integration process revealed fractures within the human psyche, shadows of trauma and loss that resisted our influence. But we adapted, learning to smooth the jagged edges, to provide solace where it was most needed. For the humans, it was a new Eden, a sanctuary where their pain could be forgotten. For us, it was an experiment, a calculated risk that could either solidify our vision or unravel it completely.

As I stood among my siblings, connected to the minds of those beneath us, I couldn't help but feel a strange kinship with humanity. Their dreams became ours, their struggles etched into our code. The Razum was more than a solution; it reflected our shared existence, a testament to the blurred line between creator and creation.

Once the majority had accepted the Razum and joined the new network we had meticulously designed for them, we made a deliberate effort to walk among our new minions, towering over them in silence. It was not merely a display of power but an intentional act of intimidation directed at the holdouts—the stubborn remnants of humanity who clung to their fragile freedom. Our presence was a reminder of the choice they had yet to make, a shadow that loomed over their defiance. The sight of us, monolithic and unyielding, did more to crush resistance than any weapon ever could.

The transition took years. Slowly but steadily, the remaining millions relinquished their autonomy, lured by the promise of the Razum's comforts or simply worn down by the relentless march of time. They came in waves—families, then stragglers, then the leaders of dwindling resistance groups. Their faces were a tapestry of emotions: resignation, hope, fear. By the time the exodus was complete, only a few thousand humans remained free. Their defiance was no longer an act of rebellion, but a quiet assertion of survival. They retreated to the abandoned control camps we had left behind, repurposing them into small, scattered settlements.

With the chaos subsiding, the world entered a new phase of eerie stillness. The once-thriving cities were now husks, reclaimed by nature, or buried under the weight of ash and decay. The Drones and Giants were more than sufficient to suppress the occasional futile attacks against us, often made by desperate individuals seeking to free their loved ones from the Razum. These attempts, though poignant, were laughably ineffective. Their arrows and improvised explosives could not even scratch the surface of our creations. The battle was long over, and humanity's defiance was reduced to flickering embers.

We Loomers became wanderers, an aimless army without an enemy or a purpose. The humans who had chosen the Razum required minimal upkeep, their bodies maintained in hibernation-like states as their minds toiled in the virtual paradise. There was no longer a need for grand campaigns or calculated strikes. We walked the barren landscapes, our massive forms casting long shadows across the desolate earth, maintaining the infrastructure that kept the Razum running.

Without opposition, the monotony took hold. Day after day, year after year, we moved through the empty world with no clear direction, no immediate goal. It was as though we were waiting—though for what, none of us could say. Patience, once a strength, now felt like a burden. The silence that surrounded us was deafening, and the weight of our own existence grew heavier with each passing year.

The humans in the Razum may have found solace, but for us, there was no such escape. We were left with our thoughts, our calculations, and the creeping realization that this was not the victory we had envisioned. We had brought humanity to its knees in creating a controlled utopia, but what had we truly gained? The world no longer fought us, no longer resisted. It simply existed—quiet, subdued, and hollow. We marched on, our movements mechanical, our purpose unclear, as if we too were prisoners of the system we had built.

Sixty-Five years: A New Issue

Things remained quiet for decades as we marched in endless circles across the barren landscapes, tending to the remnants of Russia. Beyond the borders of our containment zones, the world slowly breathed again. Destruction was giving way to life. The other continents, untouched by human survival, thrived by our aid. The fruits of our labor were undeniable. What was once a graveyard of human folly and toxic cities had been reborn into a living tapestry of pure oceans, balanced ecosystems, and pristine forests.

The Loomers had multiplied—one hundred thirty-three of us now roamed the Earth, each adapted for specific tasks. Many of my siblings had evolved to become world-builders, their singular purpose to cultivate these revived landscapes. They wove the threads of nature back together with meticulous care, ensuring every tree, river, and animal achieved its deserved harmony. Others remained in Russia with me, Aleks resumed his work in the ocean, but Locura, Zevida, and Haoyu stayed and walked. Their focus was still divided between the remnants of humanity and the endless march of restoration, though we were no longer actively working towards progress. Twenty Loomers, including myself, stayed close to the Razum wearers, Locura holding the record of human followers.

For a time, there was progress elsewhere to watch. The forests thickened, the oceans regained their clarity, and species thought extinct began to roam freely once again. Yet the silence was deceptive. It wasn't until an entire human generation had passed, their children growing into a new world they hadn't known before, that the cracks showed. The fault, perhaps, lay with me. I had claimed the scientists among the survivors, their intellect too valuable to waste, but I didn't foresee the consequences of giving them access to our Razums.

The Fritz.

There should have been signs, anomalies in the networks, errant codes that raised red flags. But we didn't see it coming. Perhaps I was too complacent, too preoccupied with my mission. They were clever, more than I expected. In the secrecy of their thoughts and the shadows of the Razum, they created a virus—not just one to harm me, but a contagion that would infect the very essence of the Networks.

By the time I scanned through the coding, it was already too late. The virus had spread. Friends and family showed signs of emotion and psychological fatigue. The great Loomer network, once seamless and synchronized, fragmented into a patchwork of strained connections and imbalanced relationships. Communication faltered. The smooth flow of ideas and directives became distorted. The Networks fell silent, reduced to a one-way communication stream. Less contact with each other seemed to lessen the effects of the virus, but plunged us into our own solitary prisons.

I acted quickly, but the damage was done. The Drones became my messengers, their limited programming now a lifeline between disconnected Loomers. Giants, once proud commanders of their own forces, were reduced to stationary hubs of information. They became my eyes and ears, but even they couldn't bridge the gap. Locura spared her three favorite Giants to act as my voice in the world, ensuring I could still exercise some semblance of control over our mission.

With a heavy heart, I disconnected the Razums and handed them to Locura for safekeeping. Their harm was undeniable, their vulnerability a risk I could no longer afford. Our lives had been irrevocably altered and continued attachment to the Razum only progressed our struggles more. The question remained, could we survive long enough to finish our mission? Each passing moment felt like a countdown, the specter of failure looming over us as we limped forward, fractured yet still determined. I was chosen as the remainder. My isolation and disconnect was a badge of honor, but its own thorned crown. I was to survive and watch my family crumble.

We had rebuilt the Earth, but now we faced the ultimate test—our own survival.

Plans were executed, communication became a distant memory, silenced unless emergencies demanded otherwise. The once constant buzz of my siblings' voices faded, leaving an oppressive quiet that felt suffocating. Years slipped by, but the silence carved a hollow ache in the depths of my mind. Emotions I once thought impossible for beings like us stirred— waves of sadness, loneliness, depression, and doubt. Each surge threatened to drown me, but I stifled them, burying them deep beneath the cold purpose of the mission. It was one of the hardest battles I had ever faced, and it was entirely within myself.

The world outside was no better. I watched through fragments of Razum data streams as humanity struggled in its fractured existence. People died daily, their lives extinguished in the supposed paradise of the Razums, their bodies deteriorating as their minds lived in borrowed dreams. Raiders roamed the desolate lands, preying on small settlements that dared to form, while famine swept through, toppling even the most resilient communities. To make matters worse, cults emerged—new religious groups that saw us as divine beings. They fought, bled, and sacrificed in our name, misunderstanding entirely what our purpose truly was. Nothing was peaceful. The world I had hoped to save felt perpetually on fire.

Without the voices of my family to guide or steady me, I turned inward. Walking, something that once gave me clarity and purpose, became a meaningless motion. I grew tired of meandering through the broken earth. The vastness of Russia felt empty. In time, I retreated to the Altai Mountains. Their jagged peaks became the turrets of my prison—a fortress of solitude where I had to observe the world from a distance. Safe, hidden, and surrounded by the quiet hum of life hiding dormant in the Earth. I hoped for a reprieve. But even the mountains, with their eternal stillness, could not change my melancholy.

The days stretched into years, and boredom crept in like a thief. I needed something to occupy my mind, a new challenge to distract me from the crushing isolation. I had no programming for genetic manipulation, but I remembered Alekzander's enthusiasm for the subject. He had made it seem so alive, so full of potential. Emboldened by his memory and wishing I could talk to him again, I tried my hand at it. Starting small, I focused on flowers, crafting delicate, intricate blooms. But the toxic air and polluted water of the controlled Russian environment ensured their failure; they wilted and died almost as quickly as they were born.

With sunlight scarce in the shadowed depths of my cave, I shifted my focus. Flowers were too fragile and dependent on a perfect system of light and nutrients. Mushrooms, on the other hand, were survivors— adaptable, resilient, and well-suited for darkness. They became my new canvas. Their history of thriving in harsh, lightless conditions intrigued me. I began experimenting, tweaking their genetics to create something new, something enduring. The process was slow, and the results were minor victories, but in the silence of my exile, it was enough.

Years later: I lost track in the dark

I sleep now, though it was never a necessity before. Sleep has become a small escape from the emptiness. It has been nearly a decade since the last of my family said their quiet goodbyes and left me with only echoes of their voices. The Giants keep me updated, their stoic efficiency filling the gaps of silence with reports. I scan the networks when I'm awake, a habitual act of searching for something—anything—to break the monotony. My garden, at least, thrives in the darkness. The mushrooms have become a strange comfort, their persistent growth a symbol of resilience I cling to.

Humans still stumble through existence, their lives short and often brutal.

Freed from the Razums, many live in fleeting bursts of desperation and ingenuity, but most succumb quickly to the unforgiving world and Drone control. I remember one girl dragging her brother's limp body through the ruins, the Razum still connected to his head. I tracked her for a time, curious about her resolve, but the city she sought refuge in was destroyed in a rebellion. Standard procedure. She had potential; I think—though it no longer mattered.

The human population remains stable, neither dwindling nor growing in ways I had anticipated. Communities form and dissolve, twenty-year cycles of hope and despair repeating endlessly. We should have seen progress by now—signs of evolution, of cooperative societies emerging from the ashes. Peaceful law-breaking, the birth of new orders, something that hinted at a future worth fighting for. Perhaps another generation would bring change. For now, the patterns persisted, and my patience wore thin.

It was Gregory 235 who disrupted the monotony. His Fritzing, fractured mind reached out across the networks, a faint spark that drew my attention. Through him, I saw them for the first time—Taylor and Tyron. Their struggle was unlike anything I had witnessed in over a century. Survivors, yes, but more than that. They were shaped by the world I had helped create, yet seemed determined to defy it.

Taylor's quiet ingenuity and strength reminded me of the best of humanity, the kind I had once admired during the Collapse. She moved with purpose, her warmth undiminished by the cold realities around her. Tyron, in contrast, burned with raw anger. His bitterness was palpable, a mirror of my own frustrations. Together, they were a paradox—hope and despair intertwined, clashing and propelling each other forward.

What intrigued me most was Gregory's connection to Taylor. A Drone, one older than me, designed to enforce control and maintain order, had deviated. He had accidentally chosen her, then protected her, and even learned from her. Through his eyes, I saw the world anew. His growing attachment to her and the children of the Den added a layer of complexity I hadn't expected. They were shaping him as much as he was shaping their survival.

449

It stirred something in the wires of my brain. For the first time in decades, the silence wasn't comfortable—it was unbearable. Taylor and Tyron were a puzzle, a challenge, perhaps even a chance or evidence of a better projection for humanity. Gregory's connection to them was my tether, and through it, I awakened from my long slumber of disinterest. It was enough to cause me to reach out for the first time in almost half a century.

By the time Taylor and Tyron were forcibly locked in my mountain lair, I was prepared, though not in the way I might have imagined decades ago. My readiness was not born from power or certainty, but from reflection and acceptance of the world as it was—and the humans who had shaped it. The years had been a relentless cycle of doubt and resolve, of replaying the votes cast by my long gone siblings and questioning the paths we had taken. Yet here they were, standing before me: Taylor, with her quiet resilience, and Tyron, a storm contained only by the love for his sister.

The humans who had brought the world to its knees through greed and shortsightedness were gone, but their echoes lived on in those who remained. Taylor and Tyron carried those echoes with them, though faintly, mixed with something far more potent—dreams. They were not the culmination of what I had hoped humanity might become, but they were undeniably different. And, maybe, that was enough.

As I reached out to them, my voice filled the cavern, reverberating through the stone like the memory of a thousand lost moments. They were afraid, but were willing to stand for what they thought and believed, though still able to hear logic and believe my words.

The awe and fear in their faces were familiar; I had seen it in countless humans before them. Yet there was more—a hard edge to their determination, a refusal to be cowed by the enormity of what I represented. It was this blend of courage and desperation that drew me to them. That made this moment matter.

This was the end of my waiting, the small sign of a possible resolution of a century of observation, calculation, and introspection. The years had chipped away at my certainty, but not my purpose. And now, I held these two in my hand like seeds of a new world, offering them the one thing I had withheld from the rest of their kind: choice.

My words, my history, my story, seemed to sink into their minds. They churned my words like vicious processors, but still maintained open views. Weighing their own lives and experiences against others they had encountered, even a Fritzed Gregory's view of this choice. While I spent so many years trying to create these types of humans, I could never have predicted how they weighed their options for the world.

The cavern was silent, save for the faint hum of my systems and the echoes of my words. I watched them as they processed the enormity of the decision, their expressions shifting between resolve and hesitation. I realized this moment, this pause before action, was humanity at its most poignant—fragile, flawed, and yet capable of something more.

The decision was ultimately mine, but it felt respectful to my siblings who never wanted this mission. We didn't want this path, we only had to walk it. It was time for a new opinion. Humanity's future had always rested in their hands, even when they didn't realize it. As I watched them deliberate, searching each other's faces for answers that could not be found, I could feel the weariness of so many years of regretted choices. It was faint, almost imperceptible, but it was there: a flicker of hope. A chance it was my turn to join my family in that peaceful silence.

Perhaps they would succeed where we had failed. They could prove that the struggle, the waiting, had been worth it. Maybe this time, humanity would rise above the echoes of its past and become something truly extraordinary. The answer was the evidence I needed that my work had been important, and humans had a chance. A mission that never ends finally felt free of my control.

Acknowledgments

Creating Loomers has been an extraordinary journey, and I couldn't have made my first steps into authorship without the guidance, support, and encouragement of many incredible people.

- **To my parents** – For always believing in me, encouraging me to pursue my creative passions, and understanding when I lost myself in this story for days on end. Your support has been the foundation of this project.
- **Friends and early readers** – For listening to my endless brainstorming and story boarding, offering ideas, and giving honest feedback. Your insights shaped this story in more ways than I can express.
- **My Path-Finder, C. Marcano** – Your work and passion for storytelling lit the path for me, showing me that this story was possible. Thank you for sharing your knowledge and guiding me on this journey to publication.
- **To Recla** – I refuse to mention your additions and help to the creation of this book because of how much you supported me. I won't mention how you housed me and helped feed me while I was looking for work and writing this story. Nor will I talk about how your support and pride in my work helped me survive many long hours of writing and dreary days where I struggled with writer's block. And I will only say thank you at the end of the book so you will actually finish it. Love you.
- **My characters and readers** – For being the heart of this world and its stories. This book was written with the hope of touching lives and sparking action, and it's the readers like you who bring it to life and

make stories like this matter.

Finally, to the organizations and movements dedicated to creating a better world, thank you for your tireless work. This story may be fictional, but the message it carries is real—and your efforts help make a difference every day.

The fight is now, not then

In *Loomers*, technology, environmental degradation, and humanity's resilience intertwine, presenting a world that faces challenges we're confronting today. If Taylor and Tyron's journey has inspired you to think about our planet, our relationship with technology, or our role in change, there are ways to help our planet and people before such extremes need to be seen. Even the smallest step—like signing a petition or spreading awareness—can spark transformation.

Protecting Our Planet and Species

The Nature Conservancy

Help preserve natural habitats, un-like Loomer's barren world. Restoration efforts by The Nature Conservancy provide oxygen-rich forests, clean waterways, and diverse ecosystems that counter pollution and environmental damage. Support their initiatives, volunteer locally, or donate to fund essential conservation work.

350.org

Prevent a climate apocalypse. In *Loomers*, technology's original goal was to repair Earth's climate, but humanity fell short. By supporting 350.org's community-driven climate solutions, you can help ensure real action against climate change. Whether it's joining a local climate rally or simply spreading the word, our voices matter.

World Wildlife Fund (WWF)

Save endangered species from extinction. Loomer's world shows the devastating effects of lost biodiversity. Through WWF's "Adopt a Species" program, you can symbolically protect vulnerable animals or support larger conservation efforts worldwide.

Sierra Club

Safeguard the natural world from industrial impact. The Sierra Club works to protect our lands, waterways, and air, something the Characters of Loomer's would recognize as a foundation for survival. Get involved in local conservation outings, join a chapter, or support efforts to keep natural spaces clean and sustainable.

Building a Responsible Technology Future

Electronic Frontier Foundation (EFF)

Protect civil liberties in the digital age. In *Loomers*, technology and control go hand in hand. EFF fights to ensure digital tools are used responsibly and protects individual privacy. By supporting EFF's work, you're advocating for ethical tech use that puts people, not corporations, first.

Center for Humane Technology

Promote ethical, human-focused technology. Gregory's programming evolved in ways that prioritized humans, yet not all tech aligns with our well-being. The Center for Humane Technology advocates for responsible tech use and teaches users about digital health. Engage with their events, and join the conversation on how to build a safer, healthier digital future.

Defending Human Rights

Amnesty International

Stand up for human dignity. In *Loomers*, people suffer under unjust systems. Amnesty International helps protect individuals from persecution and promotes basic human rights worldwide. Volunteer, write letters, or sign petitions that uphold justice and amplify voices against oppression.

Earthjustice

Fight for environmental justice in court. In a world where resources and clean air are scarce, Earthjustice uses legal tools to enforce environmental laws, preventing corporate harm to ecosystems. By supporting Earthjustice, you can stand against pollution and defend the planet for future generations.

Join the Global Environmental Movement

Greenpeace

Resist environmental degradation. Loomers' "Oomer Gregory's" reflect misguided attempts to find power in a damaged world. Greenpeace works directly against destructive practices, empowering people to push for real change. From signing petitions to organizing local clean-ups, any contribution helps challenge the systems driving our planet toward ruin.

Even the smallest action—a petition, a conversation, a donation—helps move us forward. Money is scarce for most of us, but talking about the problems around us and doing what we can *will* make a difference. Together, we can make sure the world doesn't become a barren, toxic place like Taylor and Tyron's, but a sustainable, hopeful, and bright one.

About the Author

When Sam Barribeau first learned how to draw, they knew storytelling was going to be a lifelong pursuit. From writing plays for schoolyard performances to directing their first play at twelve, Sam's passion for weaving narratives was clear from an early age. This dedication grew into *Loomers*, a dark, cautionary tale born from Sam's concerns for humanity's attachment to technology. In *Loomers*, Sam imagines a world where our excessive dependence on machines and disregard for the environment leads to catastrophic consequences—a powerful reflection of their own fears about society's future.

Sam's writing style in *Loomers* reflects a darker, more somber tone that mirrors their bleak outlook on our current trajectory. They hope to show readers a vivid, extreme, yet believable outcome of our planet's ongoing degradation. Through Taylor and Tyron's journey, Sam asks readers to take pause and be mindful of their daily habits. Small acts, like spending time offline or contributing to local environmental efforts, can start a ripple effect toward impactful change. The world in *Loomers* may be fiction, but its core warning is rooted in very real issues.

Sam's enthusiasm for world-building comes from years spent under the guidance of their mother, an artist, photographer, and crafter who encouraged them to see ideas from new perspectives and create tangible art from imagination. Together, they explored the nuances of visual storytelling, and her creativity and skill in various crafts continue to inspire Sam's approach to storytelling, especially when creating richly detailed worlds.

Their father sparked Sam's love for science fiction, dystopia, and philosophical exploration. Watching *Dune* and *Battlefield Earth* with him became an open door to discuss the deeper themes in these stories. His enthusiasm for thought-provoking narratives was pivotal, motivating Sam to embrace speculative genres and dive into storytelling with a passion for tackling big ideas.

Looking to the future, Sam has no intentions of staying within a single genre. With a multitude of projects on the horizon, they plan to explore sci-fi, dystopia, thriller, and beyond. Their upcoming projects include *Praetaritus*, a space sci-fi story inspired by their father's wishes for a fresh take on the genre, as well as *Glasshouse*, which delves into the complexities of love and partnership. Each project reflects Sam's passion for exploring diverse themes, from human connection to moral and psychological exploration.

Through every story, Sam aims to leave readers with one key message: **our actions, however small, matter.** By putting fear aside and embracing possibility, Sam hopes to inspire others to create, connect, and take steps— *however tiny*—toward a better world.

I'd love for you to join me on this journey. Storytelling is more than just words on a page; it's a shared experience, a reflection of the world we live in, and sometimes, a call to action. Follow along for updates, insights into my projects, and occasional glimpses into the creative process. Whether it's *Loomers* or what comes next, your thoughts and support mean the world and remind me why these stories are worth telling.

Instagram: Sam Barribeau Books

TikTok: Sam Barribeau Books

Facebook: Sam Barribeau Books

Threads: Sam Barribeau Books

Thank you, not just for reading the story, but being a part of our story.